ADELAIDE

Independent Bimonthly Literary Magazine
Revista Literária Independente Bimensal
Year III, Number 9, Volume One, September 2017
Ano III, Número 9, Volume Um, setembro de 2017

ISBN-13: 978-0-9992148-7-9
ISBN-10: 0-9992148-7-X

Adelaide Literary Magazine is an independent international bimonthly publication, based in New York and Lisbon. Founded by Stevan V. Nikolic and Adelaide Franco Nikolic in 2015, the magazine's aim is to publish quality poetry, fiction, nonfiction, artwork, and photography, as well as interviews, articles, and book reviews, written in English and Portuguese. We seek to publish outstanding literary fiction, nonfiction, and poetry, and to promote the writers we publish, helping both new, emerging, and established authors reach a wider literary audience. We publish print and digital editions of our magazine six times a year, in September, November, January, March, May, and July. Online edition is updated continuously. There are no charges for reading the magazine online.

A Revista Literária Adelaide é uma publicação bimensal internacional e independente, localizada em Nova Iorque e Lisboa. Fundada por Stevan V. Nikolic e Adelaide Franco Nikolic em 2015, o objectivo da revista é publicar poesia, ficção, não-ficção, arte e fotografia de qualidade assim como entrevistas, artigos e críticas literárias, escritas em inglês e português. Pretendemos publicar ficção, não-ficção e poesia excepcionais assim como promover os escritores que publicamos, ajudando os autores novos e emergentes a atingir uma audiência literária mais vasta. Publicamos edições impressas e digitais da nossa revista quatro vezes por ano: em Setembro, Dezembro, Março e Junho. A edição online é actualizada regularmente. Não há qualquer custo associado à leitura da revista online.

(http://adelaidemagazine.org)

Published by: Adelaide Books, New York/Lisbon
e-mail: info@adelaidemagazine.org
phone: +351 918 635 457

FOUNDERS / FUNDADORES
Stevan V. Nikolic & Adelaide Franco Nikolic

EDITOR IN CHIEF / EDITOR-CHEFE
Stevan V. Nikolic
editor@adelaidemagazine.org

MANAGING DIRECTOR / DIRECTORA EXECUTIVA
Adelaide Franco Nikolic

GRAPHIC & WEB DESIGN
Istina Group DBA

PORTUGUESE LANGUAGE EDITOR / EDITORA PORTUGUESA
Adelaide Franco Nikolic

BOOK REVIEWS
Heena Rathore
Jack Messenger
Ana Sofia Pereira
Scott Morris

CONTRIBUTING AUTHORS IN THIS ISSUE

Jayno Miches, Heidi Popek, Angie Walls, Kathleen Glassburn, Janet Mason, Isaac Wofford, Valerie Kinsey, Charles Edward Brooks, Richard Key, Caroline Miller, Max Bayer, CG Fewston, Edward Mathis, Sevasti Iyama, Robin Zabiegalski, Richard Schmitt, Alexa Findlay, Alex Rafael Encomienda, David Summers, Nina Wilson, Steve McBrearty, Mattie Ward, Mike Cohen, Jon Benham, David Macpherson, John Tavares, Lewis Beilman, Sarah A. Odishoo, Kate McCorkle, Joseph Eastburn, Ellen T. Birrell, Gabrielle Morales, Olga Pavlinova Olenich, David Boyle, Lydia A. Cyrus, Carrie Bailey, Rebecca Johnson, Carla Sofia Ferreira, Pierre Sotér, Donald Mager, Richard Pacheco, Larry Smith, Seamus O Sparks, Sergio Ortiz, Clint Davis, Dianne Moritz, Joseph Harms, Gayle Compton, Mark Martyre, Eduardo Escalante, Lydia A. Cyrus, John Grey, T. William Wallin, Meg Eden Kuyatt, Joseph Buehler, John Garmon, Craig Kurtz, Daniel Kenitz, Viktor Tegner

CONTENTS / CONTEÚDOS

EDITOR'S NOTES

ADELAIDE BOOKS, By Stevan V. Nikolic   6

FICTION / FICÇÃO

A MEETING IN BROOKLYN by Jayno Miches   8

DEAR MR. REDINGTON by Heidi Popek   15

TELL ME YOU LOVE ME by Angie Walls   17

DENIAL by Kathleen Glassburn   21

THE ARTISTS by Janet Mason   26

SARAH by Isaac Wofford   29

FOREVER BLUE: A TRIBUTE TO CHRIS ISAAC   33
by Valerie Kinsey

CUCUMBER PUNCH   36
by Charles Edward Brooks

THE TREE REMEMBERS by Richard Key   42

SECRETS by Caroline Miller   46

MONIQUE by Max Bayer   55

A DAY IN THE LIFE OF A GUITARIST   59
by CG Fewston

THE END OF HISTORY by Edward Mathis   62

THE HOLY FACE MEDAL by Sevasti Iyama   69

THE LAST GIRL IN AMERICA   75
by Robin Zabiegalski

MOTION SICKNESS by Richard Schmitt   82

HELL BOUND by Alexa Findlay   90

THE LABYRINTHINE AFFAIRS   94
by Alex Rafael Encomienda

THE FUNERAL by David Summers   101

A DAY IN THE LIFE OF DELLA by Nina Wilson   108

THE LATIN SUB by Steve McBrearty   118

BIG MAMA'S PORCH by Mattie Ward   125

MOTORBIKE MAN by Mike Cohen   130

NERVES by Jon Benham   135

ONE LAST CHANCE by David Macpherson   139

OVERFLIGHT by John Tavares   145

THE SILENCE OF THE NIGHT by Lewis Beilman   153

NONFICTION / NÃO-FICÇÃO

VIRTUAL PLAYGROUND: PLANET EARTH   160
by Sarah A. Odishoo

IDENTITY CARD by Kate McCorkle   163

NEW BOY RULES by Joseph Eastburn   169

SANTA CLARA RIVERLESS by Ellen T. Birrell   173

WREAK OF THE COWBOY by Ellen T. Birrell   177

SONS OF UNCONSCIOUS FATE   179
by Gabrielle Morales

WALKER by Olga Pavlinova Olenich   183

IN THE COMPANY OF MEN, MUSCLE,   186
AND MACHISMO by David Boyle

ASSOCIATIVE LEAPING by Lydia A. Cyrus   189

LOLITA'S GLASSES by Carrie Bailey   191

THE GOLD CHAIR by Rebecca Johnson   193

POETRY / POESIA

WHAT IT TAKES by Carla Sofia Ferreira   195

MOON SILENCE by Pierre Sotér   196

ANA AHMATOVA POETRY   198
translated by Donald Mager

HOMEGROWN ATROCITIES   203
by Richard Pacheco

PIECES OF A LIFE HISTORY by Larry Smith   205

I ATE MY POEM by Seamus O Sparks   208

FORGOTTEN by Sergio Ortiz   211

LUNA by Clint Davis   214

ELM STREET NEIGHBOR by Dianne Moritz   216

SAMAEL'S LYCHGATE by Joseph Harms   217

CALL ME ISHMAEL by Gayle Compton   221

THOUGHT ON A MONDAY MORNING   225
by Mark Martyre

THE WAY IT IS by Eduardo Escalante   228

IN A PEAR TREE by Lydia A. Cyrus   230

SMALL TOWN IN OHIO by John Grey   231

TRISTESSA by T. William Wallin   234

HONEYMOON by Meg Eden Kuyatt   240

PARODY by Joseph Buehler   244

CONFESSION by John Garmon   247

AN END OF THINGS by Daniel Kenitz   252

INTERVIEWS / ENTREVISTAS

A CHAT WITH PIERRE SOTÉR,   253
the Author of the
Poems & Thoughts Book Series

BOOK REVIEWS / CRITÍCAS LITERÁRIAS

SORROWS AND JOYS By Colin Ian Jeffery   258
– A review by Rev. Dr. Paul James Dunn

THE WILLOW HOWL,   259
A book of Poetry, By Lisa Brognano

NEW TITLES

DAWN: Poems & Thoughts, By Pierre Sotér   260

THE LONELINESS CAFÉ: 262
A Collection of Short Stories,
By Richard Dokey

DENNY'S ARBOR VITAE: 263
Poetic Memoirs, By Timothy Robbins

A BOX OF DREAMS: 261
Short Stories, By Denis Bell

ART & PHOTOGRAPHY / ARTE & FOTOGRAFIA

DAWN – Photograhy By Viktor Tegner   264

Front cover photo:

THE DOORS IN MATA PEQUENA I- By A.F. Nikolic

Photo illustrations in the Adelaide Literary Magazine No.9, Vol.One, Sept. 2017:

By Viktor Tegner

Editor's Notes
Stevan V. Nikolic

ADELAIDE BOOKS I

Our September Issue brings 111 authors on 600 pages in two volumes. Thirty-nine poets with over 120 poems, fifty-three short stories, nineteen nonfiction pieces, one excerpt from a novella, and three photo presentations will be quite enough to keep busy our readers until our next issue in November.

Although it is impossible to separate any of the published pieces, I would like to recommend DAWN, a photo presentation by young and very talented Portuguese photographer Viktor Tegner, an essay by Fred White titled BOOK COLLECTING AS A SPIRITUAL EXPERIENCE, a poem by Carla Sofia Ferreira WHAT IT TAKES, and DERB JOSSI, an excerpt from the novella "The Jossy Farm" by Lisa Brognano.

It seems that every new issue of the Adelaide Literary Magazine brings yet another novelty. Our last (July) Issue was our first bi-monthly publication after two years of going out quarterly. With this (September) Issue, we are announcing the launch of the ADELAIDE BOOKS.

ADELAIDE BOOKS, an imprint of the Adelaide Literary Magazine, was founded in July 2017, with the aim to facilitate publishing of novels, memoirs, and collections of short stories, poems, and essays by contributing authors of our magazine.

We believe that in doing so, we best fulfill the mission outlined in Adelaide Magazine – "to promote writers we publish, helping both new and emerging, and established authors reaching a wider literary audience."

All titles are published in paperback and eBook format and offered through Ingram for bookstore distribution in the US, and through Amazon.com, Barnes & Noble, and other major retailers for online sale worldwide. Optionally, we do hardcover editions with or without dust-jacket. Additionally, we offer the possibility of translating books into Portuguese and Spanish and publishing short-run paperback editions for distribution in bookstores in Portugal and Spain.

We offer to our authors two unique publishing contract options which guarantee full transparency of the pre-print and post-print publishing process, and generous royalties paid in a timely manner.

When starting Adelaide Books, we didn't expect much interest for our new project. Didn't make any estimates how many books and how often we would like to publish. However, the attention our new endeavor received from the authors made us think big. In the first month of its existence, Adelaide Books released four titles, with another four to be released by the end of this month, and two more set for a release in the Fall of 2017 and Spring 2018. So, the decision to put out four books a month came naturally, on its own, and that is just about what we are doing.

Authors interested in publishing with Adelaide Books can contact us and/or send their queries and proposals to info@adelaidebooks.org.

A MEETING IN BROOKLYN

By Jayno Miches

In retrospect, he wished it had not occurred to him to ask that fellow any questions. But then again, he also now wished he had asked his questions and left it at that, and that he would have been gone without waiting for answers. Instead of doing the opposite, he had gone for chatting up that fellow, and so he got himself mixed up in one of those situations we often lament as being of the kinds in which "one thing led to another." For, good things are not always connected, but bad things always are. It was, however, absolutely irrelevant now that against his best instincts he had chosen not to ignore that man. And honestly, it had long been too late for revisiting his regret. His rueful feelings had begun to gnaw at him not long after they had exchanged casual greetings, before getting into conversation. But even sooner than that, deep remorse had taken over him. That began exactly from the moment when it dawned on him that, if he came out alive from meeting Todvrodoswky for the first time, he would do so only to more strongly wish he had just passed him by, and had kept walking on in silence.

At that precise moment the late evening looked as if perforated by an uncertain darkness. Already moving towards its end, the day when Mario Rosario and Todvrodoswky crossed paths with each other had a different feel to it; nothing in it announced that daytime would soon start to get shorter and darker. Nothing was certain concerning what October would turn out to be when it finally arrived. It was through that uncertainty of the pattern worn that day by the weather that, as they ascended from the underground to the streets, the two men discovered each other. They both had been riding the same F train, and, in appearance at least, each was going his own way.

The way it seemed to Mario Rosario, Todvrodoswky looked tentative as he walked, as one would who was not entirely sure where he had meant to be going or wasn't quite familiar with the part of the city where he now found himself. But as we all know and often tend to forget, things are oftentimes not what they seem. Shortly after they exchanged their first few words an excellent opportunity would open up for Mario to see for himself that there are things which indeed popular wisdom gets right.

Cobble Hill, where they were now walking, wasn't anymore Mario Rosario's neighborhood. He had lived there, or in the proximity, for a long number of years. Presently, he was slumming around Red Hook, where renting a dismal studio was still more or less affordable; but maybe not for long. Still, after he would subtract the rent money from his paycheck, he could afford food and clothing, and pay for the utilities, which now included the Internet and his Netflix membership. And he still bought books, but now only secondhand, and since thankfully not many good books were being put out, he needed less money for that. Altogether, his monthly expenses qualified him as an old-school New Yorker; he was as a full-fledged Brooklynite. Being "Brooklynite" still came with a certain ethos back then, and Mario felt naturally inclined to offer directions to someone who was going along his way looking a bit lost, as Todvrodoswky seemed to him. Mario knew the ins and outs around those corners, and was perfectly familiar with the whereabouts where they could lead, if someone turned on the right corner at the right moment.

That's how he came to talk to the man. Rosario asked if he needed to be pointed out in any direction. But now that he was looking straight at the man, Rosario seemed to have discovered some sort of familiarity in his face, and the vague, fleeting recollection came to him that he might have seen Todvrodoswky before someplace else; if so, that must have happened before he knew his name, and then, even before he learned to shiver when he even thought of the rendition of such name in the Cyrillic alphabet. Oblivious to what he was getting himself into, Rosario charged on.

"No. I'm serious. I'd swear I've seen you before, at least a couple of times."

A blank stare looked directly at him.

"Yet that has always been in Manhattan, never in Brooklyn, that I've seen you." The blank stare was still in force.

But then, as if talking to nobody, the other man said:

"Until now."

"Obviously," he got in response.

It was true. Rosario had seen Todvrodoswky before. Yet, the latter was right in disbelieving him, for Todvrodoswky knew himself to be a distinct type of man; his being distinct consisted in his taking great care never to look exactly the same as he did the last time you thought you would have seen him. In his personal life, for not obvious reason to the unsuspecting, he consciously conducted himself much like a Shakespearian actor in a cheap production of Henry IV, who must play half the cast. For one, Todvrodoswky tended to alter his dressing habits so often that it was fair to say that the very phrase "dressing habits" didn't apply to him. His only "habit" in this respect was that quite often, although not every week, he molted his clothing two or three times in a day and sometimes more; in doing so he also took care to style himself, from morning to mid-afternoon and from evening to night, in the most diverse and contrasting manners.

Always in good taste, as if his wardrobe only held collectible articles of clothing, the best way to describe him is that Todvrodoswky appeared to dress as if to create the effect of the "unexpected." If for example in the morning he could come across as a tycoon on his way to signing a front-page worthy business deal, beyond the afternoon he could be taken to be a community college adjunct professor of English 101 with questionable left-wing inclinations. And yet, by dusk, the same man would reappear and pass you by all dressed up as a mainstream hipster, minus the beard, of course, but with jeans uncomfortably tight for his effeminate legato, and thin-soled children's sneakers, a skateboard, and a set of graphic "novels" in his backpack. He could as well be wearing makeup of some kind, and his light-brown hair, probably dyed to cover the blond, would never move to the same side of his head. That particular day, when Rosario came to give him directions, he was going around dolled up in the classical cliché of a movie director. Everybody knows somebody of this type.

The reason for his sartorial shifting would in due time reveal itself for Rosario to make a note of it; but that was still far from happening. So, when Rosario insisted that he had seen him before, Todvrodoswky wasn't exactly telling a lie when he corrected his questioner by simply uttering a "no," leaving him to his own devices, to wonder exactly what his "no" applied to.

The only thing clear about him, and only for the moment, was that Todvrodoswky, despite affecting the contrary, was not totally bothered by being approached by Mario Rosario. They were establishing a relation whose motivations would become self-evident in due time. Actually, that relation had been already established a while ago; but Mario was, between the two of them, the last to catch up, and so he wasn't up to the minute with the news. As it was, Todvrodoswky was sneakily appreciative of the help he was getting from the target of his operation, who was also his willy-nilly victim. The Russian was coming after the Hispanic man.

They let a silence pass between them. That's usually what happens with strangers, who have not much to tell to each other. Truth be told, though, Todvrodoswky wasn't there looking for someone to "tell" things to. He was more into doing things to people.

"Court Street's this way, I suppose?"

The "foreigner" to Brooklyn said that suddenly. He was implying a question without actually asking it. That could have meant that he knew where that street was, but wanted only confirmation. Or again, perhaps he didn't know, but neither did he care to know; he was "just asking," maybe to reinforce in Mario the belief that he was actually going somewhere, not hounding him down.

"That's correct."

Yet the other man continued walking, as if not caring about the answer. Later, when Rosario tried to exchange names with him, Todvrodoswky simply said that "a name is just a name." In a failed attempt to trick him, Rosario said that his name was, in fact, "Roberto Bolaño." He had been reading the Chilean author around those days, and the name had been on the tip of his tongue. He failed there, because Todvrodoswky knew what Rosario's given name was. But that didn't matter either; Todvrodoswky's undisclosed interest in Rosario made knowing his real name something of lesser importance. A man who concluded, correctly or incorrectly, that his life has up to this point been a failure, begins by wishing he were somebody else, and follows up this wish by giving himself somebody's else name, just to start over somewhere. That's how Todvrodoswky thought of his walking companion. And he was correct in thinking thusly of him.

A sudden change came when Todvrodoswky, unprompted, told Rosario that his own name was, "Sigürd." His voice made the name sound Scandinavian. This marked an unexpected development and introduced a new pace in their relationship. Whether that was really the name his family and friends, which those who knew him better called him, Rosario would never get to know. But over a meaningful span of time, time and again he had moments when all he could remember about Todvrodoswky was precisely how he pronounced his own name, which came to him as if carrying a vibrating whisper, like something ethereal precipitating from a fjord. It would soon change back, becoming more as it would be the next time they met again. But presently, still on the street leading off from the subway, his words were coming

out of him as if linked to each other through a reverberating distance. And his outstanding Slavic features ran in his face like a loose translation from the Norse language. He talked as if he wasn't there, but with no hostility in him, only with an unfriendly indifference. It was in that tone that he informed Rosario.

"I have also seen you many times, though not as often as you think you have seen me. You, like me," he continued, "often sit at that coffee place on the Bowery, where Bleecker Street's no more." He had meant to say "where Bleecker ends." The Hispanic man, which is how he thought of himself, wanted to correct him, but didn't. Rosario had been around that area as recently as the previous week.

"Exactly."

One of them had entered the coffee shop as the other was leaving, and one of them had likely held the door for the other. But when Rosario tried to remind him of that, Todvrodoswky denied it. "Certainly not last week," he said, quietly enigmatically. He offered as proof the logical argument that, if one man gets the door for another, neither can see the other without being seen by him. Todvrodoswky was emphatic; he knew how unrecognizable he was capable of making himself look.

Unable to completely rule that out, what he was now hearing wasn't as he believed it had happened just last week, Rosario subsequently began to doubt the certainty of having seen this man all other previous occasions he could have said he had. He didn't become doubtful without a reason.

Not long ago, more or less one year and a half from the day they were tensely chatting each other up, the not exactly unprovoked but completely undeserved September Eleventh Attack had occurred, which history still remembers as "September 11th." One of the lasting consequences stemming from that day, which will maybe never go away, was that the city government, working with the media and with any able bodies, was out to apprehend the culprits and to prevent copy-cats and repetitions. To that end, a Gestapo-inspired campaign got launched aiming at turning the whole city into a den of police informants. To help the city, every city-dweller got scared into being on the look-out, watchful on the streets, the trains, buses, the planes, and the buildings and all public spaces. Then people took to going around wondering what you may be carrying in your bags or on your person. For people are quick to take to paranoia, and some citizens went as far as to induct themselves as freelance spies, and started to go around nosing on other affairs and the lives of citizens, who themselves were also spying on others. Everybody was fine with that for their own safety, as they continued to be cordially invited to snitch on whatever looked suspicious in their eyes, giving no mind that snitching in itself is a suspicious behavior. With time, everybody became somebody else's suspect, and as suspicion reigned, people refrained from doing almost anything, including talking to each other, lest that looked suspicious to anybody who was ready to snitch.

Despite that, for unrelated reasons by then Rosario himself had already spent endless hours of his days and his nights in what he referred in his mind only as "the search." His searching throughout the city had nothing political in it and didn't issue from fears for the national security. His search concerned itself with, and was limited to finding a love or a sex interest of his, who went by the name "Sabrina Santo Schmidt," that being the most clear datum about her, and that she was a wannabe actress. She claimed to be from Germany, and from time to time, from Mexico.

Even though he was yet doing it only part-time, something that eventually changed, Rosario often saw the need to go to odd places, to loiter on streets and around buildings, residences and establishments of the most diverse occupations, some maybe dedicated to businesses he shouldn't have had an interest knowing about. Wearing his hat and his dark glasses, at any day time of the night or the day, Rosario could often be seen by whomever would look at him suspiciously, going about town without any itinerary or fixed destination. And so could have been seen bumming around from far more standpoints than the Empire State Building can be reconnoitered from the four corners of Manhattan.

If it were true that Rosario and Todvrodoswky kept running into each other, it would have been logical under the circumstances for either of them to assume that hadn't been happening by chance. Yet, the Hispanic man believed he had reasons to suspect Todvrodoswky of taking upon himself putting Rosario under his personal watch. If you do not believe that coincidences happen in sequences, he thought to himself, there was no room for believing otherwise, and the thought infused him with apprehension. Feeling his well-being was on the line he gave himself free range, and continued to freak out. Of course, he knew he was up to nothing that required his name to be put in a watch-list. But, taking precaution, from now on he began to weigh his words when talking to Todvrodoswky; because most people seemed to swallow whole the official explanations for the September Attack, he had become wary of words when talking to anybody at all. Fortunately, like the good books which were not being put out, New Yorkers had begun to drop the use of talking to one another. More than tad worried by now, Rosario began to ready himself up for whatever came at him from the Russian, while hoping it would be nothing. Struggling to look undaunted, he waited for the man to be the first to show fear, while also wishing something would be said that would relieve him of his. Moments ago Rosario had realized that by approaching this man he had created a situation nobody needs to be caught in. But nobody could have expected it to go that way. Unexpected situations usually take unexpected turns, so he was wishing for ways of kicking himself out of this one maybe already too late.

Still looking absentminded and as if reciting from a piece he would have many times said from a stage, here Todvrodoswky began to mention many other places downtown where the Hispanic fellow should have seen him. What he was actually doing was giving his interlocutor notice that he knew all the city nooks and holes where his fellow walking-traveler had been of late, where he was a "regular." Not that Rosario would have a clue; but a scene alike this one, so ripe with real danger, already awaited him in the near-future. The Russian had already started work on it. In the meantime, his recitation was having the desired effect. Rosario began to see that what he was trying to achieve, to pin him down, was doomed to failure, and he recognized that. Compulsive and unpredictable, Todvrodoswky was a born histrio, a hypocrite in the Greek sense of the meaning for "actor." The man could in short notice pass himself off as whatever he would choose to; he wasn't a "person" more than he was an interpreter of personas. So, good luck to whoever tried to bust him! There was going to be no success for Rosario in deciding which one was this man, of all the foggy faces from the days behind him, which he managed to summon to the present. He was already far-gone into thinking that this man, Todvrodoswky, was a dedicated psychopath, and that he had, no doubt mistakenly, become the center of his attention, a situation that if true was as pregnant with danger as very few dangerous situations are.

But maybe there was a sliver of hope? One of the associations stood out in his refreshed memory. Earlier that same afternoon when the episode took place, it seemed completely ordinary, presaging nothing but a motif for amatory disillusions. At one of the cafes missing from the tally Todvrodoswky had recited, where he had assured Rosario had been seen in previous weeks, the latter had a casual but endearing meeting with two sisters and their mother. The three of them were in the city traveling from Denmark. Although strangers talking with each other, meeting-up, and coming together around a table to share an amicable conversation was something on its way out, displaced by the computer, by gentrification, by collective city paranoia, those things still used to happen now and then. The Danish daughters were saying to Rosario that they would soon be coming to live in Brooklyn for a while; they were acting students at the Lee Strasberg. That casual piece of information decided that drama was going to be the subject for their ever prolonging but in the end inert conversation, from which nothing would come. Nonetheless, Rosario had emerged from the meeting and the talking with the feeling of a man who would have visited any part of Scandinavian mythology. In that mythology, all female creatures are goddesses, and all goddesses are marked for death, from an excess of beauty. But before he emerged onto the streets bathed in that feeling, Rosario had ventured some mild opinions that apparently worked to tick off someone who could best be described as a maniacal zealot of the performing arts, a description that later he would find out, perfectly captured his Russian assailant.

The women and he had been "just talking" and maybe to provoke them into saying more, Rosario let out this.

"If you asked me, but you would not," he said, "The Oscars, The Grammys and the others are essentially flawed; or fraudulent all the way."

"And how do you figure?"

"Well, they award actors who play for an audience, for its money, yet the audience who pays for them to play doesn't get to vote on the winner. Actors, directors, producers and so on vote for one another, and so, whoever is better at schmoozing and bullshitting is almost sure to win..."

"That usually is whoever throws the best parties..."

"Or whoever has nicer things to say about the others, and is more believable in saying it..."

"Because of that," Rosario also added, "since everybody is ready to die to get an Oscar, actors are best known for fucking their way to getting nominated, which they hold to be an accomplishment in itself..."

That was all said on the topic before the coterie that included Rosario moved on to other themes. No phone numbers was exchanged, and no word had been spoken about the vague possibility of meeting up again, which anyway, it being New York City, would most likely never happen. To whom it would have occurred that the inner, idle coffee babble of a man totally inconsequential to the acting business would come to have a near-fatal repercussion in his future, a time which seen from the perspective of the earlier afternoon of one same day, was already here, and walking next to him?

But that was, nonetheless, what was happening now.

Because to him "Sigürd" sounded like a Slav name, Rosario was thinking that the man confronting him now must have been eavesdropping, undetected being a party to that café casual conversation. Having developed an interest in the women, he was speculating, this guy was giving chase, coming to claim them as his territory, and to mark it by delivering a sound beating on him. Situations like that used to be a commonplace element of city life; but that happened mostly among blacks and Puerto Ricans. And besides, that was in times when men used to see in women good reasons to fight each other off over them. But that was before. Now, most city men seemed to have lost serious interest in women; men now preferred the childlike homoerotic company of their video gaming buddies, brought to them by Silicon Valley. And they also went for porn, instead of sex, which had fewer complications.

Rosario was still agitatedly trying to trace a mental line back to that coffee shop, to see in his mind if he had seen anybody who fit the slim, tall, blond human constitution represented in Todvrodoswky, with his pallid, somber face as of a man under the influence of a hang-over from the last season. But Rosario had not run into anyone resembling him; not while the soiree at that café was on, and not afterwards during his search. He had nothing to work with. He knew not a thing about Todvrodoswky's inborn histrionics, which he cultivated into a personal art. And so, not knowing who he was dealing with, Rosario didn't either know what he could have done to bringing about the hostility he sensed quietly amassing in the heart of this perfect stranger.

But he would better be careful. For Todvrodoswky was convinced that Rosario knew all too well what was coming to him, and why, but was acting coy, perilously playing stupid. Todvrodoswky was not the kind of man who expected people to freely acknowledge their mistakes out of their own honesty. Therefore, he would only give Rosario warning tidbits about the things that people's stupidity makes other people do unto them.

"As a matter of fact…"

Seeking clarification, Rosario restarted saying something, but was cut short. He was told that "As a matter of fact, there is nothing in the past that's a 'matter of fact'." In Todvrodoswky's way of thinking, the past is the past, and a fact is always in the present. He was showing that although his actions could appear to some to be somewhat off, despite his appearance, he was a logical man. To that, Rosario said nothing; he maintained his silence but inside himself he was in agreement. Yet again, he began to mumble something. It would turn out to be a question, to which "yes" or "no" wouldn't have advanced his chances of moving away from the other guy, and Rosario stifled that question. But, again, since it

was his turn to say something, but also because he was really confused and could not associate "Sigürd" to anything or anyone he knew and besides he had run out of memories to associate the present moment with, he linked it to "the search," and made recourse to a name he had been trying hard to keep out of his tribulation. Thus, he asked as if by chance, if Todvrodoswky knew some actress who went by the name "Sabrina Santo Schmidt."

Here, a chill descended over him. The other man welcomed his question with the coldest, most hate-filled look Rosario had ever been given. Unless Todvrodoswky was overdoing it for effect, what was going to happen to him from that moment on was handwritten in that look, and in uppercases. Already feeling the sharp edge of that look rummaging through his skin, one single blood-coagulating phrase got inspired in him, for Rosario to say. But he didn't dare: "He's a cold killer." In the next minute he grew feverish. In the glowing light from closed storefronts, his face took on a tonality that to people passing them by would have made it obvious that one of those two men was going to be the end of the other.

They had been walking on Warren Street. If you are past Smith, there comes a point at which Warren splits and you meet Court Street. If walking on its left bank, once you go across, Baltic begins. Rosario usually took that street to reach the overpass on the BQE highway, to get to Red Hook. But now, to avoid any further cooperation with Todvrodoswky, to not collaborate in his own murder, thus preventing his life ending as a crime scene, around which a post-modern "artist" would try to put a NYPD Do Not Cross Yellow Line, and call it a Human Blood Installation, Rosario decided to skip Baltic, not to lead his nemesis straight to his home.

On one of the vectors of that corner, where Warren is separated from one of its halves by the main throughway, there was a ghostly, unfrequented, but brimful secondhand bookstore. That corner used to keep odd hours depending on the season; in the autumn, it closed very late in the day and opened very early in the night. The bookstore had stood many years on the same corner, but its days were already numbered. The bookstore's owner was a friendly taciturn man who always gave off the appearance of having just woken up, and at the same time, of getting ready to go to bed. He was sitting at the entrance. He was smoking in the company of another man; but for the smoke, they looked like the reflection of each other's taciturnity. Yet, to the man running for his life, his business presented the sole opportunity of escaping horror before it could strike. Here, Rosario took the only opportunity. Once sheltered in the dusty safety of decomposing books, Rosario would try his effort to remember what the fuck had he done to Todvrodoswky.

Slowing down his pace, he had caused "Sigürd" to pull slightly ahead of him; then, indifferent to the one-way traffic, Rosario broke off running in despair, to safety. Yet, anyone noticing would have derided him; for he would have been mistaken for a costumer in a rush to get something to read before getting home when reading was not considered anymore a "cool" thing to do even in neighborhoods that erstwhile were well-read and book-friendly. Like Rosario himself, that had been diagnosed "almost dead."

Running for his life, Rosario headed straight up to the dimmed back of the establishment, for he knew the secret password to the alphabetic chaos in which the books there were arranged. Many times, not in a rush to get back home to his Red Hook quarters, Rosario had gone in at any hour of the night, sometimes just to do a little browsing. And when his search had brought him there at night, he sometimes went in and did not come out until late the next day; there had been occasions when he had ended up falling asleep there under some dark staircase. There was never the risk of getting the cops called on him and getting charged with trespassing. Unless you actually got something and decided to pay for it, the bookstore owner didn't seem to ever keep a close eye on the coming-ins and going-outs of his costumers. Rosario kept this in mind as he entered. Following a maze of dusty counters, which in all probability had been set in a place intended to be provisional but decades after were still displaying their items on a first-come, first-served basis, he found a hideout to spend the night in.

As he was making him his escape, Todvrodoswky had time to say to the flying prey that he would be "seeing him around." There was menace and revenge lurking in his words. He said it loud enough for the already running man to hear him through the fast falling darkness. After giving him that cold-blooded killer look, when Rosario had asked him concerning the object of his "search," Sabrina, wanna-be actress from Germany or Mexico, Todvrodoswky angrily had shot back that he knew not "who the fuck nor where the fuck" Sabrina Santo Schmidt was. He was lying. But that was to be discovered only much later.

About the Author:

Jayno Miches is an American writer of Dominican -Spanish ancestry. He studied Spanish at the New York University, where he received a Master's, and Philosophy and European Thought at the City University of New York, where he received a Ph.D. He writes fiction and nonfiction, but remains largely unpublished. He has lived in Germany and Switzerland, and travels extensively through Spain and Latin-America. Miches is a life-long resident of Brooklyn.

DEAR MR. REDINGTON

By Heidi L. Popek

The kitchen is flooded with sunlight that stabs my eyes. It takes a moment of slow blinking before I can look at Peter. He's slouched in a straight-backed chair, right foot on left knee, just the tip of his salt and pepper waves cresting the sports section. I drop a kiss on his bristly jaw; my hand lingers on his warm shoulder. "Morning," I say.

The paper dips, revealing a face firmly set in deep thought. "You're up early, Rose."

I slip into the opposite chair. "I can't sleep, my mind won't shut off."

I have not slept the sleep of dreamers in weeks; insomnia began with the first letter. The plain white envelope arrived in a hill of catalogs, assorted junk, and bills. I'd almost missed it.

Peter's eyebrows slant in a frown. He folds the newspaper and places it next to his empty cereal bowl. "There's only one way to sort this out, Rose."

"You'll meet him then." A glance at the stove's digital display, only seven o'clock - the day stretches before us like a panoramic view - yet the simple statement leaves me end-of-the-day weary.

"It's the only way to know for sure."

Shadows slant the walls; clouds eclipse the sunlight that had bathed the back of my neck like a lover's caress.

"You have so many projects due in the weeks ahead. When will you even have time to meet him?"

"Three o'clock."

My eyes narrow. "Today?"

Peter shrugs. "Why is today so surprising?"

"Why do you sound like my being surprised is not a reasonable reaction?" I snap. "This is happening so fast."

Peter dumps sugar and another splash of cream into his coffee and stirs a lazy figure eight pattern. He sits back and meets my eyes over the rim of his mug. Steam rises. He blows a ripple across the hot liquid. "You think it will be easier if I meet him next week, or next month?"

"Nothing about this is easy, Peter. I'm still in shock."

Concern etches Peter's face. "I know it's been hard on you. You toss and turn all night."

The shadows lengthen as thunder rumbles in the distance. A yellow finch darts between the branches of the soaring spruce adjacent the picture window. We'd planted the sapling almost twenty-five years ago, a month after moving into a neighborhood where children rode bicycles to school, and backyards had swimming pools and swing sets.

"Maybe he doesn't want anything from us, just to meet you." I say, but even to my own ears, this sounds weak.

Peter stays silent for so long, lost in his thoughts. "So many wasted years. What was she thinking?"

My coffee mug clatters against a plate of sliced melon. "You never told me much about Sandra."

Peter looks up, exasperated. "That's because there wasn't much to tell, Rose. We were only together a few months. When we split up, I never heard from her again. Not a word. She was a blur from my past until I read her obituary two months ago."

I push my hair behind my ears, close my eyes and take a deep breath. "Maybe this is some sort of scam, Peter. Have you even thought of that? Maybe he did his homework, researched everything about us." I am the voice of reason, the one with the common sense. Peter is an artist, a dreamer. Our marriage is a balance of function and fancy. "He probably knows we never had children."

"Rose." It is a whisper. Peter reaches across the table, laces our fingers. "We're going to be ok, no matter the outcome." His trademark grin, the one that usually meets his eyes, the one I fell for. He sings a line from a song he'd written on our first anniversary, his voice soft and melodious: "Baby, it's you and me, that's how it's got to be. You and me, that's how it'll always be."

That bit of song always lifts my spirits, but now I stand and clear the table without a smile or a glance at Peter. He simply believes the letters are true because he wants them to be true. I fill the sink with warm suds, gently sponge the pale blue coffee mugs.

"Do you want to come with me today?"

A mug slips my grasp; soapy water splashes my shirt. Did I want to go with him? Did I need to protect Peter, to ask the necessary questions? I rinse the plate and gently stack it in the dish drainer. "I don't think I can do that. Not yet."

Peter's chair scrapes the wood floor, a moment later his hands rest on my shoulders, his lips to my ear. "I need you with me, Rose."

The niggling guilt of my own inadequacy rises to my throat. "It would have helped to hear those words before you agreed to meet him, not as an afterthought."

Peter's hands drop to his sides. His words fall on my skin. "I didn't mean to exclude you, Rose." At the picture window, he studies the dark clouds meeting the horizon. "Storm's coming in fast." He does not turn around. "Why don't you get some rest?"

I crawl into bed as the first cloudburst patterns the windowpane. I dream of black towers that climb into silver clouds, and a tall bridge spanning a river that never ends.

When I wake, dusk fills the sky, the time of half-light. Peter sits on the edge of our bed. He hasn't bothered with the lamp. He'd opened the window; the air smells fresh and clean.

He picks up my hand and holds it to his lips. "Did you get some sleep?"

I search his eyes. "Peter?"

Gently, he cups my cheek. His breath smells of whiskey. "I would have known him anywhere, Rose. He looks just like me."

My mouth is dry. I should have gone with him. I swing my legs over the bed and sit next to Peter. "I don't even know what to say to you right now."

Peter pats my hand. "I hope you don't mind, Rose. I've invited him to stay with us for a while. Just until he gets on his feet."

About the Author:

Heidi Popek resides in western New York and works at Daemen College. Her work has been published in print in Play of Mind and Affaire de Coeur; online at sayitatyourwedding.com and, most recently, at mothersalwayswrite.com.

TELL ME YOU LOVE ME

By Angie Walls

In the next room, my mother is dying. Lights out, dark as night though it's the middle of the day. The heavy, velvet curtains are pulled tight with tape and wooden clothespins, so they keep the blue skies, blue birds, and the rest of the moving, breathing world out of sight. It's severely quiet ever since last month, when the visitors stopped coming. No more neighbors waiting at the front door with casseroles, no church folk coming to pray on Sundays, no family to help me. The mailman leaves the daily mail on the porch swing now without so much as a knock. A lifetime ago this room was not the room where my mother slept, ate, retched, and wept—not the mausoleum where she would die—but a living room. I miss when this room used to be full of people and things and didn't echo from its emptiness. There used to be a piano, where my brother and I once sat and played. The walls are barren, with scratches and dust lines where the bookshelves used to be. The dilapidated, blue-and-green-plaid couch is my mother's bed, covered in layers of blankets and family-stitched quilts. The old coffee table is buried in letters, pictures, and greeting cards that are an accumulated history of her illness: all the Get-Well-Soons when my mother was first diagnosed with cancer, the Thoughts-and-Prayers when I was driving her to the city for her treatments, the ones with white doves and PEACE in gold letters for when the doctor told me there'd be weeks and not months left.

And now it's just me, my mother, and the empty space between us.

I'm sitting in the brown leather chair on the far side of the room, a safe distance from my mother on the couch, as I did yesterday and the days before. Too early to tell what kind of day it is. A cough comes out, deep from my mother's weak lungs, reminding me that she is dying for real this time. She's calling out for help sitting up on the couch, but she's not asking for me. She pleads for my brother, Joshua, who hasn't been home in more than a decade. In the tenderest spot in my heart, I know she wishes it was anyone but me.

"Josephine, how long have I been calling you? Never mind." Her eyes close for a minute. She collects her thoughts one at a time. Only my mother calls me Josephine, and it makes me feel like I'm eight years old again, hiding under the stairs. She is gripping the arm of the couch until her knuckles are whiter than the bedsheets tangled around her feet, determined, because she has something to say. For the past few days, she hasn't eaten or spoken much, other than yelling at me for buying the wrong kind of cereal and messing up her pillows. If I try to fix them, she says they're stabbing her in the neck. If I bring her new ones, she'll throw them at my face.

"I want to talk about the funeral." She points to the notebook on the coffee table, waiting to be filled. She tells me she has to make sure it's done right, as though we're talking about planning a dinner party. The flowers, guests, food, music— she wants to have her say over the funeral—but especially how everyone should remember her after she's gone.

When I was a child, my mother used to throw parties for the smallest of occasions, and they served a purpose: she was intent on knowing all the comings and goings in her neighborhood. But there was more to it. She savored the days that followed, when she would become the envy of her friends, the talk of our small town. It was the promise of perfection; that's why she always made sure every detail would mean something. Most folks remember her brownies or cakes with perfect buttercream roses, gold-plated ivory cups and saucers, and her secret red punch—everything obsessively put in place with the hopes of being photographed and shared, cementing her win as Best Mother, Best Wife. In the summer she spent weeks to stage the house for a party. She'd go to the local nursery to strategically select her peonies; there's an old superstition that a peony bush in full bloom would bring good luck, and she made sure each flower would be right. She'd put out paper lanterns by the pool deck in matching pink and white, and her chocolate layer cake with peppermint ganache frosting was the centerpiece. For a short time before I turned twelve, I had been another thing that she could parade at her parties, dressed in pink bows and lace.

"What will I be wearing?" she asks me pointedly. I tell her I don't want to talk about it, which makes her repeat herself loudly, until her voice cracks on the last word. I can't fight my way out of the exercise, though I could recognize there's just one way this will end. When she asks me a question, it usually means she wants me to read her mind, to know what is right and what is wrong—a clear division of the world as she has defined it. I'm her only daughter so I know it wouldn't be smart to ask why it matters what clothes we choose.

I mention the blue striped pantsuit that was the last gift from my Aunt Lila but this makes her angry. "You're useless." I concede, saying that if she tells me which one is right, I will make sure she gets buried with it. She laughs, probably because she doesn't believe I can manage the task.

I have a hard time sleeping that night. In my childhood bedroom I'm haunted by the same faded, yellow-flower print, peeling and frayed by the years that have come and gone in this house. On nights like these I'd count the tiny bumps in the popcorn ceiling above the bed or use my index finger to trace the shapes I could see. The dust in the room is making my eyes burn, but I have to

avoid settling in here. The moment I start sweeping the floors, replacing the air filters, or unpacking my belongings, my future here is cemented. I can't survive here much longer.

Tell me you love me, my mother used to ask me constantly. Together, her words formed a dark, haunting melody defined in its bitterness. When they reached me, the cut was unforgiving, jagged. An open wound that could never heal and drove deeper than her words that preceded: I wish you were dead. I manage to whisper the words she wants to hear (they are the most painful to say). My mother's emotions toward me came in extreme opposites, because everything I am must be held to the same standards of right and wrong. So as quick as she could love me, she had to reject me as though I were another unacceptable flaw in the world. I was beautiful, I was ugly. I was her pride, her failure. I was precious, I was worthless.

I was eight and I loved her. For a child could eagerly love a monster, even though I had the memory that it'd swallowed and spat me out. I could cling to its razor-sharp teeth and claws in a desperation for the kindness that could follow pain. I dreamed of the night when she was in one of her worst down spirals. She woke me after midnight, dragged me out, in my bare feet, to go for a drive. *Tell me you love me.* My mother's hands were shaking; the car darted left and right on the dark road. In one swift movement she could find an end, with me a meaningless piece of her wreckage. *Tell me you'll never leave me*, she cried, pressing on the gas until the car crashed into the railing.

In the morning my mother tells me to help her get dressed. This is the first time in months she's been outside, so we argue over the idea. She says we have to go to the florist downtown. I grab the notebook as instructed, which now has MOM'S MEMORIAL SERVICE written in Sharpie across the front. My mother has an affinity for lists. When she used to get sick from the treatments, she made hundreds of them. Fifty foods she couldn't eat anymore, so I would remember to avoid them at the grocery store. Fifty names and addresses for Christmas cards, which I signed and sent from her to the people she calls friends and family—the ones who had good reason for never calling or visiting again. Fifty things for the lawyer to add or, in many cases, to remove from her Will. Fifty worst ways she might die, everything from pneumonia to being killed by a falling bookshelf.

I flip through the notebook, seeing that the first few pages of the notebook are filled with a list of scribbled names. A few of them are already crossed out, including Aunt Lila. My mother isn't the type to forget a grudge. We haven't seen my aunt since last Christmas, when most of the family came by to collect the things they'd been owed from years of overlooking her nitpicking and unkind words—the wedding china, paintings, antique furniture, and my father's first editions. They flew in for the occasion of one final family gathering, bringing gifts of fresh fruit, flowers, and photo albums to reminisce for days. Only they didn't realize until the last dinner that she'd sold the expensive things months ago for a good price, allowing my aunts and cousins the leftovers.

The florist is hard to find; she shares the space with an antique shop. My mother and I have to walk all the way to the back, past the furniture and jewelry, to the counter. The florist is a friendly woman with blond, wavy hair and a strawberry-print dress, who smiles while she introduces herself as Betsy Anne. She shows us to her "office," where there's a small, two-seat sofa, a wooden bench, folding chairs, and a table with her portfolio. My mother takes the sofa; I sit in one of the folding chairs, which is two seats away from her. There's a large floral display on the table, blocking her direct view of me. Betsy Anne is smiling at me as I'm flipping through the book of lilies, roses, and tulips. By the tenth page of similar arrangements, I realize she thinks we're here to plan my wedding. When I tell her different, the expression on her face turns somber.

"What kind of arrangement would you prefer?" she asks after removing the wedding book from my hands, replacing it with a black book. I am flipping through the pages for the right one. I can sense my mother staring right through the flowers into me, testing me to see if I know what she'd want. On one page there are tall, bright-

blue delphiniums, following by bright-pink, orange, yellow, and red carnations. One has fake butterflies.

"You know, most people choose flowers that best represent the person's life and the relationship you had," Betsy Anne says to be helpful, but she's making things so much worse. How could flowers be capable of explaining our relationship? What is the color for my mother's rage, for the blood she draws from others? I am uncertain how to talk about the life of such a woman, who has purposely driven everyone else away. Roses. I say it more like a question.

"What could be more of a fucking cliché," my mother contributes to the conversation. *Carnations? Orchids? Lilies?* I continue the guessing game. "Carnations, that's the best you can think of?"

"Carnations are a good choice too," the florist tries to chime in without success.

"They're cheap," my mother says to me, in response to the florist. "Is that how you want to remember me?"

I ask her what she wants.

"Everybody wants roses at their funeral. Nothing yellow, nothing white, this isn't a christening." My mother is flipping through the book, rejecting each arrangement by page. It's then that I remember an article about white tulips—they supposedly represent forgiveness. "Definitely no tulips. No baby's breath. Lilies are too expensive. Why waste your money if I'm dead?" I apologize to Betsy Anne, the same way I apologize to most people who have to endure my mother in public places.

★

It's two in the morning, and I can't get to sleep the next night again. On the wall opposite my bed is one of my mother's old lists, which she wrote for me when I was sixteen. It's a list of my personal flaws—for inspiration, she'd said. Nothing crossed off. For years I did try to become smarter, more beautiful, less me. With everything I could, I tried to change into something else more worthy, but I was, inevitably, her biggest mistake. I dropped out of college the first time my mother was sick. I flew from the city to come back home, left behind a man who loved me, though I was an unlovable person. When I sat by her hospital bedside, holding her hand, there was no love in her eyes. Only the regrets of a mother telling me the story I've heard since I was a child. It's a list of the fifty different ways she'd imagined killing me when I was a baby: drowned in the kitchen sink, fed with a lethal dose of table salt, carbon monoxide poisoning.

By the time we make it to the funeral home for our first appointment, my mother has filled up half the notebook with what she wants. Although most are things she doesn't want. I walk through the display room of caskets while my mother is resting in the next room, where the funeral director is trying to offer comfort to her. There's another life-or-death decision staring at me, and I know I will lose this exercise too. The caskets are stacked in rows, the lids open to reveal white cloth, velvet, and satin linings. The exterior options are overwhelming too: should I choose maple, cherry, oak, or stainless steel? Do I pick the stronger wood, or do I choose something exquisite like shiny brass or gold? One of the funeral assistants is following me as I pace slowly between shelves, letting my fingers graze the wood grains of each casket. He tells me to take my time, it's an important decision. Then, as a reminder, if I needed one, he wants me to think over which coffins make the best representation of my mother's life.

My mother is coughing up blood in the next room. There's a small audience gathering in the funeral parlor while we wait on the ambulance to arrive. The looks on their faces tell me they want to help, but I know they won't be able to. I hold her hand, cold and frail in mine. I dare not look in her eyes again, to relive the disappointments of my mother.

About the Author:

Angie Walls is a short story writer, novelist, and screenwriter who grew up in Springfield, Missouri, near the Ozarks. Many of her stories explore contemporary themes of identity, isolation, and survival in the Midwest. She is the award-winning screenwriter and director behind "Redmonton," a web series inspired by her hometown, and has published stories in various journals including Cutthroat, East Bay Review, Halfway Down the Stairs, The Helix, Fredericksburg Literary and Art Review, The Griffin, Stirring, and The Summerset Review. Her short story "Things We Should've Said" received an honorable mention from Glimmer Train, and one of her essays will be published in Carve Magazine. In 2017, she will be releasing a new book of short stories, Anywhere But Here. To learn more, visit her website at AuthorAngieWalls.com.

DENIAL

By Kathleen Glassburn

The yellow 1964 MGB my father gave me as a birthday present had been parked in front of our special place—Rose Motel—for three hours. We'd been meeting there for the past six months.

In Room 5, Nick and I sprawled across a lumpy, double bed, still naked and damp from lovemaking. One of my long, sticklike legs draped across his lower torso. My head nestled against his shoulder. I traced a hand along his stomach. Was it less fleshy? Was Nick, at seventeen, losing his pudginess? Just the year before we had been the same height of five-foot-ten. Lately, he'd been looking down at me instead of meeting eye to eye. My lips pursed into a smirk at the image of him towering over everyone in my family. The whole lot of them—Mother, my older brother Chet, my younger sister Marj, even my father— with their healthy, golden skin and compact, shorter-than-average bodies.

Picturing those sturdy, tanned people, I couldn't help but recall endless hours on Sunny Daze, the sailboat inherited from my maternal grandfather, Frederick Porterfield. The others companionably hollered back and forth above board while I hid below deck, playing my violin, going over and over difficult passages in pieces like Vivaldi's "La Tempesta di Mare."

Every half hour or so, Mother would yell down, "El - e - a - nor! Enough already!"

I had been named after my paternal grandmother—a name I'm sure Mother disliked but agreed to as a concession to my father. She'd parody it when annoyed with me, which was most of the time.

I'd take a break from my practice, feeling like a collapsed sail. Once I figured she was occupied with rigging, or whatever else happened up there, I resumed my music.

Now, moving away from Nick's warm body, I whispered, "We have to talk."

"Huh?" He roused from a doze.

"Please wake up. I need to tell you something." I placed a pillow behind my back and drew the sheet over my breasts, self-conscious even though he called them his "beautiful little lemons."

One of his brown eyes squinted open as he rasped, "What's up?"

"My acceptance from Middlebury came yesterday. I'm going to Vermont."

It was December of our senior years—mine at Oak Ridge, a private girls' school on the fringes of Porterfield, Connecticut; his at Roosevelt, a public high school in the warehouse district. August seemed an eternity away, yet I knew we had to think about this if my plan were to work, if Nick were to go with me. I had purposefully chosen Middlebury over Mother's Wellesley because it was co-ed.

"I want you to apply."

Nick sat up and I caught a whiff of his English Leather. He stuffed a pillow behind his back. "Even if I could get in, how do I pay? No one's going to give me a scholarship."

"I have a plan."

"Yeah?"

"Let's get married." We had never used protection, and I had secretly wished for a pregnancy to force the issue. But, no such luck. "Right after graduation."

"Your mother won't allow it."

"We'll elope."

"What's that got to do with you going to Vermont?" His dark eyebrows scrunched together.

"She'd never, ever want me to skip college, and you can go too. My father will pay."

"Your father?"

"Of course."

Daddy didn't have much to do with Nick, who showed no interest in Sunny Daze or playing tennis, but unlike Mother, he'd never been nasty. She made remarks like, "He's not our kind, dear." Daddy said things like, "If he makes you happy, he's all right with me." My father knew what it was like to be poor. He'd been a scholarship student when he met my mother. And, ever after, he did whatever it took to keep things agreeable for her. If it meant paying for my new husband's education, as well as my own, Daddy, who ran Porterfield Textiles since my grandfather's death, would do exactly that.

Taking in Nick's puzzled expression, I said, "Trust me. This'll all work out."

Walking around campus with my handsome husband, I felt as if I possessed some enviable treasure—like a trunk full of gold coins and jewels. Other girls stared at him, which gave me a secret smile. He was mine. Rushing to keep up with him, I could tell by his lengthened stride that their attention also pleased him. By the end of freshman year, he had reached six-foot-four, his chest broadened, his waist slimmed, and his ruddy skin, though scarred from adolescent acne, had a masculine, outdoor look, as if he spent all his spare time in the wind and spray. He'd also gotten rid of the glasses, opting for contact lenses. Along with physical changes, something else had occurred. His grandmother, whom he'd lived with since his

unwed mother was killed in a car accident when he was three, died shortly after we married. Nick was adrift except for me.

I didn't delude myself. I still looked the same—tall, with scant curves, hunched shoulders, and a plain face that, while not unpleasant, resembled the cautious demeanor of a church cleaning lady. Despite this, with distance from the family, my self-confidence blossomed in direct proportion to the clearing of eczema that had plagued me since childhood.

At thirteen, Nick and I had met in a dermatologist's office. The state paid for him to make a few visits.

While he paged through a car magazine, I sat across from him, in an otherwise empty waiting room. Thoughtfully rubbing my hand on the pebbly upholstery of a chair, I decided that this boy, with his blotchy face, seemed nonthreatening. Bolstering my courage, I moved over beside him. He didn't look up. After a minute or two, I said, "That red car's a Corvette, right?" My question started a friendship, and a couple of years later, it became our romance.

One day, the end of junior year, we took our last exam and headed across campus. I anticipated a long summer with plenty of time to play my violin, read anything I wanted to read, and explore fun places together.

"Let's sit down." Nick tossed his books on a stone bench.

"Aren't you ready for lunch?"

"I want to talk first. Here. Not at the apartment."

I sat next to him and put a hand on his knee. "Are you upset about something?"

"Not at all." He moved his leg. "I'm excited. I just don't want you to be upset."

"Why would I be upset?" I made a move to stroke his rough cheek, but he drew away and started scratching at a gouge in the bench.

"I'm not going back to school next fall."

His words sank in. "What do you mean? What will you do?"

"I'm not cut out for this stuff, El. You love it. I don't. I don't care that Michelangelo spent four years on his back painting that ceiling." He looked me full in the face. "The past few weeks have felt like four years to me."

I clutched my arms as if to protect myself from a storm at sea.

"I've been talking to Mike."

I grew uneasy when Nick talked to this Mike guy during class breaks. He was swarthy, with grease under his fingernails, not someone I wanted to be around. Meanwhile, I made an effort to talk to some of the girls, while trying to disguise how much I watched Nick out of the corner of my eye. The situation made me feel like a hovering, over-protective mother, but I couldn't help myself.

"His dad owns a garage. The old guy's sick and forced to retire. Mike's quitting school to take over. He wants me to work with him." Nick assessed my reaction, then sat up straighter. "I start tomorrow."

"No asking my opinion? What am I supposed to do while you're working all summer?" Suddenly, I felt rudderless, and my usually controlled voice had escalated to a shriek. A group of girls strolling by stopped and turned, like a flock of ducks on a pond. They gave Nick a quick once-over, then paddled away. This time their attention didn't make me feel the least bit pleased.

"I knew you'd be upset, and I'm really sorry, but I can't back down." He put an arm around my "bony frame," which he'd taken to teasing me about—in a loving way. "Let's go home. There's the rest of today. We can make the most of it."

I peered at him, almost able to touch the waves of enthusiasm emanating from his body. More than anything, I wanted him to be happy.

"Okay." I rose from the bench, already resigned to the future. The beginnings of a familiar tingle made me quicken my step.

That's how it worked—easily distracted. Whenever I grew bothered by something Nick did or didn't do, even though I seldom said anything, he sensed it, and at the earliest possible moment we were in our bedroom, where he stroked and plucked my body like a well-tuned instrument, his hands working me into a trembling, taut tension, until release was near, like the highest note on my violin, the piercing, exquisite sensation of a thin golden string running up through my insides, stretching tighter and tighter, until it could go no further...a sostenuto...followed by my soft exclamation and a tumbling down - down - down in a series of deepening tones.

I dropped by the garage every day, bringing lunch from a nearby deli. Nick seemed to appreciate each sandwich surprise. Often he would be with a customer, so I'd slip off to a corner of the grimy-smelling room, holding a brown bag and a Dr. Pepper, trying to be inconspicuous.

He'd be bent over an open hood, carefully tuning, adjusting, and pointing out different aspects of the engine, justifying services to be performed and explaining how the owner's car soon would be humming along in perfect order.

That fall, to my surprise, I enjoyed college on my own. I took appealing classes without worrying whether there would be anything remotely interesting for him. I played my violin with the campus orchestra. I attended marches against the war in Vietnam, and sometimes said to Nick, who had a medical deferment due to a heart murmur, "The U.S. government is lying to us. This is futile and senseless."

If happening to hear me, he'd mumble a vague response, then go back to his car magazine.

One day, I walked into the garage, and a girl from several of our classes the previous year stood next to him, looking into the engine of a purple Capri. Nick was in the midst of explaining the operations of her vehicle and his proposed alterations—as slowly and precisely as he did with any customer. At one point, he showed her how to test the car's oil level. After she (I remembered her name to be Heidi) pulled the dipstick out, wiped it off, reinserted it, pulled it back out, and showed Nick her results, I stepped forward with my deli offering.

"I didn't know you were here," Heidi said

in a voice that sounded as languid as if she'd been awakened from a nap.

"I brought Nick's lunch." Why had I bothered to say this?

"That's right. You two are married. No wonder you watched this guy like such a hawk." She tossed her long, sun-streaked hair and laughed as if she'd said the funniest thing anyone had heard all day. Golden skin shone with her smile.

When Nick got home that night, early for a change, I mentioned Heidi. He shrugged it off.

A couple of hours later, he was extra attentive.

That spring, I was about to graduate, and one day, I stayed home alone making a special dinner for the two of us—to celebrate. Soon, my family would arrive for their blessedly brief visit. A knock startled me. Since no one ever dropped by, I assumed it to be the landlord returning our deposit. We'd given notice and planned a move to Washington, D.C., where I would begin working at the Smithsonian in the department that planned multicultural presentations.

Putting on my pleasant face, I opened the door and found a middle-aged woman standing outside the apartment. Head bent down, she fingered buttons on her tan coat. A kerchief half covered her crimped, gray-brown curls.

"Yes?"

"You're Mrs. Duffek?" The woman raised her eyes for a moment, before casting them back to her buttons. One hung by a thread.

"I am. What is it?"

"My daughter...Heidi...she goes to the college."

"Maybe I know her."

"You do know her. She told me that she knows you and your husband."

"My husband?"

"That's why I'm here." The woman stared straight at me and took on a harsh attitude. "I want your husband to stay away from my Heidi. She shouldn't spend time with him. She's got a boyfriend to

marry as soon as she's done with this college stuff. If he breaks it off, Heidi's going to be sorry. I don't want my girl hurt."

"You're mistaken. My husband works all day, and every night he's home with me." I pushed his occasional late hours from my mind. "You're thinking of someone else."

"I saw them together, Missus. Going into her apartment. My son...he's a patrolman...he checked the license I gave him. The car they came in belonged to your husband."

"Nick would never do anything like what you're implying. You need to leave and never come back!" I slammed the door and locked it.

Breathlessly, I collapsed onto the sofa, my cheeks burning. Hands rubbing my face, I spoke to the empty room. "There's an explanation. He repaired that purple Capri and he drove her...she had someone...the boyfriend...at her apartment. She needed to get money from him for the bill."

A couple of hours later, I heard the key turn. I'd been scrambling for what, if anything, to say. But while I waited, my skin had calmed. I was wearing my prettiest blue dress, the one that he said made my eyes look as clear as a cloudless June sky. "Yesterday"—one of his Beatles' records—played. I didn't care for most of his music, but did appreciate this group. Their instrumentals were good. Sometimes, like in this piece, there were violins playing.

"How come the door was locked? I told you I'd be home early."

"Um...I must have done it automatically... after Mr. Connor came by with our deposit."

Nick sniffed the air. "Something smells great." He always took my word on money matters. He pulled me to him and danced me around the room. He whispered, "What's the occasion?"

"We're leaving soon. I wanted to have a good-bye dinner to remember all the sweet times." I pressed my head into his chest. "I'm going to miss this place."

"Me too." He twirled me as the song ended, and said, "Anything happen today?"

I chose not to mention that crazy woman who'd

been at our door. Why upset him over something as stupid as her accusations? Why spoil our meal? We had so much to be excited about. College was done. We were headed to Washington. I had a wonderful job. We'd signed papers on a house that my father bought for us in Alexandria, a short commute to the District. And, Daddy had helped Nick buy his own car repair shop, a couple of minutes from our new house. We were set. No. I won't say anything, I promised myself. What a strange woman. Spying on her daughter like that—not trusting her.

Nick put on another 45 and said, "Dinner can wait. Let's go this way." He started to sing with his deep voice, "Something in the way she moves..." He put his hand on the small of my back, guiding me into our bedroom. The whole day, along with the pot roast in the oven, disappeared from my mind as my skin began to glow, and I leaned into his gentle touch.

About the Author:

Kathleen Glassburn's fiction has been published in many journals. For examples of her stories see her website: www.kathleenglassburn.com. She is managing editor of The Writer's Workshop Review www.thewritersworkshopreview.net She earned her MFA in creative writing from Antioch University, Los Angeles. Currently she lives in Seattle with her husband, three dogs, a cat, and a fifty-year-old turtle. Her horse is boarded nearby and she rides him several times a week. Also for fun she plays the piano.

THE ARTISTS
By Janet Mason

(October, 1926)

After dinner, Nan and George refilled their wine glasses with a deep red Bordeaux and went to the sitting room where they waited for their spouses to join them. George put a record on his new Victor Victrola. It sat in the corner on its own end table. Its sound horn with its fluted edges resembled a large silver lily. The opening was turned toward the wall.

Nan stared at the fluted horn.

"I turned it to the wall so that the sound would echo through the apartment," said George.

"The music sounds turbulent," said Nan.

"That's the point," replied George. "Stravinsky's The Rite of Spring portrays the violence of the Russian pagan rites. A maiden dances herself to death in the sacrificial dance. Stravinsky uses Russian folk music in the score. He was sketched by Picasso, and Picasso undoubtedly influenced him. They both discovered artistic primitivism at the same time -- Picasso in his cubist painting and Stravinsky in his experimental music."

Nan cocked her head and listened to the strains of music amplified by the phonograph. She imagined violin bows slicing air. She heard cubism in the music. The bass of kettle drums sounded. She cocked her head so that one ear was turned to the sound horn as she listened intently to the high tones of the piccolo and flutes.

Despite what George had said, Nan didn't care for the music. She didn't say so though -- out of politeness to her teacher and friend.

Emma came in and joined them, sitting down on the burnt umber leather sofa next to her husband. Wilna was still missing.

She must be in the powder room, thought Nan.

"I hear that the piece started a riot in Paris when it debuted," continued George. "But that was because of the bad ballet dancing under the direction of Nijinsky."

Nan nodded again. She was relieved that Emma had lowered the sound. Nan could hear herself think. She had heard about the riot in the theater in Paris. The patrons undoubtedly had paid too high a ticket price for bad ballet dancing.

"John Singer Sargent did a portrait of Nijinsky," said George.

George was always mentioning other artists that he knew.

"Maybe Nijinsky was one of John's conquests," chimed in Emma. "We found out from friends in Europe that he was notorious."

"Now Emma," gently chided George. "John's personal life doesn't really matter, even if he did conduct his professional life along the same lines as his personal life. May he rest in peace."

"George means that John was a whore -- and that he sold out. That's why he was so famous," said Emma.

George chuckled. He couldn't have said it better himself. But his mother had told him to never speak ill of the departed.

He cleared his throat. "To his credit, John was the first to use light to define form in his portraits."

Emma was quiet.

Then she said, "Whatever you say dear. I say a whore's a whore."

Then there was an awkward silence. Nan was glad that Wilna wasn't in the room. Wilna would be uncomfortable and probably would interpret Emma and George's conversation as a marital spat. But Nan smiled inwardly. Using bad language was uncharacteristic of Emma. But she was defending George. She was also defending the other Ash Can artists. There was a reason the Ash Can artists didn't get as much respect as painters such as Sargent who was considered the most important portrait artist of their time. He was known for the portraits of wealthy patrons who could pay his commissions.

"Is this Djuna Barnes in this photograph?" Wilna's voice boomed from the hall. If she was an opera singer, she'd be a mezzo soprano.

"Yes, that's exactly right," said George as he rose from the sofa.

Emma and Nan followed him into the hall.

"I thought I recognized her," said Wilna. "I met her once. She's a writer."

Nan studied the portrait in front of her.

Djuna was wearing a shiny hat wrapped close to her head. It made the top of her head look larger, and it accentuated her sad almond-shaped eyes. Her triangular nose led down to her deep shiny lips. The photograph was black and white but, to Nan, Djuna's lips looked deep red, so dark they were almost maroon. She wore a dark cape around her with a high collar that came up past her ears. The cape looked like it was out of a Dracula movie.

"Berenice Abbott, who I met through one of my students, is an up and coming young photographer who lives in Paris. She took the portrait," said George. "Berenice and Djuna used to live together here in the village and now they live in Paris, but separately."

Nan looked at the photograph. She wondered what it was like to live in the Village with the bohemians. Or to live in Paris and be an artist.

"Nan and I would never live in the Village," stated Wilna. "We prefer Bearsville -- give us the mountains and the fresh air any time. And, of course, we settled there because it's so close to the arts colony in Woodstock. But we do like the sea. That's why I just bought a another property in Carmel. We're packing up and going there next month for the winter and coming back East in the Spring. While we're in Carmel we are going to do nothing but our painting. We are going to be full-time artists."

Wilna looked at the photograph dismissively.

"This is a good portrait," she said. "But it's a photograph. It's not art."

"Of course, it's art," said George. "Photography has been art for decades now. Look at Stieglitz. Many of the Ash Can artists have been inspired by fine art photography and the documentary photography such as Lewis Hine produced of the exploited child laborers in this country early in the century."

"I didn't say that documentary photography isn't important," said Wilna stubbornly. "I just said that I don't think it's art."

George pressed his lips together sternly and looked at Wilna as if she were a pupil who didn't do her homework.

"Oh, I hear Carmel is beautiful," exclaimed Emma. "And it's by the sea. The perfect place for an artist. I'm happy for you girls."

Nan smiled at Emma. How like Emma to change the subject since Wilna and George appeared to be having a disagreement, thought Nan.

"Actually," said Nan, "we just bought a property in Carmel. Wilna bought the first one. But we both own the new house -- and it's perfect for us!"

Nan realized that she was still stewing about Wilna's earlier comment that she had just bought a house in Carmel.

Wilna looked at Nan and frowned.

She probably disapproves of me telling George and Emma, thought Nan. Buying property together did make it look like they were a couple. But they were a couple. George and Emma had to know, even though they never talked about it. It really didn't matter.

George smiled. Having Nan here made him feel like he was in the classroom. He knew how to bring the focus back to his lecture.

"Bernice used to live in the Village with Djuna and the Hippolyte Havel, the anarchist who is friends with Emma Goldman. He was going around saying that he had 'adopted' Berenice. She left and moved to Paris. I suspect the Village was too bohemian for her. The ideas are brilliant -- but an artist can't work without regular hours."

"That's right, George. You are a fine example of an artist who does his artwork every day," said Emma. She radiated pride.

Nan noticed that Emma always spoke up for George when she could. She hoped that she did this enough with Wilna. It was different with George and Emma, of course, since Emma wasn't an artist. But the fact that Nan and Wilna were both artists was a tie between them, just like the fact that they were both farmers and now had a pair of goats. Nan and Wilna were here because they had both had taken classes with George and he liked their paintings. Of course, they thought the world of him. Now Emma was part of their

world. She may not make art herself, but Nan could see how she was a part of George.

George nodded.

"We just heard that Berenice has started working with an interesting French photographer -- and elderly gentleman who used to be an actor and who toils in obscurity, documenting the old Paris. I'm sure we'll hear more about him. He sounds like a true artist."

George gave Wilna a meaningful look.

"And speaking of pictures, it's time now for our main event -- the unveiling of George's newest painting Nude With A Parrot, " said Emma.

"It's just my latest work," said George modestly. "I'm sure they'll be others. But with what I have planned for us later tonight, I seriously doubt that this is the main event."

He had a real treat in store for them.

"Nonsense," said Emma. "You've been working on that painting for years. It's time for a celebration. I'll get the champagne."

"Champagne," cried Nan. She clapped her hands.

About the Author:

Janet Mason is an award-winning creative writer, teacher, and blogger for The Huffington Post. Her book, Tea Leaves, a memoir of mothers and daughters, published by Bella Books in 2012, was chosen by the American Library Association for its 2013 Over the Rainbow List. Tea Leaves also received a Goldie Award. Janet's short fiction has appeared in many literary journals including the Brooklyn Review, Sinister Wisdom, and Aaduna. Her work has been nominated for a Pushcart Prize.

SARAH

By Isaac Wofford

"What are you working on?" James asked.

"I am writing a fiction story about my toxic psychiatrist." said Dan, then he handed the detached scribbled looseleaf paper and hot notebook to James.

James looked like he was reading, rather than just pretending, but the sun was taking its tole on both of them so Dan questioned his ability to perceive pretend-reading. James said "Yeah its good, I want to see more. Give a physical description, what was her hair like, you know."

"She had hair like a stupid bitch!" Dan slapped his draft against the table then took a breath and made his hands in a prayer position. "I've processed this I'm ready to describe what happened" he said as a robotic mantra.

They were at a table outside The Drop, a coffee shop that Dan had taken James to in order to show him where he wrote. Dan wrote into a notebook with coffee and cigarettes and no water at a wooden table in the blazing hot sun several days a week. Dan looked up behind him at a recognizable figure walking by, but he didn't get the person's attention. It was England Cohen.

Dan had met England first when he was an undergraduate living on the campus at Northwestern Arizona University. They were both in a creative writing class. England had a face covered with unpopped pimples, matted dark blond hair pulled into a ponytail, and he smelled like armpit. It wasn't long before England got married, got into mushrooms and acid, and dropped out of school.

Dan and England had been in Professor Odin's class. Professor Odin taught creative writing at the local university although he had no masters degree and no creative publications to his name. It wasn't until later that Dan learned Professor Odin was dating Professor Sarah, Ph.D.

Professor Sarah substituted one day for Professor Odin. After class Dan asked her about the graduate program. Dan asked how long the submission should be, "It said two to five pages on the website" he said.

She said "As short as possible, we don't want to have to read long pieces."

"Oh. And the cover letter?"

"The less we have to read the better, just look like someone we would want to work with for two years."

Then Dan's mother went to Europe for a week and he had to visit her house downtown and walk her Italian greyhound. As he walked eleven year old Loki through the residential area with beautiful lawns he came upon Professors Sarah and Odin.

At first he didn't see them, he was looking down at the ground to let Loki sniff some grass. Then her heard a woman's low, nervous laughter, almost a growl. He looked up and there was Professor Sarah in her dusty-rose, fitted wool sweater and slacks with her dark grey heavily highlighted bob. Professor Odin was about six feet tall and about fifty pounds overweight with a striking white goatee. They were sitting in lawn chairs, and each holding a glass of champagne.

Dan said "Oh!" and then "Hello!" in the most friendly way he could. He was stoned and felt awkward.

Professor Sarah kept laughing nervously.

Dan left, though he may have spoken too long as they would not respond or speak. That was weird.

The first day Dan took Professor Sarah's class she said "take off your hood." Dan should not have kept his hood on, perhaps. When he exposed his naturally red hair she said "He looks like the Uni-bomber."

To be honest the evil professor was amazingly witty. Every day she had something newly toxic to say about someone and Dan. It could be any one of the other students in the class, and also Dan. Dan got his every day.

Finally, Dan stayed after class to confront his professor. He had to wait for her to speak to four other students first and she spoke to each for ten minutes. It was already the end of the semester, he had to ask what was going on because he might take her class in the graduate program. Also Dan was angry. It was wrong. Why did she aggrandize her own wit at the price of his pride for so long?

When he finally saw her they were alone in the classroom. He said "Sarah, why are you mean to me?"

She said "I am not mean to you Dan."

He said "Another student said she felt bad for me after you made a joke. And other students agree with my point of view I have asked them."

Professor Sarah stood up "I will monitor my behavior around you from now on." She said it like a robot, and then she walked out.

When Dan got back to his Dorm he had an email from Professor Sarah that was forwarded to the head of the English department. It said "Dan, in hindsight I find it confusing that you would want to attend graduate school with a professor you find 'mean.' Please report my behavior to the head of the English department. Sarah."

Dan responded immediately. Instead of "mean" he called her behavior "harassment" and since she had no idea Dan was disabled (due to his bipolar disorder) he threw in the word "discrimination." He included about ten examples of her doing things like comparing him to the Uni-bomber for a class joke.

In a way, Dan won. Professor Sarah had to take a class in ethical teaching or something, and one can tell because she hands out candy to the class. Dan learned from his experience with Sarah that professors that hand out candy or order pizza may have had to take a class to prevent showing favoritism.

Unfortunately, Dan could never attend his alma mater for graduate school to get the Masters of Fine Arts in Creative Writing. He could write like Shakespeare and they would never accept him now. Instead of Northwestern Arizona University he had to attend Western New Mexico University and take every class online. Dan's Masters of Arts in Interdisciplinary Studies with concentrations in english and writing qualified him to teach literature or creative writing at a community college, but not a university.

Going to school online was hard. At one point, halfway through, Dan withdrew from both of his classes and saw a private psychiatrist. This first psychiatrist tried to have sex with him so he replaced his first psychiatrist with another one.

The second psychiatrist put Dan on medication that she said would not make him gain weight. Dan called her back when he got home and said "I have been on atypical antipsychotics before, I gained so much weight I almost got diabetes." It was true. Dan had done an amazing amount of work to recover.

She insisted Seroquel would not make him gain weight. He started Seroquel that night.

The second time he saw her he told her he gained weight. He was perfectly ready to reveal that the weight was being gained on his love handles and on his inner thighs, the kind of weight gain could make a man question his sexuality if it continued. It made his thighs looser and his chest droopier. Even if he were fat naturally, Dan didn't gain weight like this. But she looked down at Dan, shrugged her shoulders, and didn't ask any questions so he gave her none of those details.

The second time he saw her it was difficult for Dan to walk the two miles to get to her office without stopping for breath. His gut spilled out from under his shirt and with no belt his large pants were tight. In three weeks Dan had gained about fifty pounds, he hadn't had the means to replace any of his clothing, and he had no car. His mother was paying for the private psychiatrist. He had no choice but to look the way he did in public.

"Well we have to take you off of the Seroquel! you're obviously gaining weight!" Doctor Sarah said. Sarah the psychiatrist, like Sarah the English professor, wore a blonde bob. Sarah the psychiatrist was more overweight than Dan, no matter how much weight he gained he could never be as fat as her. She wore dresses that fit too tightly, always sleeveless, and she had fat shoulders. Her breasts were always in her way.

Dan wondered why she didn't listen when he told her he was gaining weight. Before she could tell through his clothes, because that was before it ruined his body. Why hadn't she listened? Didn't she know that anyone would know if they've gained weight before someone else saw them in clothing?

In further sessions Doctor Sarah revealed she had an "addiction to eating," told Dan how to eat to lose weight, told Dan which exercises to do, asked Dan if he weighed himself, she replaced the chair she was sitting on with a medicine ball, and her clothing became too short.

"Since the pills turn muscle into fat why are you telling me what to eat?" Dan said "I think you are trying to give me an eating disorder. Let me re-phrase that. I think you are trying to give me your eating disorder. No! Wait!" Dan waved his hand "I think you are pretending I have an eating disorder. Dummy, I had a six pack when you met me! You are fat don't tell me what to eat you are pre-scribing the pills that made me fat what the hell is wrong with you?" Sarah was an exhausting trigger for Dan, and she seemed to enjoy arguing back, so there was no way for Dan to really defend himself from her lectures about exercise and food.

Once a medication gave him double vision in each eye. Not only did Dan look different than before, he now had to see people differently than others saw him. It was another unwelcome change to his body.

"You can't have double vision in each eye" said Doctor Sarah.

"I do." Dan said after closing each eye to make certain.

"Maybe you should see an eye doctor!" Doctor Sarah argued back.

Doctor Sarah had ordered blood work and deci-phered it incorrectly, she told Dan that he had hepatitis C. "You could get a liver transplant!" she suggested cheerfully.

Suddenly and momentarily Dan identified himself as someone with a dying body, one that would need another's organs inside of his own to stay alive. She held eye contact as he digested her words, and she smiled and looked down at her desk when she was done looking into Dan's eyes. The blood test turned out to be a false alarm, Dan did not have hepatitis. Not only that but the treatment would have been a pill, not a liver transplant.

Finally, Dan graduated. He took the cocktail of medications Doctor Sarah had prescribed him to a clinic for refills. He didn't need her anymore. The ordeal had ruined his physique, but he lost some of the weight. Rounder and less handsome facial features and the need for loose clothes were worth it for a graduate degree.

Dan saw England Cohen again when he was buying weed downtown. England still had a face full of un-popped pimples, matted dark blond hair along the scalp even though the rest was pulled into a ponytail, and he still smelled like armpit. "How are you Dan? Long time no see." England said.

"How's your wife?" Dan asked.

"Crazy bitch is in a mental hospital."

"From the drugs?" Dan remembered that England had done acid, gotten married, and dropped out of school.

"I don't know. She was just a bitch." said England.

Of course Dan wanted to say he had a Master's degree. So he asked "Gonna go back to school?"

"I already finished the program."

"Which program?" Dan asked "The one at North-western Arizona University?" Oh Hell no. Not you, you privileged little asshole. Did Professor Sarah like you? You were comfortable flirting back! I know it! You're heterosexuality was a privilege and you don't have the education to understand.

When England replied he affirmed that he had indeed finished the program at Northwestern, and then he said "I don't agree with the privatized educational system..." That was something Professor Odin used to say. Professor Odin was Professor Sarah's boyfriend, he had no graduate degree but still taught at the university. England's imitation of another professor's rhetoric got him into the program because the professors were dating.

"So do you work there? Dan asked. little slut.

"Yeah." England said. You know a friend of mine said I was bragging when I said how much I make but it was a just a statement." England said, shrugging his shoulders.

"What do you make? Thirty thousand a year?" Dan asked.

England remained silent but nodded.

"How old are you, England?"

"Twenty-Seven."

"Well I think that's awesome! Congratulations you are set for life!" You can't brag because you don't know what to brag about. Your accomplishments were gifts. You have the gift of being given gifts.

Dan sat back and drank from his cup of coffee. He was no longer thinking about Sarah the English professor that harassed him or Sarah the psychiatrist that pretended he had an eating disorder. He was no longer watching England Cohen walk past. He still felt fat.

"James check out my notebook." He said.

James was facing the other direction smoking a cigarette, the back of his neck was now brown.

Has it been twenty minutes?

They looked at one another, James' skin and hair shone in the blazing sun.

Dan said "Yeah. Too long. Let's go."

About the Author:

Isaac Wofford is a thirty-six year old emerging writer. He lived in Brooklyn until he was nine and at the Navajo and Hopi reservations until he was fifteen. He has one self-published novella, "Too Ethical for Empathy," published by CreateSpace and available on Amazon. He has a BA in religious studies (comparative religion) and an MA in writing.

FOREVER BLUE: A TRIBUTE TO CHRIS ISAAC
by Valerie Kinsey

Baby Did a Bad Bad Thing

Jay—the second Jay—is shorter and squatter than the first and has skin the color of hazelnut gelato and a layer of fat over his muscles. He tells me he spent hours in the gym bulking up when he got out of the army, but it's the way he used his muscles in the army—humping gear, lifting the bodies of his fallen comrades, working some manly shit—that turns me on. That, the musky scent of his sweat, and his tattoos. "Commit" is inked on his back in black letters in a font I'd call Old Style Medieval Badass. *Is that a command?* I wonder as I dig my thumbs into the notch of flesh on either side of his sacrum. I leverage my weight, all 110 pounds of me. Eventually, when we get down to it and he's deep inside me, my tit in his mouth, my hands holding those round, nut-brown shoulders, I'll itch for the whir of the needle and the burn of the word emblazoned on the skin of my pectoral, and why, in this sweet, sweet moment of pleasure, I crave a little pain to make it sweeter.

Somebody's Crying

This song is about the first Jay, who is on stage, horn in hand. My Jay strums one hand against his pressed white shirt, untucked under a 44L merino blazer, in time with the drum, bass, and piano. A look of aloof intensity crosses his face while he's waiting to lift that trumpet at his side, and I'm forced to look into my clear, viscous drink. I suck on a Grey Goose-drenched olive. It tastes the way my father's martini olive would have tasted, except that he drank St. Polly Girl's Nonalcoholic beer. There are only two kinds of people who drink nonalcoholic beer. The first kind is obvious.

The second is the same as the first, minus the incontrovertible proof. Jay drinks Scotch, butterscotch-brown booze, on the rocks. If I looked in his wallet, there'd be business cards for women lawyers and restaurant managers, cell phone numbers printed on the back. Yeah, it's partly his skill that's sexy, those long, thick fingers that move with agility, the sound he makes, the lock of hair that falls across his Scottish-white, perspiration-dotted brow as he leans back and into the note, the swell of his chest, but sometimes, ladies, music is just background noise. It's the desire to train that intensity, to turn a single-minded communion with horn into a single-minded communion with you. Just as I look up, he raises the trumpet to his lips. I hold my vodka-soaked breath.

Don't Leave Me on My Own

Jay the Original—we'll call him Jay-Zero—took me to the beach in Mexico. During the sunset, long and sleepy as a summer matinee, we drank Coronas from recycled bottles smooth as sea glass. Boys fished for snapper in waves that lapped at their hips. They were successful sometimes. Americans laughed loudly nearby because they were expected to, but I was in my sundress, busy making a promise to God: *If I do not have HIV and contract AIDS and die, I will be happy with this man for the rest of my life, and, if this weren't clear enough* for God, I added: *I will not sleep with anyone else for as long as I live.* Please don't let me be alone. That evening, the sun was a violent orange eye watching us fight. *I can't believe you've been with more people than I have.* He might have called me a slut, but punished me, instead, by saying nothing. My hands smelled of lime juice, sharp and acrid, and I was thinking of the birth control pill and how, in certain moments past, I believed that nothing bad would ever happen to me. I didn't really think I was sick, but I felt lucky because maybe I deserved to pay a penalty for my caprice. Truth be told, when I uttered this promise, my intentions were good. But I made a liar of myself when I found that the true danger was in keeping my word. Given the choice, I'd betray God again.

Things Go Wrong

Jay the Third stops in Albuquerque to see me on his way back to Denver. He tells me he wasn't planning to call after what happened last time, but he's a victim of his impulses. Last time, he needlessly reminds me, he ended up in a hotel room and the power went out. He warns me I shouldn't get carried away by this little visit. The light on the rooftop bar—sheathed in tent plastic to keep out the early winter cold—is amber colored and he's wearing a sweater-vest and cashmere scarf, which makes it seem like we're sitting in a catalog selling new things meant to look old. He tells me all the great beauties had a look of sadness—Audrey Hepburn, for example, or Ingrid Bergman. Because of this, I should take what he says as a compliment. Silly me, I do. It's only a week later when I'm sipping ten-day-old chardonnay by the wattage of my energy-saver bulb that I realize how much of love depends on a trick of the light. When he finally got back on the road, the morning sun was white and sharp as a blade. We giggled nervously about the dangerous snowstorm that awaited him at the Colorado border, and he disappeared, soundlessly, into that crystalline white.

Forever Blue

Winter in New Mexico. In the pre-dawn, deep purple-blue clouds billow over the tops of the Sandia mountain peaks. Brilliant lights spread like a blanket at their feet. Too often I ask *what's Jay—the first Jay—doing out there? Where is he? What's he thinking about?* Have all but given up manufacturing reasons and ways to run into him. Keep making bargains that start with the phrase, *maybe if I sleep with him...And then what? I'll like him less? I'll trust him?* Luckily, Mom offers some help:

A. You don't have to do anything

B. But you are dating

C. It's good you have a therapist

D. You have so much anger, sugar, can't this be a learning experience?

Nighttime, on the balcony, I shove my hands deep into my fleecy pockets. I can see my own breath, pale and ashen, but I can't see the mountains, only the red blinking light on top, warning hot air-balloonists, reckless fliers.

Goin' Nowhere

This club is darker than the last. You're in your jeans and black leather jacket. Two lesbians sit at the checkered-tablecloth table where your sax player sets his Stella. Everyone else—your fans—are all dressed like you: single men, former band-dorks who whistle through their teeth after your solos. Not me. I'm perched on a barstool, front and center, in two strands of fake pearls, a suede miniskirt, and a pair of stacked, leopard-print heels. There's nowhere for you to look but at my legs, pale and bare in the bruised-colored room. You find a way to gaze into the walls that need paint, the bar that was once black but is now scuffed like your patron's shoes, the music, the drum shuffle, the jumping bass, the thick notes that swill and fade into the dingy air. When you press that trumpet to your lips, what am I hoping to hear? That you still want me? How can you feel regret when I'm bare-legged in your presence and it's obvious I'm going nowhere? I see the paradox: that for you to miss me—to really miss me—I'd have to leave like I mean it, exist in a past that, for me, doesn't yet exist.

Changed Your Mind

To me, this song explains what happened with the second Jay: I chose a table by the window to eat my sandwich so I could sit in the November morning and watch the wind tear yellow, paper-thin leaves. Jay may have been waiting out of sight, but he came and sat across from me. I pushed my plastic sunglasses to the crown of my head and then set them beside the waxy white bag to reach for his hand. I stroked the inside of his tattooed forearm.

"When I mentioned I wanted to see that band Friday, I was thinking that we'd see each other the following weekend," Jay said. "I was taking the long-term view."

The long-term view?

"It's like when the circus is in town, and it's only in town every once in a while."

The circus?

"When I told X I missed playing in a band, she told me to call the guys. 'Start playing again,' she said, even if it meant going on tour."

Why don't you marry X again?

Who asked you to give up music?

Why don't you fucking marry her (again)?

"You have to make room in your life for a relationship, Jay, that's all I'm saying. It's the nature of it. You don't have to stop playing music. Or stop listening to music." I release my hand from his, open the waxy white paper bag and take out my foil-wrapped BLT. There is too much mayo, and the bread is buttered soggy and squishes against my palate. Leaves swirl in eddies and scrape on the pavement outside. Without looking in his cinnamon-flecked eyes, I chew, swallow, and persist:

"As for priorities, I get that your son comes first—"

"And you had a problem with that."

I blink in the light and shove buttery crusts and foil back into the bag and reach for a near-empty Styrofoam cup of Coke. The straw squeaks against the lid. I set the cup down and pick up my sunglasses. "You were the one who was uncomfortable."

"I was. You're right. I'm a person who needs a lot of time to himself. I don't have a lot of free time. Time I spend with my son isn't free time. My free time, I spend playing music. Music is my life. It's more important than even writing. If I have to choose between you and music, I don't want to be in that situation. My free time is, well, free. That's the nature of it."

The End of Everything

Everything ends, but not all at once. Just like the sound of one hand clapping is difficult to hear, so is the sound of a cell phone that doesn't ring

when Jay the Third says he's going to call. My Buddhist friend, Steven, suggests I might be making myself too available:

Look without looking.

Hope without hoping.

Wait without waiting.

But, I protest, if Jay the Third doesn't call, he'll never know that I'm not going to answer. It would be nice to know he's not going to call. It's only fair, isn't it?

Buddha shrugs.

My unanswered question hangs in the air, and the conclusion drags on until I forget I even asked. Almost...

Heart-Shaped World

Jay-Zero once said, When the only tool you have is a hammer, every problem looks like a nail. With every Jay I meet, I feel the almost-thereness of love. He might be the missing piece, I tell myself. He just might be, and even if he isn't, close enough. After all, I carry around a palm-sized, construction-paper red square with a heart shape missing. This is the danger of living in a heart-shaped world.

About the Author:

Valerie Kinsey lives in the Bay Area with her husband, children, and a terrier. She teaches writing at Stanford University.

CUCUMBER PUNCH

by Charles Edward Brooks

To have lost is less disturbing than to wonder if we may possibly have won.

—Thomas Hardy, The Return of the Native

The mellow bells at First Baptist Church swung into a hymn, marking three o'clock in the afternoon. At the first peal, Ollie Garston banged her walnut gavel: "The August meetin' of the United Daughters of the Confederacy, Belle Boyd Chapter, will come to order."

All chatter ceased. Coughs and throat raspings faded into attentive silence.

"Madam Secretary, will you call the roll, please?"

"Ollie Garston."

The plump, gray-haired president replied in her clear contralto voice: "Present."

"Bertie Gaster."

A tall, slim woman answered: "Present."

"Gwen Handel."

A heavily made-up matron with dyed black hair tossed her head as she confirmed her presence.

"Maxine Jethway."

As blond as the lady preceding her was dark, and just as naturally so, prettyish Mrs. Jethway raised her hand: "I'm here."

"Lois Monger."

A tart-faced redhead attested to being at the gathering.

"And I'm also present," concluded the secretary, Meta Rush, in a deep voice.

The president's blue eyes flashed through rimless glasses. "Six ladies present out of a membership of eighteen! It's an insult to the ideals of our organization! And where are those younger recruits to the Cause that we've talked about so much?"

She paused and glowered at the little assembly. The five other ladies, ensconced in Victorian lady's chairs, counted like herself between fifty and sixty years of age. As president, Ollie occupied the only gentleman's chair in the room. The Victorian style, with an abundance of velvet, claimed all the remaining furnishings as well.

At a signal from the chair, Gwen Handel rose, seated herself at the baby grand piano and pounded out one entire verse of "Dixie." The others rose in turn and stood at attention, their right hands over their hearts.

During her long tenure in office, Ollie Garston had always insisted on "lots of pow" in the rendering of what to her comprised the national anthem. The ladies now delivered precisely that. Stamping feet, clapping hands, and swinging hips accompanied the six blaring voices:

> I wish I was in the land of cotton,
>
> Old times there are not forgotten.
>
> Look away, look away,
>
> Look away, Dixie Land...

At the end, huffing with emotion, the Daughters fell back into their armchairs.

Ollie sailed majestically onward: "Are there any old business?"

Maxine Jethway, English teacher at the high school, winced. No one spoke.

"Are there any new business?"

Lois Monger raised her index finger. "Madam President, as chairman of the Excursion Committee, I've been in touch with the P.G.T. Beauregard Chapter in Richmond. They'd be glad to receive us in October."

"Thank you, Madam Committee Chairman," said the president graciously. "Work out the details as you deem fittin' and proper."

There being no further new business, Ollie now introduced the speaker of the day. "Miz Leonard Gaster is gon' give us a paper on the Battle of Jubilation Creek, a historic event that took place within spittin' distance of where we're sittin' this very minute. Madam Speaker, the chair cedes the word to you."

Bertie Gaster extracted a bundle of papers from her pocketbook and coughed delicately. She began to read in a high soprano voice: "Madam President, fellow Daughters, it is my privilege, and one that I don't take lightly..."

By the end of the first paragraph, her five listeners had all begun to nod.

Some days before the August meeting of the United Daughters, Plink and Reuben Garston, age seventeen and eighteen, had spent the hours between supper and bedtime in their basement laboratory. As the first part of a chemistry experiment, they mixed together carefully calculated portions of corn, molasses, and yeast in earthenware crocks. Afterward, they placed the containers in a warm spot near the water heater.

On the night before the meeting, the boys kept well out of their mother's way. That great lady was already arranging flowers for the morrow and working herself into a state of fervor for the Cause That Failed.

Plink and Reuben repaired to the basement and carried out the second and final part of their experiment. After filtering off the liquid from the crocks, they subjected it to a process which their chemistry teacher called fractional distillation. It took them some time.

What remained at the end of the evening filled a big mason jar: a clear liquid with an agreeable ethereal odor.

"That'll be more than enough," opined Plink.

"Lord, I reckon!" his brother exclaimed.

While Bertie Gaster droned on about breaches in the Northern left flank and charges by the Southern right one, the Garston kitchen buzzed with activity. Queen Esther, the family's housekeeper, was assembling refreshments. A cold salad made of pineapple and marshmallows in a cream sauce, homemade rolls filled with pimento cheese, and a varia of pickles made up the main course. Queen Esther had baked her unique peanut-flavored chess pie for dessert. And since it was far too hot for coffee, her mistress had concocted a cold beverage for the occasion: her beloved cucumber punch. None of the recipes for these delicacies had ever been published in the cookbooks put out by the local women's clubs to raise money for charity. Even Ollie's civic-mindedness had its limits.

That morning, the old man on the red wagon had lugged two blocks of ice into the pantry behind the kitchen. One went into the cold chest, the other into a tub earmarked for the cucumber punch.

"Plink, you an' Reuben get that punch bowl ready," Queen Esther commanded. "That woman's windin' down. And don't make no noise in the dinin' room, neither."

"Okay."

The boys half-filled Ollie's pride and joy, her mother's crystal punch bowl, with chipped ice. Walking on tiptoe, they carried it from the pantry to the dining room buffet. Only then did they pour in the cucumber punch. And at the last, they added a clear liquid from a mason jar—a substance whose very existence their mother vehemently opposed.

"There bein' no further items on the agenda, I declare the meetin' closed." Ollie Garston stood up. "And now, ladies, let's adjourn to the dinin' room." At these words, Queen Esther appeared like a genie and opened the double doors to that shadowy room, where she had closed the venetian blinds to keep out the sun.

Unique bouquets of roses, wood fern, and hollyhocks adorned the dining table, buffet, and china closet. Only Ollie Garston, among all the town's flower arrangers, would ever have combined these three elements. The dark red blossoms of American Pillar scented the room with their cloying fragrance.

"Lord, Ollie," Gwen Handel exclaimed as she passed through the double doors, "a few more whiffs o' those roses and I'm gon' be downright intoxicated."

The other ladies received this remark in silence. Of the six, only Gwen ever touched alcohol at all. And touched, in her case, was a euphemism.

Over the buffet hung a photograph of Queen Victoria taken during her long period of mourning. The turned-down mouth and bulging eyes conveyed an unspeakable sourness. Beneath the picture stood the punch bowl, with crystal cups on either side of it. Flanking these, the eatables waited temptingly. But before digging into the refreshments, the guests expressed their envy of their hostess for her culinary skills, her good taste, and the devoted services of Queen Esther. When they sensed that Ollie's need for praise had been gratified, they pressed forward to the spread.

It was Lois Monger who took the first sip of cucumber punch. She lifted her fine aquiline nose. "Ollie," she raved, "your punch really hits the spot on a swelterin' day like this!"

"It surely does," agreed Maxine Jethway. "I feel like I could drink the whole blessed bowl."

Beads of perspiration rolled down Lois Monger's face and onto her chic two-piece outfit. When she dabbed her cheeks with a delicate lace handkerchief, splotches of powder and makeup came away. But by this time, she couldn't have cared less.

"Gwen McTavish," she yelled, "I'll thank you to mind your own damn business!"

"Maybe it is my business. Or was, I should say."

Gwen spoke with a thick tongue. "I was crazy about Fred Opie all the way through high school, and it was mutual. Everybody knew it was mutual, includin' you. And then..."

Nature had more than replenished whatever color Lois had wiped off her face. Against the flaming cheeks, her hazel eyes glinted as green as an angry cat's.

"And then what?"

"You lured him away from me; that's what. Y'all lived next door to the Opies, and you had easy access. And now both of you are still livin' in those big ole family homes, rattlin' around by yourselves. All your folks long since dead and buried."

"And what of it?"

"You could've married. Had children. A real family life. But no. There you are in your house and Fred in his, both of you gettin' older every day."

Maxine Jethway wore a nasty smile that none of the others had ever seen before. Her black eyes shone with malice: "Everybody in this town knows Fred comes in your back door at bedtime and doesn't come out again till morning."

"You and all the other bitches in this town can mind their own goddamn business!"

"Lois, really!" Ollie slurred. "Language like that comin' from you of all people!"

Lois Monger placed the smudged handkerchief over her eyes and began to sniffle.

Maxine went on mercilessly: "Not that I blame Lois for not marrying Fred Opie. The man's a failure. She stole him from Gwen out of sheer meanness and then realized he wasn't worth the trouble. She's like a dog—and a female dog is a bitch;

I can't help it—that snatches a hunk of meat from another one and then just toys with it."

Lois leaned back wearily and closed her eyes. Her head began to nod.

"Maxine Garston," screeched Bertie Gaster, her green eyes flaring, "you're not the one to be criticizin' anybody for takin' up with a failure! If that word doesn't fit Caleb Jethway, I don't know who it does fit."

"Whom it does fit, you ignorant woman."

"Don't change the subject. A bitch with good grammar's still a bitch. You were the brightest thing in your class—here in high school and at Salem Academy too. You could've gone on to graduate school and really made somethin' out o' yourself. But you chose to come back here and throw yourself away on Caleb Jethway. You've wasted God-given talents, and you'll be called to account for it someday."

"Of all the silly moralizing I ever heard!" cried Maxine. Her large bosom heaved. "I suppose I could have done more with my life than I have, but then who can't say that?"

Meta Rush tottered back from the bathroom, the back of her skirt caught in her bloomers, her gray hair in disarray.

"Bertie Hart," she growled, "you always have resented it that you don't have a college degree. Claimed you couldn't afford it. Now, plenty o' folks with less wherewithal than you had went to college. But they had somethin' you didn't: willpower and gumption."

"What do you know about any o' that, Meta Rush? If we weren't in your sister's home, I'd slap your face!"

Unabashed, Meta went on: "So instead o' goin' to college, you stayed here and married Leonard Gaster, who you look down on and blame for everything bad that ever happened to you, even your lack of a college education."

"All these ladies know you wanted to marry him yourself."

"I did. It's no secret. I'd marry him today, for that matter."

"You common hussy, if I catch you even lookin' at my husband…"

The plump Meta Rush leaped on Mrs. Gaster with such force that the victim's chair fell over backward. Like Furies, the two women clawed, scratched, screamed, and spat. Drops of blood discolored Bertie's mousy hair. Gashes disfigured Meta's flawless skin.

Gwen Handel threw herself into the melee and tried to separate the combatants. "Meta Rush," she gasped, "you've never gotten over bein' single. But if you're not married, it's your own fault. Nothin' against Leonard, but he's not the only man in the world."

"Have you ever gotten over Fred Opie, Gwen?" bellowed Meta.

Gwen rolled her brown eyes. Her throaty voice sank almost to Meta's own pitch. "Yes, I have. I married Albert Handel on the rebound, but I've made do with him."

"I'd rather be on my own than just make do with somebody," Meta insisted. "My sister did that, too."

"Now wait one minute, young lady," Maxine Jethway growled. "You're talking about my brother."

Ollie burped: "And my husband."

"Well, his two sons are the most vicious boys I've ever seen, even if they are my nephews. Their practical jokes go beyond all the limits of decency. They'll be famous criminals one day, mark my words. And if 'Like father, like son' means anything, that says somethin' about their father, too." Meta smiled at her triumphant conclusion.

A few moments of quiet supervened, disturbed at intervals by discreet belches and hiccups.

Suddenly, Ollie Garston sat up straight in her chair. "All right, ladies." The words emerged slowly, with crystal-clear enunciation. "In virtue of my office, I'm entitled to call an extraordinary meetin' of the Belle Boyd Chapter at any time. And I'm callin' one right now!"

The majesty of the president's office did not fail of effect. Shamefacedly, the five other Daughters gathered themselves.

Ollie pushed a button by the mantelpiece. Within

seconds, Queen Esther materialized in the double doors, her expression a mixture of horror and indignation.

Salad sauce and chess pie filling spattered the ladies' summer frocks. Recent tears had left several faces splotched with red. Only Ollie's coiffure held up in anything like normal condition. Bertie's and Meta's plates lay upside down on the carpet, together with the fragments of a shattered punch glass. The room smelled of roses, peanuts, and sweat.

The black woman looked at her mistress, who simply nodded.

Queen Esther raised the venetian blinds and threw the windows open; at once the odor of hot freshly mown grass stifled every other smell in the room except that of the roses. With deft movements, she collected crockery and crystal and removed them to the kitchen. In a second step, she took the three remaining punch glasses, by no means empty, from the hands that held them. On her next entrance, she handed each Daughter a dainty towel dampened with cologne.

"Queen Esther," Ollie ordered with studied distinctness, "put a pot of coffee on, the strongest you know how to make."

A smile stole over the broad face. "It perkin' already."

At six-twenty the telephone rang.

A black hand picked up the instrument: "Garston res-i-dence."

"It's Caleb Jethway, Queen Esther. What in the worl's goin' on over there? It's suppertime and my wife's not home yet."

The answer adhered to Ollie's instructions: "The United Daughters is assembled in a 'straor-dinary session and dealin' with urgent business. They'll be home when they gets there."

Leonard Gaster and Albert Handel garnered exactly the same words.

When Paul Garston got home, he forbore, on strict orders from Queen Esther, to enter his own living room. Instead, he joined his two sons, the

picture of wholesome youth, at the kitchen table, where the threesome consumed the remnants of the feast. The boys had emptied the leftover punch down the sink. The punch bowl now sparkled innocently on the pantry table.

As they ate, father and sons listened to the news, through patches of static, from a little Philco radio. The German government has dissolved all the Masonic lodges in the Reich and confis-cated their assets...

"Dad blast that Hitler!" Paul cried. Freemasonry alone still aroused passion in the flabby businessman. A thirty-second-degree Mason, he had always given other fraternal bodies—and quite especially the Sons of the Confederacy—a wide berth.

By seven-thirty, the neighbors had finished their supper and sat on their porches, enjoying the relative coolness and the lingering daylight. They observed the Garstons' front door open and five Daughters of the Confederacy, followed by their president, emerge onto the veranda. One and all, the ladies were beautifully groomed.

The five descended to the liriope-lined walk, advancing with circumspection. Her features composed into affability, Ollie waved goodbye from the steps with a lace handkerchief.

Gwen Handel, who lived in the next block, made her way thither with a queenly bearing. The other four climbed cautiously into three automobiles. Bertie's Pierce-Arrow started and jerked away from the curb. All three vehicles moved out of sight with remarkable slowness. One last wave of the handkerchief and Ollie stepped back into the house.

The housekeeper was putting the last touches to the living room. "Miss Ollie, it's time for me to get home. More'n time."

"It certainly is," her employer agreed. "I appreciate you stayin' late and helpin' me in this, ah, emergency. You'll be paid for the extra time; that goes without sayin'."

"Anything else befo' I go?"

"No. Good night, Queen Esther. Thank you."

The back door closed after the black woman. Total silence fell on the house. No unfamiliar sound, no extraneous scent intruded into the now tidy living room. Every stick of furniture occupied its proper place. And yet, the order of Ollie Garston's life had been radically disturbed, shaken so hard that the sediment of lifelong habit would never wholly settle down again.

The woman felt her thoughts becoming firmer, less capricious.

I'll get to the bottom of this if it's the last thing I do, she vowed. Something went wrong with my punch. My one-of-a-kind cucumber punch! It must have gone bad in this heat…or fermented… or else somebody fiddled with it. Whatever or whoever it was, I'll get to the facts. And at the September meeting—I reckon it falls under "old business"—I'll table them.

But in parliamentary procedure, old business is brought up to be dealt with and laid ad acta. At the very moment when she was taking this re-solve, Ollie knew that the events of the afternoon would never be cleared away once and for all. As unalterable as Appomattox, they would hover about the Daughters, like a stench, for the rest of their days. For too much truth had been spoken.

Why does the truth always have to be bad? she puzzled. We lie ourselves black in the face to get through the days. We might not even get through them if we didn't. We can't stand the truth, and we hate the people who tell it to us. What a world!

Ollie felt that she should solve the puzzle, write down a solution in the neat hand she used for her UDC correspondence. But the task was beyond her. Perhaps she would find time to think about it tomorrow. Most probably not; so much else had to be done. There would be no getting rid of the problem, either. Like a huge dusty cobweb, it would hang about her forever.

Sinking back in the roomy gentleman's chair, she sensed a mire of old insults, defeats, and disap-pointments oozing about her feet. And of new fears as well. Her sister had rightly said it: Her marriage had never been more than a make-do affair. As they grew up, her sons were becoming strangers to her. Local interest in the Cause That Failed was waning. The Great Depression con-tinued to cast a dark shadow over the entire Earth. The Germans were rearming, and no politi-cians anywhere had sense enough to stop them.

Would her boys have to go off someday and fight Hitler's hordes? What a world, indeed!

Ollie Garston stood up and set her jaw. No one would ever be able to say that she had quailed before unpleasant truths. She would keep to the path she had chosen. If specters got in her way, she would just push them aside and forge ahead. She would read her paper at the September meeting, and it was high time to start writing it. Not to mention the talk she would be expected to give in Richmond. But now: Had her husband and sons had anything to eat?

She walked to the hall door and called upstairs: "Paul, are you up there? Plink…Reuben…have y'all had supper?"

When a cracked adolescent baritone answered from the back bedroom, the heaviness of being fell off her like a suddenly loosened shroud. And as she made her way to the kitchen, she felt the swampy miasma about her feet dissolving into thin air.

About the Author:

Charles Edward Brooks was born in North Caroli-na. He holds advanced degrees from Duke Univer-sity and the University of Lausanne and fellowship in the Society of Actuaries. His work has appeared in Eureka Literary Magazine, Licking River Review, Menacing Hedge, North Dakota Quarterly, The pacificREVIEW, SEEMS, Xavier Review, and many other publications. In addition to original writing, he is active as a literary translator, working in English, French, German, Italian, and Portuguese. He lives in Switzerland.

THE TREE REMEMBERS

Richard Key

We were on the outskirts of Shreveport when it became clear that the next exit or two would be our last opportunity for lunch. I had lost all my credibility for predicting fast food exits, and the troops were deep into their Valley Forge routine. My watch said ten till three.

Wendy's won by a vote of two to one over Burger King. I abstained at first but then had to break the tie. Derek lost because I knew he wouldn't grouse as much as his older sister, Stephanie. Food. They basically wanted food and here it was. If their mother were with us, she would have had snacks in her purse for just such an occasion: SweeTARTS, raisins, little bags of peanuts and pretzels saved from remote airplane rides. But we had dropped her off at her sister's house in Texas, and I was now in charge of hunting and gathering.

Few actual customers were inside, and it took no time at all to be seated with our sandwiches and drinks. A group of twenty or so workers assembled in one half of the dining room, some sitting and some standing, while a middle-aged lady with a gravelly voice lectured them on Wendy's protocol. After a minute or two, we were the only customers remaining and could not help but hear the whole proceedings.

"Some of the day shift people have complained that the chili meat is not thawed out when they come in. If you are on the night shift, it is your responsibility to take the meat out of the freezer and let it thaw out." At this point she wagged her index finger around at her audience. "From now on take the meat out of the freezer for the next shift, or you're gonna git wrote up."

Derek slurped on his straw and wagged his forefinger at Stephanie, who promptly grabbed it and bent it backward. I was savoring my spicy chicken sandwich. Nothing elevates fast food into the higher ranks of cuisine like fierce hunger. The lady manager continued her sermon.

"And speaking of the late shift, if you're on evening or night shifts, starting next week there will be unannounced visits by me or Mr. Ken, so be forewarned. If you're a supervisor on those shifts, you better have all your ducks in a row and they better be quackin'."

Derek could not help himself. "Quack."

"Shh."

"Quack." Then giggles.

"Stop it!"

"Quack-quack."

"That's it. We're leaving. Come on." I gave the lecturing woman a look of parental exasperation and we exited.

As we settled in for the next leg of the trip, I thought I should use the opportunity to make a point. "What did we learn back there, kids?"

Stephanie piped up, "That if you get French fries after three o'clock, they're cold and limp."

"No. What we learned was that if you don't study hard in school, you could end up with a job in a fast food restaurant where the manager will always be trying to sneak up and catch you goofing off so he can fire you."

"I think it'd be cool," Derek chimed in. "You could have ice cream whenever you want."

"What would be cooler would be to have a professional job like a doctor or a nurse where you get to help people and don't have managers on your case all the time."

There was silence so either the message was being mulled over, or it seeped out into the warm Louisiana breeze, aided by a couple of eye rolls.

Back on the interstate, a little east of Shreveport, we passed the carnage of an animal heaped up on the right shoulder of the road.

"Ugh!" declared Stephanie.

"It's a kangaroo!" yelled Derek.

"It's not a kangaroo," I said. "It's a deer."

"It had a long tail!" he protested.

"How many kangaroos do you think they have here in Louisiana, son?"

"One less than they used to have."

"Think about it. The only place with kangaroos around here would be the zoo in Baton Rouge. I don't know if Shreveport even has a zoo. But anyway, they'd have to do a lot of hopping to get this far away." Silence in the back seat. "And gators would probably get him when he crossed the swamp," I added to solidify my case.

Derek thought for a moment and then added, "Yeah. Gators would have got him. But it sure looked like a kangaroo."

Somewhere between Shreveport and Monroe, I developed a discomfort in my left side and back. At first I attributed it to sitting funny and spinal fatigue. But no amount of repositioning seemed to help. It was becoming hard to concentrate on the road. I stopped off at a drugstore in Monroe to get a bottle of Advil. I took three of the things, even though they tell you two is the limit.

"Are you okay, Dad?" my daughter asked.

"I think I will be after these take effect. I'm not sure what's going on."

But by the time we reached the Mississippi River, I had a pretty good idea: kidney stone. My brother had one a few years ago, and his description was much like this. I was beginning to writhe and sweat.

"Kids, I'm going to have to pull over. Stephanie, dear, call your mom and tell her I'm going to the hospital."

She did so and then replied, "She says she's coming over here."

"No. Tell her I'll be all right once they bust up this stone. Here, let me talk to her."

I told Paula I couldn't make it back to Jackson and we were in Vicksburg. My mom could come over and get the kids, and I should be out in a day or so. That way she could stay in Dallas and take care of her sister, who was recovering from an accident. She agreed but said she would fly back if anything happened. I saw a sign by the highway and followed the directions to Mercy Hospital.

"I have a kidney stone," I told the nice lady at the ER check-in station. You might think that would exempt me from the five pages of paperwork but you would be wrong. Three hours, two examinations, urinalysis, blood work, and an ultrasound later, the first doctor I saw told me, "Looks like you have a kidney stone, Mr. Gage. That's the good news—it's not a tumor or an aneurysm. The bad news is the lithotripsy machine is on the blink. They told me someone is coming up from New Orleans tomorrow to take a look at it."

I took the news pretty well. My options were to wait for the stone to pass on its own and strain my pee to try and catch it. Or wait for the machine to get fixed. Or drive to Jackson to another facility. But driving while on narcotics is discouraged, and it became clear that the only sensible option was to stay put, stay medicated, and wait for either the stone or the repairman. I started drinking tons of water. Mom came up from Brookhaven and got the children. Paula texted often to check on my status, and I sat in a hospital room watching Sunday night television.

I spent the whole next day alone with no progress, and a nurse informed me that I wasn't officially admitted to the hospital but was under "observation" so that the insurance company would pay. After twenty-four hours I would either need to be sent home or have some reason to be admitted.

I got a copy of the local newspaper, and on page two there was a sad story about a kangaroo and two wallabies that escaped from someone's farm near Bossier City, Louisiana. The two wallabies were captured, but the kangaroo was hit by a truck on I-20. Said this family had fifty acres of land where they kept exotic animals. Someone left the gate open. Dang if Derek wasn't right. I made a mental note to tell him as soon as he turns twenty-one. Oh, all right, eighteen.

I put the paper down and pondered my situation. I felt a vague uneasiness being stuck in Vicksburg, a city one of my ancestors helped defeat during the siege as part of the Ohio 47th Infantry Division fighting under General Grant. Although I was now a second-generation Southerner, these people have long memories. So even if the battle that almost wiped them off the map was the main thing that put them on the map, I wasn't sure if all was forgiven. I took the kids to visit the national battlefield a couple of years ago, and at the Ohio monument I relayed the story of their distant relative, Captain Jeremiah Gage.

As it turns out, the urologist, Dr. Ben Sword, was a Civil War buff, and his great-great-great-grandfather was the city's newspaper editor during the war.

"Is there still some animosity about the war here?" I probed.

"Well," he answered, "what's that saying? The ax forgets but the tree remembers? But you can't hang on to grudges forever. After a while they pile up, and you have to let some go. My Granny Sword, though, now she did carry a grudge. She participated in the hundred-year commemoration of the battle of Vicksburg. I wasn't even born yet back in sixty-three, but if you wanted to get her hackles up, just bring up the war. I'll never touch a fifty-dollar bill as long as they have a picture of that drunken so-and-so on the front, she used to say, except for the so-and-so, which is the sanitized version."

They must've found a reason to admit me, because I fell into a deep sleep that passed the time limit. I dreamt that Union forces had surrounded the hospital and wouldn't leave until I surrendered. Tuesday morning I was awakened by severe flank pain, and I knew this was it—I was in active labor. I strained my urine and there it was,

a cannonball the size of a BB. Not thirty minutes later Dr. Sword entered my room.

"Good news! The lithotripsy machine is fixed. You'll be the first to test it out."

I handed him the cup with the stone. "I have better news."

Mom and the kids arrived later as I was being released. The doctor came in to instruct me on things I could do to prevent stones in the future and to tell me they sent off the little troublemaker to the lab to get analyzed. Two blue-coated ladies came into the room as he was talking, checked a couple of things at the hand-washing station, and exited.

"Excuse all the hustle and bustle around here," said Dr. Sword. "The hospital inspectors dropped in this morning, unannounced of course. That's the way it is in medicine these days. Regulators and government bureaucrats sneaking around, checking on everything to make sure you're not incompetent."

"They want to see if you have all your ducks in a row?" I asked.

"Exactly," he replied.

Derek looked up at Dr. Sword. "Quack."

The doctor held his forefinger up to his lips. "Shh. Wait for the inspectors to leave before you call me that."

The doctor exited and we gathered my belongings to be discharged. I had to excuse myself for one last trip to the bathroom as the gallons I consumed continued to wind their way through my system. Monday's paper was still open on the bed and Mom picked it up.

"Hey, listen to this, kids. A kangaroo got hit by a car over in Louisiana. Isn't that strange?"

"We saw it!" yelled Derek. "Dad said it was a deer."

"Well, here's a little secret: your daddy doesn't know everything."

Stephanie fell over on the bed and exclaimed, "I'm in shock."

I finished drying my hands and yelled through the door, "Thanks, Mom!"

About the Author:

Richard Key earned his medical degree from the University of Mississippi and currently works as a pathologist in Dothan, Alabama. He has been writing essays and short stories for about ten years. His work has been published in Bacopa Literary Review, The Birmingham Arts Journal, Broken Plate, Crack The Spine, Forge, Hawaii Pacific Review, Penmen Review, Storgy, and Tusculum Review. He hopes to have a website someday. And a Twitter account, and all those other things.

SECRETS

Caroline Miller

I sank into an overstuffed chair, feeling as though I'd slipped through a time warp. Forty-eight hours earlier. I'd boarded a plane in San Francisco. The year was 1971. Now, I seemed to find myself in the Middle Ages, looking at high-timbered ceilings, mullioned windows and brass fittings that gleamed in the firelight of a large hearth. Nothing had changed since I'd last been here last, ten years ago, though my feelings about the village, located in the English Midlands, were less painful than when I'd fled the country in tears.

What a timid creature I'd been in those earlier days, an American of twenty-two who dared to cram English into the heads of blue-uniformed girls at the local grammar school. That was the year I waited for my fiancé, Malcolm Gray, to finish his degree at university. The moments he and I shared were all too brief in this land of Thomas Harding's. The constant mists, the dark moors and grey, stone architecture all served to heighten my broodiness. Malcolm was often away pursuing his studies, so no one should have been surprised that I was dogged by loneliness and a dread some blonde, blue-eyed coed might lead him astray.

After one too many quarrels in the passing of a year, I'd cried my way back across the Atlantic. If I half expected Malcolm to follow me, I was disappointed.

"You were always Marilee's favorite." Simone Pardy, the inn keeper, looked down on me. He was a large man with hands dangling at his side like dead seagulls. "She's a teacher now. I

expect you had something to do with that. Classes full of fourth formers, just like yours, but in the south. In Colchester."

I noted the pride shinning in the father's eyes and thought of my two children at home, Sean and Emily. Already, I missed them.

The inn keeper misread the frown that clouded my expression. "It'll be all right, Mrs. Sinclair. We'll soon have news of her. There's not much goes unnoticed in a village this size. She'll turn up right as rain. Now, is there anything I can do to cheer you up? More tea? Another biscuit?"

When I shook my head, my host headed for the kitchen with my tray, leaving me alone with my thoughts. I was worried about Sylvia's absence, naturally. She'd accompanied me to England but in protest, agreeing with my husband, Howard, that my travel was unnecessary.

"Besides, the Midlands in October? It'll be so cold."

Born and bred in Florida, Sylvia was addicted to the sun, evidenced by her freckles and leathery skin. What she'd look like when she reached middle age, I couldn't imagine. But she wasn't the one with cancer. I was. So when my doctor didn't object to my trip, she was loyal enough to join me -- a relief to Howard who couldn't get away, as I well knew.

Sylvia and I always got on well. In many ways we complimented each other. She was a tall, leggy blonde who could make conversation with a lamp post. I was small, dark and inclined to look inward. Money had given her a privileged life. I was the first in my emigrant family to go to college.

If Sylvia had one failing, it was her choice of men. At thirty-three, she'd divorced two husbands and was game for a third. This lapse in her character I'd noted early, when we were roommates in college, and was the reason I was deaf to her complaints about Malcolm. Malcolm had been an English exchange student during our senior year. He wore cravats and carried an umbrella in all weather, behavior which made him seem exotic. Happily, he returned my interest and showed little in Sylvia, an indifference which may have explained why she'd disapproved of him.

"Phone, mum."

I jumped at the sound of Simone Pardy's voice. He didn't seem to notice.

"The squire would like a word."

"Malcolm? But I've barely arrived..."

"The Manor's just across the Commons. Word gets round. He often stops by. Not shy about buying a pint for the patrons when he's here. Lady Margaret's been poorly for the last couple of years. I suppose he gets lonely."

"I'm sorry."

I rose from my chair and followed the sweep of the proprietor's arm as he pointed to a private parlor where I could take my call. My hand trembled as I lifted the receiver and sank into a rocker beside a glowing fireplace.

"Anne, is it really you?" Malcolm's clipped manner of speaking hadn't changed. "I can hardly believe it. Why didn't you say you were coming?"

"Yes, it's me. I should have written... it was spur of the moment, actually. Sylvia's with me."

"What's this about her gone missing? Shall I have a word with the local bobby?"

"No, no. The moment we arrived, she dashed off in our rental car to look up an old acquaintance."

"In Leek?"

His dubious tone set my teeth on edge.

"She made a few friends when she visited us. Surely you remember? She still exchanges Christmas cards with one or two."

"All I remember are her complaints. 'Where's the dishwasher? Where's the refrigerator?'"

"You settled the last when you opened a window to let in a blast of snow. Remember?"

We laughed. No doubt each of us was recalling Sylvia's stupefied expression when she discovered the drift had made hillocks of her slippers.

"We had some good times, didn't we, Anne?"

I wasn't quick enough in my reply, apparently, as Malcolm's next remark was businesslike.

"Let me ring the constable, why don't you? With all the rain, she may have stalled somewhere."

His argument made sense.

"She's driving a red Morris Minor," I told him.

"Morris Minor?" The voice at the other end of the line registered surprise. "Not her usual style, is it?"

"It's my rental."

"Ah," he said. "That explains it."

Explained what, I wondered. Did he think Sylvia's was extravagant or that I was a penny-pincher?

"As you're alone," he went on, "why don't I join you for dinner? They do a fair steak and kidney pie at the pub. I'd have you here, but Margaret, my wife, isn't well. Are you staying long, by the way?"

"No, not long, Yes, do come. If Sylvia hasn't turned up, at least I'll be near the phone."

A woman's voice filtered across the line and Malcolm's words became hurried.

"It's settled then. See you at eight."

The hall clock struck five as the telephone went dead. For a moment, I sat wondering how to while away the time. Read a book? Walk through the village?

Outside, autumn leaves, roiled by the wind, as if to reflect my mood. Had I been foolish to revisit this place, after all these years?

Hoping a nap would soothe me, I returned to my room. Howard's picture on the nightstand seemed to scowl from its shadowy corner as I entered, reflecting my anxiety. Worse, the low slung beams and puffed up feather bed invited feelings of claustrophobia. I flung myself into the Queen Anne chair beside the window, instead.

Outside, the Commons was enameled with rain and beyond it, Gray Manor loomed like a fortress in the gathering dark. Its marble halls I remembered, vaguely, though seldom had I been a guest there. Even so, I could imagine Malcolm sitting opposite his wife beside a fire in the cavernous library. He'd choose his moment to announce he was dining out, I felt certain. But would he tell her with whom?

A rap at the door brought me to my feet. When I answered it, the inn keeper stood looming in the hallway, clutching a bouquet of Blue Girls clutched against his broad chest. A gift from Malcolm, no doubt. Blue Girls had crowded in bunches outside the flat we'd shared at the edge of the village years ago. I'd loved them for their hardiness, blooming from mid spring into fall, long after the mums and marigolds had lost their spirit.

Malcolm had called me his "Blue Girl," because I'd made a habit of tucking a blossom into the button hole of my cardigan to enjoy the fragrance throughout the day. Had I been blessed with their hardiness, I might never have packed my bags and run away.

Dressing for dinner, I plucked a bloom from the vase and pinned it to the neckline of my gown, a blue crepe. Malcolm was partial to blue. I hoped the color would divert him from noticing the pallor of my complexion.

When the hall clock struck the dinner hour, I tossed a dissatisfied glance at my image in the mirror. Then I descended the stairs on wooden legs.

Malcolm was seated in a darkened corner of the dining room. Another couple huddled near the fireplace, opposite: a girl in a pink sweater and a boy with brilliantine in his hair. They glanced up as I entered, then returned to their conversation, as if I'd been judged and found wanting. Barely in their twenties, by the touching of their hands across the table, I sensed they were in love.

Malcolm pushed back his chair, rising as I approached.

"Anne, you look wonderful. You haven't changed a bit. A littler thinner, but Mrs. Pardy's cooking will soon put that right. "

I was more than thin and we both knew it. I was gaunt. My hand brushed the back of my cropped head in a self-conscious gesture. The last time Malcolm had seen me, I'd had long, lustrous hair. Chemotherapy had changed that.

"I like it," he offered, as if sensing my embarrassment. "Daring, perhaps. But with your delicate features, you carry it off." He bent as he pulled out my chair, time enough for me to notice his hairline had receded a little but the strands still gleamed like threads of gold.

"I've changed, too," he confessed as he'd seated himself opposite me. His statement sounded like a question.

"Nothing dramatic," I assured him. "More mature, of course but handsome as ever."

He flashed a smile of white, even teeth, and looked relieved.

His gaze dropped to the neckline of my gown. "You got the roses. The last of the season. I hope I'm given credit for remembering."

"You used to call them weeds."

"Only to tease." His fingers brushed the back of my hand, but he pulled away when I stiffened.

"Good news," I piped, changing the subject. "Sylvia called."

"She'll be joining us?" Malcolm's complexion grew rosy near the edge of his cable knit sweater. Was he pleased or disappointed? When I told him we'd be dining alone and saw his shoulders relax against his chair, I had my answer.

"She drove to the farm of an acquaintance," I explained. "When the storm broke and the lines went down, she stayed the night. She'll be back tomorrow."

"She always could manage a bed."

"What's that supposed to mean?"

Malcolm's eyes widened.

"Nothing. I'm glad she's all right. We can enjoy our meal without worry."

"Are you sorry she's with me?"

"Good heavens, why should you think that?" The crimson line around his throat grew brighter. "It's true she and I never got on. Too much alike, I suppose. Both spoilt." His gaze fell to his lap as if to break the flow of conversation, but I was unwilling to do so.

"You did, once."

"What?" He looked up, his forehead creased.

"Get on with each other."

"How do you mean?"

"When she stayed with us. I felt sure you'd buried the hatchet. In fact, I was a little jealous."

Malcolm's mouth flew open.

"How extraordinary. Sylvia loves herself. No suitor could compete."

"That didn't stop you from trying, did it?"

Fearing I'd gone too far, I bit my lip in consternation. Why did I never feel secure with Malcolm, never good enough...after ten years?

He brushed my barb aside as if I were an errant child.

"Look, we needn't concern ourselves with Sylvia. She's safe and chin wagging with an old friend. Good for her. Let's talk about you. I know you're married and living in San Francisco. I do catch the American papers from time to time."

Learning he'd tried to keep abreast of me softened my mood.

"Mine is an ordinary existence," I shrugged. "My husband, Howard, is a cardiologist. We have two children. A boy who's nine and a girl, seven."

Malcolm leaned forward with his eyes narrowed.

"So, you didn't become a career girl, after all?"

Inwardly, I smiled. I was about to lose an argument ten years old. I didn't mind considering the way my life turned out.

"No. Children have a way of changing plans. I couldn't give up mine to a babysitter."

His eyes crinkled with apparent pleasure.

"You know I agree, of course?"

"And what about you?" I parried, unwilling to let him to linger on his triumph. "You wanted a large family."

To my surprise, Malcolm was slow to answer.

"Margaret's not been well... No children as yet. But we do hope."

My heart knocked against my ribs. Here was the opportunity to open the conversation for which I'd come. Would what I had to say anger him? Or make him happy? I hoped it would the latter. Yet when my lips parted, what poured from me were watery banalities. "Yes, there is always hope." Inwardly, I cringed at my cowardice.

Malcolm accepted my sympathy with a nod, then let his eyes sweep the room as if he had a confidence to share and wanted to be assured of our privacy.

"It's wonderful to be together like this, Anne. I've missed you." His finger touched the circle of my wedding band, almost wistfully.

"Your husband let you come alone. May I ask why?"

"Howard has a difficult surgery to perform," I answered honestly.

The corners of Malcolm's mouth drooped a little.

"You're happy then? Coming here isn't a sentimental journey?"

Malcolm didn't wait for an answer but took my hands in his with a force that surprised me.

"Why did you leave me, Anne? I was devastated. No note, no forwarding address..."

"Malcolm, please..."

The man opposite me looked embarrassed as he released me.

"I-I apologize. I'm being a fool. But understand, after so many years.... "

The tremor in his voice filled me with guilt, even though I remained convinced I was the one who'd suffered most.

"After our last argument I'm surprised you don't have a clue."

Malcolm frowned, confronted by words so much colder than his ardor.

"We had lots of arguments. So much was at stake. School. My parents. I never imagined you'd stopped loving me "

"Stopped loving you?" I sucked in my breath. "I never stopped loving you. You were bored. Remember?"

Malcolm blanched, as if he'd stumbled across a dead body while out for a stroll.

"I never said that. And how could you think it when I was ready to break with my parents to marry you. Did my intentions mean nothing?"

"What about Margaret?"

"Margaret was my parent's doing. You can't blame me for her."

" You married her, didn't you?"

"You're being absurd. Margaret was never a match for you."

"And I was no match for her money."

Malcolm's eyes narrowed.

"You think so little of me?"

I should have laughed outright. How like Malcolm to imagine he could rewrite history. And how like him to put me in the wrong. But before I could answer him, the inn keeper arrived with our salads. If he noticed Malcolm's white knuckled grip on his chair, the man didn't let on. He poured wine into the Squire's goblet at a glacial pace and hovered, waiting for approval before filling mine.

Once he'd gone, it seemed difficult for either Malcolm or I to know how to continue. For the sake of peace, I considered offering an apology; but when I opened my mouth to speak, a squeal came from the far side of the room.

"Jeremy, you remembered!" The girl in the pink sweater stared down at a cupcake with a candled burning at its center.

Aware he had an audience, the boy tossed a wink in our direction. "A year ago today, that's when we met."

Malcolm and I smiled our congratulations and would have returned to our private gloom, but the young man had another surprise up his sleeve. Reaching into his jacket, he withdrew a small box tied with a ribbon. The ritual about to unfold was centuries old, yet one that never failed to gladden the heart.

"Go on, Chloe, open it."

The girl tugged at the ribbon. Her eyes, illuminated by the firelight, were already welling with tears.

"Jeremy, it's beautiful." When she spied the ring, her free hand pressed hard against her breast as if she feared to breathe.

Still, the boy looked uncertain.

"I-Is it 'yes', then? Is it okay?" .

"Of course, it's okay, you idiot. I love you." To convince him, the girl leaned forward and kissed her fiancé.

Malcolm signaled to the waiter and a bottle of champagne was delivered to the couple's table. They smiled as they lifted their glasses in our direction to acknowledge the gift. Then their eyes sought each other's and, for them, the world seemed to fall away.

"A lovely gesture," I whispered to the man seated across from me whose eyes had turned wistful.

"I should like to have a girl. I'd buy her pink sweaters and give her ballet lessons..."

"Not a fishing pole or a baseball?"

A smile parted Malcolm's lips as he turned to face me.

"Still a feminist, dear Anne?"

"Having a girl strengthens my resolve for equal rights, if that's what you mean."

My answer was without rancor and Malcolm smiled to hear it. .

"Your daughter likes fishing then?"

"No," I laughed. "She loves ballet."

"Ah," my companion nodded, satisfied. "I'm sure I'd like her very much."

"And I'm sure she'd be happy to allow you to spoil her."

"What about your son? Is he the fisherman?"

I shook my head.

"His passion is music, like yours."

"Really? What did you say his name was?'

"I didn't. Emily is my daughter. And...." We'd reached another delicate point in the conversation. "I hope you don't mind. His name is Sean."

Malcolm shook his head as if water plugged one ear.

"My brother died before I met you."

"I know. But I liked the name and you were so fond of him..."

"Hang on." He held up one hand and looked puzzled. "Help me to understand."

My face warmed under his gaze. We'd reached an important juncture and I found I wasn't prepared for it.

"I liked the name. That's all."

"No," Malcolm corrected. "That isn't all. You preserved a memory. You knew how much I loved Sean. And you also knew how different our lives would have been had he lived. He'd be the Squire and my parents would have allowed me to do as I liked." Malcolm took a sip of wine as if giving himself time to consider.

"Oh, Anne, what a mess we've made for ourselves."

"Not so bad, really" I shrugged, not wanting to admit any truth to his statement. "You're not unhappy, are you?"

Always a proud man, Malcolm threw back his shoulders and grew taller in his chair..

"I have my consolations, I suppose." He peered into his wine glass for a time, as if it were a crystal ball.

"Tell me about Sean, this son of yours," he said at last. "I presume he plays an instrument?"

"He tortures a guitar and dreams of becoming a Rock Star."

"What boy doesn't?" Malcolm smiled. "Does he favor you or your husband?"

"He's blond, like Howard, but I'd say he favors himself."

"Any pictures?"

Realizing I'd left my wallet in my room, I grew flustered and offered to retrieve it. Malcolm waived me back into my chair, however..

"Another time. Margaret would enjoy seeing the photo. She's eager to see you again.. You understand...an old flame. What woman wouldn't be curious?" Malcolm stabbed at his lettuce with a forced show of nonchalance.

"So, if not me, what brings you to Leek? You always hated the place. Called it 'Bleak Leek.'"

"I cared for it even less after you married."

I'd meant my words to flatter Malcolm but they had the opposite effect.

"I married Margaret two years after you'd gone. She had nothing to do with us. Frankly, I don't know what happened with us..."

To my annoyance, Simone Pardy's shadow fell across our table a second time.

"The missus makes a good steak and kidney if I do say so myself. If the storm hadn't put 'em off, I'd be fitting customers into this place with a shoe horn."

He set the warm dishes before us, then peered down into our faces with his hands folded across his broad belly. Apparently, he was used to a bit of chit-chat with the Squire but tonight he would be disappointed. We required privacy and our silence told him so. After a few moments, he left us and headed toward his bar, looking, I thought, a little crestfallen.

"Tell you what," Malcolm began once we were alone. "Why don't we forget the past for tonight? We'll talk as old friends. After ten years, there's so much I want to know."

"Agreed. But we can't entirely escape the past. In fact, I do have something I want to say."

Malcolm looked up from his plate, looking wary.

"Anne, If you think I ever meant to hurt you, you're wrong. I knew what you gave up for me. You could have accepted that scholarship to graduate school, become the writer you wanted to be. Instead, you buried yourself in this grey little outpost. But I thought you believed we had a future together. I know I did. I loved you. And thought you loved me. What more is there to say except we made a mess of things?"

"Yes. But hear me out..."

Malcolm threw up his hands like a crossing guard.

"All right. If you need me to apologize, I will. I admit I may have been too preoccupied with myself. I was young. It was in my senior year. I needed to sow some oats. You have to understand, so much rested on my shoulders at school... with my parents. I felt entitled to blow off steam. That wasn't responsible of me. I know that now. But you played your part, Anne. If I didn't rush home to our little love nest at every opportunity... To tell the truth, I felt suffocated."

"Suffocated?" I thought we'd turned a corner in our conversation, but apparently we hadn't. If Malcolm had thrown the contents of his water glass in my face, I couldn't have been taken more aback. "Well, that clears the air," I snapped. "I gave up my life for yours and it made you feel suffocated. I do apologize."

Malcolm fell against his chair, vindication flashing from his eyes.

"There you have it. Guilt. Always guilt. Did you never consider my needs? I was working for our future. That's what we wanted, wasn't it?"

Malcolm's words had a revelatory effect. Ten years had passed and yet nothing between us had changed. We continued to lick old wounds. He never listened and I was always the one to bear the blame..

"What I wanted was for you to love me," I told him with an honesty that surprised me and left me feeling gutted. "But you didn't... not enough. And then you were bored."

"That's a lie. You were the one to leave, remember?"

"After all these years, why can't you be honest? Someone came between us. If it wasn't Margaret, maybe it was that Egyptian student. She behaved as if she owned you."

"Nadia? That's ridiculous."

"What's ridiculous is that you imagined I'd swallow your deception. The long absences. The feeble excuses..."

"You're problem, Anne, is that you were always jealous. Always needed reassurance. You made it hard for a fellow to breathe."

"Did I? Yet somehow you managed. Who resuscitated you, I wonder. Or was it only one?"

Malcolm threw his napkin on the table as if it were a gauntlet. In earlier times, this would be the point when he'd stomp out of our flat, puffed with indignation, and leave me to swallow my unspoken words. But in this public place, with his fellow villagers in full view, such a display was unthinkable. A proud man, he'd never take part in a scene that would expose him to common gossip.

I watched as his eyes flitted across to the bar. Nobody seemed disturbed by our exchange, and the young couple had long since departed. Malcolm's relief was almost palpable.

"We should eat our dinner before it gets cold," he said, as with exquisite care he laid his napkin across his lap. His fork bit hard into his pot pie, spraying crust in a 360 degree circle. The evening which had begun with hope was officially dead.

At the stroke of nine I rose, glad to bring our charade to an end. Not only was I exhausted, but I was equally certain Malcolm would be glad to be rid of me. Yet when I pushed back my chair, he looked surprised. His complexion paled and he appeared to be like a man awaking from a spell. The skin under his eyes and around his lips formed a tight mask akin to grief.

"Anne, I'm so sorry. I wanted our reunion to be special and now..."

"Don't blame yourself, Malcolm," I interrupted. "I've not been well."

He complexion turned paler, if possible.

"I'm sorry. Is there anything I can do?"

Taking hold of my hand, he cradled it as if it were an injured sparrow. The gentleness of his touch brought back memories, loving ones I hadn't expected to revive in this moment. A tenderness enveloped me, one less easy to bear than my anger. We had loved one another in the past and in a strange way, we still did -- perhaps too desperately, for despite the best we meant to do, we ended up hurting one another. My body trembled as it filled with sadness, threatening my existence as surely as if poison had been poured into my glass.

How I managed the stairs without stumbling is a mystery. My eyes were awash with tears, and when I reached the confines of my room, I threw myself across the bed to give vent to them. How long I wept, I don't know. But it was late when Sylvia found me in my desperate condition.

Early the next morning, we packed our bags packed and climbed into the rental car, headed for Heathrow airport. Having settled our bill the previous evening, not even Simone Pardy was awake to wave us off.

"I'm sorry it went badly" my friend said as the rural landscape flashed past us. "You came a long way to get kicked in the stomach a second time."

"Something got resolved," I muttered without looking at Sylvia. "I decided Howard was right."

"I'm glad you didn't tell Malcolm. It might have been too much for you."

"That'll be Howard's job when I'm gone."

"Don't be such a pessimist."

I didn't argue. We both knew the doctor hadn't held out much hope for a third round of chemotherapy.

"I decided I didn't want him in my life again, even for a short while. Too much pain.... I really loved him, you know."

Sylvia nodded as she pressed her foot to the gas pedal, squinting through the rain washed windshield as she did. "He doesn't need to know, Anne. Howard is Sean's father by rights. And what a shock for the kid. Tell him when he grows up, if you must."

The hum of the car engine blanketed our conversation. Lulled by the hypnotic rhythm of the windshield wipers, each of us sank into our private thoughts. Outside the passing farmlands glistened in the rain. Nothing stirred. No workmen or cows in sight. But life was present in that still-life painting. Worms waited with a seasoned patience to feed upon the shoots of spring.

From the opposite lane, a truck passed, splashing water across the glass. Sylvia held the car steady without blinking. I trusted her and allowed myself to sink deeper into the knitted afghan she'd thrown over me. I was glad to be leaving England. She'd been right. I never should have returned.

My friend hummed quietly to herself, probably glad to be leaving, as well. What was that song? I knew it. "The Way We Were." Malcolm's favorite.

My eyes popped open. The glint of satisfaction in Sylvia's smiling profile sent a chill through me, one having nothing to do with the wind and rain raging outside.

About the Author:

Caroline Miller is a former elected member of the county commission of Multnomah County, Oregon in the United States, and a published author. Since leaving the political arena, Miller has been heavily involved with writing. She has published three novels: Trompe l'Oeil in 2012, Gothic Spring and Heart Land in 2009. Her short stories have been published in Children's Digest and Grit and Tales of the Talisman, and her short story, Under the Bridge and Beneath the Moon, were dramatized for radio in Oregon and Washington. Miller's two-act play, "Woman on the Scarlet Beast," was performed by the Post5 Theatre company in Portland, Oregon Jan 20-Feb.8 2015.

MONIQUE

Max Bayer

South of France, Summer of 1951

It was about thirty-five miles east of Nimes when Franz stopped at the small village of Lunel to have some coffee. He had his coffee in one hand and a baguette with a hefty chunk of camembert in the other. Bicycles, motorbikes, and small cars threaded through the narrow streets, darting in and out of alleys. He sipped his espresso. Franz had come to France to write feature stories for a new magazine. He had been trolling the Mediterranean coast for ideas and had just sent an article about the camps Vichy French officials had used to intern Jews, Communists, gypsies, and just about anyone else Nazi officials had ordered them to round up.

His train of thought was interrupted by the shouts of a man not more than ten feet in front of him who began screaming at a woman in a green jersey dress. The shouts in a guttural French became louder. All attention turned to the man. Franz looked on in horror. The man knocked the woman down as he waved his hands wildly while he continued to berate her. Her groceries fell from the cloth bag she was carrying. Carrots, onions, and a wrapped chop fell onto the hot cobblestones, with a half-dozen broken eggs congealing around them.

The man, who appeared to be in his late fifties, was short and stoutly built, with a deep tan. There was a furor in his eyes, leading Franz to believe that he wanted to kill her. The woman lay cringing on the pavement, attempting to gather her food as the man cursed at her. "You German-loving bitch! You lived and ate well with the Bosche, while we all starved. And you dare to

show your face here again! You are lucky we did not shoot you when they left. People like you are the scourge of France. You do not deserve to live! I spit on you and your kind."

Everyone stopped walking to watch, and traffic came to a halt. The woman remained kneeling, keeping her head down, cowering in fear. She had blonde hair which stuck out from her red scarf. She looked to be about thirty years old. She had scraped one of her knees but seemed afraid to examine it. The man kept screaming and then finally spit on her. Franz was shocked that no one standing by said a thing. No one attempted to help the woman. What was wrong with these people?

Franz could no longer sit and watch. He dropped some coins on the table for his coffee and went to assist the woman. He picked up the chop packet, wiped it on his jacket, and stuck it back into her bag. She glanced up at him with a look of gratitude that he would never forget. She was fighting back tears, while she said softly, "Merci, Monsieur." Her eyes conveyed her thanks a thousand times more than her words. Franz was pained by her humiliation, no longer cognizant of the man berating her. Or the multitude of stares.

A bystander shouted, "What kind of Frenchman are you, to help this collaborator and traitor? Maybe you are one of them too!"

Franz replied in his best schoolbook French. "Excusez-moi, Monsieur, mais je ne suis pas français, as you can tell from my accent. I am an American, a tourist enjoying your beautiful country."

"Ah, yes, what do you Americans know about these people and what they did to us during the war? Yes, help her and make your conscience feel good. But you do not know what it was like. These bitches fucked the Nazis and had plenty to eat. But we who were on rations had next to nothing. And we who fought back were beaten and starved. They tortured my friends to death."

"I am sorry, Monsieur, I am truly sorry about your friends."

Then Franz turned away from the man, grabbed his bike, and offered the woman a ride home. He instructed her to sit behind the handlebars. As he pedaled off, the crowd shouted at them but, to his relief, made no move to follow them.

"Where is your house?" Franz asked the woman in French.

"It is about one kilometer down this street. Then some turns I will have to show you if you take me that far."

Franz rode slowly with his bike rattling against the narrow cobblestone streets. They passed some old buildings, a fruit orchard. About half a kilometer they went, and she turned her head and said, "I came back only because my mother is sick. I had no choice. I must care for her."

"Of course you must," he said into the wind. He leaned forward to say the words close to her ear. She smelled clean and flowery, and he could glimpse her cleavage bouncing along on the path.

Franz could feel her body against his as she sat on the bar in front of him. Pedaling hard up the slight incline caused his breathing to increase. He tried not to breathe too hard in the small of her neck.

"Over there, Monsieur, you can make a right and then two more streets and a left."

In a few more minutes, they were in front of a tiny stone house with a red tile roof. The stones looked old, with green growth on the lower portions. Given the sunken tiny windows, the walls looked a foot and a half thick.

"Okay then, I hope you will be all right," he said as he helped her with her groceries and with no excuse to stay proceeded to leave.

"Please, young man, let me prepare some lunch for you," she said. "I want to thank you for what you have done for me. Please, I insist." Without waiting for his answer, she led him alongside the house to the back and up a very narrow spiral staircase into a tiny flat. He leaned his bike against the thick stone building. She introduced herself as Madame Monique Bisset. She was staying in her mother's flat with her young son, Paul.

Her mother was sick in bed in the back room. Monique went to check on her. Then sent Paul to sit with her and told Franz. She had met a German soldier, Gunther Niedelbaecker, during the occupation. "I gave him French lessons, and he gave me food. Just before the liberation of southern France, Gunther was taken prisoner of war and I never heard from him again."

"And Paul?"

"He has never known his father."

Facing the tiny sink with her back to Franz, "After the liberation, I took Paul to Marseille, where it was easier to live without the complete condemnation I suffered in this small town."

However, even in Marseille, though no one ever spoke of it, people seemed to suspect that Paul's father might have been a German, and many families did not allow their children to play with him. She worked as a waitress in a restaurant. She was seeing an Algerian man, she told Franz.

Less than an hour had passed since Franz had stopped for a coffee in Lunel, and now he was sitting at a tiny table across from Monique in this small kitchen. She served him a bowl of bouillabaisse with bread and cheese. He noticed that she touched his arm as she gestured to express herself. She turned frequently toward the tiny two-burner stove. In just those few steps, she seemed to exhibit her womanhood, which Franz could not help but notice. He felt himself being drawn to Monique, yet he was conscious of the awkwardness of the situation: her Algerian boyfriend she had just mentioned, her son playing at their feet, and her mother complaining from the back room.

Franz wanted somehow to make everything right for her and her family. But who was he to think he could fix other people's lives? He was a 25-year-old American man traveling through France to find stories to write, adventure to relish, and maybe love to cherish.

"Madame, I very much appreciated your lunch, but now I really must be going," Franz said reluctantly.

"Franz, please call me Monique. If you could stay a little while longer, perhaps you could help us go to the station for a train to Marseille. When we came here, Paul and I walked the eight miles from the train station in Nimes. But now that people know we are here, the walk back will be difficult for us."

"How serious is her illness?"

"She has only a bad cold and some fever and should be much better in several days."

He watched Monique as she cleaned up their lunch dishes, moving back and forth between the table and kitchen sink. He took in her tight dress, her prominent breasts, and her soft, curly blonde hair, which came into full view without her scarf. Even with her back to him, she sensed what he was up to. "I can feel the way you watch me, you know," she said with a smile. "Are you sure you want to go?"

He was taken aback by her frankness, not realizing that his lustful stare was so apparent. He stammered a bit, not knowing exactly what to say in response. "But if I did not go, where would I stay?" he asked, trying to sound practical and to make light of their situation.

"Do not worry, chéri, we can figure something out."

"Well, I guess I could stay for one night."

"Do you really think that you will be able to leave tomorrow?"

"If not tomorrow, then the next day for sure."

So, it was set. He needed to stay for at least a day, two at most, to continue to protect her and her son and to see them off safely to Marseille. From that moment on, he regarded her differently. What would she be like in bed? He had harbored a taste for older women ever since he had known Fatima.

Franz went out to the balcony at the top of the spiral staircase. Stretched out from corner to corner and using his duffel bag as his pillow, he snoozed while Monique prepared the evening meal.

Franz recalled his first visit to a whorehouse when he was a green recruit in Paris six years ago. He had come to France still innocent in the ways of women. In the Army, it seemed that all the recruits ever talked about was girls and sex. That's where he had met Fatima. She took him to a room upstairs and starting speaking French to him. He remembered a little bit from high school, and she was pleased that he understood her.

It did not take him long.

Afterward, he felt such exhilaration for having done it. He was now one of the guys. He would never have to sidestep any conversations again.

Franz spent the next two days with Monique. Her son slept in the back room with his grandmother. Franz slept in the other room with Monique. He took her son to the beach. Paul did not know how to swim. Franz taught him a little. Paul asked if they hated the Germans in America too. "Now that the war is over, they don't hate them anymore," Franz told him.

"I want to go to America," he blurted out. Franz was at a loss for words. He had lost his own father when he was ten years old, but at least he had known him.

Monique's lovemaking was very expressive. It made him feel good. But also sad that she would throw herself on him so easily. On the third day, he brought them to the train station in Nimes. He gave her three packs of Camel cigarettes when they departed, as distasteful as the gesture was. He knew that American cigarettes were better than French francs. She was very appreciative of the cigarettes and the help in getting to the train station. She smiled and kissed him on his cheek. He helped her board her train. He watched it depart and saw her wave from the window.

The experience gave him an idea for a story about the despised women of France. He traveled back to Paris and followed leads of people to interview. He wrote his story to wild acclaim by his American editor. "Great stuff, Franz. Looks like you had some personal involvement to add authenticity to the subject."

Sitting in a Paris café with his French friend Roger, Franz told him the stories he had written about the south of France. He focused on his recent one about the French women who had dated German soldiers. He was proud of the firsthand knowledge he had of these women. Roger didn't seem interested. So, Franz asked if he should tell him more. Roger answered, "If you insist." Thus he told Roger how he met Monique. He was proud of how he had helped Monique when her groceries had been splattered on the pavement and the angry man was berating her.

Roger asked him what happened after that. Franz explained everything, in detail. He even embellished upon the events, describing Monique and her physical attributes. Franz felt like a big man and was pleased with his story.

Roger was silent. He looked at Franz. Franz felt the words about to come. "Franz."

"Yes, Roger, you want to say something?"

"Yes. My older sister was accused of being a collaborator. She was hungry and was close to a German who gave her food. They shaved her head and paraded her through the streets. They taunted her. They threw things at her. My parents had to put her out of our home. She cannot marry. Maybe, one day people will forget. Her crime was to love. She loved the enemy. That was her crime. But my sister's name was not Monique."

Franz was silent. He no longer told the story of Monique to anyone.

About the Author:

Max Bayer was born to immigrant parents who fled war-torn Europe in 1942. He came to writing late in life when he discovered that his parents—Holocaust escapees—left a daughter in Germany when they fled to America. He attended the City College of New York and completed a tour in the Peace Corps in the south of India where he met his wife, Mildred of 48 years. He received his PhD in City and Regional Planning from Rutgers University and has worked as a strategic planning consultant for the Urban Health Institute while pursuing his passion for building and writing. He currently shares his time between suburban NJ and his pastoral retreat in upstate NY.

A DAY IN THE LIFE OF A GUITARIST

by CG Fewston

Riodago knew nothing on the nature of dreams, except that he had one: to be the greatest guitarist the world had ever known.

By the time he was three years old, his mother had passed to breast cancer. As he wept onto his mother's hands, Riodago knew nothing of guitar strings; the boy knew only of the invisible strings that pulled at his breaking heart to bring forth tears in childish hopes to stir his mother awake once more. Maria never woke, not even to the screams of her only son.

Riodago with his father, a British banker, buried Maria a day so windy Riodago believed his mother's voice came with it to calm him and to tell him "to go and play."

Instead of uprooting Riodago from the only home he had known in the Spanish town of Santiago de Compostela, his father remained at his lowly-but-stable position with the international banking firm and married his mistress by the time Riodago had started daily guitar lessons to counsel his grief by the age of five.

By the age of seven, Riodago had reached his fourth guitar, having smashed the first three over frustrated tantrums caused by the constant bruising of his fingertips and his inability to play from beginning to end "El Porompompero" without making a single mistake. As a clinical response to educate his son in the more formal manners of obedience and perseverance, Riodago's father doubled the daily guitar lessons.

By age ten, Riodago could pick up a beggar's guitar, close his eyes, tune the instrument in accordance to the same invisible strings he had known since he was three years old, and play "Flor de Luna" so enchantingly widows-in-black would openly weep, young maidens would descend upon him wild, passionate kisses while the men stood in ovation. Riodago would open his eyes to find the street around him full of people, return the humble guitar to the beggar—who was allowed to keep all the coins and bills dropped into the coffee tin—and Riodago would walk away from the crowds each time wishing he would one day be good enough to bring back the dead.

At six in the evening, Riodago woke from his dreams of childhood feeling an old man at the age of thirty-eight, having been forced to follow his father to London twenty-two years ago.

For the first five years, into his early twenties, Riodago had loved the frenetic pace of London—where things seemed to be happening at lightning speeds—but this false amour faded when Riodago realized the real world outside of Spain had no place nor desire for a guitarist.

His father forced him to study a more classical form of training at the Royal Academy of Music, and that resulted in Riodago being stripped for a time of his passion. The fluidity in his fingers dried up and Riodago learned alternative ways to move along the strings of guitars, which for him had become little more than an instrument to allow the rest of the world to hear the music coming from the invisible strings pulling at his heart from within.

By seven that same evening, Riodago had showered and drank a double espresso. Outside the sun had started to set and leave a low, soft light over Riodago, now a man, sitting nude on the edge of a sofa where he played a few melodies from "Nocturnal after John Dowland."

By eight, Riodago dressed, packed his guitar and headed for the underground. He had played the guitar his whole life, but he had not once come close to the perfection he had sought for so very long. In the world around him there was a nature Riodago didn't understand, and though he wanted to be great the world forced him—time and time again over the years—down and down and down until he wished simply to be paid.

Even so, Riodago knew the music that came from within could never be packaged, labeled and sold. Not really. No amount of money could ever settle the debts of his heart. The price he had paid to become the artist the world rejected, like his father, every day, could not be given a number.

Riodago exited the underground and walked the London streets as normal men and women hurried home or rushed to catch happy hour. Strangely enough, Riodago grew more alive as the night stirred into its own.

At the back exit, Riodago entered the Falconer's Club, a hotspot mixing and mingling the separated, the divorced, the naïve, and the hopeless; in other words, the dead.

Riodago did not drink alcohol but mineral water instead, and by nine he had settled onto stage atop a three-legged stool. He plucked his guitar into tune amidst the clanking of glasses and the ceaseless convo of the upper middle-class.

With eyes closed, Riodago ignored the bartenders, the waitresses, the shuffling of feet and purses, and the occasional drunk shouting at him to "play or be gone."

Even in all that noise Riodago could sense the ticking of the clocks and watches in the room, and at 9:15 he would briefly open his eyes, see his mother's form—imaginary or real, he didn't care which—sitting alone at the small table for two in the corner to his left, a little in the dark and a little in the light, and at 9:20, on the dot, Riodago would close his eyes, lean into the microphone and say,

"This is for you."

Crowds hushed at the precise moment Riodago began to play his guitar. The sensation of his music calmed the tensions of the day and pacified the restlessness found in lives lived for the wrong reasons.

As Riodago played, the separated would be reunited, the divorced would seek out marriage, the naïve would see the truth and hypocrisy overlooked in the world around them, and the hopeless would be filled with hope; in other words, they would start to live again.

For two hours not a single person thought it strange or unusual that Riodago would play his guitar without interruption to break. He'd simply sit on his stool with eyes closed and play.

By midnight, Riodago was back on the streets close to his home. When the spirit struck, Riodago might open his guitar case and begin playing "El Porompompero" from his childhood right there on the street corner. Passersby would drop coins and bills into the open guitar case as Riodago played and played into the early morning hours.

Sometimes the Bobbies would stop to hear Riodago play before forgetting why they had wished to cease from this cruel world such beautiful music, especially with what had happened in Manchester and on London Bridge. The police officers would walk away without a word and Riodago would play on.

By the time the sun was coming up, Riodago could be found on his living room floor in the nude still playing his guitar. The music poured effortlessly outward and he could sense it not wishing to be bottled up and silenced. The music wished to be played on and on and on into eternity, but that, Riodago knew, he could not do.

By ten in the morning, Riodago would settle into bed having forgotten to eat again, but dreams awaited him. He'd close his eyes and fall to sleep listening to the invisible strings playing from within, and against the music of his soul Riodago could hear his mother sing.

About the Author:

CG Fewston was born in Texas in 1979 and now lives in Hong Kong. He is the author of several short stories and novels. His works include A Father's Son, The New America: A Collection, Vanity of Vanities, A Time to Love in Tehran, and (forthcoming) Conquergood& the Center of the Intelligible Mystery of Being, and (also forthcoming) Little Hometown, America: A Look Back.

THE END OF HISTORY
Edward Mathis

I was on a walking path through the Tiergarten when a bird flew into me and pecked the back of my head. I ducked and ran for cover. He fluttered and squawked and took little nips at me until I connected with a swat and sent him flapping off into the branches. A Common Redstart. I had seen a picture on the sign at the entrance to the park. Pretty boring looking bird.

Assuming it was a freak accident, that I was a pane of glass who happened to be in this daydreaming bird's flight path, I looked up into the branches and laughed. Gee, I thought. I hope I didn't inflict any damage on the poor fellow.

Then he was on me again! A little red tornado of wings and talons and inexplicable rage. I shrieked and waved my arms in the air. This not-so-common Redstart was a million little Redstarts, a bloodthirsty swarm of bees, a dive bombing Stuka chasing me down a farm road strafing machine-gun fire, little geysers of dirt shooting up at my heels.

Screaming, I sprinted to a clearing. I wheeled around, fists up like a boxer. Then, as suddenly as he had appeared, he was gone. Nowhere in sight. No sound except for the rustle of a light breeze through the leaves and some sunny day chirps in the distance.

I turned to see a man with white hair sitting on a nearby park bench staring at me through thick lenses that made his eyes the size of half dollars. I searched for the word in German. Couldn't find it.

"Bird," I said. "A crazy bird. It was attacking me. Terrorizing me." The man smiled and walked away with his hands clasped behind his back.

I surveyed my face with my fingers. I touched the back of my head. No blood. No welts. No feathers in my hair. I laughed. "Well, that was weird," I said to nobody.

After a bit more walking, I found a place to lay out my towel and enjoy the serene Berlin summer day. A big open field with some boulders arranged in a strange formation meant to represent something celestial. There was a plaque explaining the significance of the rock formation but I was far too relaxed to get up and read it.

Hardly anyone was around, just a few frisbee tossers in the distance. I laid on my stomach and opened World Empire Lost, by General Armin von Roon, a fascinating guilt-shirking tome about German military strategy during WWII. It was only a few seconds before I was lost in Von Roon's rather psychotic point of view.

When the chapter ended, I looked up and the field was brimming with people. Naked people. Sunbathing, reading, chatting, laughing. Naked. Those Europeans!

Well, hey, Ich bin ein Berliner.

So I disrobed and moved out of the shade to get some color where the sun don't shine. I closed my eyes and inhaled that clean German air. The backs of my eyelids were a soft velvety red. A cool breeze enveloped me. I quickly dozed off.

When I opened my eyes, the field was deserted. Everyone was gone.

I looked around. There were little birds surrounding me. Sparrows, I thought. Sparrows seemed a ubiquitous bird. They had cute little beaks and were hopping around on cute little legs, picking off invisible bugs from thin blades of grass. They were adorable. I propped myself up on my elbow and watched them, feeling a bit like St. Francis as they hopped closer and closer.

I sat up, thinking they would scatter from my motion. But they didn't. They only moved closer. I could see at least ten little birds in my immediate periphery. Darting their heads back and forth from bug to bug, taking no notice of me.

One hopped on the corner of my towel. I karate chopped to scare it off but it barely moved. It hopped casually back into the grass, not acting at all like a creature that had almost been karate chopped into oblivion.

"Hey!" I yelled. "I'm the human here. I'm in charge!" They sparrows on hopping, kept on chirping. They had no fear. Panic crept up from my stomach.

I craned my neck like an owl to assess the situation. Jesus, there were hundreds. They formed a perimeter around me, systematically hunting for every morsel of food in their ever shrinking circle.

One landed on my foot! I kicked and screamed and he fluttered off lazily. But not before snatching a microscopic insect from one of my big toe hairs. He landed in the grass, tossed it down his gullet, and continued on his way.

Given my vulnerable state of undress, you can understand the primal fear that took hold of me. Fear for my life. Or at least life as I knew it. I bunched my clothes under my arm, and broke through their wall of fire, their Siege of Stalingrad, whipping my towel in all directions as if engaged in the most vicious of locker room melees.

I didn't notice if they fled, my eyes were closed. If I squashed one, too bad. They had it coming. The gall of those little fuckers!

I threw on my shorts, shirt, and shoes mid-stride. I chucked my undies and socks in the bushes, there was simply no time. I jumped on my bicycle and didn't take a complete breath until I

was inside the door of our apartment building and collapsed on the cool tile floor.

"I'm not crazy. It happened," I said. My wife, Alice, was in the kitchen chopping squash. I laid on the couch in the living room, staring up at the chandelier. We'd owned the apartment for six months and I was still quite taken with that chandelier.

"Well." She sounded bored. "I'm just saying you must've done something to provoke it. Rustled the nest or something without knowing it. You are quite tall."

"No, I told you. It was completely unprovoked. It was cruel and undeserving. It was Pearl Harbor. It was, I'm sorry, I know they don't bring this kind of thing up around here anymore but it's true, Alice. It was Poland in 1939. It was blitzkrieg, I tell you."

She turned from the cutting board. "Jesus, give it a rest. Nobody says that kind of thing anywhere. There is no one in the world as obsessed with relating everything to that war as you are."

"What about the sparrows? How do you explain their actions? Their aggressions?" I asked.

"It sounds like they didn't actually do anything to you. They were just— what was the word you used?"

"Threatening."

"Yes, they were threatening little sparrows weren't they?"

"Please don't make fun of me. Let's ride our bikes over there and I'll show you. If it happens again then we'll really know something is up."

"I can't. My bike is in the shop."

"Again? What happened this time?"

"The, uh, chain broke."

"The chain broke? Geez, what a hunk of junk. That's the third time this month you've had to take it in."

"Yeah, I don't know. Maybe I need to get a new one."

"Well, listen. All I'm saying is the whole episode

was weird. Nothing like that has ever happened to me before. The whole thing felt, I don't know, off. And scary. Like they were really out to get me."

"Oh, honey." She loomed over the back of the couch, an upside-down head floating over me. The knife was still in her hand. I couldn't tell if her tone was patronizing and even if it was I lacked the energy to do battle. I hoped that maybe she actually felt sorry for me and this could lead to some sex. It had been a while.

"I'm sorry," she said. She kissed my forehead in a sexless way. "I'm sure you were just in their territory and didn't know it. You're still acclimating to our new life here. Don't worry, it'll get better."

Alice comes from Mercedes money. She was born on her mother's farm in Pennsylvania but her father was German, a very imposing blond-haired man named Wolfgang. Alice's mother met Wolfgang in the 70's when she was an Army nurse stationed at the American base in Stuttgart, the home of Mercedes-Benz. Wolfgang was, and still is, a big exec there, a real hotshot engineer.

Something about the American farm girl caught the Bavarian big wig's eye at the schnitzel restaurant where he first saw her. Alice was the fruit of their 24-hour romantic harvest.

Wolfgang wasn't the world's best father. He was much too consumed with being filthy rich on the other side of the world and then, later, with a family of his own. But he wasn't the world's worst either. Every summer of her youth, he flew over to scoop Alice up from the farm in Pennsylvania and take her on lavish, exotic vacations. Exchanging a year's worth of inattention for a week's worth of overindulgence.

Alice lived in two worlds. She spent most of her childhood years mending barns, milking cows, and fixing tractors. By all accounts, she was a resourceful, appreciative, polite little girl. But she knew, all the while, that come summer she would be whisked away to a life where any desire was fulfilled before she even knew it existed.

Thus, Alice became a paradox, an amalgam of her two parents: somehow equal parts modest and spoiled, selfish and generous, perfectly content with life as it was and feeling entitled to so much more.

Alice and I met in college in New York and got married shortly after graduation. We both worked in advertising. We spent our weeknights taking walks together to pick up Chinese takeout. We spent our weekends brunching and instagramming. We talked with our friends about how much cooler our Brooklyn neighborhoods used to be back in the day. We argued about at which albums our favorite bands had peaked. We were happy.

There was only one little splinter that burrowed its way into our marital flesh. Alice constantly wanted to take trips to the farm in Pennsylvania. She said she needed the air. But farm life wasn't for me. What's appealing about pulling ticks from your butt? I almost always refused to make the drive and she'd get all sullen and withdrawn for a day or two. But splinters only hurt if you poke them. I wouldn't bring it up and eventually the matter would disappear. Our blissful marriage lived on.

That is until Alice got this big promotion at work and started making way more money than me. At first I was excited for us. Hey, more money. We renovated our brownstone and really upped our dinner party game. We turned the downstairs bedroom into a combination office/jam room decked out with gear galore. I bought a kick ass Les Paul and learned every single Pink Floyd guitar solo note for note.

But soon it wasn't fun anymore. Our income disparity became an acid that dripped between us, eroding our union from the inside-out. Not unlike the Wehrmacht in 1944 when Hitler started making some wacko tactical decisions. Everyone knew it was over but nobody dared say a word.

I dared.

"Are you comparing me to Hitler because I make more money than you?!" Alice said. Honestly, you drop the big H and everyone thinks you're saying they are Hitler.

"No, no. Clearly you misunderstood. I'm comparing the feeling inside our marriage right now to what it must've felt like inside the German

Army at that time. If you want, I can explain why it was rotting. You see—"

"That's insane," she said, interrupting me. "You're the one that feels that way, not me. I'm perfectly happy."

"Yeah, well at the end of the war if you compared the perceptions of the generals on the field with those of Hi— look, never mind. That's not the point. The point is I want to save this thing, Alice. The clutter is killing us. Our jobs, New York, this apartment, it's all clutter. Our marriage is bigger than all that."

"What are you saying?"

"I'm saying we drop all of it. Quit our jobs, move away, be crazy, be adventurous! See if we can survive it, you know? Together."

Maybe I didn't expect her to agree. Maybe I actually wanted out altogether. Maybe it was all a bluff. Either way, she called me on it.

Germany seemed the obvious choice. Alice had dual-citizenship and had always wanted to get to know her father. Stuttgart, though, was dreary and industrial. So we set our sights on Berlin. A city bursting out of its skin like a growing serpent, electric with youth and newfound ambition. Plus, I thought I would dig all the historical relics from WWII.

For awhile, it really did feel like the excitement of the move was a panacea for all our marital woes. Wolfgang got me a job at the English-speaking advertising firm that works with Mercedes and Alice decided to take a break from working to see the country. Shortly after we arrived, we found our beautiful little apartment in the charming neighborhood of Kreuzberg.

Alice had gone back to the kitchen and I was still on the couch dissecting the day's events when there was tender knock on the door. I got up and walked through the kitchen to get it.

"Careful, it might be Big Bird," Alice said.

"Ooh nice one," I said, really ladling on the sarcasm.

It was a man. A young, handsome man. His skin was caramel and his beard long but neatly groomed and flecked with grey. He wore a starkly white tunic, blue slacks, and brown leather loafers. He was smiling. But not the kind of door-to-door salesman's smile I would have expected. He smiled like he was holding some juicy piece of gossip.

"Grüss Gott," he said after a moment of silence.

"Oh, um, yes. Gross Gott. Sprechen sie English?" I asked. I hadn't yet progressed from common greetings on Rosetta Stone.

"English? Yes, I speak English. You are American?" His accent was intoxicating.

"I am. We are." I opened the door wider. Alice looked over smiling. "Um, come in, come in. This is my wife, Alice. Alice, this is— I'm sorry, sir, what was your name?"

"Mustafa, madam." He took her hand affectionately and bowed his head. Alice put her other hand to her chest and giggled.

"It's very nice to meet you, Mustafa." she said. We all looked at each other and smiled, nodding, not saying anything for a few moments.

"So Mustafa, are you a neighbor? Is there something we can help you with?" I asked.

"Oh no, not a neighbor." His pearly whites caught the light of the sleek Edison bulbs I had recently installed in the kitchen. "No, this is my apartment. Well, it was my apartment. Now you live here," he said, nodding his head. "So clearly it's not mine anymore."

"Yes," I said. Alice and I looked at each other and laughed nervously.

"May I?" He gestured toward the couch in the living room.

"Yes, I'm sorry, of course. Take a seat," I stumbled. "Would you like something to drink? Coffee? Tea? Water?"

"Coffee sounds splendid," Mustafa said, situating himself in the other room. I reached for the French press on the shelf above the sink.

"I got it," Alice said.

"No, I got it," I muttered.

"No, really, I got it," she said through clenched teeth. We both grabbed the French press and began tugging it back and forth. Mustafa noticed the commotion and looked over the back of the couch.

"Water is quite fine if coffee is a problem," he said.

"You are making a fool of us in front of Mustafa," Alice whispered. "I got it."

"Fine!" I growled and let go. I turned and flashed Mustafa a grin. "Nope, no problem. Three coffees coming up! So Mustafa." I took a seat across from him on one of our austere minimalist chairs. I was dabbling with a Donald Judd thing in the living room. I adjusted my butt in all sorts of ways but I never could find a way to make that chair comfortable. "Mustafa, I gotta say, your English is great. Fancy words like splendid and quite. Makes you sound British. Are you British? You certainly don't sound German. No offense."

"No, my friend. I am Turkish," he said.

"Turkish! Hey, you know a thing or two about coffee then. Hope Alice doesn't screw it up." I smiled. He stared at me. "Lots of Turkish people around here, aren't there? It's wonderful. If I open the windows, we get a scent of incense from the street. Have you seen the line for that shawarma stand on Friedrichstrasse? It stretches around the block!"

He nodded and stroked his beard.

"You, uh, used to live in this very apartment?" I asked.

"What do you know about Kreuzberg?" Mustafa asked ominously.

"Aha!" I wagged my finger at him. "Okay, I see what this is. You think I only know that it's the hippest neighborhood in Berlin. But I did my research." I paused to let his misjudged assumption sink in.

"Let's see," I said. "Most of these buildings were originally built in the latter half of the 19th century. In the days of Otto Von Bismarck. The Iron Chancellor!" I stood with my fist in the air. Mustafa didn't seem moved so I sat back down. "And, well, most were destroyed during the war. It's sad how everything in this country is just a

replication of its former self, you know? I mean, all the old stuff is not actually old at all. Kinda weird, right?"

"This building survived," he said, gazing out the window.

"Well, there you go, what do I know? Actually, I really do know quite a bit. In fact, I like to think of myself as a bit of a history buff. Are you a fan?"

"A fan?" he asked.

"Of history. Do you like history? Do you study it?"

"Worrying about now keeps me busy enough." He offered a faint smile.

"You know, that's a good point. Gee, I should apologize. I got all wrapped up thinking about 19th century Prussia, I forgot to ask what you do. What keeps you busy, Mustafa?"

"I have a bike shop. Near here. It was my father's before."

"A bike shop, I love it. There are so many bikes in this city! Hey, Alice is getting her bike worked on this very second. Alice," I called into the kitchen. "What's the name of the bike shop you went to?"

I guess she didn't hear me over the sound of the kettle.

"Well, maybe it's your shop," I said. "Small world, huh?"

Mustafa examined me. Then he took in the room. I wondered what he noticed. Besides for a few of those aforementioned minimalist touches, the room hadn't changed much from when we bought the apartment.

"This was the furthest eastern neighborhood in West Berlin when the wall was up," he said. "Kreuzberg was nestled into the wall, was touched by it on three sides. Some people didn't like to be near it so they moved away. Others had no choice but to stay. You do know about the wall?"

"Oh yes, of course. Now that I could really say a thing or two about."

Alice came in then and set two steaming mugs in

front of us. She smiled at Mustafa and walked out of the room without looking at me.

"Yes," he continued after a tentative sip. "This neighborhood changed quite a bit when the wall came down."

"Of course it did. The world changed. This city returned to its former self. Ah, Berlin," I said, dreamily. "The place where everyone has a marvelous roommate. Sometimes two marvelous roommates." I winked at him.

"Pardon?"

"It's from Cabaret. Broadway musical. Takes place in swingin' Berlin. A pretty happening place back then. And, hey, now it's back! I went to a rave a few weeks ago and, phew, let me tell you, Berliners know how to throw down. Actually," I whispered. "Let's keep that one between us. I never did tell Alice about that rave."

Mustafa reclined into the couch with his mug and crossed his legs. "I see," he said, sipping slowly.

"Wanna know something interesting about the fall of the Berlin Wall, Mustafa?"

"Certainly," he said.

"When the wall came down, people called it The End of History. It was that big of a deal. Can you believe that?"

He nodded slowly.

"The idea was that we had been fighting and dying and living shitty lives for all these centuries in order for that very event to occur. For humanity to be saved. All of time was funneled toward that moment when the last brick hit the ground. The wall was the definitive representation of an epic battle between good and evil. And it was finally over. No more wars. No more struggle. Kind of a nice thought, isn't it?" I asked.

I sparked something. Mustafa sat up and put his mug back on the table. "Are you a religious man, Louis?"

Louis? He knew my name. I quickly retraced the mental trail of crumbs back to the knock on the door. I definitely hadn't said my name. A faint thought began to bubble up in my mind and settle at the top: Mustafa knew some Turkish voodoo shit. That's how he knew my name. And he set a curse on me that made all the birds in the city want to peck my eyes out.

"You're curious how I knew your name?" he asked.

"My name?" I said, nonchalantly. "I introduced myself, didn't I?"

"No, you didn't. But it's here on the mug." He turned the mug so I could see the picture of me making an X with my arms across my chest and backward W's with my fingers. My lips were pursed. It was my hard-ass pose. Under the picture it said Louis: Number One Stunna.

"Oh, right," I laughed. "I have a softball team back home that, uh, well it's an inside joke I guess. No, Alice and I are not very religious. Why do you ask?"

"Do you believe in destiny?" he asked.

"As in, do I believe that I'm meant to be here in Berlin, married to Alice, working for her father, having this conversation with you at this very moment? That no matter what I do, my path has been preordained? No, I don't believe in that," I said.

"Do you believe that we are at the end of history?"

"Oh, that idea went out of fashion pretty quick once people started hacking each other up again. But I do think there was some truth to it. I think humanity ultimately wants peace and freedom for all."

"Is that what you want, Louis? Peace and freedom for all?"

"Well, yeah. Don't you?"

He stood and walked to the window with his hands clasped behind his back like the old man in the Tiergarten. "It isn't possible," he said. "It seems to me that one man's peace has always been the currency for another man's way of life. Your end of history idea says that the crumbling wall was supposed to bring us freedom and prosperity. You say that peace is our destiny, peace is the norm, but something went wrong along the way. No, I don't think that is so, Louis."

He turned to face me. "Suffering is the norm," he said. "Peace and freedom are fragile. When each of us finds our quiet corner, we must hold it dear, Louis. Because it can always be taken away. Bought by someone else. Or taken."

"Okay, okay Mr. History Shark, pretending like you don't know anything so you can bust a history egg on my head. Here's my money." I threw some euro coins on the coffee table and smiled. "You're lucky I don't break your thumbs like Paul Newman," I joked. He didn't get it.

Mustafa stared at the money then pulled his tunic to the side and revealed a screwdriver. He walked towards me and removed his shoes.

"Uh, Mustafa? What are you doing there, my good man?"

He stepped up onto the coffee table. "This was where I lived, Louis. This is the apartment where my children were born and raised." He reached up to the ceiling with the screwdriver.

"Oh, well, I didn't know anything about that when we bought the place. Really, Mustafa, what are you doing?"

"People are quite good at finding ways to absolve themselves of blame. Aren't they, Louis?" He said to the ceiling.

"Oh yeah. I mean, look at Nuremberg. Hey, can I help you with something, Mustafa?"

"Louis, I came here because I forgot one thing when we were forced to move. This is mine." He stepped down from the table holding the chandelier he had pried from the ceiling, the little crystal pieces singing their sweet tinkling song. He stared at me, challenging me to speak. I pointed at the chandelier and opened my mouth but no words came.

"Do treat this home well, Louis. And do thank your lovely wife for the coffee for me."

He turned and walked through the kitchen. I followed him to the door. Alice wasn't in the apartment. She must've slipped out. He opened the door for himself then turned to face me. With a vague, fleeting smile he asked, "Louis, have you enjoyed your time in Berlin so far?"

"Yes, very much," I said. I squinted my eyes and tried to read his expression. "I've only had one strange little incident. It happened this morning, actually. Some birds attacked me. It happened twice."

He nodded slowly. "Yes, that is strange. Birds can be quite territorial. Be careful." He offered his hand. There was bike grease under his nails I hadn't noticed before. "Good day, Louis."

Now I'm laying here on the couch staring up at the bare spot in the ceiling where the chandelier used to be. I look out the window. The sun is low and casts a latticework of shadows on the facade of the apartment building across the street. A pigeon lands on our sill. He paces back and forth, looking inside the apartment, looking at me on the couch. Then another pigeon joins him. Then another.

I lay back and close my eyes so I don't have to see the blank spot in the ceiling. I plug my ears so I don't have to hear the pigeons' incessant cooing. I lay and I wait. I wonder how long it will be until Alice comes home.

About the Author:

Edward Mathis is a teacher and writer from Austin, Texas. He is a MFA-Fiction candidate at Texas State University and is currently at work on his first collection of short stories.

THE HOLY FACE MEDAL

Sevasti Iyama

I park my old T-bird in front of Wendy's. Puffs of smoke pour out of my car, which coughs like it's in the final stage of COPD. A mechanic told me that I need a new catalytic converter, and there is no way in hell that my car is going to pass smog next year but that's 12 months away.

One day at a time.

I learned in AA that's how to deal with life.

I have to believe that, or else I will go crazy.

I also have to be of service to fellow alcoholics and addicts who are still suffering, or so my sponsor Mitch tells me. This whole crazy idea of my sponsoring this 40-year old rich ex housewife was his idea.

I walk by a row of cars, and spot Colleen's brand new white luxury Cadillac Escalade EXT crew cab.

I brace myself, and approach Starbucks, clutching my stupid Big Book, like a religious zealot clutching a Bible.

She sits outside on the patio. Her back is faced to me, and I can see her long blonde hair cascading over her shoulders. Colleen is a dowdy, plump woman, and yet somehow she manages to get all the guys in AA to drool all over her. Maybe its because she is a newcomer or maybe its because she always wears tight little spaghetti dresses with hems that go way up over her knees, revealing suntanned legs. And she always wears sandals that show off a fresh new pedicure.

Today she looks like she is hanging out at a country club, waiting for a waiter to bring her a pina colada with a plastic cocktail umbrella propped in the glass.

There is no else sitting outside at this Starbucks, which thanks to globalization, looks like a thousand other Starbucks all around the world.

This particular Starbucks is located in the Antelope Valley desert. How the hell did I end up in the AV? Oh that's right, I moved up here in a blackout ten years ago, with a fiancé who walked out on me the day our electricity got shut off, due to nonpayment. Seems like he had some younger woman waiting for him, in some candle lit villa somewhere in Albuquerque.

Up ahead, a woman driving a black BMW is passing through the drive-through. She has sunglasses and dyed red hair. I hear the barista ask, over the speaker,

"Hello, welcome to Starbucks. What can I get started for you?"

The woman's face scrunches up like a walnut and she bleats out of a grape lipstick colored mouth, "Caramel macchiato with low fat soy."

Colleen turns, as if she has sensed that I am standing behind her. Her face breaks out into a wide grin, and her long teeth are as white as her new truck. Her lip-gloss shines, and she has makeup on, highlighting her big blue eyes. Today she boasts a bright red pedicure, and matching manicure. She wears a short blue dress that has pink hyacinth and blue bird prints. Around her neck, she wears a gold medal, hanging from a thick gold chain.

"Hi," she says, and gets up to give me a crushing hug. I smell perfume, shampoo and wine. The medal catches onto my knit blouse, and for a moment Colleen and I become Siamese Twins, connected at the chest.

"I am sorry," she laughs, and then bumps her forehead against mine, like we are two bulls in a rodeo.

"I am sorry!" she says, again.

"Stop moving, I got it," I say.

I disentangle the pendant, and get a good look. It's a holy face medal, showing an image of Christ on the shroud of Turin. Honestly, Christ's face reminds me of a 19th century post-mortem photograph.

Finally, I am free of Colleen and her medal. She collapses on a chair and guffaws, like a shopping mall Santa Claus.

I stare down at the table. She has a brand new copy of the Big Book, a notebook, pens, the 12 and 12, and a compass. Why the hell does she have a compass? Does she think that we are going to be drawing circles and studying Euclidean geometry? She also has a pack of Marlboro Lights, that she has not opened, and a brand new green lighter.

"I bought a pack of my own cigarettes," she says. "This way I don't have to keep bumming off yours."

Does she really smell of booze or am I just imagining things? Should I say something or just let her admit the truth to me? What the hell do I do?

"This morning I got a 30-day chip," she says, and pulls it out of a Michael Kors handbag.

I want to call her bluff, but I don't.

She is too excited about the damn white chip that is hanging off her key chain.

"Would you like a coffee?" I notice that she has not ordered, and I figure that hey, I should be nice and get her something. Besides, maybe the coffee will sober her up.

"I would love a hibiscus iced tea." She reaches for her bag again.

"It's okay, I got it," I said, and walk inside the Starbucks. Suddenly, I feel like running back to my crappy old T bird, and driving off, letting white exhaust pollute the air. The Native Americans used smoke signals for communication. Three puffs mean something is wrong. Maybe if my stupid car emits three puffs of white smoke, the universe will reach out and help me.

An hour later, after I have drunk two iced Americanos, and I watch Colleen chain smoke her Marlboros and chomp on the melting ice cubes from her pink colored iced tea, I have heard so much about her life. We have done everything except talk about the steps, which honestly seems like a moot point. How can I take her through the steps if she is drinking? She got a DUI six months ago, which is why she is in AA. Some judge in Santa Clarita mandated her to go to 12-step meetings, but she was able to get her license back, since it was a first time offense. She is newly divorced, and just moved back home with her mother. During the week, her daughters live with her ex, because of the DUI, but she has the girls on the weekends. Then, she tells me she works for the FBI and that she walks around with a Glock 43.

"Where's the gun?" I ask.

"It's on my upper thigh," she says.

I peek at the hem of her bird and flower-covered dress, which is way above her thigh, revealing too much skin and nothing that looks like a weapon.

"Listen, don't tell anybody else I work for the FBI. That's classified information."

"I won't tell a soul," I say.

I stare at the medal around her neck.

"That's very pretty," I lie. The medal gives me the creeps.

"My mom gave it to me, when I moved back home. I'm Catholic."

"I am Greek Orthodox," I say. "But right now I like to think of myself as spiritual."

Colleen nervously lights a cigarette and fingers her medal. I don't think she is listening.

"What do you think of Stan?" she asks.

"Stan?"

"From AA. Blonde Stan," she says.

"He is a nice guy. He used to date my friend Amanda," I say.

"She died," Colleen says.

"Yes, she hit her head on a coffee table one night in her living room and fell over dead. They think it was a stroke. She just lived alone with her cat."

"Stan misses her," Colleen says.

"Well, she was my hairdresser. Now I just go to Supercuts."

Colleen lights another cigarette and says, "He asked me out, I mean, Stan did."

"He is a nice guy," I say, and stare off into space.

I refrain from telling her that he had broken Amanda's heart, and had dumped her several months before she died. This is because she had started using again, and people in AA told him to leave her to fend for herself. After she died, Stan seemed interested in asking me out. One night, he wanted to have dinner, but I told him I was writing a PowerPoint presentation on Diane Arbus for a History of Photography class. At that time, I was working towards my Associates in photography, and I was a full-time student at Antelope Valley Community College.

Stan expressed interest in Arbus, so I sent him the presentation, which included many of her photos. He said her photography was way too weird, specifically the photo of the Boy with the Hand Grenade. He said that I looked like Arbus, with my short hair. After I told him Arbus killed herself and sometimes I entertained suicidal thoughts, but would not kill myself because I had too many pit bulls, and God only knew animal control would confiscate them if I croaked, he backed off.

I seem to have an unsettling effect on men.

Honestly, the thought of being in a relationship makes me feel numb. I'd rather be independent and pay my bills, and make sure the electricity is always on. I don't like the dark.

The next time we meet, she can't stop crying. It is a cool overcast day in October, and she wears a jean mini skirt and a tight white t-shirt. I have cowboy boots on and she wears sandals, revealing a black pedicure.

Her red fingernails are chipped, and she is not wearing the holy face medal.

"I am not drunk," she says. "But I don't know if I can do this. Work these steps. I don't believe in God. My mom and I had a big fight, because I lost the medal. I have no idea where it is. But I am not drunk."

I stare at her. She does not smell of booze or perfume.

"You don't have to believe in God to work the steps," I say. "Just a power greater than yourself."

"Does that mean I should collect crystals, and meditate in front of a Better Home and Gardens rock fountain?" she asks. "I have no idea what you are talking about! Besides, I'm Catholic!"

"Well the truth is I have a hard time wrapping my mind around a higher power. Being Greek Orthodox has really installed the idea of a Jesus who looks like a terrorist, ok? When I first got sober, I took an astronomy class, and just knowing that the galaxy was eternal made me visualize something greater than myself. Anyway, surrendering to a higher power is in the third step. We have time to talk about that. But lets work on step one," I say.

"Ok," she says.

After she admits that she is powerless over alcohol, and that her life is a total mess, I ask, "What's this whole thing with the FBI?"

"I am a school teacher," she says. "Working for the FBI sounds better, don't you think? The truth is, I don't even own a gun."

We look at each other and laugh.

"I have something for you. You said you were studying photography, so maybe you can use this," she says.

She hands me a bulky camera bag.

"It was my father's," she says. "He's been gone for almost 20 years."

I zip open the bag, and there is a Minolta film X-570 SLR, along with a huge telephoto lens, inside a black tube and a few other lenses, and a flash. Everything is so neatly arranged, and the camera has a brand new strap.

"I know it was a long time ago, but I miss him."

She looks up at me. Her eyes are full of tears.

"It feels like yesterday that he died. Anyway, I found the camera. It's yours."

A few days later, I see her at the Palmdale hall. She is outside, while the meeting is going on. Stan and a few other men circle her. I walk towards the hall, and she sees me. She breaks out into a large grin. As usual, she wears a little mini skirt. I look terrible. She has a fresh new manicure, and her high-heeled sandals reveal an equally fresh pedicure. I look at my hands. There are remnants of duct tape and dirt underneath my nails. This morning I was served with a three-day notice, which I ripped off my gate like a crazed animal. I didn't want the neighbors to see it. The papers were taped with duct tape all over the gate. Even though I have washed my hands ten times this morning, scrubbing them over and over like Lady Macbeth trying to rub blood off her hands, they still feel dirty.

A month ago, I had a job an hour away in Lake Hughes, where I worked as a kennel assistant at a dog rescue. And then I started having serious problems with my car, and a local mechanic warned me not to drive long distance. I couldn't get to work because this place was miles away and so I got fired, and couldn't pay my rent this month.

Colleen hugs me. I smell the booze, and I flinch.

"Stan and I went on a date. He is so wonderful! I love you!"

"Ditto," I say.

During the break, I pull Stan aside, and I said, "Is she drinking again?"

He nervously combs his fingers through his long brown hair. Stan is tall, and looks like George Washington without wooden teeth.

"That's her choice. All I can do is take her to meetings, and maybe she will catch on. When I was with Amanda, too many people had too much to say, and I was stupid to listen."

His face turns red, from anger or from guilt, I can't tell.

"It's your life, Stan."

"Thanks for being her sponsor, " he said.

Her sponsor? The way he said that made me feel like I was some kind of hospice nurse, and Colleen was my terminally ill patient.

The next time, we are supposed to meet, she is there, waiting for me at Starbucks, and I have overslept and I have stood her up. It's two in the afternoon, and I huddle under the covers, shaking. I was served with an unlawful detainer the day before. That means I have to go to court and respond within five days, or else my dogs and I will be out in the streets. And today is the second day and I haven't done jack shit.

Prior to meeting Colleen, I had planned to be at the darkroom at the college, where this semester I am taking one film photo class because that is all I can afford. Over the weekend, I had used the Minolta, and had taken some black and white shots of a Joshua tree. It was a simple depth of field assignment. I shot the same damn tree on different F-stops. In one pocket of the camera bag, I found a Fuji color roll that had been shot yet not developed. It probably belonged to Colleens' dad, and he never got a chance to develop it.

I mean to call Colleen but I fall asleep again, and I am walking through the desert. The sky is yellow, the way I imagine Hiroshima to have been after the Atomic bomb. There is a man up ahead, wearing a white robe and sandals. He kneels down and prays. Up ahead is Colleen, and she has a Polaroid camera. She takes a picture of the man. Then she hurls the photo on the desert ground, and I run and pick the print up. I wait for an image to develop and I hear her up ahead laughing and I can't see the man anymore, he is gone.

Close by I see a rattlesnake. Colleen yells out, "How did you find me here?"

The snake has approached me, and if I get up, it will bite. An image develops on the print, and before I see it, I hear, "How the hell did you find me?"

Colleen told me later that she had waited for me at Starbucks for two hours.

"There was this nutty red headed lady in a BMW. She was such a bitch," Colleen says. "She went through the drive through. After she ordered her stupid drink, it was a caramel macchiato with low fat soy. I mean what the hell is low fat soy? Isn't soy already low fat? Anyway, she told the guy that I was smoking on the patio, and didn't they have some new law that prohibited smoking on the patio?"

Colleen slurs her words.

"So I told the bitch to fuck off, and they threw me out of there. Guess we have to find another Starbucks."

"Colleen, you are still drinking."

"I had a slip," she says.

"I can't help you if you are still drinking."

"What are you telling me? You don't want to be my sponsor anymore?"

"No," I said. "I can't."

She bursts into tears, and wails like Andromache, when her child was thrown off the walls of Troy.

After I was evicted, my dogs and I lived with a guy who I had met at an AA meeting years ago. He said he was sober, but I found empty bottles of Vodka hidden under piles of sweaty clothing and dirty socks in the living room. Thankfully, we had our own room, and my pit bull Zeus safeguarded me from this guy, the way the Sphinx guarded the city of Thebes from travellers, unless they could solve her famous riddle. Zeus had no riddle, he just barked. We lasted there for a tortuous month, and then I found a small trailer up in the Mojave.

We have been here a year. The desert landscape that was in my dream surrounds me in real life. I wonder if the Mojave is purgatory, and I am paying for past transgressions.

Guilt compels me to call Colleen's cell. A Hispanic male picks up. He doesn't speak English. I suppose she has another cell phone number, but I have no idea how to find her. She is not on Facebook or any other social media sites. I connect the cell phone to the charger, which is in the bathroom, which is as claustrophobic as an aircraft lavatory.

I feed the dogs, warm up a slice of pizza, and watch House of Cards. I am so tired, but I have to brush my teeth. Inside the bathroom, I notice that there is a text. It's from my sponsor, Mitch.

"Stan said last night at the meeting that they were supposed to take Colleen off life support yesterday at 4. She drank herself to death I guess."

The camera and the lens are all tucked away inside the bag, safe and sound. I find the Fuji color roll that belonged to Colleen's father. The next day, I drive down to Lancaster and drop the roll off at the one-hour photo department. I am not sure what I am hoping to find.

After I pick up the photos, I skim through them. Most of the prints are a brownish black, like mud after a rainy day. I find an overexposed print, and I see a grainy image of a man's face. His eyes are shut. While Pope Benedict XVI once said, that in the shroud of Turin, we see a reflection of our suffering in the suffering of Christ, all I see in this man's face is stillness. This is what I imagine for Colleen. Inside her coffin, which will shelter her like a cocoon made of metal, she will be sealed away forever, buried six feet under, but she will be safe, and protected from a world that only gave her torment. Perhaps the suffering that I see in this image is not Colleen's, but rather my own anguish.

For Shannon

About the Author:

Sevasti Iyama is the blog writer for Cycles of Change Recovery Services. She has written for RehabReviews.com, the Antelope Valley Press and the Kern Valley Sun. She's also the co-author of How I got Sober, 10 Alcoholics and Addicts Tell their Personal Stories. Presently, she is working on a novel called, The Pomegranate Cowboy, which is loosely based on the myth of Persephone and Hades. She is pursuing a Masters Degree in Creative Writing from Southern New Hampshire University. Sevasti is from the Bronx, and Los Angeles. She lives in the small town of Lake Isabella, California but being a city girl at heart, she plans to go back to New York City, in the not too distant future.

THE LAST GIRL IN AMERICA

Robin Zabiegalski

23 days. 23 fucking days. That's how long it's been since those boys left me in this glass room. Like a goddamn pet turtle. They don't know what else to do with me. Until they found me in this glass room, they'd never seen a girl. They'd probably never even seen a real woman. Only female bots. They're only ten or eleven years old, too young to remember what the world was like before.

I was out hunting when I heard their voices in the woods. I was miles from the cabin off the coast of Oregon, where my mother and I had lived for almost as long as I could remember. We'd been in hiding since right after the Revolution, or The Uprising as the Administration calls it. The victors always get to decide what events are called in the history books.

I'd been hiking all day. I'd been hunting too often and the animals were slowly disappearing. Mom had tried to warn me, but I didn't listen. In the few days before I'd had to go further and further from the cabin to find game.

I'd heard the snapping branches and crunching leaves before I heard their voices; thin, high voices. Children. I hadn't heard a child's voice in years. They weren't trying to hide their presence. They clunked on heavy feet, as if they were sure the woods were their kingdom to rule.

I should have turned around. I should have quietly crept back to the cabin, to Mom, to safety, but I wanted to see them. I hadn't seen a child since I was small. I had almost forgotten they existed. Alone and isolated for so long, the outside world seemed distant, unreal, like a show we watched on TV. I just wanted to see their faces, even from a distance.

I crept closer to their voices, peeking around the edges of thick, ancient trees. As the voices grew closer I stepped more cautiously, keenly aware that to be seen would be disaster. I peered around a tree trunk that stood on the edge of a clearing. I slipped the bow and quiver filled with arrows off my back, placed them on the ground, and covered them with dirt and leaves. I judged the distance to the next tree big enough to conceal my presence. I listened and tried to estimate their distance from me before stepping out from cover. I took a deep breath and bounded in to the clearing.

Less than halfway in to the clearing I heard a whooshing noise. I was confused, but I didn't stop running, until I smacked face first in to an invisible barrier. I lay on the ground stunned for almost a minute. Eventually, my hand made its way to my face. My fingers touched warm stickiness coming from my nose, which ached and throbbed.

I shakily got to my feet and reached out to touch the invisible barrier I'd hit. It was a glass wall. I let my fingers graze the surface and began to walk around the edges, constantly touching it as I went. The walls formed a square. I counted my steps as my mother had taught me to do to approximate distances, and judged that the room was about 8 feet square. I looked up, trying to see the outline of a glass ceiling, but I couldn't. I tried jumping to see if I could touch the ceiling, but I felt nothing. I went to one of the walls and jumped, trying to see if I could catch the edge of the wall and hoist myself over the top, but I just slid back down the wall.

Three boys burst through the trees. They were busy chatting and none of them had raised their heads yet. I sat on the ground and waited, panting with fear. They all seemed to lift their heads at the same time and I heard their excited gasps and shouts. They all broke in to a sprint, headed toward the room, but they all stopped just short of the wall.

"I think it's a girl," said one of the boys excitedly.

"There are no girls anymore stupid," one of the other boys snapped back.

"Maybe it's someone's bot," replied one of the other boys.

"They don't make kid bots. Only Mom bots and Wife bots," said the third boy with exasperation. I stood up and they all instinctively backed away from the wall. I walked directly to the wall and breathed heavily. My hot breath fogged up the glass. I heard their collective gasp.

"It's breathing! It's alive." They all stared at me for a minute in silence. I stared back at them imploring them with my gaze. Please. Please just let me out. After a moment of silent staring, comprehension flashed across the face of one of the boys.

"But look at how old she is. She's way older than us, right? Maybe she was born before the Uprising."

"All the girls born before the Uprising were sent away with the women," the same boy retorted, "so they wouldn't brainwash boys with their feminism." His face twisted as he spat out the word "feminism."

"Maybe she got away," chimed in the third boy. They all paused for a minute, considering this argument, considering my existence and all the contradictions it proposed.

One of them finally spoke, authoritatively, "It must be a girl." They looked at each other and nodded, then turned their attention back to me. I nodded as well. He walked up to the wall and tapped the glass, like a child at the zoo. I rolled my eyes and tapped back. He jumped backwards,

lost his balance, and fell on the ground. His friends exploded with laughter. His face twisted with anger and embarrassment as he shoved himself off the ground. He shot me a venomous look then turned his back to the glass.

"What should we do with her?" he asked harshly.

I finally found my voice and whispered, "Please let me go home." None of them turned, so I said a little louder, "Please let me go." They looked up, their faces gone white. Perhaps they didn't know I could speak. I realized that though they'd concluded I was a girl, they did not consider me to be like them, to be human.

"Go where?" one of them asked.

The word left my lips before I could think, "Home." I gasped and clapped my hands over my mouth. I felt hot tears in my eyes. I crumpled under the weight of my mistake.

"You live around here?" the same boy asked incredulously.

"We can't just let her go," said the boy who'd fallen to the ground. "She's illegal." He paused for a moment, then said with finality, "We have to keep her in here." I began to cry.

He continued over my sobs, "What if she gets caught and she tells someone we saw her? We could get arrested. Or deported. Or maybe killed. We can't just let her go home." The other two considered this carefully.

One said quietly, "Why can't we just take her back to your house and tell your Dad? He'd call the police and have her arrested." The other nodded in agreement, but the boy who fell shook his head.

"My dad would kill me if he knew we'd gone this far in to the woods. Besides how would we explain where we found her? No one but us knows about this room. We promised it was our secret. She can be our secret too." The other two looked at him and then at each other. Resignation came over their faces. I continued to sob, shaking on the ground.

"We have to get back before my Dad gets home," he stated firmly. They turned their backs on the wall, on me, and walked away.

As soon as they left I began throwing rocks and

slamming them against the glass, but they never even left a mark. I tried climbing the glass walls, but I slid down. I tried jumping until my legs felt like they would fall off. My hands never found something to hold on to.

I combed the forest floor within the room. It had occurred to me almost immediately that I must have stepped on some sort of weight sensitive trigger that caused the walls to raise. I walked heel to toe over every inch of the room, but the walls did not come down. I crawled on my hands and knees moving every leaf, but found no button or device that would move the walls.

The trigger mechanism must lock after being triggered. It could only be disengaged by someone who knew the trick. My best guess was that the police had placed the room there years ago, to catch people like my mother and I as they tried to flee. The boys must have found an animal trapped in here on one of their illicit adventures. They must have worked out the trigger and set the animal free in the process. Now they held the secret to keeping me trapped.

I gathered leaves in the corner of the room and crafted a makeshift bed. After I laid down I huddled in to the leaves and brushed some more over me until I was almost covered and closed my eyes.

I am small again. Three or four years old. I'm in my own bed, in the cabin where I've lived most of my life. I'm supposed to be asleep, but I'm not. The voices down the hall are too loud. Mimi and Poppy are here. We snuggled on the couch all day. I buried my face in Mimi's neck and smelled her sickly-sweet perfume. She ran her fingers through my dark brown curls. I curled up in Poppy's lap and smelled the rich tobacco he used in his pipe. Everyone was smiling, even Mom. But it doesn't sound like she's smiling now. I slide out of my bed and my feet land softly on the floor. I step deliberately, soundlessly. Ninja steps, that's what Mom calls them. We've been Ninja stepping my whole life.

I creep down the hall and stop just outside the living room. Mom says sometimes I'm too good at listening, which is confusing because she's the one who taught me to listen all the time, for every little sound.

I hear Mimi tensely say, "I just don't understand why we can't come anymore."

"It's too dangerous," Mom spits back at her.

"But the police never connected you to the Revolution," replies Poppy. "I never understood why you thought you had to hide out here. And why you had to take our granddaughter out here with you. You covered your tracks so well."

"It's been over a year sweetheart," Mimi says calmly. "If they haven't figured it out yet, why would they now?"

"Do you even watch the news?" snaps Mom. "Haven't you heard about the arrests? The deportations?"

"Of course we have," exasperation edges in to Mimi's voice.

There's silence for a moment before Mom says, "They got Nadia. That's a direct connection to me."

Poppy inhales sharply, then replies, "She wouldn't say anything, would she?"

Mom's voice lowers and fills with quiet anger. "You have no idea what they'll do to her." Mimi begins to cry.

She chokes out, "Can we at least say goodbye to Eva?"

"In the morning," says Mom. "I don't want to wake her. We've had too many sleepless nights already." The voices stop and all I can hear is Mimi softly crying. I creep back to bed and close my eyes.

I woke up on the ground, shivering. I sat up, for a moment disoriented. Why had I fallen asleep in the woods? How far was I from home? I wiped my runny nose and it ached. Slowly, I remembered running in to the glass, and the boys, and desperately searching for a way out. I crawled forward until I touched the glass, reached down to the earth and began to dig. I scooped small bits of earth in to a pile next to me.

After a few minutes of digging my fingernails scraped on a rough surface below the dirt. I yelped and stuck my fingers in my mouth. I leaned down over the gap I'd created between the earth and the wall and tried to make out what my hand had hit upon. I reached down and slowly ran my fingers across the surface and realized it was concrete. I moved to another spot and started digging, until my fingernails scraped the concrete again. I moved through the rest of the room, digging until I hit the concrete floor with my hands. I didn't stop until I heard the sound of footsteps coming toward the room.

I looked up and saw the boy who'd fell the day before. He glared at me contemptuously as he approached, carrying a bottle of water in one hand and a granola bar in the other. He stopped just short of the glass, looked up, and tossed the bottle and the bar over the top of the wall. I tried to watch their trajectory and judge where the top of the wall was, but he'd thrown them so high and they came down in a large arc. I scrambled toward the food and water, scooping it up greedily. As I picked them up, the boy began to walk away. I dropped the bottle and granola bar and ran to the wall.

"Wait! Please don't leave me in here." He didn't even turn. I slammed my body against the wall, screaming obscenities at him until his figure disappeared from sight. I slammed my open hand against the glass wall, angry tears streaming down my face.

After I ate, I resumed my digging. By the time the sun was setting I had uncovered most of the bottom of the room. It was a solid slab of concrete. I crawled around the room, running my fingers over the concrete, feeling for a trigger to open the door, but found nothing. Exhausted, I curled up in one of the piles of dirt I'd made while uncovering the floor and passed out.

I spent the next morning gathering the piles of dirt I'd made in to a small hill near one of the walls. I packed it down as much as I could, trying to make a surface that would support my weight.

Late in the afternoon, I heard feet tromping through the forest. I stopped digging and headed to the wall closest to the sound. Another one of the boys emerged from the tree line. As he approached, I saw that he was carrying a bottle of water and a large bag of Doritos. He stopped just short of the wall and stared at me. It was the boy who'd suggested turning me in. I glowered at him

through the wall. He examined the bottom of the room and his eyes darted to the small dirt pile I'd made. He smiled a little. I slammed my palm against the wall and he involuntarily jumped.

"Are you giving me the food or not?" I snarled. He looked up toward the top of the wall and then chucked the water bottle. The bag of Doritos followed. I grabbed the water bottle and bag, then turned to watch him walk away. He hadn't moved. He just stood, staring. I walked back to the wall and stared him down.

"I'm not a fucking animal in a zoo. I'm not here for your fucking entertainment. I'm trapped and you little cowards won't let me out." He was silent, watching me the whole time. I screamed, but he didn't even flinch. I sat, opened the water and the Doritos, took a drink, and ate. He sat on the ground and watched me. When I'd finished the water and half the bag of Doritos, I turned my gaze to him. I stared him down, willing him to get up and leave, but he didn't.

Eventually, I stood up and went back to the dirt pile I'd been constructing. I continued to move the dirt from all around the room. He watched me work, studying my every movement.

"Do you think you'll get it high enough to jump over the wall?" I started at the sound of his voice and turned to face him.

"I wouldn't have to if you would just let me the fuck out of here." He stood up slowly and walked away.

By nightfall I'd finished moving all the dirt to the pile. It only came up to my waist. I tried to climb up it, but the dirt crumbled under my feet and I slid downward. I yelled and kicked the dirt pile hard, stubbing my toe against the wall behind it. I sat down and cradled my foot, staring blankly in to the trees.

Mom and I are in the cabin, sitting in front of the TV. The flashing image shows women being dragged out of their houses in handcuffs, their families screaming behind them.

The anchor announces, "As the Administration's investigation in to the Uprising continues, more connections to women's groups all over the country are being discovered. Those found to be involved in the Uprising are being taken in for questioning. Those found guilty of participating in the Uprising will be charged with treason, which carries a death sentence since the recent passing of the 'Domestic Terrorism Act'."

Mom picks up the remote and hits pause. We've watched this footage over and over in the past twelve years. She turns from the TV and looks right in to my eyes.

"The Administration created a narrative in which feminist groups throughout the country were responsible for the Uprising. They televised the 'confessions' of hundreds of women who had been abducted from their homes and tortured until they were willing to say whatever they had to in order to avoid execution. The Administration used these confessions as 'proof' that women were a threat to national security. They exploited pre-existing misogyny and fear to justify annihilating an entire gender." I let out an exasperated sigh.

"Thanks for the history lesson Mom. Not like I've heard it a hundred times or anything." Her eyes harden and her fingers clench in to a fist.

"I risked my life to prevent this. I risked my life to try and give you a world where this wasn't real."

"But instead we've been alone in this cabin my entire life," I snap back. Her fist raises, but she immediately drops it.

Through clenched teeth she says, "Let me tell you about some of the other people who risked their lives, and lost them, fighting the Administration." She gets up and leaves the room. I consider escaping in to the woods, but it's not worth the screaming match that would ensue when I came back.

Mom reenters the room, stands over me, and tosses a small book in to my lap. I've never seen it before, which is saying something, since the cabin is so small and we've been isolated here so long. She'd hidden this well.

"Open it," she barks. I open the cover and see a photo staring back at me. How quaint. I didn't know anyone kept photo albums anymore. I stare at the faces of two women, one olive skinned, wearing a hijab, the other dark skinned and voluptuous. Their faces beam at me. As I stare at

their faces, faded images pop in to my head. I vaguely remember the soft fabric of the hijab against my face, the dark-skinned woman blowing raspberries on my belly as I laughed uncontrollably.

"That's Samira and Aamino. They were my college roommates. Aamino was deported after the Immigrant Registration Act was passed. Samira was killed six months later by a mob, in the street, in broad daylight. They screamed 'ISIS bitch' as they beat her to death." My heart does somersaults and nausea overwhelms me.

"Turn the page," she commands. I comply and find a photo of two handsome men in suits, kissing under a flower covered arch. "Gary and Mason. When the Administration repealed gay marriage, they were no longer legally married. When Gary got cancer, Mason wasn't allowed to make medical decisions for his husband. Gary died alone, in the middle of the night, because the nurses wouldn't allow Mason in the room." I feel hot tears in my eyes.

"Turn the page." I see a man and a woman in front of a small storefront. "Hannah and Rob opened that store together right after they got married. Turned out, Rob was an abusive asshole, but Hannah never left him because the Property Acts stated that she couldn't own the business without her husband's name on the paperwork. And he would have gotten all her assets if they'd gotten a divorce."

"Mom, please stop."

"Turn. The. Page." I see a thin, pale woman, trying to smile, but her attempt is insufficient. "That's Mary. In our senior year of college, she was raped. She took her rapist to court, but he was cleared of all charges because the jury didn't believe a 'mistake' should ruin his future." Tears roll down my cheeks.

"These are people who fought in the Revolution. Revolutionaries. The Administration took everything from them, and they took it legally. They used the systems already in place to strip these people of their basic human rights. When these people, and hundreds of others fought back, they were slaughtered on the steps of the Capital building in D.C. during a peaceful protest. The cops told the media and the media told the world that these people fired first; that they were violent degenerates who just wanted to see the world burn. And the people were so scared they believed it. These are the people I fought next to. These are the people I watched die." She crouches down and takes my chin in her hand. "Don't you ever, ever take for granted the fact that you and I are still alive."

For the first few weeks one of the boys came every day to toss me food and a bottle of water. Sometimes they stayed for a bit and sometimes they didn't. The boy who'd fell the first day never stayed. He barely even looked at me. He just threw the food and water bottle, then left; like I was a chore that needed completing.

The boy who'd watched me continued to just watch, from a distance, studying me like a mad scientist. If he could have snuck in at night and built a maze for me to run through I'm sure he would have. After that first day he'd come, I swore to myself that I'd never do anything even vaguely interesting while he watched. I didn't look at him, I didn't move, I just sat. A living statue. My body almost vibrated with anger in that stillness. He never spoke to me and I never spoke to him.

The third boy came the most often, four or five times a week. He would toss the food and water over the wall and then sit right next to the glass and watch me eat. He just sat there, silently, and watched me for what seemed like hours. He would look straight in to my eyes. It was unnerving until I realized that his eyes were always sad. Sometimes there were tears trying to spill over the edges. He never cried. The tears were suspended on the edge of his eyes, making them glassy.

I kept trying to build up the dirt in to a hill that would support my weight. I started saving some of my water and mixing it with the dirt, hoping that if the mud dried it would create a stronger surface. The hill still collapsed under my weight. I tried piling the dirt on top of the water bottles to give it more structure. This helped enough for me to be able to stand on top of the hill and reach up. Even standing on the pile, I couldn't feel the top of the glass walls. I tried jumping, praying my fingers would catch on the top edge of the wall, but they didn't. I realized then, for the first time, that I maybe I wouldn't ever make it out of the room. Everything went numb.

A few days later, the teary boy came back. He tentatively approached the wall and placed his palm on the glass, with all of his fingers spread. At first, I ignored him. I sat in the corner of the room, and stared at his hand. He kept his hand there for a few minutes, then dropped it, maintaining eye contact with me the whole time. He placed his palm on the glass again, and stared at me expectantly. Cautiously, I crawled over to the glass. I stared at his hand, and then lifted my eyes to his eyes. Today, for the first time, the tears spilled over and slid down his face. I lifted my hand and placed my palm against the glass, exactly where his was on the other side. My fingers stretched out past his, and I realized for the first time how young he actually was.

As we held our hands together on the glass, I just barely heard him say, "I'm sorry. I'm so sorry." I put my other hand up and pressed my forehead to the glass. He mirrored me. Our hot breath fogged both sides of the glass.

"Please let me go home," I said, staring in to his eyes, so close to mine on the other side of the glass. He looked away, bowed his head, and began to sob.

"I don't know how to open the room. They won't show me." All the air was sucked from my lungs. I dropped my hands from the glass, curled my arms around my knees, and began to rock. The boy on the other side of the glass got up and ran.

The crying boy never came back. The other two boys started coming less often. The hateful boy only came every once in a while. The mad scientist came more often, for a while, but still less than he had in the beginning. They were getting bored with me. It was becoming too much of a chore to keep me alive.

Then, they stopped coming at all. It seems like forever ago, but maybe it was just last week. I can't tell anymore. Everything is getting fuzzy.

They haven't come for a long time. Well, it seems like a long time, but maybe it was last week. I can't seem to remember anything anymore. I can't seem to keep my thoughts in order. They run around, then stop midway, and don't come back. Then it's empty, until different thoughts start running around all over again.

I hoarded food and water. I made it last as long as I could, but it's gone now, and it's been gone for a while. I can't figure out how long. When I can think clearly, I know that I'm going to die if they don't come back. When I can think clearly, I know that they're not coming back. I know that I'm going to die in this glass room.

I sleep a lot. I still dream. My dreams seem to be the only place where my thoughts can organize themselves coherently. I dream of Mom. I dream of being wrapped up in her warm arms in front of the fire in our cabin. I'm so cold all the time now. I dream of Mimi and Poppy. How I used to sit in their laps, before it was too dangerous to see them. I dream of inhaling Mimi's perfume, Poppy's pipe smoke.

I hear Mom's voice, loud in my ears, telling me about the Revolutionaries and how hard they fought. I hear her speeches about feminism and human rights. I used to roll my eyes and tune her out. Now I wish she would lecture me forever. I swear I'll listen Mom. I promise I'll listen.

The dreams stop coming. Her voice fades from my ears. I lie on the cold leaves and stare up at the sky until everything goes black.

MOTION SICKNESS

Richard Schmitt

"It is the unforeseen upon which we must calculate most largely." - Edgar Allan Poe

Our trip to the coast in October, a rented beach cottage, a fall break from school, was disrupted by a recent hurricane. The cottage owner called, there'd been flooding, we won't be able to use the washing machine.

"We could postpone," I said to Katherine. She sat upright at the piano in our living room, hands paused over the keys.

"Stick to the plan," she said. "We'll take your car."

"My car?"

"We took mine last time."

"My car, with the dog?"

"What about it?"

"Oh, nothing." But last time was a concert in Philly, someone Katherine had to see, she's a composer. And we didn't take the dog to the city. So this trip seemed, to me at least, different.

"What's the difference? Does it matter? If it matters we can take my car."

"No, no. It doesn't matter. I like to drive anyway."

"You don't want me driving your car?"

"I didn't say that. I usually drive is all, you're better at navigating. I'm not a good navigator, I mean. Right?" She flashed a squinty-eye

look, evaluating, measuring, slowly settled her hands to the keys, one note, ping, then another, pong. The thing about the dog, I hate to say it, is puke. Her dog, Lila, gets carsick, especially in the mountains. You can't get to the coast from where we live without crossing the Appalachian Mountains. So there was that to squint about, consider, mull over, the mountains and the puking.

And the other thing was cars, mine was new, Katherine's was less new. They were both suitable vehicles. Subaru the two of them. Mine had fewer miles on it. But that wasn't the thing. Okay, maybe that was part of the thing. The thing is we're grad students. We share rent but pay for our own cars, gas, upkeep, so when we go on trips for rest and relaxation the equitable nature of our relationship is paramount. We work on campus, teaching assistants, Katherine in the music department, myself an MBA candidate, so a car is a big thing to buy and maintain. One must be mindful of the miles, wear and tear, and her car was more torn up than mine. But that wasn't the thing either. The thing was sharing, taking turns, fairness, and possibly dog puke. Things unspoken because neither of us wanted to be seen as petty.

"Then it's settled," I said.

I folded down the back seat in my vehicle, coated the space with rugs and blankets and plastic sheeting, and with the dog installed among the beach chairs and sleeping bags, we set off.

I had the back covered with triple-layer puke protection. But Lila, a shelter-rescued hound, she really likes us. Not uncommon. Dogs in cars mostly resent being in the back. Mostly they want to sit up front. Everyone else is up front, all the important people, the driver, the navigator. Up front is the place to be. I don't like being a passenger in a car at all, front or back. I always drive because everyone else's driving makes me sick. Lila and I have that in common. I too am prone to motion sickness. I too, like to sit up front, nose to the windshield, sniffing out the incoming. Because that is the future and looking forward seems like the thing to do. Especially if you are upset about present stomach churning, as Lila is, stuck in the back with her head hanging over the seat. She hates car trips. She'd rather be home with her dog sitter and her doggie door so she can zip out into her own backyard and roll in her familiar grass and romp with the birds and squirrels. And who can blame her?

When I was a kid I hated car trips too, for the same reason, motion sickness. Subject to it my whole life. Not behind the wheel, drivers don't get sick. A driver can anticipate. A strategy for passengers prone to car sickness, is to do everything the driver does. I mention this to Lila. "Li," I shout, "pretend you're driving, you won't get sick." I show her how to hold the wheel, elbows out, ten and two, check the mirror, honk the horn. She gives me that sidelong look dogs do when they think you're nuts. Humans are fucking crazy she thinks emitting a hopeless sigh.

Heavy into the mountains, the road winding around, up and down—it was too much for her. She let loose. And when she did, not all the upchuck ended up on the triple layer protective barrier. A substantial portion shot over the seatback, filling the cup holder, running down the crack onto the floor carpet.

It wasn't a surprise. I knew Lila would puke. It didn't upset me. But Katherine, well, she had hope. She's a hopeful person, more so than myself I think, she's a gifted musician, faithfully committed to touching out notes in sound-proof booths. She'd given the dog Dramamine, she'd prepared, she planned on Lila not puking. I was ready for it and calmly pulled onto a gravel strip bordering the steep road when the retching began.

Katherine was distraught. "I'm sorry. We should have taken my car."

"It's okay, Kate," I said. "I don't care."

"Oh, I'm so sorry."

"Forget about it. We knew it was going to happen. Get the towels. I'll walk her around."

On the leash up and down alongside the road we walked, deep in the Monongahela National Forest, the fall leaves in full-flight, a beautiful blue-sky day, no cars in sight. The hurricane hadn't touched this area. It was quiet and serene with the sun spotting through the leaves of the trees, Lila happily sniffing and pissing everywhere. Katherine didn't find it pleasant. She was bent over the floor, scooping and soaking up, one hand holding her hair from the partially digested dog food and stomach juice, whatever that foamy yellow stuff is that smells like garbage. "Why didn't we take my car? We should have taken my car."

"Stop worrying about it," I said. "We knew this was going to happen."

But she wasn't to be dissuaded from being distraught. She can be obsessive sometimes when caught by the unexpected. We've gone on many enjoyable trips she's planned like military incursions. And at times she gets frustrated when planet earth doesn't conform precisely to Google Earth, or when the GPS sends us astray, or when I callously drive off course asserting without a shred of factual evidence "I think it's this way."

"Now it's going to smell," she said.

"We've got windows," I said. "It's a nice day. It could be raining."

"Well at least that's it," she said. "She'll be okay now, Lila never throws up twice."

"Right. We're home free."

"Except for the smell."

"Don't worry about the smell, it doesn't smell, we've got windows."

"We'll go to a store, I'll buy some Oxy Pet Spray, a brush and a sponge."

"You don't have to buy Oxy Pet Spray. It can wait until we get home."

"We're almost out of the mountains for sure," she said when we were rolling again.

But the mountains went on longer than expected. What went down went back up. And the thing is, I did my best for Lila's sake, but my lead foot is no soothing salve to a stomach. "Are you getting queasy too?"

"Not at all," Katherine said. She never gets car sick. I'd have been puking for sure if I wasn't driving. And for the record, it was true, the dog never puked twice on any trip we'd taken. We were almost out of the mountains too, we knew it. "It's all downhill from here," Katherine said. "Lila never throws up twice." Right then: Barfaroo!

"Oh, shit."

"Ah well."

"I think she got your sleeping bag."

I pulled over, again. Walked the dog again. This time we had a fine view of a green valley, red barn, white house, cows grazing. Lila, dejected now, tramped alongside the road above the farm, sniffing and pissing half-heartedly while Katherine went at the mop-up again. "I'll buy you a new sleeping bag," she said, shaking it out. "I'm so sorry."

"It's washable," I said. "We'll hit a laundromat when we get there. No harm done."

"I've ruined all the beach towels now."

"Laundromat."

"Spending our holiday at the laundromat is not how—"

"It will be an adventure, Kate." It was clear she was getting, like the dog, dejected.

A double puke was new terrain, not part of her plan, we were totally off-grid, and Katherine, well, she's a grid person, she calculates, computes, she knows notes and formulas. She likes things carried out according to melodious design, parts to whole, things played out in unison. She writes scores for symphony orchestras. You can't do that slipshod, you have to be organized, disciplined. Yet, I've seen the way she works. Weekday afternoons I walk over to the music department to find her in one of the recording booths. I see her through the window, hair tied back, eyeglasses, focused. She works on a keyboard, feeling her way along, touching out a phrase, a few notes

then stop, two more then stop, stutter stepping, backing up, going on again before an array of blinking and blazing equipment: synthesizer, sequencer, sampler, a triptych of monitors. Her work, very faint, comes through the wall. Ping-ping-pong. Pong-pong-ping. Back up, start again. She's finding her way, I can see it. Exploring. When I tap on the glass she smiles, holds up one finger, I watch her finish. Pinging and ponging through the forest of possibilities.

We were off again, Lila sleeping now, exhausted from puking and the sheer anxiety of puking. "How can this happen?" Katherine said. "We gave her Dramamine."

"It's a mystery."

Nobody knows why motion sickness affects some people and not others. Doctors say it's a sensory mismatch. Expectations and reality out of alignment. Our stabilizing system senses motion where there is none, senses none where there is some. That's why we get sick with our butts firmly stuck to an IMAX theater seat and also standing on the rolling deck of a fishing boat. Motion sickness is conflicted senses. A sense that makes no sense. Your eyes tell you one thing, your inner ear says another, it's barf away.

I'm convinced Katherine doesn't get car sick because she's a planner. No matter what she does, cooking a hamburger or writing a concerto, she charts her course and does not vary. She plots and sticks. Nails the dates and times. She doesn't wander, waver, add or detract. Once she commits to an idea it's granite. Consequently, conflicting senses don't collide within this woman. Expectations and reality stay aligned. Hope and result don't mismatch and things remain on an even keel, nothing rocks the boat. She lives on the salt flats of stability.

Faith is the thing. She believes well-made plans yield predictable and satisfactory results. I figure her inner ear is like a crystal ball, she sees a future that can't be altered because, well, it's the future. It exists as fact in spite of conflicting facts like roads not taken, decisions second guessed, options passed, minds changed.

"This is it," she said. We'd dropped into the green valley and were passing the farm, the cows, the chickens. She was bent over her Google printouts, her direction sheets, her notes and maps. "We're out of the mountains, flat from here on."

She's a map person of old school variety. Rand McNally is her bible. Current issue well-worn in her lap, she consults, considers, compares it to the GPS, walks her fingers through the pages, finds her way, and becomes impatient when I suggest—nose to the windshield—a disparity between her research and incoming signs and signals from the open road. Parsing the world coming at me sometimes leads to disagreements that disrupt the equitability of our relationship. This may sound minor, but, when we are traveling at high speed in traffic and I decide based on fast-arriving intel to abruptly exit stage left, or bear right by the Burger King, when I zip tootle-loo one way or another on instinct, ignoring her carved-in-stone directions, her fingertip pressed firmly to a blue or red or black line on the Rand McNally, then, we are no longer equitably aligned. We are off charted course. And that is a sensory disruption for my dear girl, the here-and-now isn't documented. The maps no longer align with rolling Subaru, the plan is thwarted, meaning no safety net, meaning before you know it, we could be—lost!

But, we were not lost, not yet. As we neared the coast, piles of debris appeared alongside the road. The hurricane came ashore just south of here. Hadn't affected us on the other side of the mountains but these folks on the coast had been slammed and were still cleaning up.

Katherine insisted we stop for the spray, the brush, the sponge. Major scouring and scrubbing ensued. When she was done the carpet was like new. Her hands, red-raw, smelled of bleach. There isn't much you can do with a woman like this except love her. So I do, I did. I hugged her and kissed her and brought her hand cream. "To hell with the laundry," I said, "let's hit the beach." She smiled and the trauma of the trip was behind us. For the time being.

She packed the beach bag. I grabbed the dog leash.

Though the cottage was advertised as "ocean front" a more accurate description would be once ocean front. Once upon a time waves lapped the sand a stone's throw off the porch.

But then came condos, developers paved a road, slapped up pastel towers of steel and cement and signs saying Private. This departure from detail irritated Katherine. "The website specifically said ocean front," she said. "That's what we booked, that's what it said. 'Frontage' was the word used, 'ocean frontage', that's what we paid for."

"It's okay, Kate. It's close. Let's walk."

Front or frontage the path to the beach was convoluted. A hand-drawn map tacked to the cottage wall showed the correct route across the road and down the sidewalk to public access. Then a few wooden steps up and over the dunes. It felt stupid since the water was a straight shot across the road from the cottage. There was a driveway with a duplex at the end of it and whoever lived there hadn't taken in their empty trash barrel. Everyone else had taken in their blue county-issue containers except this place directly across from us. "No one is home there," I said, "let's cut through."

"There's a sign," she said. "No Trespassing."

I didn't mention it again but for two days the trash barrel stayed at the end of the driveway and the house appeared vacant while we walked the correct way per instructions. It wasn't far and it was nice to walk together with the dog, something we rarely do at home. The thing was, every time we left the cottage, no matter who held the leash, Lila pulled in the direction of the vacant house. She knew where the beach was. Dogs know, and I too was follow-the-nose prone, but Katherine, that wasn't her way so we stuck to the mandated path.

On the morning of our last day she was up early sitting in the kitchen with her coffee and logistical gear: Rand McNally, laptop, phone, notepad and pen—studying, evaluating, weighing options and odds, determined to find a stomach-friendly route through the mountains. "We can go north or south," she said. "There must be a way. What do you think?"

"We're going to the beach," I said. "Me and Lila."

Her fingers hung over the keyboard. "Good idea, you guys walk, I'll figure this out."

Hooked to the leash Lila bounded off the porch pulling hard and dragged me straight across the road to the empty trash barrel where she stopped before the vacant house. The leash hung loose, she gave me the sidelong look, tentative and guilty. She was laying this one on me. If I even breathed in the direction of the house we'd be straight at it like a shot. But no, it was already decided, we turned toward public access.

The beach was cold and the wind blew hard turning the tops of the waves into clear silver spray in the rising sun as we went sniffing and pissing about, watching surfers in black suits out on the waves.

Back at the cottage Katherine was triumphant. "I've got it!" She said. "Look at this."

She went over her itinerary step by step, route numbers, scenic overlooks, stop for lunch. Her plan had twists and turns, byways and highways, down and around little towns. But not up. The goal was to avoid upheaval. "There are a few choices," she said. "What do you think?" She often asks me what I think but just as surely her mind is already made up.

"You're the navigator," I said.

Roadmaps are neither here nor there. Red lines to blue lines to black lines. The connection to movement is suspect. I prefer point-nose-and-go, laden with faith that I will land someplace better than what might be conjured up using the fixed coordinates of a cartographer at Rand McNally. According to her strategic plan we were to go down into the counties south of here, then swoop back north, and that was enough to get us packed and out the door.

Pulling away from the cottage, Lila's head hung over the seatback, Katherine's head buried in navigational mire.

Soon we hit snags, complications, misalignments. The road south was strewn alongside with piles of wreckage getting bigger, very big, calamity size. Finally we weren't exclaiming about them but staring slack-jawed. FEMA contractors with immense clawing and scooping contraptions worked with dumpsters the size of in-ground pools full of appliances and furniture bent and twisted. Household goods pushed and piled helter-skelter into heaps. Kitchen tables, living-room sets, waterlogged mattresses bloated in the sun. Flat screens and computers crushed and flooded. High end stainless steel refrigerators, doors hanging open. Katherine peered down at her maps and up at the devastation as if there must be a correlation, discernable sense, something to make random hurricane damage part of a logical plan.

"This is unexpected," she said.

"Looks like an Allstate commercial."

A flagmen directed us through a pale beach town, condos and shops, where all greenery had been uprooted or buried by fine buff sand washed and blown from the dunes across the highway. The sand lay molded, caked in ribbed waves and eddies, tiny mockups of the wind-driven ripples that created them. The air had not dried the sand enough to take it up and send it airborne to drift like caramel-colored snow against walls and bridges. The condos had roll-down shutters but the low-lying shops on the other side of the road seemed sandblasted, as if grown from a tawny desert. Some were boarded with plywood while the owners of others worked with claw hammers and pry bars and some had their barriers torn away by the storm. Everything was plastered with the same biscuit-batter sand except the black-hole windows and doors.

A sign said coffee and we had to pee so we pulled in. The little shop had lost both front windows. "Open?" I said to the woman behind the counter.

"More so than usual," she said happily.

They had no power but they had bottled water and were firing it up on a gas grill to make rudimentary drip. "Can't use the bathroom," she said. "It's backed up."

I walked Lila behind the place away from the road so we could pee. For Katherine it was more complicated. The coffee woman said FEMA had porta potties up ahead. Good news added to the bad news about the detour. "Road's washed out," she said.

We took the coffee and went to find the lineup of portables. A cop kept eye on them. "Go back to the fork," he said, "then drive west around the preserve."

"It must be this green spot on the map," Katherine said, head in the Rand McNally. "Doesn't say what it is."

"Terra incognita."

"A blue spot in the middle of a green spot,"

"It's a detour, there will be signs."

But after we took the fork and drove inland around a large brackish body of water we didn't see any signs. We didn't see anything but wiry wetland bushes and high water and birds. I sensed Katherine getting panicky. The road had that federal highway look, like in a national park, high and dry and winding around to eventually end back where you started. She couldn't locate us on the map and her phone had no signal. "You can't have a detour and then drop people in the middle of nowhere," she said.

The road began to rise and the saltmarsh smell subsided and the wetland scrub gave way to solid ground and trees. "Terra firma," I said. "We're getting someplace."

But the place we got wasn't good. The road deteriorated and cut into the side of a slope gradually rising to the north. Far off to the west we saw inland hills. The phone came on just before we hit the town. "I think, I might see," she said, "about where we are."

On the south side of the road a river ran dangerously high. Deep water moving fast, deadly quiet. Small clapboard houses on the north side were swollen, as if pumped full, the joints strained, the edges gaped. The homes were packed solid with mud that had slid loose from the hillside and dried like cement. Whatever wasn't crushed inside the houses had been rammed out through the windows and doorways and shoved across the road through the guardrail and into the trees lining the riverbank. Couch cushions, kitchen chairs, a bicycle, were caught high up in branches like a bizarre art installation.

"God," she said. "This was a town—"

"I smell gas."

The road had been plowed of red mud. In places asphalt slabs had been upsurged and carried away leaving deep holes in the blacktop.

Telephone wires, poles knocked askew, lay scrambled in ditches. We passed a yellow CAT road grader mudded over and a heap of cars and trucks pushed together and piled off the roadway. There were no birds, no people. Nothing moved but the river.

"Don't stop," she said.

This wasn't a place anyone could ever live again. Entire households were razed, garages and mobile homes were rubble. There was nothing to clean up, nothing salvageable, no one would be coming back here. The place was erased from the map.

I sensed tears welling up next to me—she was staring. We were lost and tired and there was something wrong with the daylight. We experienced the devastation out of proportion to our situation. Lost and loss are close on the map of emotion.

We picked our way along, the road rose gradually, relatively straight. Lila slept in the back unconcerned. Up front we were concerned. Katherine frowned, fretted, shifted her attention between her navigational aids and what was coming at us through the windshield. She blamed herself. "You're not responsible for mountain ranges and hurricanes," I said.

She wouldn't talk.

We came to a T-junction and I waited, staring straight ahead at a stand of trees stripped of bark. We had no idea where we were. Whichever way we went the land had a dour basted-in-mud look. Swatches of black trees toppled as if by the swoop of a giant hand, laid out all in one direction, an acre here an acre there, pelted down. A hurricane is a system like any other, given to patterns, paths predictable, chartable, which can be planned for. And if calamity follows cleanup is the course of action. I felt the seams straining across the front seat that had grown much larger, the air between us charged, pressure building, things about to rupture.

We drove on through an abandoned land using the compass on the phone to head west and came finally to a wide crossroad intersection. A blinking red light that wasn't blinking, a stop-and-go juncture jammed with signs pointing north, south, east and west. It was one of those perplexing concurrency road networks where one physical road is burdened with multiple route numbers. Three concurrent routes faced us heading in four different directions. A triplex times four of confusion. It was breathtaking. Or maybe I just held my breath.

That's when I heard the pages, the shredding, the thump. She'd torn apart the Rand McNally, slammed it to the floor. She was in tears.

"Let's take a break," I said. "We have to pee."

I pulled over and got Lila out. There were no cars, no homes. The higher elevation air had lost the sewer-gas smell. "Kate," I said, opening her door. "Get out and walk around. Stretch your legs." She cried and wouldn't budge. This wasn't like her. She's generally calm under pressure, doesn't get flustered easily. At school she deftly handles a multitude of administrative and academic tasks. "Come on," I said, "everything's fine." I reached out for her but couldn't get close enough with Lila on the leash pulling hard for a gooseberry bush. Nose to the ground.

"This is all my fault," she said.

"It's not your fault."

"We should have gone home through the mountains."

"We wanted to go this way."

"We're lost."

"We're not lost—Lila stop pulling!"

"We don't know where we are."

"We do know where were are, we just don't appear on those silly maps." She cried childlike tears, silent, and more heartbreaking for that, streaming and dropping off her cheeks. I reached her with one hand.

"This wasn't the plan."

"Kate, honey, look, just relax. Does there always have to be a plan?"

I shouldn't have said 'relax', she doesn't like being told how to feel. "Planning," she said, slowly, as if talking to five-year old, "is the quality separating humans and animals."

What could I say to that? I was being dragged away by a dog following her nose.

Katherine isn't like this at work. It's only when we have time off, days untethered from academic tedium that she gets tense. When there is no obligation or agenda relaxation is hard for her. And I wonder why. "I've watched the way you work," I said. "You don't plan your pieces, you pick your way through."

"That's different."

"It doesn't seem different."

At home she works the old fashioned way, a battered upright, a batch of staff paper, a few fat pencils. But the quest is the same, mapping uncharted territory, decorating our little house with notes, knocking one down, hanging up another, sounding out the way, making something in the air like bicycles in trees. Whisper and growl, catch and sustain, ping-ping-pong, pong-pong-ping. Stop. Pick up the pencil. Scribble little birds on wires. She once told me notes were portals, one opens another, no space between them, no crossroads. We're tired now. Jammed up. I'm too tired not to say: "Kate, which way?"

And from my navigator: "Fuck if I know." Very unlike her, the language. Her senses are scattered, she feels the churning stomach, the bile rising, the upheaval of being unmoored. Lack of control is the ultimate misery for her. She fears the present becoming the regrettable past. We've been together since undergrad, five years now, so I've seen all her facets, turned many corners with her, and I know the roads to come will not all be well charted. We will take them together, find the way, of that there is no doubt.

This distress she feels—anxiety about the elasticity of all possible futures, the fogged crystal ball, the conflicting facts of roads not taken, decisions second guessed, options passed—this is a different kind of motion sickness. The unplanned is a sense that won't align for her. The straight line broken, the course muddled, the blueprint corrupted. She fears breaking new snow. So maybe that's my role, point man, arrowhead, eye at the helm. Forging the way, following the nose. A symmetric sense to her contrasting sense, the white space between grid lines, between the notes imprisoned on the staff. Together there will be alignment then, no sensory mismatch here, rather sensory complement, whole notes only, forms coupled, complete.

And just at that ending, shocking us out of our daze, roaring through the intersection north to south, not even thinking about stop-and-go, raising a whirlwind of promise, a fleet of power & light trucks. "Kate," I said. She perked up. "Power trucks don't go nowhere." They were going fast, with a sense of purpose. We cranked up the Subaru and fell into the slipstream. Keeping up with the convoy, electric, charged, windows wide open, map pages flew. "We're pinging along now aren't we?" She gave me a smile. "Pinging and ponging our way home." Lila's head hung over. "Li," I said. "Check it out—this is how you drive, ten and two, eyes up, nose to the road."

About the Author:

Richard Schmitt is the author of The Aerialist, a novel, and has published fiction and nonfiction in Arts & Letters, Cimarron Review, Gettysburg Review, Gulf Coast, North American Review, Puerto del Sol, and other places. His story, "Leaving Venice, Florida," won 1st Prize in The Mississippi Review story contest. He has been anthologized in New Stories of the South: The Year's Best 1999 and The Best American Essays, 2013.

HELL BOUND

Alexa Findlay

It's happening. I get the message when mom calls us downstairs. Just when I thought life couldn't get any worse. First, mom and dad separate, then we have to move, and now my sister, brother, and I have to go visit my mom's sister, whom we have never met before. From what I've heard, she is crazy. You know mentally crazy. Apparently, she was put in a mental hospital when her and my mom were teens. Great, now we have to stay with Miss Crazy for two weeks. Who knows what she will do. She is unstable and unpredictable.

To think my mom of all people, who is extremely overprotective and worries a lot, would let us go stay with her whacko sister. She must really need some time alone from us. To get things straight, when I say "us" I am referring to my five year old sister, Luna, my ten year old brother, Luke, and I of course. Luna is too young to understand the meaning of anything. She just plays with her dollies and cries when she doesn't get her way. You know the typical childhood behavior. Luke, on the other hand, is oblivious to anything that goes on around him. He doesn't listen, nor care about what mom and I have to say. He just ignores us and plays his video games. You know the typical ten year old boy behavior, I guess.

Mom finally finishes her candid speech about her sister and how much fun we are going to have. Ignoring her deceitful tongue, I leave the room. Mom calls for me, but I don't budge. As I walk away, I can hear Luna jumping up and down, laughing excitedly to go see her aunt. Rolling my eyes, I try to think up a scenario of ways to somehow get out of this mess, but I've got nothing.

Mom continues to holler for me as I gradually pack my luggage, trying to delay the trip. From the corner of my eye, I see Luke walk into my room. "You know mom's going to have your head if you don't hurry up." "So!" I shout back hoping to persuade him to leave me alone. "So...hurry up slow poke. It doesn't take that long to pack." "Just get out!" I shout once more, but he doesn't budge. "What's your problem?" "I don't want to go, o.k. Mom's sister is crazy." "How do you know? We have never met her before." "From what mom has told me, I just know she is," I say with confidence. "Whatever Layla. Just hurry up please."

By the way, I forgot to mention my name is Layla and I'm seventeen years old. If you haven't already noticed, my parents really like names that start with L. I'm not really sure why, but I never cared to ask. I figured they had a reason.

After hours and hours of being on the road, we finally arrive at Aunt Cecilia's home. Oh, by the way, my crazy aunt is named Cecilia.

She walks out of the small house wearing a pink fuzzy robe with matching pink fuzzy slippers and rollers in her hair. I can't seem to take my eyes off her face. Her black eye makeup is dripping down her pale cheeks and her red lipstick is smeared all over her mouth. I can't help but chuckle as mom turns the car off. Mom gives me "the look" in the rearview mirror. You know "the look" that all moms give when they are extremely upset with you and want you to shut your mouth. Well, I got "the look."

Mom wraps her arms around her sister whom she hasn't seen in ages. Aunt Cecilia returns the favor. Luna smiles and jumps up and down ready to give Aunt Cecilia a giant hug. Luke stares down at his phone, swiping his fingers across the screen as he plays his games. I roll my eyes in disgust dreading the hug I am about to receive from Miss Crazy.

I can feel Aunt Cecilia's long claw like nails dig into my back as she forces me into a tight embrace. She leaves a red lipstick smudge on my cheek as she kisses me. I cry a little inside wanting to break free of her clutch.

We help mom unload our luggage from the trunk as Aunt Cecilia stands by and watches. She pulls out a cigarette and lighter from her pocket. She begins to smoke. Mom sees and doesn't say a word. Before I can say anything, mom covers my mouth and whispers, "Layla don't say a word about her smoking. She gets really angry. Got it?" I nod my head in agreement.

Mom kisses us goodbye and gives us one last hug before she leaves to go back home. Gosh I wish I could go with her.

Aunt Cecilia invites us into her small messy two bedroom home. Luna and Luke walk in, completely oblivious to Miss Crazy's outfit and smoking habits. I can't stand the stench of cigarettes, so I plug my nose hoping not to inhale the murderous fumes as I take a dreadful step into her godawful house. She shows us the bedroom that the three of us will be sharing for the next two weeks. Great, not only do I have to stay with Miss Crazy, I have to share a bedroom with my siblings. What could be worse?

Night time arrives. Aunt Cecilia turns off the lights and closes our bedroom door behind her as she leaves our presence. There is a reflection of bright light from my phone as I turn it on. I try to get relief from this painful trip by checking my social media accounts. Out of the blue, Aunt Cecilia comes barging in. She flips on the lights. "What was that?" Aunt Cecilia shouts with fear in her voice. "That was just my phone," I say confused. "Turn that damn thing off." "Why?" "Once I turn out the lights, it's time to go to bed. No devices. Period," she yells with pure anger in her voice. She grabs my phone from my hand. "Hey!" I shout. "Where is your device boy?" she asks Luke.

Luke hands her his phone, fearful of what might happen if he doesn't. She leaves our room with our cell phones. The door shakes as she slams the door behind her.

The smell of bacon and eggs fills the air. Luke and Luna spring out of bed excited for a decent morning breakfast. Luna tugs on my arm to get me out of bed. Giving in to her tugging, I decide to get out of bed. We walk into the kitchen, seeing Aunt Cecilia spreading butter on a few pieces of toast. "Hi lovelies. Breakfast is served. I hope you can forgive me for the little incident last night. I don't know what came over me," she says kindly. "It's okay Aunt Cecilia. We forgive you," Luke answers. "Oh bless your heart," she says sweetly. "Can we get our phones back?" Luke asks nicely. "No! Don't ask again! You don't get them back until the end of your stay," she says with a livid tone. We stare at her puzzled. She stares at us right back in a state of trance. "Sit and eat," she says in a kind but forceful way.

We spend the night playing old board games, because that's all that Miss Crazy has in her house. No television just board games. I swear she still thinks this is the early 1900's. We decide to go to bed to relieve the boredom.

Barely awake at 3 a.m. in the morning, I hear scratching noises just down the hall. I try to ignore what I am hearing, but then the scratching noises begin to get louder. I throw myself out of bed and open our door as quietly as I can, hoping not to wake Miss Crazy. I creep my way down the hall and I peer into Aunt Cecilia's room. She is scratching at her wardrobe door like a cat. Immediately I go to help her, but within seconds she scratches my arm, leaving four deep scratches. I head for the nearest bathroom, hoping to make sense of the situation. But I've got nothing. I knew she was crazy, but not this crazy.

Our alarm goes off. Eyes barely awake, I glance and the alarm reads 6:00 a.m. What the hell? I don't remember setting it for this time. "Luke did you set the alarm for 6 a.m.?" I ask barely being able to get the words out. "No," he responds half asleep. Aunt Cecilia comes barging in. "Get up, get up kiddies. It's time to plant some flowers with me," she says as she jumps on my bed like a little kid. "Aunt Cecilia, what are you doing? Get off my bed!" I shout angrily. "No! Make me!" she says sticking her tongue out immaturely. I jump out of bed, hoping to make her get off my bed. She jumps off my bed and lands on the hard wooden floor. She touches my shoulder. "Tag, you're it," she says running out of our room down the hallway, hoping I will chase her. "What was that about?" Luke asks astonished. "I have no idea," I say shocked.

Aunt Cecilia lets us know that she is going to be out for a while. Convinced that I might be able to find our phones while she is gone, I begin to look around the house, but I have no luck. Where in the heck are our phones?

Once again I awake and it's 3 a.m. I swear this is becoming a nightly occurrence with this lunatic. I can hear that something is going on in the kitchen. Who knows what Miss Crazy is up to at this late hour? Oh well screw it. I don't want to get scratched again, so I will just go back to sleep and pretend like nothing is going on.

Luke and I wake up around 10 a.m. hoping to grab breakfast without Aunt Cecilia annoying the shit out of us. We slowly creep our way into the kitchen. She is nowhere to be found. We look in the fridge. Nothing in the fridge but stale milk, a jar of tapioca pudding, and a jar of pickles. We look in the pantry. Nothing in the pantry, but bags of old chips and an old box of cereal. I swear there was just food in here a week ago when she made us breakfast. Oh well, we better make a run to the nearest grocery store, if there is one in this god-forsaken town. Mom gave me fifty dollars of emergency money. I definitely think that this is an emergency.

Aunt Cecilia notices the bags of groceries on the kitchen counter. "What's all this?" she asks bewildered. "We are hungry. There is nothing to eat in the fridge or the pantry so we did a little shopping. I hope you don't mind." "Yes I do mind. Who gave you permission to leave this house? Huh?" she says livid. "Well...uh no one. But I thought..." she cuts me off before I can finish the rest of my sentence. "You thought nothing. You stupid, stupid girl." "Excuse me?" I shout. Luna and Luke stare at me fearful of what Miss Crazy might do for disobeying her. She slaps me across the face hard enough to leave a bright red mark on my cheek. Luna covers her eyes. Luke stands there in astonishment. "All of you go to your room now!" she screams at the top of her lungs. She shoves us into our bedroom just down the hall. "Don't come out until I say so or else!" She shouts as she slams the door behind her.

The next day, Aunt Cecilia opens our door. She looks at us as we sit up in our beds. "I'm so sorry my darlings. That was totally out of character for me. You can come out of your room now. I made some toast and jam. Come, come into the kitchen for some breakfast," she says trying to be all sweet. We stare at one another, angry at what Miss Crazy has done. Forcing us to stay in our room. "No thanks we are not hungry," Luke answers angrily. "Excuse me boy?" Aunt Cecilia says with fury. "We don't want any," I say agitated. She enters our room forcing each one of us to get up out of our beds. She pushes us into the kitchen. "Sit down, now! You little brats. I want to see all your plates' empty," she shouts.

That evening in the middle of the night, Luke and I hear screaming and yelling just down the hall. We decide to check out what Miss Crazy is up to this time. We sneak our way down the dark murky hallway trying to follow the noise. It leads us to the living room where Aunt Cecilia is looking up at the ceiling yelling at someone or something. We don't see anything, but apparently she does. She continues to chant, "Kill the boy! Kill the boy!" Luke and I glare at each other, horrified. "What the hell is she saying and doing?" Luke tries to whisper, but Aunt Cecilia hears him. She turns her head and looks straight at Luke. She darts right for him, with her hands out right in front of her hoping to grab him. I stand in front of him, hoping to protect him. She wraps her hands around my neck with her grip getting tighter and tighter. I can barely breathe. From the corner of my eye, I see Luke. He jumps on top of Aunt Cecilia's back. She instantly lets go of my neck. She tries to push Luke off, but he won't budge. Finally I am able to catch my breath and then I push Aunt Cecilia, which forces her to fall to the ground. I grab Luke's arm. We head back to our room shutting the door behind us. Within seconds, she bursts into our room. Luna and Luke sit next to me on the bed as Aunt Cecilia comes right for us. "Don't come any closer! Step away!" I shout. Aunt Cecilia lunges right for me. I urge Luna and Luke to get out. As she wraps her hands around my neck once more, I punch her right in the neck, forcing her to release me. I escape with Luke and Luna. We head to the closest house. We knock on the door. A woman answers the door. She invites us in, locking the door behind her.

The next morning, there is a knock at the door. It's mom. She throws her arms around us with streams of tears running down her eyes. From the corner of my eye, I see Miss Crazy being escorted to a police car in handcuffs. I chuckle once again, but this time it's for a good cause.

THE LABYRINTHINE AFFAIRS

Alex Rafael Encomienda

Paul felt a sense of longing at the gates that surrounded a tainted home where he remembered watching Alyssa undress through the gap in his bedroom door. Back then, the house smelled of sourness and residue of wet boxes mixed with the fish that was often cooked there but in his mind, it was actually the scent of transformation from a child to an adult. Paul peered through the windows of the lonely place and remembered when he and Alyssa used to play Sue and Allen. She was warm and soft underneath the white cottons and he was too shy to ever finish playing but one day that changed. It was a day neither of them would forget and he remembered pondering in his navy blues about the turbulence that came with loving someone.

He stepped over the crooked walkway and lamented the dear old days of mother and sister in the living room den; soft and unaware of his desires. He could only grasp the very silent twelve year old's thoughts so much until they too were just as foreign to him as love. The essence of that word was so difficult to break down that it almost seemed as though it never existed. Perhaps in his corridors of lust and woes it never did exist.

It was 1996, Paul slept in his olive knitwear at the Robinson's home; his parents had been gone for the weekend with most of their trinket machines. They would say that the towns in Normandy were better than every Cliffside bank near Nova Scotia and Cape Breton but Paul was a soothsayer by the ear; he knew they were somewhere between Honeymoon's Island and Residents Inn. He hoped they would not come back peculiar; all friendly with deep sighs and a reddened mark on his mother's neck. If their two night stand was

anything like the time in Budapest, he was certain he'd run away from his family and never be at ease.

Paul was only a child of ten and the true identity of sex was still behind closed doors; it had not a face of woman or man, human or animal; life was peaceful and quiet just like him. He would skip with Sarah at the park, play house with Judie and John at recess and even had sleepovers at their houses on the weekends. At night, Judie pretended to kiss John because he was her "husband" but Paul wondered what would happen if she really kissed him. There was another time afterwards where it was his turn to be her husband and he was frightened. There was a certain way he saw his friends and they appeared to him as notable characters that did not shape shift. If Judie was bossy and arrogant at school then she was also like that everywhere else.

When he played the role of her husband, he was shy; distant. He remembered her asking to him, "Do you even want to play?" and he nodded his head with flushed cheeks. They blanketed stuffed animals and called them their "children" and after they put them to bed, Judie looked at Paul and said, "This is when we kiss."

Paul saw her coming closer to him slowly- footsteps quiet and soft; she was looking at him with deepness and then she really kissed him on the lips. He never noticed that he liked Judie. She was always the bossy one with a Lucy Van Pelt attitude until he kissed her. Afterwards, he remembered thinking about it quite often and wondered to himself, "Kissing Judie is just like kissing mother and Aunt Gina. Their lips felt the same and they kissed the same way... why did Judie's kiss feel different?"

Paul woke up today at 9:15 am in a home devoid of memories and warmth; staffed with rocks and willows, a patch of grass at the corner and a little coil of greens beside his bedroom window. The air was not very stiff but it did get thick every now and then when Paul was left to his thoughts and his wine. It would have been a very beautiful morning and an even better first of October if he was not entangled in such a mix of sentiments. He planned on taking a stroll down memory lane and began to think about where that last glass of wine took him last night; if he remembered correctly, it was Alyssa's house. Yes, he remembered every detail from slightest to boldest in scenes like a film. Summertime was strong and fierce in his thoughtful mind.

There was a knock on the door. Paul was startled for a moment and then he looked through the peephole to see a thin young woman standing by the frame. He wondered to himself, "Should I open it?"

He then twisted the doorknob and greeted her, "Hello."

She gave him a look of disaffection and said, "I forgot my cell phone."

She let herself inside and then grabbed the tiny trinket by the bedside and smiled at him with slight hollowness before leaving. Suddenly, he remembered what happened last night after that last glass; she was his night toy. Memories then came to him and they were not from last night but much before when he was a child of ten; young and shy.

It was a summer day in 1996; Paul had just come back from school and briefly went home where his mother asked if he was hungry. He replied, "No, mother. I'll eat later on at Judie's house."

Later on, he went to his neighbor's house where Judie and John were watching reruns of bland television cartoons. They were all quite bored with what they had in front of them until that topic came up somehow. John asked Paul if

he ever had a girlfriend and he replied, "No, have you?"

John stammered, "Yeah, I always have girlfriends." Clearly he was lying because Paul had never even seen him holding hands with a girl. John then asked, "Have you ever done it with anyone?"

Paul gave him a sudden look of shock; unprepared to talk about this secret knowledge.

"Oh, leave him alone. I doubt he's ever done it with anyone," said Judie.

Paul felt his face blush and then he answered nervously, "Yes, I've done it before. It was no big deal."

John remained quiet for a moment and then said, "So you know how it looks?"

Paul nodded and then gave a look at Judie because she seemed so unfit for the topic yet she was so interested.

He then asked, "Do you know how girls' things look?"

John nodded and Paul felt his body tense up because they probably knew he was lying. He never seen it; he never knew how it looked but something told him it was secretive, bad and dirty. The occurrence that came afterwards took him completely by surprise. Judie stood up and dropped her pants to her ankles and showed them how it looked. Quietness... stillness; a collective sentiment overthrew them and perhaps even Judie. For the rest of the day, Paul could only think about Judie. He could not eat, play or speak for a while until he figured out what he was feeling and that night he tossed and turned in confusion.

Nowadays, Paul often dreamed of his adult endeavors; only he was a child in his dreams. Sometimes he was an adult like in waking life but for the most part he was a virgin; warm and shy.

Paul removed the bed sheets and thin cotton blankets from the bed and threw them in his washing machine. He poured himself a glass of wine that was probably more nutritious than he was and then he peered outside at passersby who knew nothing about his lamentations. He began to wish he lived in his dreams instead of living in waking life because the places he saw and the women he met in his dreams had the quality of a hundred widows and single mothers put together in waking life. The validation he would feel when having an affair with a woman in his dreams was omnipotent; difficult to fathom yet righteous enough to consider it a strength. When he woke up, he was always so downhearted about his loneliness and he would clutch his heart and lie awake until morning came.

After recovering from a one night stand and eleven glasses of wine, he threw on his overcoat and left the house. As he did so, his cell phone rang twice. He picked it up and answered, "Hello."

"Hey, big brother!" said his sister on the other line.

"Hi Emily, how was your weekend?" he asked.

"It was alright I suppose. I took the children to New Glasgow on Friday and they loved it. You've been there, right?"

He suddenly remembered a recent affair he had in New Glasgow that ended awry and replied, "Yes, I've been there."

"Great, well I'm not sure how I've been though. The doctor says I have an infected gallbladder. I should have gotten it removed years ago but I was just too scared. What do you think I should do?"

"Well, you should do what's best. Talk to Dr. Carmen and see if he can remove it. I think you'll be better off. No pain, no worries," he replied.

She sighed, "Yes, I knew I had to go. I was just too scared. I guess that's why mother used to say don't think too much about things. I've been thinking about it the whole night and because of that I couldn't sleep."

Paul continued to listen as he walked down the roadside.

"What have you been up to these days?" she asked.

"Nothing really, I just worked forty hours last week and slept the whole weekend. I've been a little tired lately."

"You haven't been drinking, have you?" she asked.

"No, mother," he replied sarcastically.

"Don't get all smartass on me, dumdum. Well, I'll give Carmen a call and see if I can get this devil removed already. Oh, by the way- guess who I saw the other day?"

"Who did you see?" he asked.

"Remember Debbie? The girl next door?" she asked.

Paul thought long and hard; he could not pick up a memory of a Debbie however.

"I'm not entirely sure I remember."

"Well, you know- Debbie... the little girl who had a crush on you," she said.

A brief scene of him and a little blonde haired girl by a garden crossed his mind.

"Oh, now I remember," he responded.

"Well, she was in New Glasgow. She has two children and she's married now!"

Paul faked a laugh and said, "Oh, that little Debbie. I remember she used to be so shy. It's funny how things can change."

"Yes, isn't it so odd? I could not imagine her even kissing a boy back then; now she is married and has children. What a woman!"

Paul didn't have the desire to fake laugh anymore so he just cleared his throat and said, "Alright, sis. I better get going. You take care now!"

"Thanks, Paul. Love you!"

"Love you too."

It was 1998, a time when quiet became hostile and that safe place in Paul's mind was no longer safe. Somehow, his safe place became vulnerable to influences so foreign to him until he decided to dig deeper. The influences were attracted to him and so they clung to him and never let go but the more he dug, the more he began to realize, he was attracted to them as well.

One night the town was subjected to a violent thunderstorm. Paul was sitting on his living room couch and his mother was cooking fish in the kitchen. Judie came over with her backpack and she was soaking wet from the rainfall. At first,

Paul's mother was irritated that Judie walked in the house with wet clothes but then she just exclaimed, "Dinner will be ready in half an hour!"

Paul took Judie to his bedroom and for what seemed like hours, they sat at the edge of his bed and spoke awkwardly about school. Judie mentioned that she despised Mrs. Henrietta and Paul asked if she did her homework. Judie complimented Paul's Hot Wheels collection and he offered her a granola bar. She declined and the room became quiet... so quiet that they heard each other breathing nervously and Judie turned to Paul and kissed him but it was not like before when they played house; she kissed him differently and he began to tremble with anxiety but he never asked her what she was doing because then she would stop and he didn't want her to stop.

The moment felt like only a few minutes but it was actually longer and Paul's mother opened the door to find Judie on top of Paul with a look of guilt in her eyes. She gave a nervous laugh and jumped off the bed. Paul was frightened, confused as if this never happened and it was only a daydream. After that day, Paul's mother never let Paul and Judie see each other out of school again.

Now and then he thought about Judie and even looked her name up on the internet to see if they could finish what they started but he soon realized that people change like seasons. He liked to think Judie was his girlfriend in middle school and that she liked every inch of him. He wanted to think that Judie was attracted to his gestures and his lips and when she showed him her untouched body parts, she wanted him to be her lover and there was nothing that could stop this undeniable connection between them but that was not true. Judie was twelve years old and she was curious to know about closeness; she would have done it with anyone at the time.

As Paul approached Acacia Street, he saw the home of Debbie Presley (or what used to be anyways) and remembered how she spoke with a lisp. The day he rode his bicycle down to her house was the day he began to feel. Her face was pretty and pink underneath the summertime sky that day in the garden. Her mother was taking a nap inside and the two children went out to the garden to play Ring around the Rosie. Debbie was

a sweet little girl who never showed the slightest sign of disobedience. She got good grades and ate her veggies when girls like Judie would poke fun of those things.

This was the same year that Paul discovered the word horny and even though he held back on sharing it with friends in school, he certainly shared it with Debbie. Part of him wanted to just see her reaction and another part of him was looking for answers.

"Do you ever get horny?" he asked her.

At the time, she was softly bouncing up and down on the trampoline and when he asked her that, she stopped and stared at him.

Paul could not remember what happened afterwards but he was certain she told her mother and her mother told his mother and he got scolded.

Paul stood there and peered into her old house that seemed much more like a film than a memory. Things were wider then; prettier and deeper. Her backyard used to remind him of an open field somewhere in the Midwest and now it looked just like every other house he passed by on his way to the liquor store down Windmill Road.

Once, he had dreams and paintings, things that meant he would be adored by others and loved by himself; and even if he had no love for himself (since he never identified it) then tolerance for himself at least. Now his life seemed merely like a picture book with blank pages for years and years until he had someone to hold again and then it would go back to blank pages. There were women that passed in and out of his life but he supposed they were looking for someone else because they never returned.

Was he robbed of the closeness? He seemed to know everybody from a distance; an observatory distance where only the hummingbirds fed. Paul gazed at the house long enough and saw a red truck approaching, so he walked away and returned home. There, he watched television and drank some wine. After his seventh glass, he began to think about the girl from the other night. If only he could remember what he had to offer her and what she meant to him. The smell of her breath stayed with him the night he slept with her but now it vanished. He could always work overtime, find a hobby in modeling clay, learn piano or even join a club and socialize with others in Dartmouth but he had no desire for any of that.

This heart of his desired closeness but he grew weary trying to find what would quench his thirst. He thought he found it years ago in a woman named Ida and she fell off his radar and he never went searching for her. Every night when he would catch a widow at the bar, he was so sure that his heart would be tamed but it was every morning after when it felt lonely and vulnerable. He went through several women in the past ten years and all of them disappeared in the labyrinth of love. Paul clutched at his pants as he drifted into an unconscious affair and before he was completely out, he pondered;

"How did I let myself become so vulnerable? When was the last time I was at peace? If love is peace and peace is love, am I deprived of both? Will I ever find peace of mind or have I lost my peace loving someone else?"

When he woke up in the twist of white linen, he found that he was lost again. He didn't know how he lost his perception of himself or how it happened but he woke up wondering what he was missing. On Saturday, he met Janice. She gave him something to chew on when she asked him what he thinks about purity. He desired both purity and sin like day and night, only he knew that one would always outlive the other in him. On Sunday, he slept with Maria. She didn't say much but she had eyes he never dreamed of. She was high dollar and even the most peaceful couples would feel slightly envious of his affair with her. Through her eyes, he could see who he was supposed to be. They gazed and they pondered; they overthrew his romantic overtures the next morning and now today he woke up alone and vulnerable with no sense of peace.

He wondered where this entanglement would lead him to if it ever ended at all.

Paul drove through an acre of trees that had colors of red and orange and he used to remember when they were green and he wore his button ups. They were now the colors of his innards; fiery and burning with desire; closeness.

His innards used to be blue and green; serene and careless even; living like he was at peace with his past, present and future only he didn't care to bother too much with his future. After all, he was only seven years old back then. If he remembered clearly, it was the last time he identified with the concept of peace.

He began to remember a time when he and Judie were in school and they were at recess. It was the second to last day of middle school and he was feeling some kind of change in his world.

"Aren't you supposed to be hanging out with your boyfriend?" he asked her.

"Oh, Steve is playing football. I was supposed to be helping Mrs. E with the room but I didn't feel like it today. Why are you sitting way out here away from everyone?"

"I just have a lot to think about."

"Like what?" she asked.

Just when he was about to make up an exceptionally believable lie, she gave him the answer he was looking for.

"Sex?"

He looked up at her with the sunshine in his face and he could barely see hers. Her freckles were not as visible like when they were making out in his room. He saw every graphic detail of who she was that night.

"Yes," he replied.

"Sex is a complicated thing. I think everyone is pretty clueless when it comes to sex. It's no wonder why most people don't end up having sex until they're an adult," she said.

"I want to understand it more though. Why does everyone act like it's the best thing in the world? Where does that feeling come from? Why do I feel so empty when I'm not against someone else?"

Judie did not respond right away because perhaps she was wondering the same thing. Perhaps it takes two to make sense of things or perhaps everybody must find that sense of understanding themselves and she did not share his turmoil.

"You'll find the answers soon enough, Paul. At

least you're one step ahead of the rest of those jerks. You actually got a taste of it."

Judie smirked as she leaned in and gave Paul a hug and he embraced it because without words, without speaking and coming to terms with things in the naked eye, the warmth of another soul can be the remedy to a thousand hurt feelings. However, Paul remembered that night he vowed to never be open again.

Paul visited a bar he always saw from the road because only this one time he wanted to drink someplace where there was no trace of desire. Of course, the bartender smiled at him as he was a new customer and of course he smiled back at her but he was almost destined to drink something that would make him forget he ever saw her just like every other day. He wanted something thick; difficult to swallow, almost like eggnog. He wanted to dissolve into his drink and make it the melting pot of childhood fantasies, wet dreams and the bitter taste of losing time.

However, midway through drinking and dwelling over the stages of his life, a woman sat beside him and asked him where he lives. He looked around before answering and replied, "I live two blocks away from here."

The woman sighed, "I was wondering if you can give me a ride. My friend and I got pretty wasted and she bounced without me. Pretty please with a cherry on top?"

Paul looked at her and she resembled an actress he used to watch on television in his preteen years so he answered, "Some friend you got. Sure, I'll give you a ride."

Within the next half an hour, Paul and his new mistress drove through the pines across Herbert St. and instead of dropping her off at her house, he asked if she would like to spend the night at his and she agreed by saying, "Only this once."

They kissed upon the living room couch and he took off his belt and his cell phone and put them on the table. She asked if he had protection and they shared an awkward laugh before he nodded and said, "Yes, of course."

Paul was born on June, 1985 in sweet and simple Nova Scotia. He went to school until he was sixteen and met so many people since then. The woman underneath him must have been born around the same time and had her own path leading to this night of sweat and sighs. As he pushed himself into her, he began to think; this woman had been following a path all her life and so has he; if this was not destiny for them to be making love then what was? If he was not at peace now with her warm and tender body against his, sharing something so private that neither of them expose to the public, then what is peace?

A memory flashed through Paul's mind as he focused on the woman's face and he recalled the day he lost his virginity. Angels of broken wings must have not saved him from that summer day. He and Alyssa were in the bedroom pretending they were married. She turned off the light and got under the covers with him. When he asked, "Are you really naked?" she replied, "Yes. You should be naked too. That's what real married couples do."

Paul remembered being afraid, anxious and observant. He took off his clothes and moved closer to her. He knew that the summer days were going to be over soon and Alyssa was going to find someone else to play with just like Judie did. He was never very good at keeping his frame of mind and he admitted to her that he was lost so she helped him find some kind of bliss in pleasure and he knew that after that day he would never be the same. He knew that what was once lost could still be found only with a new name and a new face from another womb.

There could have been a seed that night; there could have been something so special and sacred to him that he would go the rest of his life not caring about anything else but the seed in her flesh that was killed too soon. She was young and he was lost and they were both too young for parenthood so why were they not too young for sex? Paul knew it was something neither of them could resist and it came with pain. If there was another face today that mirrored Paul's thirteen year old face, he would be certain he'd found his peace in this logbook of lust.

To become one with another soul, to feel their warm blood beneath their flesh and taste the places they hide from others, to grow up in different towns and follow different paths but connect for that one brief moment of passion, to share something so personal and mortal with another person with hopes and dreams, fears and desires and know that they will die someday just as they were born; it is a drug to die for in itself.

After Paul was finished and their faces were flushed and sweaty, he kissed her and rested his head against her bosom. For a brief moment, he recalled a time before his turmoil; before the labyrinth of love tossed him into its pit. He was a child of only seven, wearing the denim overalls his mother bought him and eating some animal crackers by the lake. His eyes gazed at the water and he saw ducks fighting for a piece of bread. The sky was unclouded and the sun shined happily just for him.

"Come here, Paul!" called his mother.

He turned around and smiled at her as he ran across the garden.

About the Author:

Alex R. Encomienda is an author of fiction and poetry. He has written content for journals such as The Opiate, Kaaterskill Basin, Adelaide and more recently Bindweed. Alex often expresses the concepts of love, peace, lust, freedom and escapism in his work and likens his pieces to pages from his life. Alex writes and lives in sunny Arizona with his family.

THE FUNERAL

David Summers

They were setting up chairs just outside the church for the extra mourners. He left the car and joined them. One of them stopped and waved him over.

"Is it David?" he asked.

"Yes" said the newcomer. "I'm David. I...I'm not sure we've met. It's been so long."

"Of course" said the man. "You wouldn't know me. I'm Steve. Emma's husband. It's all right. We haven't met before."

"Steve. Emma's husband." David repeated carefully, committing the name and the face to memory.

They shook hands warmly.

"It's good to meet you at last. How did you know it was me?"

"Oh, you were expected." grinned Steve. "Emma and her sisters were talking about how you were coming. 'The cousin', they said. 'The tall one', they said. Knew you as soon as you got out the car. It was obvious."

"Can I give you a hand?"

"Oh we've got this. No problem. You go sit over there. You've come a very long way for it. Farther than anyone, so they reckon."

"Please, it's all right. It will give me something to do while the others arrive."

"All right. Grab that stack of chairs over there."

Together with the other men, they set up the rest of the rows of chairs.

By the time they were done, others had arrived. Friends of the family. Townsfolk. People from all across the state and beyond. Auntie Rosalie had been a much loved and respected figure. The funeral was shaping up to be quite an event. A very sizable crowd.

"David?"

"Yes, it's me. Is that...? Georgia?"

"Yes, Georgia. "

"Hello, Cousin."

"Cousin."

They embraced.

"I'm sorry. Everything was so last minute."

"You are here. And right on time. Everything is fine now."

They stood silently, taking in the size and shape of the other. The different hair and the extra wrinkles. The eyes that marked a person with the burden of years lost.

Each cousin knew the other. In moments, the new image of the other was updated and imprinted in the memory for future recall. Twelve years is a long time.

Another woman approached.

"David? Is that you"

"Yes"

"I'm Cora"

"Cousin" he said.

"Cousin" she replied and they too hugged each other. Again, they disengaged and each frankly regarded the other. Taking stock. Everything committed to memory.

"Emma, Evelyn, and Nell are in the back." she said. "They have their hands full with the kids. You know, your other newer cousins once removed and all that."

"Ah" said David. "I can see this is going to get complicated very quickly. I'm terrible with names."

"Oh no worries" chipped in Georgia. "Plenty of time to make introductions after it's all over."

"Of course. Looking forward to it"

"Would you like to see her? Mum's in the church. The viewing before the service itself gets underway."

"Would it be alright?"

"Oh you dag! You are family. Of course, it's all right. Mum would have been very happy to know you could make it."

She grabbed him by the hand and led him into the church.

There were only a few people inside. The pews were mostly empty for the moment.

The open coffin was just up ahead.

Standing vigil was Uncle Len. A farmer. A businessman. A beloved father. A man of solid strength and determination. Yet now, he was simply old. An old, small man burdened by terrible grief. A widower struggling to say goodbye to the woman he loved.

He turned and moved to greet his nephew.

"Oh David, thank you for coming. So very far. So very, very far."

They embraced.

"Uncle Len, I'm grateful to be included. Thank you. I am so sorry. I had to come to say goodbye."

"Of course, my boy" said Uncle Len gently. "It means a great deal to us all. She would have wanted you to come."

David slowly let go of Uncle Len and hesitantly approached the open coffin.

For the last time saw his Auntie Rosalie.

She was so tiny. A withered and small thing. Unrecognizable.

Yet it was her. There was no doubt. This was real. Aunt Rosalie was dead.

He had known it all along, of course. He had known it on the long plane flight coming here. He'd known it during the six-hour drive getting to the town. He had known it as he saw the church and greeted family for the first time in oh so very long.

But this confirmation still had the power to shock him.

She was gone.

Tears welled up unbidden. He tried to choke them back. This was not about him. He should be strong for the sake of Uncle Len and the girls.

"It's all right" said Uncle Len, reaching out a farmer's calloused and strong hand. "It's all right, you know. It's perfectly all right. We all loved her very much"

David nodded vigorously in agreement. It was the only thing he could manage to do and not break down completely. Uncle Len understood the words unspoken. He was always a man generous in his strength and, standing side-by-side at the coffin, he gave it freely to his kin.

The service itself was animated.

To a packed church, the girls told stories about their mother. Stories of the land. The struggle and eventual success to build a farming empire up from the harsh wilderness. Raising daughters in nothing but a shed in the beginning. Surrounded by scrubland. Building a homestead by hand. Her travels around the world later in life. Her triumphs. Her songs that she wrote and performed, and of course, her two battles with cancer.

Sadness was an unwelcome guest here.

There were moments where the eulogy abruptly halted.

Tears of loss and pride and love.

As one sister faltered, another would come and lend support to carry on. And then another and another, until all five stood together, united.

David watched quietly from the pews up near the front and marveled at their strength. How open the the daughters of Auntie Rosalie were in their love and memory of their mother. The crowd in the church surged in response, hanging on every word. A great lady had gone. A tough woman. She would be remembered for a very long time.

The funeral wake was held at the local Football Club Reception Hall. It had the space and the welcome luxury of air conditioning.

The hall buzzed. Children rushed about underfoot, completely ignored by their parents. People ate and drank and mingled. Tables were moved strategically. Extra chairs moved in. All had their stories to tell and introductions to make. Gossip was exchanged and little snippets of history were revealed.

Every so often, someone would pass by and nod at David in recognition or come up and shake hands. Each face he attempted to catalogue and put a name to.

Friend or relative? Distant or near? Forgivable to forget or unforgivable to forget?

Smile now. Remain confident.

Volunteer your name at every opportunity and hope they volunteer theirs.

Suddenly he was ambushed by a grand dame of the family.

"David, isn't it?"

"Yes. Forgive me, my memory is bad. It's been so..."

"Oh you wouldn't remember me. Last time we met, you were only a baby. No bigger than my forearm. I'm Pauline, your mother's cousin. From the Tiver side of the family. Your grandfather was a Dasborough, wasn't he?"

"Oh yes."

"Lovely man, he was. Died of pneumonia. You never had a chance to know him really, I suppose?"

"No, I was still a baby."

"Yes, that would be right. Your grandmother always had a bag packed and ready to leave him, you know."

"Nana?"

"Oh yes. Lurl was quite the handful. She did love him of course. But it was complicated. Ups and downs. She never did get around to getting a divorce and moving to the city."

"I...I had no idea."

"Oh yes. Your grandparents had a lively time of it. Come with me. Something I want to show you."

At the back of the hall, a projector was silently displaying pictures on the wall at random from the family photo albums. A vast array of old black and white photos, 70's era Polaroid shots converted awkwardly to digital and wedding photos and holiday snaps from happier times. It was a huge collection.

David recognized some of the pictures, of course. Farming homesteads owned by different parts of the family. Wedding photos of his Aunt and Uncle. It was easy to guess a youthful Auntie Rosalie and her husband looking back at the camera with half-surprised smiles. Other photos of presumably distant relatives. People he couldn't place, to his embarrassment. The family was too wide and too scattered. To learn all the names and their relationship to each other and the various histories would have taken a lifetime in itself.

"Wait for it... There! That man in the photo. You see him?"

"Yes, I do. I've never seen that photo before. He's a relative, of course?"

"That's your grandfather on you mother's side. Spitting image of you. Only in that photo, he's a young man. Easy to see you are a Dasborough. No doubt about it."

David looked again intently at the photo. This old new snap shot from the past. This man he had never known. And yes, something was indeed there. The nose, of course. Tall, lean built. There was an awkward familiarity to the features of that young man. He would have to speak to someone and get a copy of that photo for later.

Food was eaten, time passed and people eventually made their goodbyes, got in their cars and drove away. The town was very far from practically anywhere. The return journey could take hours or even days for almost all of them.

"David! I have a surprise for you."

David turned to see his cousin, Emma. At last she was free of the children.

"You grew up at Rupara, didn't you? It was always yours and Nana's place."

"Yes, that's right. It's where I grew up. You and your husband are in charge of Rupara now, is that right?"

"Yes, it's ours now. Mum wanted it that way. We've been fixing it up for a good while now. New fence line put up. A couple of new dams. That sort of thing."

"I'm glad. Good to know it's all in safe hands."

"It's still yours, you know. You will always be welcome there. Anytime you want to visit, you should just come over."

"I'm grateful" said David." It means a lot to me to hear you say that."

"Well, that surprise I mentioned." laughed Emma." You'll never guess. We were cleaning up the old place years ago and we found something of yours."

"Oh?" said David. "What did you find?"

"Your appendix, if you can believe it. In a plastic specimen bottle. Labelled by the hospital and preserved in alcohol."

"What? My appendix?? Oh my goodness, I remember that thing! I was eight years old. It nearly killed me. We got to the hospital just in time. They gave it to me as a souvenir. You still have it?? How....odd."

"Well, yes. Couldn't very well just throw it away after it surviving for all this time, now could we? Piece of history it is now, you see."

"Ah" he smiled sheepishly." Yes. My appendix of all things."

"Plus there's your measurements on the door frame from when you were growing up as a small boy" Emma added. "Date, height, in Nana's handwriting. We've remodeled the house but we made sure to keep that doorframe, I can tell you. It's all there. You've left your mark on that place."

"Oh my. I remember. " he murmured.

Rupara had been his home. Far from the city. Hills and trees, sheep and dirt roads, even a modest mountain poking up against the sky. Lonely and isolated. Just him and his Nana for many years.

"The cedar tree at the front of the homestead?"

"Gone. Fell over in a storm years ago. Huge monster of a thing."

"Yes, a real giant. The apricot tree around the back?"

"Still there" she smiled." The children raid it every summer."

"The grape vines up at the shearing shed?"

"You remember? Why yes. Still growing wild."

"And the swallows? They still have their nesting places under the veranda roof?"

"How did you..? Yes, the swallows are there. Every year they return like clockwork." she said softly.

" I can still see the place. Just talking to you here and now. I can still see it.

"Yes. Yes, you can." She gazed at him in wonderment.

"Thank you, Cousin. Perhaps one day."

"Of course" she replied, hugging him fiercely.

Early next morning was a farewell BBQ breakfast up on Auntie Rosalie's farm, a few miles out of town. Just for the family and maybe a handful of close friends before final departures. This was the only real chance to properly meet the new cousins. The next generation. Thirteen in all.

They were a cheerful lot but the focus was not on David at all. No, that was reserved for their other cousins. The cousins of their own age. They too were busy renewing acquaintances since their families also lived far, far apart.

David would have to wait his turn with the rest of the grownups.

So he sat on his lawn chair and quietly observed his small cousins at play. Every so often, one of them would be caught by their mother or father and dragged to the breakfast table so that formal introductions could at last be made. Then, their family obligations fulfilled, they would wriggle free or beg to be excused; leaving the grownups to their boring stuff.

David made a mental note of which cousin belonged to which parents and which were brothers and sisters. It was a thankless task. He knew fully well that, while some names might stick to faces, given enough time he'd be back to guiltily only knowing of them rather than properly remembering the actual specifics.

There was one cousin who was apart from the rest though.

She was definitely interested in this stranger that her parents, mysteriously, did not treat as a stranger.

She was shy. Shy but curious. She kept looking at him and then turning away when David, returning her curiosity, tried to make eye contact.

Her mother noticed and decided to force the issue.

She called her over.

"Mel, over here. Come sit with your mother. Someone I want you to meet."

Mel slowly approached, giving the mysterious stranger a wide berth.

Evelyn scooped her up and sat her on her knee.

"This is your Uncle David."

"Uncle?"

"Well, he's your cousin really. But.."

"But.....He's too old to be my cousin!"

"Well he...It's...." Evelyn frowned in confusion. "David, how does it go?"

"I did a bit of study on the terms before I arrived. I knew this question would come up. I didn't know myself so I made a special effort and looked it up.

So...you and I are cousins. We know that. That's the easy part.

However, your children are my cousins too. Only they are cousins once removed. Once removed in generation, you see?"

"Ah. What about second cousins then?"

"Well, if you have children and I have children, then they would be second cousins to each other."

"Ahah, so....Mel, this is your cousin once removed."

"Mel?" said David. "I'm very pleased to meet you. But you are right about me being too old. I am. It's probably easier if you just call me Uncle David. It's....just easier that way."

"Uncle David. Hmm, ok." said Mel and shook his hand just like the grownups do.

"Uncle David?"

"Yes Mel?"

"Why do you have a big nose?"

David stifled a giggle, gave Evelyn a significant look and then in his best official 'wise adult voice' sagely announced "Well, I recently found out that would be because of your great-grandfather Dasborough. But it makes me look rather handsome, don't you think?"

Mel was thoughtfully silent.

Then, diplomatically she asked "Mum? Can I go back and play now?

And in a flash, she was gone back playing chasey with the others.

"How are things back over there?" Evelyn asked.

"Not so bad." he replied, helping himself to another sausage. "Things are a bit tight at the moment but I'm still hopeful I can make it work out."

"You could always come back home to Australia. You could set yourself up here. Someone with your skills and background could do alright here in this state, for example."

"Perhaps" he said doubtfully. "I'd like to come back home. Live at least a bit closer to you and the others. Would have been easier when you were all girls and still all living here at your parents' farm. But now, you are all married with children of your own. Even Nel. She's got that new one. Clayton, isn't it?"

"Yes, Clayton. Three months old."

"Ah, remembered that one."

He paused.

"When I come back, I want to come back with money in my pocket. Having done something. Been a success at something. Buy my own home and some land perhaps.

I look at you and the girls, your parents and...I can't tell you how proud I am of you all."he said" You've all built lives for yourselves. Made good decisions in life. Made a real go of things.

You know, when I try to tell foreigners about my home, about where I am from....I always end up talking about you and your sisters and Auntie Rosalie, and Nana and Rupara. All of it.

I'm no farmer. " David admitted. "Your lives are not something that I can emulate. Growing up on Rupara never made me a farmer. It was my childhood home, not my future career. I always felt destined to try something else. Not sure how it will all end up, to tell you the truth, but I need to see it though."

They sat quietly for a while, only half-listening to the chatter about them. The wind stirred the trees surrounding the homestead. The morning was no longer new and soon it would be time to part company.

"You were sent here as a baby, you know." said Evelyn.

"Oh?" said David.

"There was a problem with your mother not long after you were born. You needed a place to go until things settled down. So they sent you here for about four months. You and me were almost the same exact age. Both babies. So taking care of you too was pretty straightforward. She treated you like a son."

David turned to Evelyn in astonishment.

"As a baby? I...I didn't know. Nobody ever told me. Four months? Here? I never knew."

"That makes you a bit like an absent brother then, you see? Mum always wanted a boy. She ended up with a team of girls though."

David couldn't think of a suitable reply so he nodded dumbly. He was still trying to comprehend this new revelation. Auntie Rosalie had always been important to him. The one he most admired. The one he liked hearing stories about.

Her and Uncle Len and the girls. As a boy, he had a dim memory of staying here for a few days. The tennis court. The cousins that showered him with attention. The noise, the excitement and the activity.

That he knew. Uncle Len's and Aunt Rosalie's farm he knew. But as a baby? Long before? Here?

That was a different, hidden chapter and Auntie Rosalie was now gone.

Her loss pricked at his conscience. He would never have a chance to thank her.

By unspoken agreement, the guests slowly started murmuring about the time and how far away all their homes were. They got up to leave and began to make their farewells. He too, followed along with the rest and made his goodbyes. One last round of handshakes, hugs and wiping away of tears.

Uncle Len, the girls. The respective husbands. The younger cousins.

He hated goodbyes, preferring a discrete and unmentioned exit stage right. But the forms must be obeyed, especially at such a time and occasion.

Finally, he was in the car, driving down the long dirt road that connected to the country highway.

From there back to the city, then to the airport, then a flight to Brisbane and then, in turn, another flight far away from Australia itself.

This was...the end?

Is this how it ends? Really?

Possibly. Statistically, it was even rather likely.

Yes indeed. He might very well never see them ever again.

There was no way to know for sure. People die. Blink twice and twenty years pass by.

All too brief. All too fast.

Something could easily happen to him far away and, well, what could his extended family be reasonably expected to do about it? They would mourn him briefly and then move on. He'd fade from family history. Remembered only as a slightly fuzzy photo on a projector in a hall during a wake for some other relative's funeral, if he was lucky.

It was inevitable.

The tyranny of distance, even if he did miraculously return back home to Australia in triumph, the distance would always be the deciding factor in his relationship with his cousins and other family. After the first few hundred miles, adding on a few extra thousand made little effective difference. It was all the same relentless isolation and separation.

He looked in the rear view mirror at his family. Already they were breaking up and heading back into the house, getting out of the heat and dust. In his mind, he reviewed their names and faces.

He would eventually forget most of the details, that was certain. Yet it would not be due to lack of effort on his part.

Georgia, Emma, Cora, Evelyn, Nell, Steve, the other Steve, Stuart, Graham, and....and...Clayton! (of course) Mel and.......

Soon there was a bend in the road and the farm was lost in the trees.

About the Author:

David Summers hails from Australia and has worked steadily as an English teacher in Korea for many years. His interests include acting, history and travel. He writes stories from time to time but only as a result of persistent nagging from his closest friends

A DAY IN THE LIFE OF DELLA

Nina Wilson

A buzzer started sounding off. My heart jumped a few beats and I jumped out of bed, terrified. The world spun for a moment, making everything blurry. Confused by my surroundings I was wrapped up in the blanket and smacked into the carpet. I sucked in a breath and tried to get free, but it was no use. I cried out.

Milk. Toast. Butter. A few moments of peace. I looked at the clock with the red blocky letters right above the stove and under the overhanging Amana microwave my coffee still sat in. Then I panicked. 6:59, in a matter of a minute my alarm would go off...

I ran towards the bedroom and down the hallway only to hear the buzzer briefly and Della smack the ground. "I'm coming dear!" I said, hurrying as far as I could as fast as I could. "Della?"

"It's me, Della, it's me, James." I said. I knelt next to her. She was all wrapped up in her memory quilt. She hardly looked at it anymore. There were photographs printed onto it and pieces and bits of old clothes from all family members. I thought when this all began it would ease the memory loss. Nothing did, nothing could. It was these disease, it was evil. It was sucking the life out of her.

A strange old man wearing a fluffy blue robe walked in the room and stood over me. "Who are you? Who are you? Get away from me!" I cried, pulling myself out of the blankets. I stood up and walked out of the room and headed for the bathroom. It smelled like soap. I must have already showered. There were bubbles in the bottom of the tub and the lime green loofa wasn't in the place where it was supposed to be. I needed to

wash my hair. Of course, I needed to wash my hair. Where was that cream rinse, the pale blue bottle that was supposed to be right under the cupboard right next to the pile of extra toilet tissue? "Where's the cream rinse? What happened to it?" I asked. The little cat came up and rubbed against me. It had really pale blue eyes, just like the bottle I was looking for, but it wasn't the bottle. It was the cat.

Now the poor thing was asking about her cream rinse. We hadn't been using cream rinse since it would always get in her eyes and sting. I walked into the bathroom. She was knelt down almost collapsed into a pile in front of the under-sink cupboard. We had gotten a simplified bathroom two years ago when she started forgetting her name. At least the disease had been slow.

James came in. "Well good morning," I said. "Where have you been?" He was quiet. "Cream rinse. I need cream rinse." He handed me a bottle. "Thank you." James turned on the water in the bath. It made a funny clicking noise before smoothing out and water started to fill up the tub.

"I've been making breakfast." I said to Della. Her eyes made contact. They were becoming a creamy, milky blue. They used to be crystal clear and bright. The brightness was fading. Something caught in my throat for a moment.

I felt the water. "It's too cold, it's too cold." I said. I turned the tap to the right. "It's getting colder." He nodded slowly, yawned and turned it the other direction. The cat was sitting on the toilet watching us. She reached out and touched the man's butt. He looked behind him and smiled a bit.

I handed her a bottle of baby shampoo in an orange, clear bottle that was shaped like a teardrop. We had been using this for a while since it wasn't going to hurt her eyes.

"What's the cat's name, Della?" I asked.

"Why are you asking me that question?" she answered.

"What's the cat's name, Della?" I added again, but then her face changed a bit and she looked like she was trying to remember.

"Well, I don't think it matters. It answers to kitty, now doesn't it?"

"Her name is Kelly." I said quietly, helping her into the bathtub.

The water was nice and warm now. "Go away!" I said, waving at the man. He closed the door behind him. I sat in the water and watched as it started pouring from the faucet.

I sat outside the bathroom on an old kitchen chair had moved there and listened closely. She was babbling about her cream rinse again.

Then I heard the water start hitting the floor and I bolted in and turned off the water. The entire tub was filled with a massive cloud of suds from the sweet pea soap that I had bought her for her birthday. At least nothing changed in that respect, she loved her pink soaps.

"Where's my cream rinse?" I asked, looking around for my pale blue bottle. The only thing that was around was shampoo. I couldn't just shampoo, my hair would become all dry and brittle. I didn't want dry and brittle hair. I liked my hair soft. So I washed my hair out. It smelled really nice and sweet. My hair felt better after and it lathered up. I liked the smell. It smelled like the pink soap in the clear bottle. That smelled nice too.

That man ran in again, while I was in the bathtub. "How rude!" I cried, trying to cover myself up. He was polite though, and helped me to get out of the tub and I wrapped myself in a towel.

I smelled some toast. I was hungry. The kitchen light was on too. Why was it on? There was food already on the table. I must have already started. So I sat back down and started eating the toast. It

was a little cold. I grimaced and smeared more butter on it. Butter could always fix things. Tasted ok. Needed some orange juice. I was thirsty.

James sat down in front of me with a plate of food in front of him. "Do you want some food?" he asked. I nodded and reached for a piece of toast.

"Some of yours." he pointed to the plate.

"I am eating some of mine." I responded. He sighed and shook his head. "What are you sighing about old man?"

"Old man? Who are you calling an old man?" He started to laugh.

"Well look at you, bald and liver spots and all. That's old. You're all wrinkly. I hope getting that old isn't that bad."

"I'm sure it won't be for you." He nodded in my direction and raised his glass.

"Well, it better not be."

The man then went over to my record player.

It was a miracle that she didn't slip and fall and break a hip or something. Then she just walked right out like nothing had happened with a distant look in her eye.

"Della, you need to take your medicine!" I called. She looked at me, confused. "Della, what's my name?" I asked.

"What's your name?" she responded.

"What's my name?"

"Bread. No... I didn't mean that." she said, there was a piece of toast in her mouth.

"James."

"Well, I knew that."

After breakfast, I put the dishes into the dishwater and turned on some music. Her favorite artist was Michael Jackson. ~

He put something in it, but I didn't see the cover. Whatever it was, it was terribly catchy and I caught myself dancing to it behind the sofa. "Didn't this just come out on music video?" I asked. "On VH1, right?"

"Well it did come out on music video, do you

remember all the men running around in the parking garage?" James asked.

"Have I seen the video?" He then asked if I wanted to see the video and he brought over a computer. "They sure have made those things small in the past few years." I touched the screen and the video started. "Now how does that work?" Shocked I stepped back a bit and put my hand to my mouth. "It's not magic is it?"

"Oh no, Della, it's just what they are doing with technology these days."

"It's that pop star, James!" I exclaimed when the video started. "M... M... he was in a bigger band... Jackson... Michael Jackson!"

"You remembered, good."

When she first heard him singing in the sixties with the Jackson Five her face just lit up. I remember going to a dancing club and she dragged me right onto the floor with such pizzazz in her eyes and we went dancing. At forty years old I didn't know she had that much energy still in her, but she never really was all that low on energy. Right at the moment she was dancing to 'Bad'. Even if she didn't remember the face attached to this song, something clicked in her. One thing she was never judgmental about in this world was that man and his dancing skills. Even with the scandals and the bleaching and the plastic surgery, she still called him a genius and the King, which was impressive because she really loved Elvis too, and only a person incredibly worthy of the title King would get it from her.

"Well how would I forget?" I asked, starting to sing along to the song. "Would you dance with me?" I took his hand and we started to dance in my kitchen to the song. The song changed to "The Way You Make Me Feel." I wished I was wearing my high heels. "Well, I sure do love you James." I said giggling, feeling all giddy. I started singing along and twirling around the kitchen.

When we started dancing I couldn't help but think of the past, it was something I still had access to and there were glimmers of Della's past self still in her eyes. We first met during the Second World War while we were in a small rural liberal arts college. She was studying history to be a school teacher, while I was studying any number of

things before I eventually landed on religion. She always laughed about me being focused on things that I couldn't see, and I laughed that she had some fascination with dead things. She went on saying that apparently, I was incredibly infatuated with supernatural beings, and when comic books became a thing, we both started getting into those. To Della, they played quite heavily into history, at least in a modern sense. We rewatched our childhood play out during Captain American, and throughout many other periods such as the Cold War; growing gracefully into our old age through them. At least we agreed on something we liked. Most of the time we were that genuine bickering old couple that never 'got along', but we settled down just fine.

James took a hold of a pink ball that we kept on the shelf and he bounced it on the ground for me to catch it. With a lot of concentration, I got it. "Good job!" he said with a chuckle. I threw the ball back to him and he caught it in one hand. But when he threw it back at me I missed it and it bounced off my hands and onto the kitchen countertop where it knocked my glass off and it hit the floor. The noise was shocking. "What happened? How did that get there?" I asked.

"Stay back, Della, I need to clean this up." *The mess caught the light from the window so well. It just sparkled just like a jewel or a diamond. It looked so expensive. I wanted to hold a piece of it, and so I lifted one of the smaller shards and held it up to the window. It was really sunny outside, no clouds today at all. That must have been why the birds were very chatty. The birdfeeder was empty. That wasn't ok. They needed food just like anyone else. A squirrel must have eaten up everything, but those guys were hungry too.*

Pleasantries never lasted very long and when we accidently broke a glass while throwing a ball (an exercise the doctor had suggested to us) the peace just flitted away. While I got the broom and swept the mess of glass, she clearly didn't listen and just went on picking up a shard, but within moments she just wandered right outside and stood underneath the big oak tree in the front yard and stared at the branches. "Della, dear? What are you doing?" While there I picked up the paper lying on the porch.

It was spring; they just woke up. "Birdseed... we

need birdseed..." I said. We had lots of birds in this yard of all different colors. There was a blue jay who wasn't very nice though, and he would come and scare everyone away. It wasn't fair though; the way the other birds were treated. At the moment though, there was just a robin and a female cardinal sitting on a branch together. They sure got along. If they didn't, they'd be fighting right now. Then I'd tell them to stop. James gave them some food and the chirping kept on, maybe happier than before. The cat came outside then and sat on the porch. The birds didn't seem to like her being around, but I hoped they would get along.

"Della, what is it?" I asked. "What are you doing?"

"The bird seed, we need bird seed. Would you go get it?" she asked. Her feet were firmly planted on the ground. She wasn't even wearing her slippers. She never went around barefoot before. She used to be paranoid about those sneaky little parasites. Accepting the situation at hand, I just went and got the birdseed in a container on the porch. If I didn't keep a good supply of it, I'd regret it. She'd really throw a fit.

All of a sudden my hand felt like it was burning and there was blood coming all out of it, just everywhere. Dripping from my hand and down my arm. "How did this glass get in my arm?" I asked, pulling out a cloudy red piece. "What happened?" I threw it on the ground and James pulled me inside. He took me to the sink and the water washed off all the red. James wrapped the cut up. "Well how did all this happen?" I asked.

Then she did throw a fit after I filled up the birdfeeders. She started to cry and held up her hand. The she had grasped the glass in her hand so much that it must have cut her palm. Blood was just about everywhere on her left arm. I sighed and took her hand in mine and led her inside to get a bandage. She didn't remember how this happened, but that was becoming a normal occurrence. At first it started with her forgetting where various things were, turning in the wrong places on her drive home from work. She had stayed at the high school as long as she possibly could because she was scared of... well, this happening to her. That was always the fear, she had five younger sisters, all of which had already died due to Alzheimer's complications. So, until she was forcibly retired because of her increasing age,

she remained pretty well mentally intact, just a few bumps here and there. Then she went downhill slowly. She found plenty of things to keep her mind active. Between gardening and volunteering to help clean up the cemeteries around town, she always was better than I at those things. Maybe I was too comfortably with passivity. I needed to be prodded to get things done. Her activeness was healthy for me too.

"You weren't being careful." he answered. "Do you want to do a puzzle? You like puzzles." he asked.

"Well, sure, why not?" He led me to sit down at the couch and I did and he brought out a box. It was just a 100-piece puzzle. "I can do better than that."

"Let's just start with this one first." James said, sitting down next to me, opening the box and emptying it on the coffee table. I always wondered why it was called that, neither of us drank coffee. We thought it tasted bad. It was just like a drug too; it wasn't good for anyone's heart. My heart already had me to deal with, it didn't need any other stress on it. I knew someone who had died of a heart attack, but I didn't remember who, someone important.

Just then I wanted to talk to my parents. They didn't visit all that much. I supposed it was because they were getting older and were busy with all their new friends, but it would be nice once in a while to see them. Then James told me that they were still on vacation. They had been on a cruise ship somewhere south of here for a long time. I suppose that's what some people do with their retirement. Father was a dentist, maybe he made a lot of money and could spend all that leisure time in such an expensive way. We had to be careful with money around here. Things were expensive.

"Where's mom and dad? I called them yesterday and they didn't answer me." she said. I looked over to her, a bit surprised.

"Well I don't know, I think they were going vacation, remember? They don't have phone service." I responded. I always said the same things. In truth, her father had died a good fifty years ago from a heart attack, and her mother had died a good twenty years ago from cancer of the colon.

"Can I call Janet?" she asked. Her sister. Died of the disease Della currently had. "She's on vacation with your parents."

"Well why didn't they invite me? That's not very nice." she said, crossing her arms, looking hurt. "Well why didn't we ever go on a vacation?"

"We did, remember when we went to Las Vegas? You danced on that table." I laughed. I went over to the bookcase and showed her a picture I had taken of her. It was about fifteen years ago, but that was the best vacation we had. Just us going from casino to casino, watching all the shows we could. She even wanted to go to a male strip club, I didn't allow that.

Then I heard that my sister Janet was with them. I had never been on a cruise ship; it would have been nice to see that and part of the world. Traveling wasn't something that James and I could ever afford. All of a sudden James showed me a picture of a woman dancing on a table in some ugly yellow dress. "Who's that? Why is she acting so foolish?"

"Dear, Della, that's you." he said with a chuckle.

"What? Where? This doesn't look like home."

"We were in Nevada, in Las Vegas. Don't you remember?" I shook my head no.

"You must be lying." I said. Nothing came to me. "We never went to Las Vegas, we talked about it, I know we talked about it, but we didn't go. We don't have the money. We were saving to go see the concert so we can hear the songs in real life."

"You haven't been to a concert?" he asked, looking through the fridge.

"What are you looking for in there?"

"You haven't been to a concert?" he asked handing me the jug of milk.

"What's this for?" He didn't answer, only sighed. "James? What's this for? Are we drinking milk? I'm not really that thirsty right now." He poured the milk in a plastic cup. "Why aren't we using the nice cups? I don't like these ones. They feel cheap."

It was true that back in the day we didn't have money to go on a vacation. Teaching theology wasn't a lucrative business and neither was being

a schoolteacher. We hardly had enough to pay rent and eat, but Della was desperately wanting to go to a Michael Jackson concert that I was secretly saving up money for her 66th birthday to do so. I remembered that it was her first concert. She was so shocked of seeing him in person, on stage that she was jumping up and down and yelling like all the young people there who were holding the glittery signs that said 'We love you Michael'. She slapped me on the arm and said we should have done that so he could see that the fans that started being fans when he was little were still here kicking and rocking out. It was hard to hear him over all the screaming and yelling of the fans, but his dancing was still right on point and unbelievable. I was sure that man wasn't affected by gravity.

Della cried so much the day we heard he died. We were at the public pool that day, soaking up the sun. I never thought I'd be comfortable lying on one of those white plastic pool bed, bench things, but there I was, flab, age spots, white hair, balding head and all with a Stephen King novel, Salem's Lot, in my hands. Della had just read it, her first Stephen King novel, and she wasn't much of a fan or horror and gore, and this wasn't an exception. I was almost done with the book so right next to me was Bag of Bones to read next. She was reading the entire works of Victor Hugo which only comprised of the Hunchback of Notre Dame, which she had serious issues with, and Les Mis, which she said was far less depressing than the musical. Then the real depression hit when the overhead radio which was playing some awful country music went to news and we were told that Michael Jackson died.

"They are cheap." he answered. He looked tired.

"But I don't like them." I said sternly.

He shook his head and poured the milk into a glass and handed it to me. "Better?"

"You don't have to get snippy with me." I said plainly. James went right to the couch and sat down, pointing the clicker at the TV. It turned on. The set we had was brand new. It was so flat and... not shiny. James turned it onto the news. "Why do you have to watch all that horrible stuff, James? Doesn't it make you sad?" I asked.

"It's what's happening in the world. It's ok if it

makes me sad." he responded, taking my hand. "It's nice to be informed."

"Well what if they're making it all up, journalists do that sometimes."

"You don't have to believe it, Della, but there's some truth in everything. You used to tell me that all the time."

"I used to tell you that? Well what baloney." I said, picking up a magazine that was sitting on the side table. I pointed to the front cover. "Who is that?" It was some weird looking man with a leather coat and red shirt that needed washed.

"You know him. That's Stephen Tyler."

"I don't know who that is. I just know he needs to brush his hair out, maybe use some cream rinse and… and less drugs. He looks as high as a kite."

"You know him; he sings in the band Aerosmith. You like Aerosmith."

Her eyes welled right up with silent tears. She set her book aside and just sat there, staring at the waterfall in front of us where mindless children were splashing around. "They don't care." she said then, pointing at them. "They don't know who just died. God made some mistake. It's too soon." She was really quiet the rest of the day, and Della was never quiet. Never was, still isn't.

"Aerosmith…" He turned off the TV and started to type away at his little computer thing that fit on his lap and a song started to play from it with mellow guitar. "All these lines on my face getting clearer… the past is gone…" I began to sing along, a smile crossing my face and I sang along.

"Half my life's on books written pages, lived and learned from fools and from sages……. Dream on!" James started to sing too. His face looked all nice. He was nice and clean and shaved, and he didn't need to worry about cream rinse or his hair. He didn't have any!

He fell quite when I sang, "Sing with me if just for today, maybe tomorrow the good lord will take you away." He looked sad. I kissed his cheek. He looked happy again. "I thought this was the man named after the blimp."

"Led Zepplin?" he laughed, smiled and shook his head. "No, no, this is Led Zepplin." He kept tying

away on that flat black keyboard until some old timey music popped up.

"This sounds like it belongs in the Middle Ages." I said, crossing my arms.

"Give it a moment, Della." he said patiently. I nodded and listened. Voices started and there was guitar in the background. I kept nodding, hoping that the song would come back to me, I was sure it would, I could feel it in the back of my head. It was familiar. Eventually it hit me, "All of our thoughts are misgiven…" I began.

"There you go, you remember!" James said, and then he began to sing along with me, carefully though. Maybe he didn't remember it well either.

She only went to two other concerts since the Michael Jackson concert, and was greatly disappointed, at least in comparison: Aerosmith and Bon Jovi. I couldn't get her into her other favorites, Guns n. Roses, and Metallica. They never came anywhere near us geographically or in terms of the budget. She sang along to every single song by those ones, mostly because she was conscious when it came to them rather than enraptured. I never understood her amazement with music. She only laughed and told me that if her parents ever heard something like this, they would deem it heretical, demon music. No one when she was little would have ever imagined that she would see anything like that, that anything in terms of Kiss, Alice Cooper, or Twisted Sister would ever walk out on stage. Men wouldn't have the 80's hair band hair, the makeup, the ripped shirts, and painfully tight jeans. She didn't necessarily find it glamorous, she thought it more humorous. The early days of Bon Jovi could have been the funniest though of all. She thought of it as cliché, but the lyrics always stuck with her longest. You Give Love a Bad Name was our ballad for some time, then she switched it to Bad Medicine. I thought she had gone a little odd in the head thinking that way for a woman her age. Who would have thought being so old could feel so young and free?

Most of that young and free feeling dissipated, even as long as it lasted. Mom always said good things don't last forever, but if you ask God nice enough, they can last longer and end easier. I wasn't sure that this was a nice easy ending though. Della was clueless of her illness this far into it. Her nervous fears she held all her life came through and there was no fear anymore. There was just living life in specks of time now. For her, it was simple. For me, it was hell. I wasn't sure what I did, or what she did, or what anyone did, or would have done to be cursed.

"Ooh, It makes me wonder... and a new day will dawn for those who stand long, and the forests will echo with laughter... your head is humming in case you don't know, the piper's calling you to join him... dear lady can you hear the wind blow? And did you know that your stairway lies on the whispering wind?"

That's what this was, a curse. At night, lying in bed, sometimes I'd stare at the ceiling and think that maybe a demon crawled inside her and started gnawing at her personality, leaving bits and pieces behind, but also large gaps and holes. As farfetched as it sounded, it was the most logical explanation. Her brain literally looked like it was being eaten in those scans they showed me. Or a parasite had crawled up in there and just started eating up all the things a brain needed. For the brain to go first or last, it was a tough question to face. She was still physically healthy. Everything was in good if not near perfect order, well everything else at least. It was just this damned brain issue that basically took my wife away from me. At least she recognized me most of the time. I was told that eventually she wouldn't. How something could take away life itself, the soul, without removing the body, I didn't know. I had always thought about death as being the destruction of the body and the leaving of the soul, not the other way around. Yet I wasn't God, I didn't know what sick sense of humor he had, and I was sure coming to believe that.

He showed me a picture of them from the computer. "They look much cleaner, maybe not healthier though, they need to eat more, smoke less. I don't know why all these people are smoking so much, don't they know it kills their lungs? Lungs are important."

"They sure are." He stood up and said, "Do you want to do something else?"

"No, mores songs!" I demanded. "I like the songs. I remember them."

"Yes, you do. It's nice to hear you sing." he said, kissing my cheek.

"Well isn't that nice." I said and kissed him back. "You're a good kisser. Always have been." Then I pointed at the computer. "More songs." I touched the screen on a familiar name "Queen."

"There's no way in hell you forgot this one." he said with a laugh. "Remember, you saw them on some television program. Thought they were ridiculous."

Once the music started I said, "Ridiculously good, James. Good... carry on, carry on. Gotta leave you all behind, and leave you to face the truth... goodbye everybody, I've got to go..."

At first Della asked if it was a punishment, but I tried to convince her it wasn't. She had never done anything wrong. Then she started to go all evangelical on me and asked, "Have I ever lied? Have I ever coveted? Ever taken the lord's name in vain? That makes me a liar, a coveter and a blasphemer, that makes... that makes me not sound all that good." She was panicking and pacing around our bedroom. All the sheets were torn off the bed. I told her she was being too hard on herself and she said, "I'm literally losing my mind!" I told her that she was right, that's what was happening, but that didn't mean she did anything wrong and responded with, "No one deserves this happening to them, Della, but it's just... it's just how it is."

"Just how it is? Just how it is? What kind of answer is that?" she spit, throwing the pillow to the ground. I had just ironed all the pillow cases for her, and made the bed perfect... but ok.

"We should really do something else." James said.

"No, please, please," I begged just as the sweet guitar solo took hold.

"You know if your mother heard this music, she'd die."

"Well, she's not going to hear it... where is she anyways? Why hasn't she called?"

"I told you this morning, they are still on their cruise."

"We didn't talk about them this morning." I said, shaking my head.

"They are still on the cruise Della." He looked to the screen and said, "Here's one we both like and we can sing together. We can dance to this one." He took my hands while the guitar kept on going. "Guns n Roses."

He began to sing as loud as he could, and with a pretty nice voice going on, "She's got a smile that seems to me, reminds me of childhood memories. Where everything was fresh as a bright blue sky!" He spun me around and we were both giggling and I started to sing along too. "And if I stared to long I might just break down and cry!" he belted out, kissing my cheek. "She's got eyes of the bluest skies!" He touched my brow and framed my eyes. "I hate to look into those eyes and see an ounce of pain." His voice quieted a bit into seriousness. He always got so serious so quickly.

I admitted that at times I would get weak kneed around Della still. When the life returned to her eyes, when she knew who I was, the stone wall I built to keep myself safe from her tantrums would crumble. Her warm smooth hands caressed mine. If I closed my eyes, I could pretend everything was fine. I could ignore the locks on every door in this house, the plastic covers on door knobs and plugs, the soft corners added to the walls and countertops... I had to baby-proof a house for my wife. This was the first child I had ever taken care of. I nicknamed the demon, a five year old rage monster 'Gyda', which if we were able to have a child, it would have been named Gyda. I did this to keep myself calm. My only saving grace was a dwindling sense of humor, and her music. Her music was her only saving grace, the only thing she could truly remember without fail. It lodged itself in her brain better than I had after all these years. I could be jealous of it. Sometimes it said things better than me. "Through the sleepless nights, through every endless day I'd wanna hear you say, I remember you." That was my hope. My goal, each day, for her to recognize me at least once even though I knew one day it wouldn't happen at all. That distant, confused, blank stare would look past me and that'd be that, she'd be gone.

The glimpses were all I had.

"Do you want any food?" James asked.

"I want to listen to my songs" I said.

"Let me make a play list."

"A what who?" I asked.

He sighed and said, "Like a fifteen track."

"On that thing? How do you do that on that thing?" I poked it and something moved. I jumped back. "Is it magic or something?

"It's not magic, it's just how they make things these days." he said. He began poking around on the screen.

"That's absurd. Why can't you use a clicker?"

"They don't make clickers for these, Della."

"No need to get snippy." I said.

"Just let the songs play. Don't touch the screen. It might mess something up." he said. Then he walked off.

"Here I go again on my own! Cause that's the only road I have known.... Hangin' on the promises of songs of yesterday. Though I keep searching for an answer. I never seem to find what I'm looking for."

As the day dragged on, her obsession with the music grew. I was exhausted. After dinner, I told Della, "Watch your program, I'm going to shower." She didn't acknowledge my presence. She was too amazed at the library of songs available to her.

Relieved I left her in the living room, lights on, doors locked, fed, watered, and otherwise content. I hadn't showered in days. There wasn't enough courage to leave her alone that long enough, even at night.

With some time to myself, I breathed in the hot steam, holding onto the matted silver bar to keep myself sturdy. Age hadn't been kind to me either, I just didn't have the time to notice it or deal with it. I washed with my Dial soap, aware that if I didn't smell like she expected me to smell, it'd be harder to get her to recognize me. Dial Gold.

I heard a chirping from the window, and turned to see the bird. It was blue, happily going about its day. I stood up to go say hi to it. It flicked its tail and jumped to the tree. The door was locked, so I unlocked it and stepped outside, quietly closing *the door behind me in case James had fallen asleep.*

The bird kept singing to me. Though it's been a while now, I can still feel so much pain. Just like every night has its dawn... every rose has its thorn. It knew my songs.

Sixty years of using the same bar of soap, no hope of changing now. I tried that. There was a box of the 'mountain fresh' scent bar soap, but the results were surprisingly disastrous. For two days she fought against me like I was an intruder. Going back to the gold bar seemed to fix things.

"Do you know this one?" I began. "Carry on my wayward son, there'll be peace when you are done, lay your weary head to rest."

Don't you cry no more. Once I rose above the noise and confusion, just to get a glimpse behind this illusion.

The bird flew from its roost on an empty birdbath to the road. That birdbath needed water put in it. A bird might want to clean itself off. The bird called to me again. It was hovering above someone. I didn't see who it was just yet since it was getting dark outside, but the streetlights hadn't flipped on yet.

Feels like I'm knock, knock, knocking on heaven's door, yeah, yeah, yeah, yeah, yeah, feels like I'm knocking on heaven's door.

"You know Guns n Roses?" I called to the bird. It only chirped back to me. The person standing in the road was getting clearer. "You really shouldn't be in the road!" I called.

Times have changed and times are strange, here I come.

When I stepped out of the shower, the music was still playing softly in the background, Michael Jackson's 'Scream'. I listened for a second to the pained yelling. At least it wasn't Della's. After a quick brush of the teeth and getting my warm flannel back on I stepped out. "Della, do you want any hot chocolate?" I asked. There was no reply. "Della?"

Panicked I ran to the living room and Della wasn't there. She had left the playlist going. The front door wasn't opened but unlocked. It had been a week since she could last comprehend how to

turn the lock, much less pay attention long enough to do so. I pulled my slippers on and went outside with a flashlight I had near the front door in case this very thing happened. Night mares had been plaguing me about this... I was about to install alarms on every door in case she wandered around at night, forgetting where she was.

"Mama?" I said, trying to approach her. "When'd you get back from your vacation. You were gone so long. You should have called." She just kept walking like she didn't hear me. "Mama, it's me, Della! Mama!"

I've seen your face a thousand times every day we've been apart. And I don't care about the sunshine 'cause Mama I'm coming home. I can't stand to say goodbye; Mama I'm coming home."

Finally, she stopped walking, but as she did so it started to rain. I pulled my shawl tighter and tried to get closer. "Mama! Wait for me! We should get you inside!"

She said, "For I must be traveling on now. 'Cause there are too many places I've got to see."

"Even you know Free Bird. James would love to hear that. We can listen to music back at the house."

She started walking again. She usually was difficult to talk to at night. She was stubborn.

"Della? Della, where are you? It's James!" I called. She would follow the lights... she wouldn't wander around in pitch blackness, she knows better. I turned right and followed the street lights, looking for her small frame hobbling around barefooted.

"Della!" I screeched desperately, the heat beating through me viciously. I can't do this... I can't do this... she needs more than me. I'm not enough. "Della!"

"It's raining. Mama, you know Guns n Roses? Do you?" she didn't answer.

"Cause nothing lasts forever, and it's hard to hold a candle, in the cold November rain... and no one really knows who's letting go today. And when the fear subsides... we can still find a way."

"Over here!" A voice called, it wasn't my wife's, but it was a woman's voice.

"I'm coming!" I called back, trying to quicken my pace. Despite the adrenaline, I was losing my breath.

Della stood in the middle of the street, babbling, staring ahead, groping the air. A woman was holding her in place, trying to keep her calm with a soothing voice. The woman was older, like us, a small, scared dog huddled behind her.

"I apologize." I said. "Della, look at me, you're safe, you're safe." I embraced her tightly, feeling her tense body claw onto me.

About the Author:

Nina Wilson is a locally published author and photographer who recently received her BA in History and Writing. She has been previously published in "The Pearl", "Coe Review" "The Fishfood Magazine" and for Camp Fire Heart of Iowa. In the realm of poetry she is mainly interested in writing found or cento poetry because of the ability to piece together lines and phrases from other works to make something new. In fiction, she is deeply interested with exploring illness and how it effects individuals and their families.

THE LATIN SUB, IMPURE THOUGHTS, AND ONE MAN'S DEFINITION OF MORTAL SIN

By Steven McBrearty

There was a sub that day in freshman Latin class at St. Aloysius High in suburban San Antonio, Texas, so all hell had broken loose. Spitballs were flying, there were arm wrestling matches on desks, a trash can basketball game had broken out in a corner. Desks were rearranged for impromptu conference groups. The sub was a painfully-thin, prematurely-balding man who lose control of the class immediately. His protruding Adam's Apple bobbed up and down spasmodically. The underarms of his starched white discount store dress shirt were soaked in perspiration, his shiny black polyester slacks were hiked up high over white sports socks and brown tasseled loafers. His name was Mr. Waldo, the name itself the inspiration for put-downs and derision. I felt sorry for Mr. Waldo. I pitied him. I identified with him. He was somebody who was never going to command respect or command an audience. He had a wife and young child, he had told us, and I felt sorry for them, too. You could only hope they would be blinded to what a dufus their husband and father was.

I sat rigidly at my desk, letting my thoughts wander. It was all I could do. It was like a Zen exercise, walling myself off from the chaos surrounding me. I didn't like chaos. I didn't want disorder. Maybe there was something wrong with the adolescent me, but I didn't want to spend the day feeling as though I had accomplished nothing. Time was limited, after all. Life was short. Besides, disorder provided ample opportunities for my classmates to zero in on criticism of my personality, my character, my fragile ego, my looks. .

Classmates swarmed around me as in the climactic scene from Little Big Men, but I remained stationed at my desk, pretending to be absorbed in the fascinating world of Latin parts of speech.

St. Al's was an all-boy's Catholic high school located in Castle Hills, a ritzy new suburb outside the "Loop" in far north San Antonio, a zip code laden heavily with doctors and lawyers and split-level ranch styles with three- and four-car garages, small houses themselves. (My dad being an accountant, we lived seven or eight miles away in a less glamorous subdivision, with only one level and a two-car garage, driving in each morning through a hectic freeway rush hour). The school was a brand spanking new facility, designed in a clean-line, cheerful 1960s contemporary style, a sort of space program/Southern California amalgam motif, with a glassed-in entrance and dark reflective windows all around like some cool character wearing sunglasses. A slender, representational, unmanned cross adorned the entranceway, high up. Two-story ceilings on the inner corridor and a glass wall around the library provided an airy, hi-tech feel, almost as if the library were a command center for NASA, with students and librarians striding around inside like programmers and scientists working to keep the mission on course. Classroom walls were painted vibrant, life-affirming colors. The desks were table arms, with space beneath for storage. The school was staffed by Christian Brothers—they're the ones who make the wine—with lay teachers filling in the gaps. There was a companion girl's school, St. Agatha's Academy, but it was separated by a half-mile of uphill no-man's land, wooded hills and jutting rocks and cactus. At the end of the school day, students from St. Al's trekked through this thicket to visit St. Agatha's girls on the other side. It was like a journey to Valhalla. Unfortunately, I had been unable to go there recently, due to football practice.

Mr. Waldo stood facing the white, dry-erase writing board, conjugating Latin verbs in a low monotone and with a printed scrawl. One large spitball, then another, hit the board beside him. Then a volley of spitballs came, with one striking him on the back of the head. He whirled, marker in hand, face contorted in anger and surprise.

"Who threw that?" Mr. Waldo demanded. Nobody came forward. He stood there, pinching the marker hard between two fingers of his right hand.

"Fire!" somebody yelled. A paper fire had erupted in a trash bucket in the back corner of the room.

"For heaven's sake," Mr. Waldo said, his head shake a sad, sarcastic commentary on our pampered pedigree. "What kind of families do you kids have?"

"Get some water!" somebody said.

"Use your shoe!" somebody said.

"Use your Latin book!" a third person said.

"Fire! Fire! Fire!" It was like a football chant.

It was at this precise moment that the school principal, Brother Ramsey, entered the classroom—or, rather, materialized in the back doorway of the classroom, like Banquo's ghost. Brother Ramsey was a simian-like man, a man we compared to Neanderthal Man, with a prognathous jaw and long, dangling arms and an intimidating, perpetual five o'clock shadow. He was feared by all, students and faculty alike, for his pugnacious style, his combative approach to the most neutral of interactions. He entered unobtrusively, unannounced, standing silent in the doorway. He stood unnoticed for a long while, the madness inside continuing. Smoke from the now-extinguished trash can fire (somebody had actually used his shoe) drifted around the room, pushed by currents from ceiling-mounted air conditioner vents. Mr. Waldo tried shouting to restore order. Order was not restored. But as eyes turned and word about Brother Ramsey got around, the classroom turned eerily, unnaturally quiet. It was like the silencing of a crowd at a play when the opening curtain rises. Somebody coughed. Somebody sneezed. Students scurried back to their desks or stood frozen in place, like figures in wax. Brother Ramsey stood with a commanding posture, grinning diabolically. There was going to be mayhem. There was going to be bloodshed.

"So it seems that the children play while the elves are away," Brother Ramsey said, in his precise, guttural monotone. Never had that little nursery rhyme seemed so ominous.

Then he moved in, preternaturally quick, picking up one of my classmates by the shoulders and depositing him in an empty desk. He grabbed another classmate by the ear, dragging him to a desk. Everyone who wasn't in a desk went there immediately, as in a deadly serious game of musical chairs. Brother Ramsey's eyes roamed the room, searching for miscreants. His eyes were like destruction rays focusing on victims. For the remainder of the class period, he sat scrunched-up in a too-small classroom chair, like an elephant in a bubble bath, long arms dangling. Mr. Waldo's Latin conjugations were received now by a chorus of eager, responsive students, waving their hands energetically for attention. There was never such an alert, attentive Latin class in the history of humankind. As the buzzer ending the class period sounded, everyone filed out in a somber, submissive tone, as in a religious ritual. You could almost smell incense in the air.

Fortunately for us, Brother Ramsey was an anomaly at our school, a throwback to a dying era of hard-ass, Baltimore catechism, sin-and-confess Catholicism. We were changing along with the times, with Vatican II, with the counter-culture movement, with new technologies and TV and transportation advances. We were about as peace and love now as the hippies, as communal as an Israeli kibbutz. Imbued with the enlightened tenor of the times, most of the teaching brothers were sensitive, forward-thinking, progressive-minded men, earnest in their desire to impart a sense of genuine Christian love to their young charges.

Brother Xavier was the freshman religion teacher

at the school. I've never forgotten his first class that September, my very first day as a high school student. Brother Xavier was a handsome, broad-shouldered man, probably in his mid-30s, with tight golden curls on his head and bulging biceps, an athlete in his own schoolboy days, he had suggested modestly, as a point of orientation. He wore his plain brown cassock casually, jauntily, even roguishly if that were possible, his knees pushing through as if to establish that he could have been a first-rate lady's man if he hadn't dedicated his life to serving God.

As we settled into our desks that first day, Brother Xavier played a popular folk rock song on a portable turntable stationed on his teacher's desk: "A World of Our Own," by The Seekers. The refrain reads as follows:

We'll build a world of our own that no one else can share
All our sorrows we'll leave far behind us there
And I know you will find there'll be peace of mind
When we live in a world of our own

After the song had played several times, Brother Xavier camped down on his desk, right leg swinging. Throwing the room open for discussion, he requested opinions on the song's message, did we think this was the ideal, what we should all strive for? Romantics all, everybody emphatically said yes, we wanted to find somebody to love and to be with that person exclusively—in effect, to build a world of our own. Brother Xavier's leg stopped swinging. He placed his hands beside him on the desk top. No, he said, God doesn't want us to wall ourselves off from the world. He wants us to strive to make the world a better place for others, not just seek selfish pleasure for ourselves. It was a punch to the jaw, a profound, sobering revelation that I took to heart.

This day—the day of the Latin sub—one of the students asked Brother Xavier for a definition of mortal sin. A mortal sin was one that condemned the perpetuator to an eternity in hell if not repented (properly) and forgiven. Mortal sins ran the gamut from murder and grand theft to impure thoughts, with impure thoughts seeming to loom large in the sin hierarchy. (That's what the nuns taught us, anyway.) Considering adolescent boys were assailed constantly by impure thoughts, we lived in constant fear of going to hell. Brother Xavier fingered the oversized black rosary sashed around his waist like a belt. He seemed to consider his words carefully before responding.

"Mortal sin?" he said. "I wouldn't worry so much about impure thoughts and sexual desires. I'll tell you what's a mortal sin. I was riding the street car down Canal Street in New Orleans one afternoon. The street car stopped by a group of black kids playing penny-pitch in the gutter. Some old white guy leaned out the window and spit, and said, 'Niggers!' That's a mortal sin."

I understood. I felt liberated. A thrill of comprehension ran up my spine. I felt alive in a different way, an upbeat, optimistic, newly-cognizant way. Destroying somebody, destroying somebody's spirit was a mortal sin, not some random, fleeting, natural brain wave of desire. I left class walking on air. I wasn't going to hell, after all.

Buoyed by my free pass, my new lease on life, I decided to make the trek up the hill to St. Agatha's when the school day ended. Normally, I was unable to because of football practice, but with a flare-up of an asthmatic condition (and a small bit of play acting), I had a doctor's excuse to skip that day. My mother couldn't pick me up until 4:30, so I had some free time on my hands. I had told her I would be studying. The thought of heading up the hill to St. Agatha's filled me suddenly with optimism and hope. The path to St. Agatha's represented hope itself, the rank, ribald possibility of love and acceptance—and maybe more. I hadn't been up there since the first days of school back in early September. And after Brother Xavier's religion class, I felt that I was doing the Lord's work; I was doing this to save my soul.

As I crossed over railroad tracks before entering the woods I stood briefly watching the football team toiling away on the practice fields in the distance below. I could hear the coaches shouting, the piercing bleat of their whistles, the grunts of the players and the thud of their pads as they hit each other or the blocking sleds. I could see the players flop onto the ground and roll around while the coaches preened over them in their tight white shorts and cleated shoes. Watching them from this vantage point football seemed meaningless. I had joined the team because I enjoyed playing sports, but also because I thought it would make me a heroic figure, a popular big man on campus. But I discovered quickly that there were others who were stronger and faster than me, who cared more than me, who seemed to relish the hustle and the horseplay of the locker room. I hated the locker room hijinks. I disbelieved the claims of character-building, that treating players like a piece of wet dog crap somehow created strong-willed, upstanding individuals. I thought it created a distrust for all authority, a breeding ground for rebellion.

After a fifteen-minute hike I surfaced onto the St. Agatha's campus, high atop a plateau overlooking a broad swath of northside San Antonio. You could see cars moving along Loop 410—from this vantage point they appeared to plug along at a slow and stately speed—and the newly-constructed spate of office buildings lining the roadway.

The school itself was a throwback to an earlier Catholic school style, with a statue of St. Agatha, Martyr, on a pedestal out front and florid paintings of our Holy Father and Jesus and the Apostles on the inside halls. It was a different world here, a feminine world animated by nuns and permeated by the delightful (if unsettling) sights and sounds of adolescent females. (The unsettling part was the reason why our two schools were segregated by sex.) The girls wore plaid uniform skirts and starched white blouses, unintentionally sexy. After school, those blouses became untucked, hanging loose. The top buttons were unfastened. The nuns here were a different breed from the ones who taught me in high school, a bit looser, a bit more hip. Their habits were less confining, almost like regular clothes. Their wimple was really just a scarf, allowing wisps of hair to be revealed, humanizing them. Even the calves of their legs showed, and their shoes were ordinary tennis shoes, not orthodontic-looking clodhoppers. They stood sleeves rolled up, hands on hips, feet spread, surveying their charges in a relaxed and self-assured manner. They had a sense of humor. They had a

sense of irony. Some nuns seemed to have developed a kind of level-headed woman-to-woman relationship with their students, a bluff and bantering back-and-forth with an implied understanding of hormones and adolescent mood swings. And though they were protective of their girls, they accepted us St. Al's guys gate-crashing here as a natural, normal course of events. If they learned your name, they called you "Mister Kevin" or "Mister Steve" or whatever, in a tone that made you feel honored somehow, valued. There was even one young, pretty-ish nun, Sister Rita, for whom I harbored a romantic fantasy, that she would throw off her habit and renounce her vows and run away with me. She would have to drive, of course.

"Nice day," I told Sister Rita, observationally. Very adult-like, very mature.

"Nice say," Sister Rita responded. Smart, snappy conversation!

St. Agatha's was hopping that day, swarming with St. Al's students, angled afternoon sunshine interspersed with the long, soft shadows of autumn. It was a fall festive atmosphere, almost, a zone of laughter and merriment and bonhomie. The girls in their white blouses, St. Al's guys in our own uniforms of white pullover shirts and black slacks. This was where I belonged, I thought. This was how I could please God, save my soul. To hell with football practice. I quit the football team in my mind, right then and there.

After finishing my chat with Sister Rita—I thought there were subtle signs of a future rendezvous there—I took off in pursuit of love, joy, hedonistic pleasures. Or a smile, at least, from a pretty girl. I wandered into a crowd of guys teasing some girls. They laughed in tittered in response to schoolboy jibes, but they were holding their own, firing back jokes and risqué banter. I tried to think of something smart and clever to say, some way to pitch in, but my brain had gone into shutdown mode. I couldn't think of a single thing. I moved onto another group, standing on the fringe, hoping that a different vibe would give me some kind of entre there. It didn't happen. I felt shut out.

Several failed forays later, I was beginning to feel like an imposter there. I blundered from group to group, hoping to make an impact. But it was as if I didn't know the code. I had been away too long. I seemed invisible. I hadn't paid club dues. I hovered on the edge of groups of guys talking and bantering with girls, confident and cocky. I wished I could be confident and cocky. I began to wonder if I was even quite human. People walked by me, oblivious. I said things nobody responded to. Girls avoided eye contact. Even Sister Rita seemed indifferent to my plight, turning her head cruelly when I stopped by for an encouraging remark.

Depressed, defeated, I tried to rationalize my situation as just bad luck. The wrong crowd there today. In a different crowd, I would be a star. But I wasn't sure who I expected the right crowd to be. I turned back to the woods for a long, solitary hike back to the St. Al's parking lot, where my mother would pick me up. There was nobody to say goodbye to. Nobody who cared. My spirits were crushed. I felt like some sad animal, slinking back to its solitary den.

Then I heard my name called: "Kevin. Hey." I turned to see a girl I had met last summer, Denise Biancardi. She was standing apart from the other girls, smiling, fingering her crucifix. Her top button was unbuttoned. Her shirttail was untucked. It was as if the afternoon sun were a spotlight shining on her, illuminating her, making her special. A thrill of expectation shot up my spine.

"Remember me?" she said.

"Denise!" I said. "Hi! What's going on?"

We had met once back in mid-summer at a barbecue mixer for incoming St. Al's and St. Agatha students, outside on the infield of the St. Al's baseball field. Wearing aprons over their cassocks, and wielding spatulas, the Christian Brothers barbecued hamburgers while St. Agatha's nuns circulated about in chaperon style. It was a vastly different vibe from my grade school experience, a promise that life going forward could be something more than simply following rules and confession and five Hail Mary's afterwards. Sizzling hamburgers and barbecue smoke afforded a festive air. At some point, Denise and I bumped into each other in an open area near the first base line and started talking, mainly as two people who weren't talking to anybody else. Her hair was straight and very dark brunette, almost black. Her eyes were dark, too, laughing but impenetrable. I remember thinking she was pretty, in a wholesome but savvy and smart-girl kind of way. And there seemed to be a cast of kindness in those dark eyes, some safety there, a guarantee of non-judgment, unlike some of the other girls I had known who seemed to thrive on biting, injurious remarks. We were shy together at first, but warmed up quickly, relating stories about our parents and families and dogs. She told me that her father owned an Italian restaurant on Broadway, one of the main strips into downtown, and that her entire family worked there, five kids and uncles and aunts included. It made me admire her even more, that she was a working girl. I could see that in her—or thought I could, anyway. I told her that my father was an accountant and a cheapskate, so cheap that we had only one telephone, centrally located so that everybody in the house could eavesdrop on you talking. She was the oldest child in the family. I was, too. She liked to play tennis. I did, too! "Let's play sometime," she said. "That sounds like fun!" I said. It sounded like a romantic adventure, just me and her out on a court together. As afternoon morphed into night, the semi-darkness and the surrounding cacophony of voices seemed to create a kind of shroud of intimacy around us. We could do and say things we had never said or done before. Sitting on the grass, half-eaten hamburgers on paper plates beside us, we touched each other off and on, experimentally, on the arm, the shoulder, the face, the foot. It was as if a kind of spell had come over us, a witching hour where anything goes. As darkness descended, we entered a skit contest with the subject matter: "Students Entering High School." Our entry was received with laughter and applause. But in the confusion afterwards, she slipped away and I never got a chance to get her number or tell her goodbye. I hadn't seen her again until this day.

"How are you doing?" she said now.

"OK," I said. "How about you?"

"I'm doing OK," she said. "I haven't seen you up here before."

"I always have football practice," I said. I shrugged. "I'm kind of sick today so I couldn't go."

"I hope not too sick," she said.

"No," I said. "It's just some allergies or something that I always get. Sometimes I get asthma. The doctor said I shouldn't run today."

"Well, glad you're here, then," she said.

"I'm glad I'm here," I said. I stood still, facing her, feet planted. I wasn't going anywhere now. She fingered the crucifix around her neck. We seemed to be treading on new ground here, a paradigm for a different kind of relationship.

"I had fun talking to you at that mixer last summer," she said.

"You did? I had fun, too."

"I thought our skit was pretty good. I thought it was the best one, really."

"I thought so, too!"

We had edged closer to each other, facing each other tentatively, uncertainly. She held her hair behind her head with one hand. I stood staring into her eyes, eyes that seemed to confirm my own feelings, feelings of longing and affection. Desire rose up in me like an unstoppable force. For just this little while, everything seemed right. Neither of us was moving. Neither of us wanted to move. Neither of us seemed uncomfortable. It was a sweet, unexpected feeling, not being uncomfortable with somebody. I was uncomfortable with everybody.

Without really thinking then, I lunged forward, aiming for something I had heretofore only dreamed about—a kiss on the lips with a girl. She came forward to meet me. Our lips puckered and touched. I pulled back, then went in for a more comprehensive follow-up kiss. It put a charge in me. It was like a jolt of electricity, a surge of emotion, maybe a foretaste of heaven itself. It was something I felt through my entire body, in my chest and my lungs and my heart. I felt alive in a way I had never known before. We moved back, staring at each other, staring in wonderment and delight. We lingered briefly, wanting more—at least I wanted more—but fearing that a nun would intervene and then we would be put through an interrogation that would no doubt rival those at the height of the Spanish Inquisition.

Then I saw the watch on her arm. I returned to reality.

"What time is it?" I said.

"It's 4:30," she said.

"Oh, crap," I said. "My mom's picking me up back at the St. Al's parking lot. I better go."

"You better go," she said.

I grasped her fingertips briefly before tearing out for the woods. We had made no plans for the future, no proposal for another meeting, nothing. It didn't really matter. I didn't need anything else just the. I was totally happy. My life was pretty much complete. I scrambled through the trees and brush downhill to the St. Al's campus in a state of near-ecstasy, senses alive to a new dimension, a new world, a world where I was actually a respected and respectable human being. As I emerged, crossing back over the railroad tracks, I saw our car, our white Pontiac Bonneville station wagon, 400 cubic inches of unbridled 1960s-era horsepower, parked in the side lot by the gym. I saw my mother in the driver's seat, waiting. Her window was rolled down part way. Like everybody back then, she was smoking, exhaling out the open window. She was a typical mother of the times, I suppose, hair cut rather short on the sides and back and permed into an impenetrable hive glued together by industrial strength hair spray. She was over-reactive and over-protective, perpetually worried, a bit of a nut. I considered her as a kind of amateur Erma Bombeck, firing off one-liners on issues of topical importance. I don't think she really had much of a life outside our house. I don't know what kind of a life of the mind she had. It all seemed fine to me. I was too young to question her life-style. I had no idea what adults went through. I guess I thought they had most problems solved.

I slowed down when I was within view, combing my hair, tucking in my shirt, wiping perspiration from my face with a handkerchief from my pocket. I entered through the passenger-side door of the car without greeting my mother. She craned her head around to see me. She held her cigarette loosely, precariously, with a long ash, at an angle that threatened to ignite the interior car fabric. Her face had taken on a concerned and suspicious appearance that made me raise my hackles against any release of data. It was like she was peering into my soul and finding everything bad and nefarious there.

"There you are!" she said. "Where have you been?"

"I just took a short walk," I said. "Coach thought it would be good."

"You're not supposed to be running."

"I wasn't running. It was just a walk."

"You're bleeding," she said.

I glanced down at my arm. Blood was trickling down from a scratch on my wrist where I must have caught it on a thorn or bush. I hadn't noticed in my ecstatic state. I pushed down on it with my fingers.

"I brushed against something," I said.

"You'll need to clean it up."

"I will," I said. "I'll clean it up." I frowned, as if to display concern for my own carelessness and slipshod approach to my health.

"Well, how are you?" she said. "How did it go today."

"Fine," I said. "OK. There was a sub in Latin class."

"How was that?" she said.

I shrugged.

"OK," I said. "I don't like it when there's a sub." She nodded, but in a way that seemed design to ferret out additional information. I didn't want to give her any.

"I never did, either," she said. "Is that it?"

"That's about it," I said.

Nodding not too certainly, she started the car and began to back out slowly. With a car that size, and my mother at the controls, the backing out procedure seemed to require immense quantities of time and concentration. I slumped back in the back seat, separating myself from her, scanning the freewayscape as it flew by. My life was good now. I was ready to go out into the world and save souls.

About the Author:

Steven McBrearty has published more than 35 short stories, humor pieces, and non-fiction articles and has received several honors. His story collection, "Christmas Day on a City Bus," was published in 2011 by McKinney Press. Most recently, "Christmas Eve" was published in the April 2016 edition of 34th Parallel literary journal and "Pray Hard, Kick Ass Hard" was published in the April 2016 edition of the Paragon Review. "East of Paris, West of Berlin" is listed in the "Editor's Selections—Best of Potpourri" on the web pages of the magazine. "The Sacker," which appeared in Short Story Writer's Showcase, was selected by a high school student for a statewide Texas University Scholastic League reading contest entry. "Skipper and Kevin Visit Barbie's Pad" was selected as a finalist in an Austin Chronicle short story contest, and published. "Turning Blue" was published in the May 2007 edition of Chick Lit Review. "*62" was published in the January/February 2008 edition of Chick Lit Review. "Kingston: The Lizard, The Man," was accepted for publication and recording by Stories That Lift. "The Shorthorn No. 3" was published in Flatman Crooked magazine. "Christmas Day on a City Bus" and "A Situation Comedy" appeared in Disappearing City literary magazine. "Christmas Day on a City Bus" was honored as "Featured Prose" in the January 1, 2009 issue of Disappearing City. "Thanksgiving for Sex" was published in the April quarterly edition of Freight Train magazine. "Jane Fountain" received an Honorable Mention in the Coq and Bull literary magazine contest and published in the June 2009 edition of the magazine. "Night of Hope" was published in the inaugural issue of Concisely magazine. "Roadside Restroom" received a Finalist/Honorable Mention in the April 2009 Glimmer Train Family Matters contest; "Roadside Restroom" was also published in the May 2011 edition of Straylight literary magazine.

BIG MAMA'S PORCH
Mattie Ward

Big Mama (Lula) and Big Poppa (James) were the matriarch and patriarch of the Wright Family which included seven daughters, six sons and thirty grandchildren. They were born, raised, worked the fields and married at an early age on the Smith's Plantation in Tunica, MS. After the death of their parents, they moved twenty-five miles from Smith's Plantation to Robinsonville, MS; and this is where they started their family. The house was a four room shanty shack with splinter floors, kerosene lamps, woodstove, an outdoor pump and an outhouse.

But the front porch of the house is where I learned the fundamentals of life and survival. This house emitted love, happiness and a sense of well being to all who had the privilege of being there.

Big Mama's first ten grandchildren were all born in her home or two houses down the road. My name is Ana Bell, and my mother Georgia Mae was the middle child born to Big Mama and Big Poppa. Big Mama got up at 6:00 every morning to make breakfast for the adults who dropped their children off each day for her to care for, before going to work. Once breakfast was served and things calmed down, Big Mama would load us in her wagon and pulled us to her garden. While there, she picked the vegetables to be cooked and eaten at dinner.

Although we had a frugal life, never in my wildest dreams would I have thought we were poor. We were never hungry because Big Poppa raised all kinds of livestock, including chickens and cows. He also grew many types of fruit trees and as a supplement to these delicacies; he would go hunting and fishing. In addition the items he grew independently, Big Poppa was also a share cropper.

Not a day went by without a lesson from Big Mama. After working in her garden, she would sit in her rocking chair and while holding whomever happened to be the baby at that time she would sing old spirituals like 'Amazing Grace or Twelve Gates to the City' to all of us who surrounded her in a semi-circle on the porch. Her melodic voice covered us like a security blanket and we would soon all be asleep; perhaps dreaming of angels, and streets paved with gold, which were often the subjects of her songs. When she wasn't rocking and singing, my Big Mama read to us from her Bible, or entertained us with family stories, i.e. how she met Big Poppa when his family moved to the Smith's Plantation. Although we did not realize it at that time, these stories were our way of learning family history.

Sunday mornings were different. On Sunday morning, Big Mama would take all of her grandchildren to church. We were dressed in our best clothes and she wore her favorite blue suit and wide brim hat. Although she was a grandmother, her Hershey smooth skin was flawless. We entered the church like a mother duck and her ducklings, and all eyes were on us. At every Sunday service, the pastor preached a dynamic sermon which had people shouting, jumping and running up and down the aisles.

After the sermon we returned home to devour the dinner that Big Mama had prepared before leaving for church. I can still taste the biscuits, fried chicken, greens and chocolate cake that made our eyes water and filled our bellies.

When I turned five years old my father was transferred to the Navy Military Base in Colts, N.J. and our family moved to Princeton, N. J. On the day of the move, my father called out to me "Ana Bell it's time to go, come and get into the car." I cried out "no, I don't want to go to no old New Jersey!" I wanted to stay with Big Mama: to pick vegetables, help feed the animals, run the rocky roads but most of all I wanted to sit near her on the front porch while she rocked and talked about her family. When my father came to get me, I ran to Big Mama and as he took me in his arms, as I kicked and screamed, "Let me go, Big Mama help me." Those words were the last I remembered prior to crying myself to sleep.

The city had streets but no yards; there were no houses like Big Mama's house only buildings like the one we had moved to - my mother called it an apartment. My parents had enrolled me in school, and I was in the kindergarten. While in Mississippi, my cousins and I spent the day with Big Mama, we made up games to play, even after work and on week-ends. Big Mama's house was filled with family to share love, joy and have fun.

However, while in the city school, I didn't talk or play with the other children because they laughed at the way I talked and at my happy nappy hair. I cried or wetted my pants daily so I could go home but this would upset my mother because she had to leave work in order to pick me up. Here in the city learning to trust strangers proved difficult and soon I knew the meaning of "homesick." I regretted the fact that I could no longer see my grandparents and cousins on a daily basis and felt like a caged bird, but whenever I was told that a trip to Mississippi had been planned, I became a free bird.

I was seven years old when I took my first solo flight to see Big Mama. My aunt and uncle were picking me up from the airport. Once the plane landed, the stewardess had to grab my hand to stop me from taking off like a late freight train. I ran and jumped into Aunt Flora Mae's arms. Uncle John was waiting for us in the car. Thinking like the youngster that I was, I simply assumed we were driving back to New Jersey – but when I saw the "Welcome to Mississippi" Sign, I slid from one

side of the back to seat the other side so many times; Aunt Flora Mae said "Ana Bell be still and sat in one place." When Uncle John turned down the gravel road; I had my hand on the handle; and before the car came to a complete stop I jumped out ran up on the porch and hugged Big Mama.

It was one day during that visit, as we sat on the porch, Big Mama was reading and telling one of her Bible stories, I happened to look up and saw that the bible was upside down. I soon realized that she wasn't reading; she had memorized the entire Bible. I looked up and her face was glowing. It was then that I knew what I had to do. I smiled and asked "Big mama will you help me read the bible?" Knowing that I was the one who would probably be the teacher, I wondered, "how did she memorize the stories of the Bible as they had been read to her over all these years?"

Big Mama smiled and said "yes, Ana Bell," which gave me all the reassurance I needed. It was then that I begin to appreciate the strength and pride women Big Mama's age possessed. I knew that during their youth on the plantations, it was illegal for them to learn to read but, in spite of that, they adapted to the times and memorized those things most important to them - learning and living their life for God!

Life changed for me as I grew older, and my time with Big Mama became limited to summers only. When Big Poppa died six months after my visits, I cried because Big Mama was all alone now and she needed me. I wrote my Cousin James every week to get information about her, until my next visit. Everyone in the family said that Cousin James was special, he was a loner, and he loved working with his hands and with the many animals on the farm. He gave names to all of the animals and he talked to them. My fondest memory was, he didn't eat meat!

One of my most memorable summers with Cousin James, occurred at the age of eleven. I would run and hide behind the trees or the barn to watch his interaction with the animals. Cousin James caught me and called "Ana Bell gets your butt here now! Why are you sneaking like a thief behind me?" My reply was simply, "I wanted to see how you talk to and feed the animals." His reply was "Well why you didn't just ask to come with me?" He went into the barn, and when he came back out, he gave me a pair of gloves, boots, a heavy apron, a basket and a pail. "Follow me and do exactly what I tell you", he said.

In the hen house James called the chickens to him and I collected the eggs. We fed the pigs and finally, he walked into the barn. James took Bess (the cow) out of her stall he placed a stool near her body and a pail under her udder and said "sit Ana Bell, put your head against her body and pull down on one tit at a time." Milk splashed in my eyes the first try; but, I stayed until my pail was full. I was so excited that I jumped up and shouted, "Yea". My shout scared Bess and she kicked the pail of milk over.

Later that evening I watched Kitty deliver five kittens and helped Big Mama care for them. Early the next morning we found Kitty had died. At that moment I decided working with animals was my forte. I decided to become a veterinarian.

As I grew older, it became easier to assimilate the city life. I met new friends and was happy with those who became important in my life. As expected, I also began to do the things that young adults worldwide learn to do, I started working at 16. Although working had its benefits, it also had downfalls – my time in Mississippi now only occurred during the Christmas Holidays. I would lock myself in my room after work and cry. Shedding tears became a familiar experience in my life. But as many youngsters do, I found other aspects of life to make things better. I went to the movies and parties with my new friends.

It was at a party that Lawrence Sullivan glided into my life. He had a voice like Smokey Robinson, he was a look alike of Will Smith and had sway like Denzel Washington! He told jokes and was well-liked. He took my hand and swirled me around before he asked me to dance. When the music stopped he said "I'm Lawrence, what's your name beautiful?" I smiled and said "Ana Bell." He asked for my telephone number and called me the next day that evening we talked for hours. He informed me that his father was a retired Marine, his mother was a home technician and he had three older sisters. After three months of telephone conversations, I invited Lawrence to meet my parents.

My mother cooked fried chicken, collard greens, candied yams, cornbread and German Chocolate cake for dinner. After dinner, Lawrence asked my dad if "he could he court me and my dad asked him what his interests in me were." Lawrence looked my father square in the eyes and said, "I'd like to get to know her better because in my heart I know she'll be my wife." My father simply said "Respect my daughter" and Lawrence and I became a couple.

It was quite different when I went to meet Lawrence's family - his mother and sisters pounced on me like a herd of female tigers. I actually felt like I was the subject of a police interrogation, their questions went "from what do your parents do, where are you from to do you know Lawrence is going to be a doctor?" The questions were fired so fast that I was light-head. Lawrence reentered the room, took one look at me, turned and asked his mother and sisters "what's going on in here?" I stood up and politely said "please, just take me home." His response was "wait Ana; I need to let my family know that you are going to be my wife." His father smiled and said "in time that can be a wise decision, son".

Two weeks before my graduation from high school; Big Mama died. Lawrence and my friends came to my house, helped me packed and listened to my Big Mama stories. The emptiness that I felt after her funeral was replaced with the love from Lawrence which awaited me when I arrived back home. He held my hands and allowed me to cry on his chest.

Soon we were off to different colleges, but we made a pact to wait for each other. It was stressful trying to maintain my 4.3 GPA, working and making time to see Lawrence. Those four years were the longest years for both of us. When we were home we were always eager to see each other. We knew the next four years would be easier, we both had been accepted into the same University.

One particular visit home stands out in my memory, my father was there and I ran and jumped into his arms hugging, kissing and crying tears of joy. My mother came into the living room and joined in on the celebratory crying. Mother really out did herself with dinner. We talked late into the night and it was then that she hit me with the news that my father was very ill.

As a result, I spent most of my time with him, trying to catch up on his activities since he was at home every day, i.e. how was he enjoying retirement?

Lawrence called my father and asked him, mother and me out to dinner with his family. My father agreed to meet them at Don's in Newark, N.J. on Saturday evening at 7:00p.m. My parents and Lawrence's parents hadn't met and I hadn't discussed my terrible experience with them.

I couldn't sleep or eat thinking about my parents meeting them; but Lawrence reassured me that things would be okay. At the end of dinner Lawrence stood up and asked me to come stand next to him, I was puzzled, my father was smiling. Lawrence got down on his knee in the middle of that restaurant and said "Ana Bell, I was hit by Cupid's arrow, the first moment that I saw you, I fell in love. I can't see my life continuing without you, and I hope you feel the same about me."

As he continued, tears flowed down my face, "I love you! Will you marry me?" "Yes, yes" I shouted? Everyone started clapping, my mother hugged me, but Lawrence's mother and sisters jumped up, rushed out of the restaurant and waited outside for his father. Although Lawrence played it off, I could see the disappointment and hurt in his eyes. Lawrence's father gave us his blessing and left.

My parents, Lawrence and I sat down to have desserts and champagne to celebrate. The following Sunday I received a call from Mrs. Sullivan, she informed me that she had had a headache and the pain was unbearable, and she thought it was best for everyone if she left. This was just the beginning of a wedding war! Mrs. Sullivan didn't like the colors that I choose for the wedding party, my wedding dress or where the wedding was taking place. She basically refused to cooperate with my mother.

Although I had not lived in Robinsonville for many years, I could not fathom being married anywhere but in my much-loved beginnings.   Knowing where my heart rested, Lawrence agreed to have our wedding in Mississippi and we all including Lawrence's mother and sisters trekked to Robinsonville for my wedding.

I knew that I would be going back to New Jersey.

But the joy to be backed home for this occasion was awesome. I became a 'married woman' in the place that I loved and cherished most – on my grandparents' porch. The trip back to New Jersey had a different feeling, because I knew that I had received the blessings of both Big Mama and Big Poppa.

Many years have passed since I sat on Big Mama's porch watched her rock and listened to her songs and stories. My respect for Big Mama has tripled and I still wonder how she and the women of her time coped and made it through the storm of life they were given. Although she had physically left, she always remained in my heart. The rocking chair is empty, but my heart was filled with love and admiration for Big Mama. It is often said "Home is where the heart is," my true home was always Robinsonville, MS – sitting on my grandmothers' porch.

When I was two months pregnant with my second child; I sat reminiscing with my four years old daughter and I could not stop crying. I didn't know if it was my hormones or if I was missing my mom, who moved back to Robinsonville, to live with Aunt Flora Mae a year after my father died. Lawrence who specialized in Obstetrics and Gynecology was away at a conference, and I missed him too.

The ache in my heart grew daily. Soon after, Lawrence strolled into the house with a dozen of roses in his hand and he said "Ana Bell can you guess what I have in my pocket for you?" I asked gloomily "movie tickets?"   "No," he said and pulled out airline tickets to Memphis. I began to scream with joy and all I could think was Christmas had came early that year.

As the plane banked and began to land in Memphis, I felt like a little lost child who was finally going home!

The road to Robinsonville was still long and the countryside hadn't changed. The gravel road was paved, and there was a blue fence surrounding the property. A sign dominated the entry, and I asked Lawrence "What is this?" Lawrence didn't mumble a word and continued to drive. As I continued to survey the area, I noticed that the shotgun house had been replaced with a modern ranch style and the sign in front read "Wright's Plantation."

I observed other buildings, a garden, and numerous forms of livestock. As I looked further, the image on the porch resembles "Big Momma" sitting in her rocker. A closer look reveals it's my mother. As I jumped from the car she came to meet me with a smile on her face and pointed to a banner that said: WELCOME HOME ANA BELL. As the tears began to flow, Lawrence took me into his arms and whispered "now you can feel complete, let's go in and see your new house".

Confucius said "Wherever you go, go with your heart." My cycle of life was completed and my dreams came true. I was home doing the things that I love to do and my heart was leading the way.

Mattie Ward is a retired educator. She relocated to Atoka, TN with her dog, Theo several years ago. This is her first published story.

About the Author:

Mattie Ward is a retired educator. She relocated to Atoka, TN with her dog, Theo several years ago. This is her first published story.

MOTORBIKE MAN

Mike Cohen

Bernie Rivkin told his son, Arnold, about Mike Crook, the crippled motorbike man, as they walked back to Arnold's car after a Husky-Cougar football game, the last football game of the fall. Bernie loved the fall football games, loved to join the crowd whooping and hollering when the Huskies rushed out of the horseshoe end of University Stadium. Each fall season Bernie's rubbery, lined face would light up when the newest batch of hard, fast kids dashed to the Husky sidelines in their burnished gold and purple-striped Husky helmets. Arnold had never heard Bernie speak of Mike Crook before this day.

Bernie and Arnold had started watching Husky football games together at University Stadium ten years ago, more or less, after Arnold's mother, Adele, separated from Bernie, late in their lives.

"He's too tight for me," Adele had said. "He is as tight as a tick, and you know it. From now on, I am going to live and spend my money in my way."

The Husky season tickets were in Adele's name because she was a university alum, and she chose to keep the seats. Not wanting his father to unnecessarily lose anything more of great value from the dissolution of the marriage, Arnold had bought two replacements for Adele's two tickets, and thereafter, he and Bernie had sat together at the Husky home games.

When Bernie had serious surgery and had lain recovering, Arnold had bought him a satin, gold Husky-booster jacket trimmed in purple. It was a son's small effort to boost his dad's desire to make it through, to make him think about life

after his operation. Bernie had mended well and had worn the satin jacket to each Husky game ever since.

As he had sat with Bernie each successive year at Husky games and observed his dad wearing that gold satin jacket with purple stripes, Arnold had tried to feel that somehow he and his dad possessed an uncommon bond. Yet, Arnold realized—not without a mixture of sadness and envy—that he served Bernie simply as a convenient surrogate for Adele. Bernie never had buddies. Adele had been his only companion.

Bernie was no spring chicken—ninety years old and pretty much deaf. He and Arnold didn't walk to the football games anymore because Bernie's shrinking thigh and calf muscles, their arteries clotted and clogged, did not work very well.

Bernie still drove, and there was a pay parking lot for the disabled nearby the stadium. However, Bernie chose to drive to Arnold's house before each game. Then they would take Arnold's car to the parking lot for the disabled. That way Arnold would be paying for parking when the game was over.

It was Arnold's practice to drop Bernie off at the disabled pickup point before parking the car. From there, Bernie would get a free ride in a golf cart to the Rivkins' seats. After the game, it was still possible for Bernie to hobble the short distance to the car by leaning on Arnold's arm.

In the past, when Arnold had lived near University Stadium and Bernie's legs worked better, they had walked to and from the Huskies' home games. Arnold remembered those fall Saturdays as mostly sunny. He could recall his father and himself strolling together down Stadium Parkway, with its flower beds bedecked with new yellow and auburn chrysanthemums, strolling together down to the old brick stadium bridge, kicking at drifts of crinkled fallen leaves, and smelling the musty puffs of aromas floating in the air from the summer's last blossoms.

Arnold always bought a couple of crimson Delicious apples near the old brick bridge, right before Bernie and he would fold into the mob of Husky fans dressed in purple and gold. The Delicious apples were fresh from the fall harvest, and vendors sold them out of unpainted wooden crates. Arnold would stop for the apples while Bernie continued to walk alone, moving on past the stacks of apple crates. After paying for the apples, Arnold would catch up with his dad. At halftime the Rivkins would sit there in the stadium and chew away on the crisp red fruit Arnold had bought.

"These are the best I have ever bought. Ever," Bernie always said, juice welling up in the happy wrinkles at the corners of his mouth, clearly forgetting that it was Arnold who had bought them. As hard as he tried, Arnold could never remember a time when Bernie had bought the apples.

There always seemed to be a crowd of politicians in front of University Stadium running for this council or for that judgeship and glad-handing the crowd. Their volunteers gave out free printed game lineups with the candidates' names plastered on both sides. Bernie would always collect a smattering of free lineups, choosing to keep the one with the biggest print, the one that was easiest to read.

"What a bargain," Bernie would say with a leer. "I might even vote for the guy this year who puts out the best-quality job."

At first, years ago, Bernie had taken the Huskies' lineup from the Seattle Times with him to the games, but he had stopped subscribing to any newspaper. Bernie maintained that the Times was too expensive at eight dollars a month.

"I remember when the paper was a nickel a day," he said in defense. "I can get the news on TV."

A few years after Adele had left Bernie, Arnold had asked his dad to pay for his share of the Husky tickets.

"How much are they?" Bernie had asked. Arnold had held out a Xerox copy of the invoice for his father to read.

"They're twenty bucks each," Arnold said, "but the seats are available only if you join the Husky Tyee Club. That adds fifty bucks per game."

Bernie had looked as if he had witnessed a shooting.

"That's over one thousand bucks a season," Bernie had said, shaking his head in disbelief, his hands staying at his side. Bernie's hands were those of a wrestler, which he had been in his youth; his hands were the size of baseball mitts.

"Look at the bill, Dad."

Arnold held out the invoice to Bernie, offering to let him read it. Arnold remembered the old adage that once the consumer gets the bill in his or her hand—big or little—the salesperson can close the sale. Bernie must have heard that one too, because he did not reach for the invoice. His baseball mitts stayed by his sides.

"I had no idea," Bernie had said. "Your mother always took care of them."

"Took care of" was so far away from "paid for" that Arnold had smiled in spite of himself.

"If I have to pay that much, to hell with it," Bernie had said, his face flushing, his lips pouting Mussolini-style. "I'll just read about the Husky games in the sports section." He still had not reached for the invoice.

"Dad, you don't take the paper anymore."

"Then I'll watch game reruns on TV."

"Reruns are on cable. You wouldn't buy cable."

"Then to hell with the Huskies," Bernie had said, his eyes stupid with anger over the money. Arnold imagined that Bernie's outraged face would look the same if at that moment Bernie were the victim of a stickup.

"We have to join the Tyee Club, Dad."

"I'll pay for my ticket," Bernie had conceded, "and that's it."

But Bernie never got around to giving Arnold a check for the tickets.

On the Saturday Bernie had told Arnold about Mike Crook, the motorbike man, they had watched the Huskies manhandle the Cougars. As they returned to Arnold's car in the disabled lot, Arnold was in a hurry to go. He attempted to speed their pace by supporting Bernie's arm while they walked. His father's arm felt curious and thin, Arnold thought; the veined forearm muscles had vanished. This was the same arm that had seemed so huge to Arnold when he was a boy.

Bernie did walk slowly. What was left of his ninety-year-old legs was cramping on him. His right leg was the worst. Bernie dragged it along as if it were a willful pet on a leash trying its best to head off in a different direction.

Bent at the shoulders, Bernie prodded the ground with his cane at each step, looking for cracks in the asphalt, searching for potholes and loose gravel. They were as dangerous to him as land mines. Arnold had successfully persuaded his dad to carry a cane, although Bernie didn't know which of his huge mitts should grasp the handle in order to support his uncooperative right leg. Arnold suspected that his father fell frequently, but Bernie had not been willing to admit it.

Arnold steered his dad around the clumps of college boys and girls who were hooking up for some later events. The roiling sounds of the slowly moving purple and gold crowd did not bother Bernie a bit because he could not hear them. Bernie's hearing aids, recycled older models, were not a matching set. Bernie plugged them into his huge liver-spotted ears, from which wild hairs stuck out like twigs. Arnold had urged Bernie to buy a matching set of hearing aids, but Bernie would not consider it.

"None of them are worth a damn," Bernie had said, "so why should I spend any money on them?"

The letter s was a particularly tricky sound for Bernie. When they were alone, Arnold would have to shout so that Bernie could hear his s's.

After drifting for a block or so, Bernie stopped to rest for a while. "The right leg is worst," he explained, talking about "the leg" as if it were a separate creature.

Parked to the side were fancy motorcycles: Harley, Honda, and Yamaha motorbikes—real eye-catchers with satin black, chartreuse, red, and orange fenders and bodies, and engine parts covered with chrome. Bernie eyed the bikes.

"I always wanted to try one," Bernie said, "but never had the courage to do it. Way before the war, there was a bike shop in Sioux Falls, next door to Rivkin's."

Rivkin's was Grandpa Rivkin's dry-cleaning store in Sioux Falls, South Dakota. Bernie worked there for over a decade after he graduated from college. Then he started his own cleaners in Minnesota when he and Adele married in 1941.

"The bike shop was owned by old man Crook," Bernie said, staring at the parked bikes. "The motorbike repairs were done by his son, Mike. Mike was a real daredevil. He drove one of their motorbikes all over the place. Mike really knew how they were put together. He just loved them."

Bernie stamped his right leg on the ground, as if a few whacks on the earth would make the limb feel better. His nose was running a little; his draining sinuses gave his voice a warbling sound and added a sentimental quality to his story.

"There were bikes like these—not so fancy, of course—parked all around the Crooks' door, leaning on their kickstands. Mike's friends used to hang around there, too, cracking jokes and laughing. Every once in a while, someone would tinker with one of them and then jump on and take off to see how it would go and would tear around the block, swerve back onto the sidewalk, bang down the kickstand, and hop off, leaving the bike there, steaming hot."

Bernie smiled at an inner memory.

"When there was no one around, I used to go out and swing my leg over a bike, plant my butt on the seat, grab the handles, and pretend I was streaking down River Street at top speed, shooting out of Sioux Falls, past the city limits, flying off on the county roads, past all those old farmers on tractors."

Bernie pulled out a handkerchief from his pocket and tooted his ample nose. With his perpetual nasal drip, Bernie needed a lot of handkerchiefs. This handkerchief was one of thousands collected during his years as a dry cleaner. Bernie would find handkerchiefs in the coat and pants pockets of his customers, and then he would dry-clean and press them for his own use. After he retired, Bernie kept a lifetime supply of free handkerchiefs in a giant box in his garage.

Arnold had tried to get his dad to take antihistamines to dry up the drip, but Bernie maintained that the drug was too expensive.

"If I just knock off drinking cold water, it'll stop. I know it," Bernie would say. The nasal drip went on, as did the warble in Bernie's throat.

A Husky fan jumped on a Honda and cranked on the starter pedal. The motor grunted and popped as it wobbled off past the home-going crowd. Bernie watched the Honda with admiration.

"Mike Crook would just climb onto a bike just like that kid did, kick-start the thing, and take off down River Street, not even looking to see if there was any traffic coming at him. He looked so wild to me—wild, a real daredevil. I envied him, I guess. I guess I just envied his nerve."

It was getting dark, and Arnold wanted to get going. He pulled at Bernie's arm.

"Let's try it again."

Bernie shook his head.

"Too soon. It's still resting." His right leg, his old loyal dog, was resting.

"One day," Bernie mused, almost talking to no one, "I heard that Mike Crook was in an accident; his bike got caught between two cars. Must have tried to squeeze between them. Got crushed but good. He barely survived. His legs were shot. Couldn't swing them over a bike."

Bernie was looking back at University Stadium, not at his son. Arnold had never heard this story before.

"Actually, after the accident," Bernie said, "Mike barely walked at all, only with a set of crutches. I could see him scraping down the street past Rivkin's into Crook's shop, past the motorbikes parked outside. He never got better. I never saw him without crutches. Then your mother and I got married, and we moved to Minnesota."

"Can we go now?" Arnold said. He worried that it was too late, that they were certain now to get caught in the traffic jam on Stadium Parkway.

"OK, OK." Bernie laughed, coughed, and banged his foot with his cane. "Maybe it's ready to work now." A pat for his pet leg, and the Rivkins started walking again with Bernie still talking away.

"A long time later, after the war, I was going down Fourth Street in Sioux Falls near your grandma's house, walking to the grocery store to get something. Your grandparents weren't able to do much for themselves anymore; your grandpa was pretty sick by then.

"When I went into the store, I passed a man in a wheelchair outside the entrance. He wasn't going in; he was just sitting there outside the doors in his wheelchair. He was begging, actually, I think. I didn't want to look at him, but it was hard not to. He looked like Mike Crook. I'm pretty sure it was him. Pretty sure."

Bernie wiped his nose with his handkerchief.

"He didn't recognize me, but he asked me if I could spare a quarter. I said no, and then I looked past him and walked into the store. I think I knew it was him, knew it was Mike Crook, all right. But I still wouldn't give any change to him."

Bernie hobbled to a stop and put a puzzled finger on his lip.

"I don't know why I wouldn't give Mike a little change. I think that was one of the most shameful things I have ever done. Just shameful."

Bernie's head bobbed down as he began to drag his right leg—his misbehaving pet—and look for potholes and loose gravel—look for land mines—while he and Arnold walked toward the parking lot.

Out of nowhere, Arnold felt an urge to tell off his dad.

Why don't you pay for your share of the tickets? Arnold wanted to say. Why haven't you paid at least for the apples or for the parking or even bought a game-day newspaper? All of a sudden, after fifty years, when it's safe to bring it up, you pick on yourself for stiffing a cripple. You bring it up fifty years later when there is no way you will have to shell out any dough to Mike Crook. You just want me to think what a nice guy you are, even though you won't pay for a single thing. Nice move, Dad. Real nice move.

But Arnold said nothing; he remained silently in step with Bernie while holding his dad's withered arm as they walked to the car. Bernie pulled open the passenger door and entered his seat, butt first.

When we get to the tollgate, Arnold thought, I'll just pull up, block the road, and sit there. Maybe my dad will get the idea for once, and maybe—despite his unreasonable cheapness—maybe he'll pay. Maybe he'll be a mensch about it for once.

Arnold drove to the parking-lot exit, and the toll-gate attendant stepped up to the driver's window. Bernie's eyes were locked on the floor mat, his arms crossing his chest, a safe distance from his wallet pocket.

The ticket taker smiled and said, "All right now. Was it good today or what? Go Huskies!"

Bernie made no sign that he heard the cheer. His eyes were cast down, his huge hands locked tightly into his lap. Arnold saw that his father was cash-mute, money-blinded, dollar-deafened. The sun could go down and we would sit here. And my father would never lift his eyes off the floorboard.

Arnold took out a ten-dollar bill and asked the toll taker, "How much is it?" Three dollars came back. Bernie just sat, hearing nothing, his eyes now shut, his hands, as huge as baseball mitts, folded in his lap.

With the car brake on, Arnold looked down at his own hands, the hands that clutched the three dollar bills. His hands were his mother's—no doubt about that—small and dimpled. As different from Bernie's baseball mitts as they could be.

The raging heat that Arnold felt toward his dad dissipated with the setting afternoon sun. For the first time, he could see that there were things out there that Bernie, his father, would not buy and could only envy.

As the afternoon shadows surrounded them with darkness, a snort and then a mechanical snarl from a gaggle of motorbikes started up. Arnold saw Bernie look up with a start and then, with unmistakable longing, gape as the bikes passed their car—grunting, puffing, and popping, each with its own unique voice.

The amplified sound of the bikes, like a squad of bumblebees, seemed to fire up Bernie, whose breath and chest rose to a matching rhythm as the bikers accelerated down Stadium Parkway and around the flower beds filled with yellow and auburn chrysanthemums.

Arnold felt the excitement too. He could tell that Bernie was filled with unalloyed admiration for each helmeted rider, a little of Mike Crook in each biker, each unencumbered by fear and incredibly free. Each the person his dad had always wanted to be.

Bernie broke the spell.

"Can you imagine what one of those rigs must cost?" he said, first frowning and then looking relieved as he touched his wallet, reassured that it was tight and safe and unopened in his hip pocket.

Arnold watched it all as he waited for the gate to open, knowing full well that the old man had been talking to himself. Yet he considered answering his dad's question.

Cost a bunch, Dad. One of those bikes would probably bankrupt you.

But Arnold smiled in silence, grinning for the first time that day as father and son sat in their own places with their different hands, one small pair holding change and the other pair, as large as baseball mitts, utterly empty.

About the Author:

Mike Cohen practiced law for over four decades and now specializes in estates, trusts, and related litigation. He attended the Portland State Hay-stack Summer Workshop Conference from 1992-96 and the University of Washington Extension Writing Workshop from 1995-98. He studied with Craig Lesley, Tom Spanbauer, Whitney Otto, and the late Robert Gordon. Mike recently self-published his first novel, Rivertown Heroes. He holds a JD from Georgetown Law and a BA in Zoology from the University of Washington. His short story, "The Cantor's Window" was published in Streetlight Magazine. He lives with his family in the Pacific Northwest.

NERVES

Jon Benham

"Take your time," she said. Her mouth looked so dishonest as it forced itself to create words she clearly didn't mean. Patient? Having patience for one moment does not mean you're patient.

"Okay, I know what I'm doing," I replied. I did. That's what they always told me at least. Every rebellion, thoughtful conversation, lie, breakdown. They told me I knew what I was doing. At the very least, they told me to stop doing that. As if I knew what I was doing in complete honesty.

The questions on the paper were there. Just waiting for me to answer. Why can't she just ask me these questions? That would be easier, wouldn't it? Instead of having twenty-five questions looking for one umbrella answer to the inquiry, "am I good enough for this?" Of course I am. Not. Of course I am something that they are looking for. A baseline. A success. A failure to determine the definition of the other two. Everything I am has a purpose. That's also what they told me. Just not in those words.

"Sorry, I'm just a little nervous," I said as my eyes darted from the paper to her symmetrical face. No, no. Those eyes keep changing sizes. I'm thinking too much.

"That's okay!"

I smiled and went back to the paper. It was begging me to answer. Every question made me analyze myself, and because of that I had to lie.

I am an optimistic person. Strongly agree. Agree. I don't know. Disagree. Strongly disagree.

I'll just say agree. I filled in the bubble. But it didn't look good enough. I colored it in again. It looks better, but still not perfect.

"This isn't the whole interview, right?" I asked and immediately regretted it.

"No, no. You will give me the paper and I'll proceed with the regular interview."

"Oh, okay."

"Do you want the order in reverse?"

Of course.

"No, this is okay."

Why did I sound so rude? I guess I always do, huh? Quick... Look at her and smile. I did. She returned the smile. I'm okay. Unless, of course, she changed her mind and started frowning as my head went down. Stare at the paper. Stare at the paper. Why is she judging me so much?

I answered a few more questions. It took a short time. Maybe too short? No. It's just right. I imagined what her face looked like. Staring at the wall so seriously, with so much intent. An intent to throw me out of the room while knowing she couldn't legally do that. She's also probably too weak. As she stared at the wall she probably thought of what she could say to make me leave. Her thinking that was all I needed.

I started to stop analyzing my answers. I started to give what my first thought was, and that first thought is probably the one I wasn't lying about. There were two questions left.

I am a happy person...

I tend to work harder than my co-workers.

Well, I've never worked a day in my life. So how can I be happy? How can I be fulfilled? I looked up and she was in fact staring at the wall even though she had a computer right in front of her. If this test was to determine the ability to find fun stuff to do on the internet I would annihilate her. I would... Probably crack under the stress and get annihilated.

Why do I struggle?

It's because I always know what to do.

She's writing something down. I'm sure it's nothing.

I answered the two questions and then gave it to her. I handed it in. I'll probably get an F. No, no, I'll get a C minus. They're looking for A's at this job.

She looked down the paper. I prepared for the next part of the interview.

"I'm sorry, you don't seem like the right fit for this job. Going on to the next part of the interview won't be necessary," she said.

"Oh, okay, I'll see myself out."

"Good luck on your job search!" She said like she was actually excited for me. She probably was. She probably thinks I'm meant to have a cool job meant for the joke I am. Nothing could be farther from the truth. Being a joke means people like you even though it's only for their own good. I'm not a good enough joke to actually be able to make other people's lives easier.

I can't even do that right.

I was already outside of the building. I had to call my mom to get me. God, how disappointed will she be? I'll just lie. No big deal.

"Hey, can you come get me now?" I asked

"Yeah, okay."

I walked over to the bench and didn't look where I was sitting and landed right in a puddle of water. It was the only puddle on the bench from the rain storm the previous night. I got up and decided not to sit anywhere else on the bench. Why? Why not? It's a stupid bench.

The parking lot was mostly empty. There were only six cars in it. One of them must have been her car.

Her face wouldn't get out of my mind. It was a look that just wanted you to succeed. That's what it was. I had seen that enough in my life. I truly didn't want that job from the moment I saw her. That's why I didn't really try. She was nice. I hate her for that. Can you really blame me? I'm twenty-one-years old and have never had a job.

The directions I go in may seem obviously wrong, but to me I am obviously right. I can do anything I see as right, is that not a decent standard to live by? It's what everyone else does. Or am I just an idiot?

I looked again at the cars. A light blue car caught my attention because, who drives light blue cars rather than any other kind? Successful people who don't want to look like everyone else, that's who. And if it's a shitty car, you will drive it just trying to not look as novel as you can be. Everything comes down to being you. And everyone is a hypocrite for trying so hard not to look like everyone else.

She seemed that way. She seemed like someone who wanted to be original. She certainly had the money to have a choice in a car. Not like anyone my age, and unfortunately, not like a lot of people older. She has a good job. She surely must have a good life.

I walked over to the car and looked inside. There were magazines on yoga in the backseat. Maybe she was trying to calm herself down when she was looking at the wall. Maybe that's why she got angry when I interrupted. Because you know she did. I really made her angry for messing with her zen.

She likes to think she's important. Like she makes a difference. If she really wants to make a difference, why did she turn away someone who obviously needs help? Yeah, I'm a joke. An unfunny one on top of that. I deserve nothing but courtesy from people who want to help others. Everyone deserves that, I think.

Did I have to cry? Would that make her feel so compelled that she would give in? She wants to make a difference. She hires people to go out and make a difference for her. She hasn't struggled enough to know how to help kids who are going through what they go through. She faked her way to the top so she won't have to worry. Why the hell did she ask me if I was happy? Do they just wait for you to become unhappy after dealing with the job for a while and is that how they manipulate you into thinking that nothing has changed?

Do they put words in your mouth?

I realized my Mom couldn't be that far away. But I couldn't just leave the car like this. I couldn't leave this situation just like this. I'm irrelevant, and in that moment I was sick of it. I'd been looking for a job for two months, they all seemed idiotic. I would quit within two months. I didn't need them and they didn't need me.

God forbid I look for something I can tolerate and get it. I'm an idiot but I can talk to people about their problems. I can get people through anything. No one was there for me, but that wouldn't stop me.

Am I happy?

Would I be in this predicament if I was?

She's looking in the wrong places for someone who is right. She's not a good person. She took the job because it's all she could lie about being good at.

It's kinda easy.

"Oh yeah, I love people and I care about their happiness. All my friends tell me I'm good to talk to."

Sure, I'd be lying even if I said that. But I have no friends. I can be a great one to people who need it. They will reciprocate only with their happiness. At least I think.

She should have talked to me. How many times do I have to lie about happiness before I get anything out of it?

She would leave work and get into this car, drive home. Get her life handed to her. She will go to bed thinking not about me, but about how easy it is lying to people about how much you care.

I was so done.

I took out my house keys and keyed the car on the driver's side. I didn't care if the alarm would go off. She fucking deserves it. I could have written something.

Fuck you.

Hypocrite.

Liar.

Fake.

But I didn't. I wasn't thinking about how to punish. I just knew I had to do something in order to feel better.

I saw my Mom's car coming. I ran away. I didn't even get a chance to look at the damage to the lady's car I caused. I got into my Mom's car and we drove off. I saw another car park right next to the car I keyed, and the alarm went off. Finally. The guy driving looked afraid. So he drove to the other end of the parking lot even though the walk to the building was farther.

"How did it go?" My Mom asked.

"Oh, you know. I think I did well."

"That's good. We have a surprise for you since you if you don't get the job."

"What is it?"

"You'll see."

I doubted what it could be. It couldn't be something that would make people see me differently. Something told me it would be nice, something sweet, something...

"Why can't you just tell me?"

"Alright, Mrs. Sagan wants some yardwork done this summer," she said. "She's gonna give you her old car for it plus forty dollars a day," she said. "Sounds good, huh?"

"I'll think about it."

I never wanted to be one of those kids who only works during the summer. They're the ones with absolutely no future. They're just looking for weed money, aren't they? Unless they're going to college, and they usually are. Well, they're also looking for weed money.

"No, I don't want to," I said.

"You have to do something," she said. "This is a good opportunity."

"But I don't want to subject myself to that."

I put my arm out the opened window and touched the side of the car. I started to scratch it so hard that I forgot I was even scratching it. I wasn't making any marks of course. I'm not that much of an ass-hole.

"You need to do something."

"I know, but not that."

We pulled into my driveway and Mrs. Sagan was walking around in her yard. She looked so content with what she was doing. It was kinda very annoying. I hate people who don't worry about every little thing they should worry about.

"Did your mother tell you about my offer?" Mrs. Sagan asked as I walked out.

"Yeah, I'll think about it."

"No rush," she said.

I walked into my house and then my room. What if I did that? What if I finally got a car and could hang out with people. I have no one to hang out with now, but that will change. I promise that will change.

Am I Happy

Will a car make me change my answer to that? Will subjecting myself to that kind of work change that? Will anything?

Sometimes I feel like I'm doomed, and what is more of a dead-end than that? I looked out my window and got a glimpse of the car she was willing to give me in her garage. It was blue. I guessed that would be perfect for me.

I will only find happiness if I get a car, get successful, and have someone else be the one to scratch my car. I'd be fulfilled.

About the Author:

Jon Benham is a twenty-year-old writer from Connecticut. He focuses heavily on realism and the drama that comes with it. This is his first published story.

Jon Benham is a twenty-year-old writer from Connecticut. He focuses heavily on realism and the drama that comes with it. This is his first published story.

ONE LAST CHANCE
David Macpherson

Edward Richter stood in the heat at the metal scrap yard. Sweat dampened the prominent folds of fat on his chest. He might have sold the gun for a handsome amount. No, much better to remove it forever from human hands. To place the Lugar in a car about to be crushed cost him fifty dollars and a favor from his high school friend, the yard owner. Without emotion, the monstrous iron machine first flattened the vehicle top to bottom then compressed it front to back and side to side. Edward's thoughts drowned out the whine of the hydraulics and shrieks of grinding metal. The yard owner grasped the car's remains in enormous pincers and placed it among a stack of twenty similar lumps of auto corpses. The cube's metal surface showed random recognizable car parts like abstract art. The weapon lay hidden in its metallic grave soon to be melted, the freed molecules scattered into something new, something better.

In the summer of the year before, an old man flanked by his wife and daughter, Edward's first appointments of the day, sat alone in the waiting room near the airport ticketing atrium. Notices on the gray cinder block walls shouted annoying (Cell Phone Use is Prohibited-TURN IT OFF!) or grave (No Guns, Knives or Other Weapons Permitted on Federal Property) warnings. Edward had reviewed the couple's application a few minutes earlier. Nothing worrisome – a 96-year-old Polish immigrant and his wife – perhaps a last visit to the old country. This man might be his

oldest among the clients seeking a global entry card that would allow him to skip the long lines in immigration and customs when he returned to the US.

As Edward walked up the hallway to the waiting room, the old man leaned forward in the chair. He held a wooden cane with both hands in front like the start position for a nonagenarian hundred-yard dash. Neat thin laces secured shined black shoes to his feet. Strands of thin white hair draped over his black coat collar. His wife sat next to him. Her mouth sucked in rhythm like an infant – Edward guessed little went on in her brain. The other woman, younger and heavier in comparison, but still gray, scrolled a cell phone. Edward might chastise her for breaking the posted rule.

To a waiting room empty except for these three, he announced their names, "Zbigniew and Ruth Dudek."

The middle-aged woman raised her hand. "We're here." She rose first and leaned to the old man's right ear. "Come on, Dad." He turned to Edward. Dudek's eyes widened as if he recognized someone he did not want to see.

Strange. Edward did not know this man and sensed no risk – even if Dudek considered harm toward others, age made him impotent.

Without instruction, Dudek followed him into the interview room. The old woman's sucking rhythm accelerated as her daughter escorted her behind the patriarch.

In the interview room, the couple sat in front of

his desk. He allowed no more than two clients in his small office but the daughter held the residual brains. She stood behind them.

He began the usual spiel. "You're here to be interviewed for a global entry card, correct?"

The old man said nothing. He leaned forward and rolled up his sleeve to his forearm. Edward recognized the six-digit tattoo of a Holocaust survivor.

The daughter leaned over her mother and pushed her father's sleeve down. "He doesn't need to see that, Dad." She handed Edward her parents' passports. "I'm their daughter, Mary Olson. I applied for them online."

Edward sensed Dudek's hostile eyes. He had dealt with angry customers after he rejected the application, not before. Dudek's wife made random wet popping noises.

Edward's non-traditional interview style led to two types of responses, hate and delight--never indifference. Once every few months, his supervisors, an ever-changing group of bureaucrats, offered feedback from angry customers. "He told me crazy stories." "How could you hire a nut to do security checks?" "He talked so much while he entered my data, I'm sure he made mistakes." Edward didn't quibble with the first two comments-both accurate to a point. But, he never made data entry mistakes. His ability to talk on one subject and type on another took years to perfect. In security, he had to judge to perfection. One miss out of the thousands he interviewed would result in a catastrophic public failure.

Fluent in three languages, Italian, German, and English, he let the German inflections loose at work. His accent put some off. "Why is a foreigner working in US security?" He could hide his Deutsch roots if he chose but the language's rhythm and force reminded him of his father.

During interviews he hinted at his agnosticism. "Who knows what our purpose is? Maybe God, if She exists?" The innocent showed uncertain smiles, surprised that such a topic be raised. But a religious zealot might stare in anger or even counter his assertion. He poked at government. "I am part of the huge bureaucracy – I hate it, but

they pay well." Too much of a smirk or too enthusiastic agreement might lead to further exploration. He tried to tap into each client's emotions at least once during the interview. Distraction allowed the true character to escape.

Edward turned to his computer screen. Just move through – Dudek wasn't going to engage in distracting conversation. An hourglass appeared on his monitor. He waited for the program to load. Silence sometimes uncovered deceit, but Edward's armpits felt moist from the old man's stare. Why did this old Pole worry him? He did not suspect terrorism. Something else. End the awkward silence – engage the daughter.

"Will you be traveling with them?"

She was ready to talk. "Oh, yes. They can't travel on their own. I already have a global entry card. My father is a Holocaust survivor – Bełżec prisoner camp. He met my mother in the US in the fifties. He insists on going back to Poland once before he dies. We have relatives there to stay with--cousins. They live in..."

The forms finally loaded. He stopped her droning story and finished processing them in ten minutes. The old man never said another word but continued to stare at Edward. Though the air conditioning worked well on this August day, Edward wiped his brow after they left.

In December, the old man returned. Edward found him waiting outside the locked entrance thirty minutes before opening time. His application had gone through – no reason for him to be there. He stood by the entrance in a gray raincoat and black hat leaning on his cane like he might have stood there overnight. "Show you something."

Edward unlocked the door to the waiting area. "What is it?"

Dudek carried a scuffed leather briefcase with scratched metal corners. He placed it on the floor and tipped it flat with his cane. The briefcase struck the floor with a loud shot that echoed in the airport atrium. Edward flinched. A TSA agent in the atrium glanced at them, then away. Dudek pointed with his cane for Edward to open it.

"No, let's go inside." Edward struggled to bend over to pick up the briefcase. He grasped the handle and lifted it to Dudek. The old man grunted something. Edward guessed "thanks" in Yiddish but wasn't sure.

In his office Edward moved the five pictures of his children, three daughters and two sons, to make room for the briefcase. The old man's eyes followed each face. He placed his cane in the corner and leaned forward to click open the briefcase. Edward had been searching his brain for the man's name – it popped into his head - Zbigniew Dudek – strong name.

Dudek shuffled through papers in the briefcase. "Ah." He pulled a photograph from the briefcase and laid it in front of Edward. A small black and white photo showed four people, a prison guard and three prisoners. They wore the garb of German concentration camp inmates, dirty gray shirts with a single triangle patch. They stood on mud. All in the photograph attempted smiles but their faces did not brighten the scene. The blurred background of the photo revealed nothing. Mr. Dudek reached across the desk and retrieved a pen from Edward's penholder and pointed at the guard's face.

Edward stiffened at his own face, though thinner, in the photograph.

Like a prosecutor, Dudek pointed the pen at Edward. "You, yes?"

Edward was not alive when this picture was taken seventy years ago. But the prison guard's reluctant smile was his own. He knew who he might be.

"No, not me. When was this taken?"

"Bełżec camp—1942."

"I was born in 1955."

"Ja, ja. Not you. Father?"

"No, not my father."

"Why not?"

"My father was born in 1932. He would have been ten years old in the photograph."

"Your father from Germany?"

"Yes." Edward's father had emigrated from Germany after World War II with his mother.

"His father?"

Edward had the same thought. His mother had told him his grandfather was a farmer and had died in World War II. Nothing more. No good could come of this. "I don't think so."

"Why not?"

A small lie might resolve it forever. "My grandfather left Germany in 1935."

The old man looked hard at him. "You are sure?"

"Yes. I've got to get ready for my next appointments."

Dudek pointed to one of the other figures in the photo, a gaunt teenager with dirty pants and no shoes. "Me." Dudek grabbed Edward's arm and shook it. "See? Me."

"Yes."

"Others dead. Shot in head. I saw."

What could he say? "I'm glad you survived."

Dudek stared at the picture. "Fucking Nazi. He was animal." He spit into the wastebasket and looked up at Edward as he wiped his mouth with a gray handkerchief. "Nazi looks just like you."

"I have customers waiting. You really must go."

"Ja, ja. I go. You want copy of picture?"

Edward wanted a copy but this would imply too much. "No, thank you."

He followed the old man out. The waiting room remained empty. As Dudek walked through the entrance door he turned back and propped his cane to stop the door from closing. He sneered at Edward. "Yah, many customers waiting." Dudek released the door. It shut and latched. Though the wired glass, Edward watched him shuffle away.

Two weeks later, the airport atrium, when Edward arrived at 7:30 AM, bustled with lines of travelers. An airline computer system had crashed causing long lines of tense adults and whining children. A terrorist seeking maximum carnage would choose to detonate now. As he unlocked the waiting room door, he sensed eyes on him. He turned around to look at the lines but saw nothing suspicious. Each day when he arrived, he left the entry door unlocked for the first customers. Today, he locked it behind him—for reasons he did not understand, he needed more security.

But nothing happened – a false alarm.

February that year hinted no clue of spring. Weeks of dense clouds obscured the daylight's lengthening. Edward read the Saturday newspaper at the small wooden table in front of a sliding glass door that opened to a balcony in his apartment. A gray teak chair covered with old snow obscured his view of other apartments in his complex. Edward read the obituaries every day. The section started with one or two longer stories about locals who had died. How did the editor decide whose life merits a more detailed summary? The locally famous made the cut but often the accomplishments seemed weak. Somebody has to fill the space. Edward predicted he would not make the cut above the small-font capsules of life. He would be beloved by his daughters and sons. The newspaper would struggle to write much more.

Edward's scanning stopped at Dudek's obituary. Despite being a Holocaust survivor, he rated small font. But, the obituary was lengthy with the names of many who predeceased him including four brothers. He was beloved by a long list of children, grandchildren and great grandchildren. His wife had died in January. Edward must have missed her obituary or they chose not to publish one – nothing to write about a homemaker who died demented. Dudek's survival in the war and his subsequent career operating a shoe repair shop filled out the rest of his story of resilience. He had repaired shoes so that no one would suffer the months of wet feet he had in Bełżec. Even the strongest succumb – the funeral would be on Sunday.

After Edward had seen his grandfather's face as a prison guard, he had worked to determine its accuracy. Edward's father, an only child, had died in 1965 and his mother in 1980. Edward and his sister were the only remaining family. He told his

sister about the photograph. "A farmer who died in the war. That's all I know," she said.

He had contacted a few Nazi hunter organizations. They focused on living Nazis – Edward's grandfather, Gustav Richter, had to be dead – he would be 115 now. The third organization agreed to do the search. They called back in two hours. A prison guard named Gustav Richter served at Bełżec. He was killed when the prisoners were freed. Gustav Richter was a common name but the physical resemblance was too great – Edward's grandfather had been a Holocaust concentration camp guard.

Edward read the weather forecast, heavy snow predicted. His usual Sunday drive into the hills and ravines of western Pennsylvania now would be misery. Should he attend the funeral? He did not owe this man or his family anything. Edward abhorred Nazism both for the monstrous acts and for the stains set for centuries on the Germans who followed. But he had nothing better to do, and perhaps the funeral ceremony would end his ruminations about inheritance of personality traits.

Edward stamped his black shoes to remove the snow and salt and shuffled to enter Temple Emanuel. A hand grabbed his arm and pulled him to the side – the grandson of a Nazi caught at the temple so soon? Edward turned to face a clean-shaven middle-aged man with a kind face presenting him with a yarmulke. He placed it on his head. The usher helped him position it. His intent to stay inconspicuous already had failed.

He sat alone in the second to last row. Most of the other rows were filled. Edward understood little of the prayers and none of the Hebrew during the ceremony. The rabbi's eulogy made him think more about his dark ancestry. He regretted his decision to attend. At the end, the congregation heard details of the Shiva.

Dudek's daughter caught his eye as she processed past him. She leaned to him. "Please come to Shiva."

On his drive home, Edward decided he would not accept her invitation – just let this die with Dudek. But, she never left his mind for the next two days. Why would she want to talk? Perhaps his grandfather had not been as evil as Dudek stated? Some redemption? He would attend his first Shiva.

Dudek's home, a 1960s ranch, half covered in yellow brick, stood on a hill in a subdivision with curved streets. A winter sun in a cloudless sky did not chase away the frigid, still air. Edward imagined many children playing in these streets in the past. Today, no sleds or other toys decorated the driveways. Old people watching daytime TV sat in these neat little houses.

Edward climbed the seven concrete steps to the front door. Rock salt crunched under his shoes. Dudek's daughter opened the door before he rang the doorbell.

She smiled at him. "I'm so glad you came. Please come in."

Plastic covered the entryway floor. She took his coat and introduced herself. "I doubt you remember my name. I'm Mary Olson. My maiden name was Dudek."

"Edward Richter," he said shaking her hand. He stuttered on "Richter". "Should I remove my shoes?"

"Yes, please. The salt destroys the carpet."

Edward grunted as he untied his laces – should have worn the loafers.

She led him into the living room, small but neat with beige shag carpeting. Edward hadn't been shoeless in someone else's home in many years. He worried about foot odor. The closed front curtains hid the sunlight from the room. Three candles burned without scent on tables in corners of the room.

His eyes adjusted. Hundreds of pictures on every flat surface in the room emerged like stars at night. Their faces began to judge him.

She motioned him to a low couch. "Can I bring you something to eat? We still have cookies and some fruit left."

"No, thank you." Idiot. He should have brought something. He never was any good at these things.

"How about some coffee or tea? I'd be happy to make a fresh pot."

He foresaw an urgent need to urinate in her home. "No, I'm fine."

Mary sat in a chair next to the couch. She smoothed her skirt. "My father showed me the picture of your grandfather. That was your grandfather, right?"

Edward would not lie again. "Yes."

She waited for more.

"I don't know much about him. Actually, I knew nothing of him until I saw that picture. I knew only he died in the war."

"My father was shocked to see your grandfather's face on you. It's a remarkable resemblance."

"But you must understand it's only a physical resemblance. I am not a Nazi and abhor the Holocaust."

"Of course. I never thought you would be. I can see how upsetting it might be to learn of your grandfather's past."

Either she was a saint or there was more. He spoke the words he had rehearsed. "Though I did not know my grandfather, I would like to apologize to you and your family." Weak. Never enough.

She reached forward and touched his knee. "You don't need to apologize for a man you never knew. I want to show you something." She walked to the hallway.

Waiting for her to return, Edward sat surrounded by the photographs of Dudek's life – large family reunions and the shoe repair store. Even as a young man after the war, Dudek appeared old.

She returned with a small black case and set it down on the couch next to him. "I don't want to alarm you, but this is my father's gun." She opened the case. It contained a Luger pistol. Edward's heart pounded. Why did she want him to see this? "After he died, I removed all the ammunition." Not just a relic – loaded recently.

Edward shifted his weight. "Did he ever use it?" He wished he could take it back – what if he committed suicide?

"He never did for which I am so glad."

"Not even for target practice?"

"No, but I must tell you something." She dropped her head and leaned forward holding her hands as if she would pray. "He planned to shoot you."

The room seemed to darken in the silence that followed. The many faces of Dudek and his family witnessed this confession in the flickering candlelight.

"He only told me this a few days before he died. He told me to apologize to you. He got all the way to the airport. He said he watched you open your office door. But, he changed his mind."

Edward returned to that unsettling morning. The gun that almost killed him now lay still before him.

He needed to hear more. "What changed his mind?"

"He said he imagined killing Nazis his whole life. He never searched for any – he worried he would follow through. But he knew he would die soon, and he came across you. After my mother died, he thought he had nothing left to lose."

Edward shivered understanding how close he had come.

"What stopped him?"

"He saw the pictures on your desk. When he imagined your children's faces at your funeral, he couldn't go on. He said the bitterness should die with him."

Surrounded by the still faces of Dudek's life flickering in the candlelight, Edward stared at the gun.

"He wanted you to have it."

His eyes asked why.

"He said it would be safe with you."

About the Author:

David Macpherson is a retired internal medicine physician living on a small farm in western Pennsylvania. He retired in 2016 as a Professor of Medicine from the University of Pittsburgh and as a Chief Medical Officer for the Veterans Health Administration serving as the lead physician in a mid-Atlantic region. He is proud to have focused his medical efforts on US veterans. He is married and has two adult children who serve as part of his network of reviewers who critique and help to improve his writing. Most of the time, his family's thoughts on his writing are correct—but not always. Dr. Macpherson's interest in writing fiction dates to the mid 1970's. During his medical career, he accumulated near thousands of excuses why not to sit and write fiction. Since retirement, almost all of these excuses have vanished and he has drafted more than fifteen short stories and several flash fiction pieces under consideration. In addition to numerous scientific publications, he has published two nonfiction pieces online in the Pittsburgh Quarterly and two short stories published in Scarlet Leaf Review and Adelaide Literary Magazine.

OVERFLIGHT

John Tavares

Miles was coming home to Beaverbrook. As he flew the crippled jumbo jet towards Flying Fortress Lake, he remembered Lisa with a sense of nostalgia tinged with sadness. Afterwards, Michael read in Macleans newsmagazine, Toronto Star, and Winnipeg Free Press that the bomb, made from plastic explosives, embedded in a cassette recorder, burst through the luxury suitcase. The blast blew a jagged hole through luggage compartment and cargo hold at the fuselage of the jumbo jet. Meanwhile, Middle Eastern Airlines Flight 642, which originated in Vancouver, en route to Tehran, Iran, via Toronto, flew at thirty thousand feet over the border of the province of Manitoba and Ontario. The only Canadian born pilot with Middle Eastern airlines, Miles feared the damaged jumbo jet would plummet into an uncontrollable dive if he veered and turned to fly in the opposite direction to the Winnipeg international airport to make an emergency landing.

Believing they needed a longer airstrip, Miles and his Saudi co-pilot scrambled through a list of nearby airports and ruled out the municipal airports at Kenora, Dryden, Sioux Lookout. The only Canadian pilot that captained aircraft for Middle Eastern Airlines, Miles suggested they fly over the territory around his hometown until they found a suitable frozen lake. An avid angler, Miles knew at this time of year, towards the end of winter, the ice was of maximum thickness and safety.

"You honestly think we can land this plane on a lake of ice?" his co-pilot asked.

"Yes," Miles said. "They land smaller planes every day during winter."

"I'll feed you information, airspeed, altitude, wind speed, from the instruments, and you better focus on flying. Please keep talking; this is stressful, white knuckle flying for me."

Later, envious of his acquaintance's accomplishment, Michael read another article that suggested it wasn't possible to land a fully loaded 747 jumbo jet on a frozen lake with ice less than two meters of thickness, but he remembered what he witnessed, as Miles brought the aircraft down on the lake. Apparently, the ice was slightly beneath two meters in thickness in most places on Flying Fortress Lake.

"We haven't been talking to each other. I shouldn't say that precisely, that we're incommunicado: It's just she hardly speaks to me, except when drunk."

Lisa said that wasn't surprising: her friend losing her disinhibitions in regards to verbal communications except when she was intoxicated. Lisa often spoke in a formal, stilted manner: something as simple as talking was "verbal communications," but she was a registered nurse, and Michael respected and appreciated her precise, clinical manner and unconsciously emulated it around her.

"That's unfortunate," Lisa replied. "I didn't realize you two were having relationship trouble."

"No trouble: We're just not getting along; we're not talking to each other except when she's intoxicated. I mean, I don't get drunk. I can't afford to—psychologically or physically. We just don't carry on the kind of conversation we should have except when she's drunk. I go to the bar with her and try to negotiate. I drink cranberry juice, or lime-and-soda water, or diet Coke, while she has rye-and-ginger ales or rum-and-Cokes."

Lisa placed a container of cranberry juice in her grocery cart. "If you're not living with her in the house, where are you staying these days?"

"I've got a bachelor apartment in Flying Fortress Manor."

"Across town?"

"Right across the street from where we rented the house."

"I lived in a one bedroom there once with my ex-boyfriend, Miles," Lisa said, raising her eyebrows suggestively.

"Yes, Miles, the pilot—the young airline captain pilot who flies 747's for Middle Eastern Airlines. Isn't he a captain? Doesn't he fly jumbo jets?"

"We haven't been together for a year."

"I just find it amusing. Mary still talks with me—when she's drunk. There's definitely that therapeutic value to alcohol? I guess alcohol loosens the inhibitions, so those pathologically shy people who normally wouldn't speak or meet and greet are suddenly like chatterboxes after they've had several drinks."

As a health-care professional, Lisa rolled her eyes upward, thinking she didn't need any lectures or information on psychopharmacology of alcohol or aspects of health science from somebody in a supermarket, particularly an unsuccessful semi-professional hockey and low wage small town commercial radio broadcaster. "Uh-huh." Lisa did think it was noteworthy he was now single and potentially available for a one-night stand, but he sounded as if far more pressing matters crowded his narcissistic mind. She thought at the very least he and Mary had an unusual relationship, but who was she to judge. Lisa tried to give him the impression she was no longer interested in discussing their difficulties and separation, but he said: "Yes, fiancé you're separated from won't talk to you—can't talk to you—except when she's drunk. Only after she's binged on alcohol, do you get along perfectly."

Lisa forced a laugh. "How can she be your fiancé if you're separated?"

"I don't know, but she does a pretty good job avoiding me when she's sober."

Lisa reflexively raised her shaved eyebrows and thought of her ex-boyfriend Miles who had gone from a bush pilot in his hometown to flying passenger jets for Middle Eastern Airlines out of Toronto.

"When she does see me, say, downtown, at the gym, or at the convenience store, or here at the supermarket, she pretends I'm not here or don't exist."

Lisa glanced down the counters of fruits and vegetables in the supermarket produce section, the sweet peas, baby carrots, apples, oranges, bananas, in their neat geometric and linear arrangements. Then she perused more carefully, the nutrition information on a label for a canned cranberry sauce.

"I'll say, hi, but she goes on about her business as if she's deaf or as if I'm a complete stranger or homeless person she doesn't know." (Once Lisa told Mary she thought Michael looked like a homeless man with wild scraggly hair and untrimmed beard. If that was her impression, Mary retorted, why did she keep suspecting she had a crush on her boyfriend or wanted a one nightstand with him and that triggered one of their many arguments?) "I mean, it's a small town—"

"Of course, it's a small town—not that tiny, but small enough."

"We can't avoid bumping into each other."

Grimacing, pursing her lips firmly, she said flatly, "I understand."

"We have the same likes and dislikes and the same habits and practically the same schedules. Since the food co-op closed, so now there's only this supermarket, we can't help avoid bumping into each other in Comida when shopping for groceries or fresh produce. We're both birds of a feather."

Lisa raised her brow again, pushing back her tightly wound bundle of hair. Talk of birds made her think of her pilot ex-boyfriend Miles, particularly at a time when she desperately tried to forget. She put a carton of asparagus in the basket of her grocery cart. "I see what you mean."

"Then, on a Saturday night, there's all that action at The Flying Fortress, seeing how nobody wants to go to The Whiskyjack anymore."

Having given up on the bars and other drinking establishments after she broke up with Miles, when he left Bearskin Airlines and took a job with Middle Eastern Airlines, she lost hope in the whole local after hours and singles scene in Beaverbrook. "Yeah, I see what you mean."

"So, by the time I get there, she's already smashed. She sees me, comes up to me, and starts talking, and she's full of life and vivacious talk. She tells me everything that happened to her that week. She tells me things she's never told me before, stuff she should have told me long ago, and I think she never would have told me except when she's drunk. That's sort of peculiar, but it only makes me love her more than I ever loved her before. Then we end up going to her house, our old place. We talk and we talk. We talk and we have sex, and we have sex and we have sex all night and it's the best sex we've ever had. Maybe it's the best either had because neither had sex all week, when we're used to it at least once, if not, twice, a day. Anyway, for whatever reason, it feels like the best sex we've ever had. Then, early in the morning, before she wakes, I leave, and, it seems we're both happy, content, temporarily. Then, next time I see her, usually on a weekday, and, for the whole week afterwards, she has her frigid, cold, I-don't-know-you attitude. She does her   I-don't-know-who-the-hell-you-are-and-I-don't-care act, as if she doesn't know me at all, as if I've never been her boyfriend, her fiancé, as if she never intends to speak with me, unless I happen to go to the bar at Saturday night, and she's half-cut, and the whole cycle repeats itself."

"Wow. That almost sounds weird, almost, but it also sounds all too human."

"I suppose. I'm beginning to think maybe sex was the only thing that held us together."

"I'm certain you wouldn't be the first couple that found lovemaking a glue bonding them together."

Sex as glue: Michael never considered their relationship that way.

"But you do love each other." Lisa blurted the words as if it was a question and she possessed an intensely personal interest in the consequences of the answer. She realized she was not playing her cards closely enough and she was already revealing more than she originally intended to say. Her inability to forget her wayward pilot boyfriend unhinged her romantically, she thought.

"We still do, I think."

Unused to having conversations of this nature in the supermarket, never mind the café or bar, she suddenly worried about shoppers or store employees overhearing. She wondered how she managed to spend and waste so much time talking to him, but it always seemed that way with him. She told Mary she thought he was an odd fellow, who wore his heart on his sleeve. She thought Michael was too open, that he opened his mind, revealed his emotions and psychological state, to anybody, including complete strangers, whereas her own ex-boyfriend hardly said anything, which, he claimed, served him well in his occupation as a pilot since he only spoke when necessary. When he started a conversation, she complained, he sometimes spoke for long, protracted periods. She theorized his loquaciousness originated when he was lonely, when he possessed no one towards whom he could express concerns and vent bothersome emotions. Touching on every personal topic, no matter how secretive a normal person might think such matters, no subject being taboo, he spoke unendingly. Since they shared the same outlook, philosophical viewpoints, and attitudes about many things, albeit she only admitted this to Mary, who, in turn, became jealous, oftentimes she didn't mind.

"How do you get into town? I thought you didn't have a driver's license.

"I do have a driver's license, but I walk and I prefer to walk because the exercise keeps me fit and in shape." Michael motioned to his backpack. "I just hike the snowmobile trail across the lake into town and throw my groceries and mail in my backpack."

"The ice has melted, though—it looks scary. It could be dangerous. Is it safe walking across the ice this time of year?"

"Extremely safe. The ice is very strong, over a meter thick. They could land a jumbo jet on that lake ice, if needed. The ice will be safe enough to walk or snowmobile across for at least another month, and you can walk across the ice with your sneakers the trail and ice is so hard and packed."

"Wow."

"I'm finally getting some exercise, too. I lost about twenty pounds over the past couple of months."

She visually appraised him. "I noticed."

"You know, I always loved walking, too, and I've really gotten out of shape. I lost ten pounds in the past few weeks alone. I always enjoyed hiking, but once I started living with Mary I found I was always riding in her car even when I wanted and needed to get some fresh air and exercise."

As she glanced at her wristwatch, she realized they spoke for over forty minutes straight. She better get going; she was scheduled to have dinner with of all people later that evening Mary, who she needed on her side as an ally in a dispute about overtime pay she was having with her shift supervisor. For consolation and comfort, she thought she might even try telephoning Miles at his stopover in Toronto after he flew across Northwestern Ontario with Middle Eastern Airlines, even though he had warned her about calling her while he was flying.

"Listen, Michael, I don't mean to be rude. But I really should be going. I have to cook a healthy supper for myself tonight."

"Sure. Just—Lisa, I know you see Mary practically everyday, so please don't speak to her about these things."

"Of course not; we're not even on the same shifts."

Shifting her weight from one high heel shoe to another, Lisa felt pleased to see him eyeing the tight skirt around her waist and hips and her long legs below the hem of her short dress. Earlier she suspected he might have gay tendencies, but then she figured he was merely not aggressive enough in asserting his masculinity. Knowing the way he would answer, she asked, "You sure you don't need a ride tonight? It is pretty chilly."

"No. I'm fine. I could use the exercise, but thanks for the offer."

That Saturday evening, he thought she should avoid the bar, if only to save money and not

bump into Mary, to avoid any contact and communication with her. But what other activities did he have for entertainment and diversion, particularly on a Saturday night? Did he really want to watch reruns of the hockey game featured on television earlier that evening? Besides, he lost interest in watching ice hockey when The Detroit Red Wings eliminated his favorite team from playoff contention. From the squat brick building, where he resided in a bachelor's apartment, he hiked along the snowmobile trail across Flying Fortress Lake. He cautiously tread along the hard packed snowmobile trail, careful not to get caught in the grip of panic induced by the foreboding mental prospect of breaking through the ice on the surface of the lake. He envisioned himself falling into the frigid waters, swallowed by the dark undertow, suffocated, drowned under a huge mass of ice, but while he felt that fear he realized the prospect was unlikely. Within twenty minutes of brisk walking, he reached the local town beach. He strode quickly along the main traffic artery that ran along the beach and into town on the pedestrian walkway under the railroad bridge, and arrived at a hockey arena. He tugged at the frozen handle of the steel doors, frozen, frosty, solidly locked, so the fitness center, the weight room, the sauna, or the gymnasium he was forced to rule out, since the municipal recreation facilities were closed for the night early. Then he walked downtown to The Flying Fortress nightclub, but he was ambushed and didn't stand a chance, since Mary waylaid him as soon as he stepped into the bar. Intent on carrying out full force a violent quarrel, she appeared drunk, definitely not amiable.

"What business have you discussing my personal life and private issues with Lisa? It's none of her business what's going on with my ex-boyfriend."

She ranted and raved, gritting her teeth, hissing, clenching her jaw, so the muscles and tendons in her neck revealed themselves in a most unfeminine manner. On and on went her verbiage, digging into him, criticizing his ragged clothes and scuffed shoes, berating him for growing his hair and beard long, and leaving it untrimmed, curly, and scraggly. She complained about the money he spent on books and compact discs and warned she donated his books and music collection to the women's shelter, homeless shelter, thrift shop, and friends. She pushed, slapped, and backhanded him, and he worried about attracting attention, although most patrons were drinking and distracted by dancing, billiards, shuffleboard, music, and loud, boisterous conversation.

"What kind of future does a man who spends so much of his income on useless books and music? Huh?" She slapped him on his hairy arm. "Tell me!" She slapped him on the face and tugged on his beard. "Huh?" He pulled on his gloves and toque and ripped off his parka, but a pilot friend who remembered him from high school rescued him. He spent the last of his cash to buy a glass of orange juice and then a diet Coke and a few Molson Canadian beer for his friend. He played pool with his high school buddy in another part of the tavern far away from the bar, while Mary stayed at the bar, glowering, simmering.

A few hours later, towards last call for alcoholic beverages and closing time, Mary approached him. As if none of her disputatiousness transpired earlier, she asked him if he'd take her home. Did she want him to drive? No, she didn't drive her motor vehicle downtown that night; her Honda Civic was getting serviced and she got a ride into town with Lisa, who dropped her off at the bar after they met over dinner. In the middle of a labor dispute with their supervisor and employer over overtime, undecided as to whether the nurses should call representatives from their union, what she called the heavy guns, the pair discussed strategy. He asked why didn't she just take a cab?

"I don't have the cash for a cab, and these guys don't take credit cards."

He didn't want to admit he didn't have cash for a cab that night. "All right," he said, trying not to sound grudging, "I'll walk you home."

"Walk? It'll take hours."

"Not if we take the trail across the lake."

"The trail across the lake? Are you crazy? Ice melts, especially in the middle of March."

"We can still walk. The ice is safe, hasn't melted enough. Trust me. The weather's fine and it's a beautiful night."

"Then we'll get run over by the snow machines."

"The snowmobiles have headlights. It's not as if snowmobilers are drunk and driving like they're blind or mad."

She said softly, as if to warn him, "Ice melts in the spring."

After he bought her a hot dog from the vendor on Railyardside Street, they walked along the wide brick inlaid sidewalks on the south side of the main traffic artery. She checked the parking lot of the hostel for the train crews, freight conductors and locomotive engineers, and the train dispatch office to see if any of her male friends could drive their cars to lend her a ride home that night. They strode down Railyardside Street until it turned into Lakeshore Parkway at the train overpass, and then approached the snow-covered beach.

"I'm afraid of the lake, walking on the ice," Mary said.

"So am I, and that's the reason you don't have to be afraid or worry. I wouldn't dare put you in danger."

"What if we hit an air pocket?"

"We hit an air pocket."

Their feet crunching, the couple walked along the packed snowmobile trail, as it swung out onto Flying Fortress Lake. To relieve the tension and break the monotony of their footsteps chomping the ice and snow, he spoke: "Do you know why they call this Flying Fortress Lake?"

"I think I may have heard a story or two about the lake name," she said. "They once called it Pelican Lake, I believe."

"Yes, maybe we heard the same story. Anyway," he said, as he led her along the snowmobile trail across the packed lake ice, "they say that towards the end of the Second World War a formation of Superfortresses, fully armed with bombs, machineguns and cannon, was flying from an army airfield outside Chicago to Alaska and then forward to air bases in the Pacific to bomb Japan. One bomber in the formation started to experience mechanical troubles, lagged behind, and was forced to make a crash landing. There was an airport in Sioux Lookout nearby, still in use, busier than ever, but the pilot chose to those ditch the plane on the lake, which had a landing strip, because he didn't think the airport landing runway was long enough, and he wasn't sure if he could maneuver the big bomber in that direction. It was a smooth as far as crash landings go, except the wheel in front landing gear locked up and the bomber skidded along the frozen lake. The plane crash landed in the middle of the spring, as the lake ice began to melt. By the next morning, the big bomber started sinking through the lake ice and soon the Superfortress caved through the ice before they could launch a rescue. They didn't even have time to evacuate the bombs and munitions. There was nothing the dumbfounded aircrew and locals could do to save or rescue the plane, and it sank several hundred feet to the bottom of the lake. It sank in water so deep the U.S. Air Force and Canadian army never made any effort to recover the plane, despite the live ammunition and bombs aboard the plane. Apparently, that Superfortress, fully loaded with bombs and ammo, sits at the bottom of the lake, around which the town was built, to this day.

"I think you're full of bull," she said, "but it's certainly a beautiful night. Anyway, if it was a Superfortress plane why would they call it Flying Fortress Lake? If I understand my history correctly, the Flying Fortress was actually a different bomber, smaller, shorter range, but very effective."

"I didn't know you knew World War Two history."

"I think I mentioned to you a few hundred times before my grandfather was a veteran of the RAF and before I decided to go into nursing I minored in history at university. I actually loved my World War One and World War Two courses. In hindsight I think partially because I was fascinated by the fact that humanity could deliberately commit so much carnage in modern times."

"Well, maybe the plane was actually a Flying Fortress."

"I guess that makes more sense, but it doesn't sound as dramatic as Superfortress, does it?"

"Well, I think with your flair for the dramatic you'd know more about what grabs a person's attention—"

"What are you talking about? Are you trying to start an argument?"

"Listen, I don't want to fight," he interjected, when he suddenly realized the direction in which the conversation headed, "I was just trying to tell you a story."

"Anyway, what does it matter? Pelican Lake is named for pelicans, but when was the last you saw pelicans around the lake or town."

"I think DDT killed them all back in the postwar boom days."

The thought of insecticides silenced them. The skies were clear and crisp and the constellations were sharp in outline, sparkling like diamonds, with no contamination from artificial lighting to diminish the visibility of the sources of natural light. As they continued hiking, the northern lights, green glowing, snaking, swirling, soaring, twisting, twirling, danced across the broad expanse of the night sky above the frozen lake, fringed by the small buildings and roads of the town. Mary held Michael close and tight. By the time they reached halfway across the lake, a kilometer from the shoreline and the park trail that led to the cul de sac where he currently lived, she stopped walking, looked through the darkness about her, sighed deeply, got down on the hard ice of the frozen lake, and reclined, sitting on her bottom and then stretching out.

"What are you doing?"

"I'm resting, star gazing. It's warm anyway."

"I didn't think it was that warm."

"It is fair, the temperature hospitable." She patted the crusty frozen snow on the lake with her damp mitten. "Lie down beside me."

"You're acting strange."

"It's nice out here. We're finally having some spring weather, and it was your idea to walk across the ice originally."

"My idea to walk you home, not to lie down on a frozen lake."

"If we're going to walk on the lake, why can't we lie down on the ice and gaze at the stars, the constellations, and the northern lights?"

He conceded her point and sat down beside her. She unbuttoned her ski jacket, tugged at the sleeves, slipped if off, put her arms above her head, and pulled off her sweater. "Make love to me."

"Make love? Here?"

"Yes. I've never done it under the stars or northern lights before."

She took his hand and placed his cold fingers on her warm bare breast, the nipples firm, erect.

"What if a snowmobile comes speeding across the lake?"

"There's no snow machine driving around at this hour."

"You should know them better. What if a bush plane with skis came along for a landing?"

"Who cares? I'm not worried."

"I think we're directly in their flight path. The landing strip is just over there."

"I don't think their aircraft are flying this late or early." Lisa said the planes only flew during the daylight hours because they don't have the navigational or flight instruments for nighttime flying. And it's probably too late in the season for the ski planes to land on the ice."

"I saw one land a few days ago."

Peaceful, quiet, and relatively warm, he lay beside her. She muttered something about how she couldn't believe how warm it was at this time of year for these parts and he allowed her to rest her head on his stomach.

"After I left the Ontario Hockey League and missed the National Hockey League draft, when I was nineteen or so, I walked along the railroad tracks west of town, to the rapids at the end of the Flying Fortress Lake, near the reservation, where I sometimes fish for pickerel. Now it was actually a very long walk and you could access these narrows at the end of the lake by road, but I didn't have a car, just as I don't have a car now. If I worked for the sawmill, I'd earn plenty and could afford a car, but instead I decided to play hockey and made just enough money to survive. Now I'm not sure why I wanted to take this walk late at night along the railroad tracks, but I think I wanted to end my existence by getting crushed by a freight train. So I hiked and marched along the tracks to the narrows—if I didn't get crushed to death by a train, I could drown myself in the rapids at night—it was a nice scenic spot to die. But

no matter how long and far I walked for some strange reason there was still no train, no freight or passenger, came along to drive me over and squish me to juice. It was very dark, but clear, and there was no moon—at least not until later. The moon, at a crescent, didn't rise until a much later in the morning. So there I was, after midnight, walking along the tracks, which ran beside the lakeshore, through this beautiful wilderness, with this incredible view of all the stars and constellations, with no artificial sources of light, just like tonight. And you couldn't really see into deeply the bush, because it was so dark, but you could look dimly across the lake, and you could see the gleaming railroad tracks a bit ahead of yourself, and the amount of noise, from the wildlife in the bush and on the lake, was incredible. Frogs, insects, nesting waterfowl—they were making a symphony of sound. It was almost deafening, and, on top of all those sound effects, there were all those stars and constellations in the black night sky. So it was eerie, hair-raising. Then there was every now and again there was this solo sound, this lingering, lonely cry of the loon echoing across the lake. And I thought, Wow, how could I want to miss this? I need to hear those lonesome loons calling, that haunting sound, again. The loon's cry over the lake in the middle of the wilderness was amazing. But I certainly wouldn't be able to hear it again if ... and I think that was the last time I thought that way."

Michael looked at Mary's face and realized she had fallen asleep. He noticed her closed eyes as she nosily breathed through her mouth and made funny nasalizations, snoring in her own idiosyncratic way. "Mary?" He nudged her, realizing she was recovering from her drunkenness, her torpor, and sighed. He was ready to tell her that he was joking, that the actual truth was he was forced to walk home, after his friends left him without a ride at a bush party late on a Friday night miles from town, outside the gatehouse to the First Nations reservation and residential school. So he ended up taking the only shortcut he knew home, along the railroad tracks back to town. He had been in a sermonizing mood, but as usual many of his comments and words to her were lost on her.

After fifteen minutes or so he, as the late winter air grew chillier, he gently woke her. She stirred and stood up from where she passed out on the ice and, amnesic, wondered what had happened to herself. They continued to walk along the trail to the opposite shoreline and the roadway to their homes as the horizon started to lighten.

When they looked up, they saw a sight they would remember for the rest of their lives: The jumbo jet with rocking wings flying dozens of meters above the lake as fire spewed from a gaping hole in the forward cargo hold. The huge jet passenger plane landed smoothly on the lake and skidded several hundred meters across the flat smooth snow and ice before the doors flew open and passengers slid down the chutes and slides to escape from the aircraft. They both rushed towards the aircraft as a local ambulance and a fire truck sped down the lakeshore road and drove onto the ice road and broad snowmobile trail, speeding towards the sight of the immense passenger plane parked on the frozen lake at sunrise.

Born and raised in Sioux Lookout, Ontario, John Tavares is the son of Portuguese immigrants from the Azores. He's a graduate of General Arts and Science at Humber College in Etobicoke with concentration in psychology, journalism at Centennial College in East York, and the Specialized Honors BA in English literature from York University in North York. His hobbies include cycling and photography. His writings have been published in variety of North American magazines and literary journals.

About the Author:

Born and raised in Sioux Lookout, Ontario, **John Tavares** is the son of Portuguese immigrants from the Azores. His education includes graduation from 2-year GAS at Humber College in Etobicoke with concentration in psychology (1993), 3-year journalism at Centennial College in East York (1996), and the Specialized Honors BA in English from York University in North York (2012). His writings have been published in various magazines and literary journals. Set of his short stories has been broadcasted at the Sioux Lookout's CBLS/CBQW radio.

THE SILENCE OF THE NIGHT

Lewis J. Beilman III

Jack grew suspicious. He thought he heard footsteps behind him—but, when he glanced over his shoulder, he saw an empty street. He shook his head. He never liked this stretch of Asylum. It led through a series of ramshackle tenements, and the characters he encountered there were often strung out or degenerate. They were not like him, he thought. He thrust his hands into his coat pockets, leaned forward, and hurried down the asphalt sidewalk. The street lights threw a yellow haze on the remnants of muddied snow, and a full moon illuminated the sky. A gust of wind struck his face, and he raised his arm across his nose and mouth to shelter them from the cold. He didn't have much farther to go. The bar he planned to visit was a few blocks away, and he quickened his pace to get there.

This Friday night seemed like any other. Tired and empty after a busy workweek, Jack intended to blow off some steam. He would soon walk into his favorite bar and wave to Mary, the bartender. Then, he would hang his coat on the rack to the right of the entryway and sit in the barstool closest to the door. Mary would come to him and ask him if he wanted the usual—a shot of bourbon and a beer. He would say yes and watch the sway of her hips as she sauntered to pour him his drinks. He liked the way her backside filled her jeans, and he often stole a peek down her blouse when she set his drinks in front of him. She would wink at him when he paid her. He figured she knew what he was up to, but it was innocent enough. He never got out of hand and never crossed the line with her. He felt there were certain boundaries in life, and pretty bartenders were like pretty relatives—you could look at them, but you had to keep a certain distance.

As he approached an alleyway, he slowed to light a Lucky Strike. The tobacco sparked, and a vagrant, who was walking in the opposite direction, asked to bum a cigarette. Jack obliged, and the man requested a light. Jack struck a match, lifted it to the man's cigarette, and watched it cast its glow on the creases of his face and the streaks of dirt on his beard. Without meeting Jack's eyes, the man thanked Jack for the cigarette, coughed, and continued on his way. Jack took a deep drag of smoke into his lungs, exhaled into the chill air, and started again toward the bar. Suddenly, as he passed the alleyway, he paused. A woman's voice echoed from the empty space. He heard whimpering first, followed by full-throated sobbing. Intrigued by these sounds, he crept between the two dilapidated brownstones that bookended the alleyway.

Although Jack understood that someone crying in the privacy of her room was none of his business, he was drawn to the mystery of the moment. Knowing little of sadness himself, he desired to see its face. He thought this woman and her tears might teach him something of a world he found incomprehensible. He lurched forward a few feet. To avoid the eyes of neighbors who might be peering from their windows, he crouched low and crept into the black alley. About twenty yards into the passageway, he stopped. A soft moaning wafted from a half-open window above him. The woman's voice was low now—muffled. He listened for several minutes. Despite his better judgment, he needed to see her. Holding his breath, he turned and stood so only his eyes rose above the sill. A candle lit the room dimly. A raven-haired woman with light-brown skin sat in a wooden chair by a small, round table. He saw her in profile, her back to a couch that faced a television and small stereo. Jack guessed she was thirty-five, about five years older than he. Wearing a black dress cut above the knee, she hunched forward and let a cigarette dangle from in between her index and middle fingers. On the table rested a glass filled with ice and, presumably, some type of liquor.

She stared forward, with Jack in the periphery of her sight—but Jack was safe. Even if she turned to face him, she would see nothing but the darkness outside painting black her view of the alley. She continued crying, unaware of the voyeur by her window, and Jack tracked her tears as they drifted from her eye over the ridge of her cheekbone. To Jack, her sorrow imbued her with a solemn beauty, and, the longer he watched her, the more he longed to speak with her. Something strange within him needed to understand this sorrow that had shattered the silence of the night. She halted her tears briefly, tilted her head back, and finished her drink. Afterwards, she crossed her arms on the table and rested her head on her forearms. A few muted sobs escaped, but she looked as if she might fall asleep. Afraid he would lose his chance to speak with her, Jack straightened himself enough to where his mouth met the open window. He watched her for a moment before he spoke. She did not move.

"Are you OK?" Jack said.

The woman sat bolt upright. She looked in Jack's direction, her eyes bulging. Before he could speak again, she blew out the candle. "Who's there?" she said, her voice groping through the darkness.

Jack could no longer see her. The only thing he saw was the tip of her cigarette as it moved toward the window. The light vanished once she took the cigarette from her lips. He spoke again. "I heard you crying as I walked down the street. I wanted to make sure you were all right."

To allay her fears, he took his matchbook from his pocket, struck a match, and held it to his face. The flame revealed his soft features, sandy hair, and pale eyes. He still could not see her.

Soon, however, the cigarette rose from her side to her lips. She inhaled, and the tobacco crackled. "I'm all right," she said sharply, letting the smoke float through the open window. He could hear her breathing. She stood only a few feet from him.

Jack listened to the sound of her breath. He didn't know what to say. He feared she would call the police if he lingered. He awaited her rebuke. Instead, when she spoke, her tone softened. He detected a slight Puerto Rican accent. "Would you like to come in?" she said.

The invitation surprised him, and he wondered if some trap lurked for him within her apartment. Regardless, the potential of a random encounter with a stranger excited him. "Yes," he said.

He heard her footsteps cross the floor as she walked away from him. "It's the third door on the right," she said. "Be quiet when you enter." She lit the candle again and sat in the same chair she was in before.

He waited briefly in the alley—the darkness blanketing him like a shroud—before he moved back toward the street. He stepped gingerly to avoid making noise and again crouched as he passed the neighbors' windows. When he reached the sidewalk, he thought—for a moment—of walking away, but the allure of the evening was too strong for him. He felt an intense exhilaration from this break in his routine. He reminded himself that he was not a man who crouched in dark alleys or entered strangers' homes. Most days, he worked in a tidy office, ate a bland dinner, and watched the evening news before going to bed. He lived in a tony apartment building that had been built as part of an urban renewal project. He occasionally masturbated to online pornography, but he surely was no peeping Tom. He sensed that somehow a strange world was opening to him. As he ascended the gray stairs to the building's entranceway, he glanced from side to side. Taking a deep breath, he entered the building's vestibule and proceeded into the dim hallway. A roach scurried under a tenant's door, and one of the ceiling lights flickered on and off. He noticed the peeling wallpaper and ceiling stained yellow from cigarette smoke. The seediness of the building—unlike anything he had previously encountered—simultaneously disgusted and aroused him.

Jack proceeded to the third doorway on the right and stood at the woman's door. It had chipped paint and a crack in its center where someone appeared to have struck it. At first, Jack thought to knock, but he decided against it. Instead, he turned the doorknob. The door was unlocked. He pushed, and the door opened. He paused before he crossed the threshold. As he entered, the wall to his left prevented him from seeing the woman. The floorboards creaked beneath his feet. His eyes darted around the parts of the apartment he could see. He noted that the floor needed sweeping and the furnishings were sparse. To his right, the kitchen, with its rusty sink and decades-old appliances, looked decrepit. A toaster oven and microwave sat on one of the counters. After a few steps, he looked to his left and saw the woman sitting at the table. She was smoking a cigarette and drinking what smelled like bourbon. A candle sat in the center of the table, next to a cell phone, and cast a bronze glow on her face. It was an attractive face that was beginning to show the first creases of middle age. She looked at Jack with dark eyes that were red from crying.

"Take a seat," she said, sizing him up and down.

Jack set his coat on the chair at the head of the table. He sat across from the woman. "I'm Jack," he said.

"Jack," she said, nodding her head. "Call me Luz." She took a sip from her drink.

Jack stared at his hands and fumbled with his fingers. At first, he had trouble meeting her eyes. "Just so you know, I don't usually do this," he said.

Luz smiled. "Do what?"

"Enter a stranger's apartment," Jack said.

Luz rose from her seat and put her hand on his shoulder. Her fingers caressed the back of his neck. "That's all right," she said. "There are first times for everything." She walked past him to the kitchen. Jack looked back at her and watched her grab a bottle of Old Crow from a cabinet. She filled a tumbler with ice, poured a drink, and returned to the table. She set the drink in front of him.

"Thank you," Jack said.

Luz lifted her glass to him, winked an eye, and said "Salud."

Jack said "Salud" in reply, clinked glasses with her, and took a sip from his glass.

Luz shook her head from side to side, motioned for Jack to drink up, and finished her drink with one long sip. He obediently finished his. She took their glasses, returned to the kitchen, and poured two more drinks. She turned around with a drink in each hand. Through the fabric of her dress, he could glimpse the outline of her nipples. When she returned to the table, she set both glasses in front of him and began to massage his shoulders. He relaxed his neck and looked up at her. He became noticeably aroused.

"You like this?" Luz said.

Jack nodded. She leaned forward and breathed on the back of his neck. He turned his head and brushed his lips against hers. He stood, pushed the chair from between them, and kissed her. They kissed for several seconds before she bit his bottom lip. He pulled away and rubbed his mouth. He looked for blood on his fingers. There was none.

Luz laughed.

"What did you do that for?" Jack said.

"You have a girlfriend, Jack?" Luz said, slurring her words. She straightened her dress.

"No," Jack said. "Not for a year."

Luz reached around him to get her drink. She gulped half her bourbon and placed the glass back on the table. Jack took a sip from his drink, too. He remembered what had drawn him here in the first place. He took her hand in his. She pulled away, but he tightened his grip. "Why were you crying earlier?" he said.

"You have beautiful eyes," Luz said. "They are pale—very lovely." She placed her hands on his lower back and drew him toward hers. His hands settled on her hips. Her pelvis pressed against his erection.

"You didn't answer me," Jack said. "Why were you crying?"

"You have a girlfriend, Jack?" Luz repeated.

"I already told you I didn't," Jack said.

"Well—my man is out tonight," Luz said.

"Oh," Jack said. He cocked his head and shifted his feet.

"He's out with friends," Luz said.

Jack nodded. He understood now. "But you don't think he's with friends."

"He has another woman," Luz said. "I know it." Shuddering, she clenched her jaw and shut her eyes to fight back tears.

This mix of fury and sadness increased her vulnerability, and Jack found it irresistible. What is it to me if she has a boyfriend? he thought. Luz kept her eyes closed, and he kissed her again. With the kiss, her anger subsided, and she collapsed into his arms. His hands explored her body, working from her back, to her rear, and down her thighs. The kissing grew more heated, and he started to work her dress up her legs. She stopped his hands and pulled away from him. Breathing heavily, she fanned her chest.

Jack took another sip from his drink. The alcohol coursed through him. "This man of yours," he said. "If he's so good, why isn't he here? He sounds like a fool to me."

Luz withdrew. Jack sensed she was content to play this game the rest of the night. He would comfort her, take her in his arms, and bring his lips to hers. She, in turn, would relent at his touch, pull him close to her, and let his hands stroke her body. When she felt he had gone too far, she would pull away. Then, the game would stop briefly while they regained their composure. Soon, however, they would start up again. And so on. Jack believed the night would ebb and flow like this until they got bored or tired and decided the encounter should end. But, for now, Jack intended to play the game a little longer. He took Luz in his arms, and let her head rest on his shoulder. She began to cry again.

"He is a fool," Luz said. "He is a fool."

Jack patted Luz's back to comfort her and let her tears wet his shirt. Struggling to comprehend her emotions, his mind drew a blank. He had limited experience understanding women's feelings. Relationships in his past had satisfied his physical needs, but the emotional aspects of these relationships had frustrated him. Usually, when a woman pressured him to open up to her, he moved on. Once, after a lover's quarrel, a woman whom he had dated told him he was cold and incapable of love. He agreed with her and dumped her on the spot. More recently—to avoid nasty complications—he limited his encounters to one-night stands or short-term conquests, generally with women he met online. He preferred the lack of attachment these relationships afforded him, even if they were few and far between. The absence of commitment in these affairs seemed liberating to him. He hoped tonight's liaison would become another sordid memory. His initial thought that he would learn something new from Luz's sorrow faded like smoke in the wind.

Jack desired only one thing now. He began to knead Luz's back. She cooed and looked into his eyes. Her tears formed rivers in the candlelight. He hoped now to prove his prior impression incorrect—perhaps she will relent after all. Women are weak in moments like these, he thought. If he were lucky, he could still become the beneficiary of her anger at her man. He kissed her again, this time allowing his tongue to explore hers more deeply. She closed her eyes and relaxed. The looseness in her limbs contrasted nicely with the stiffness between his legs. He moved her body slowly as he kissed her. He led her the few feet from the table to the sofa. Once there, he pinned her rear against it and drove his hips into hers. She gasped. Encouraged, he worked his hand under her dress and slid it up the back of her leg. When he reached the fleshy part below her buttocks, his fingers glided across her moist inner thigh. Ripe for the sticking, he thought.

Jack moved his lips from Luz's and drew them across her cheek to her upper neck. He nibbled on the muscle behind her ear, and she lolled her head back, breathed audibly, and opened her thighs. The time to act was now. His hands still beneath her dress, he slid her panties down. She didn't resist. Now, now, he told himself. As he maneuvered toward the coup de grâce, a low sound buzzed behind him. Luz's phone vibrated on the table. The sound caught her attention, too, and broke her trance. Her body suddenly grew rigid, and she pushed him away.

"I must see who it is," Luz said, brushing past Jack.

Jack threw back his head and stared at the ceiling. An equal mixture of disbelief and disappointment overcame him. All this for naught, he thought, shaking his head. He kept his back turned toward Luz. He knew his chance was over.

"You must leave," Luz said.

Her voice was serious. A text from her man, Jack guessed. He turned around. She looked pale. "What's going on?" he said, exasperated.

"You must leave now," Luz said. "He'll be here any minute. He can't find you here."

Jack held his breath and bit his bottom lip. "Whatever," he said. A bitterness burned in his stomach. He grabbed his coat from the chair and looked once more at Luz.

"Please leave now," Luz pleaded, her voice quavering.

Jack said goodbye. Luz held the phone in her hand, staring at it as if it had rung her death knell. He left quickly, pausing only briefly as he closed the door behind him. As he crossed the hallway, another roach scurried across the floor. He kicked out his foot and crushed it with his shoe. It wriggled as it died. He felt no excitement now, only disgust. He entered the vestibule and opened the front door. A man was coming up the steps. Jack held the door for him. The man was stocky, with a hard face. He wore a gray cap and had a scar underneath his right eye. His shoulders reached Jack's ears, and his chest stretched twice as wide as Jack's. He grunted to acknowledge Jack. Jack watched him enter the building and make for Luz's apartment. It was her man.

Relieved, Jack sighed. He realized the hulking figure he had just encountered would have pummeled him if he had been found with Luz. He stood on the front steps, took a Lucky Strike from his back pocket, and gazed at the moon. He still had plenty of time to make the bar before last call. After drinking with Luz, he was eager for a nightcap. A lone car passed, throwing its exhaust into the air, and he descended the stairs toward the deserted street. Once again, he

encountered an eerie quiet as he approached the alleyway. The silence lasted only briefly, however. This time, it crumbled beneath a cacophony of shouts. He was unable to understand the Spanish he heard. He slowed at the entrance of the alley, listened to the bickering voices, and finished his cigarette. The back-and-forth raged. Once again, curiosity got the best of him, and he crept into the alley. Crouching beneath the neighbors' windows, he slunk from the alley's edge to the now familiar spot outside of Luz's apartment.

The verbal barrage continued. Jack could only imagine the meanings of the epithets they hurled at each other. The tone and ferocity of the words burned with rage. "Perro sucio!" Luz yelled after several minutes of vitriol.

"Maldita puta!" the man responded.

A silence ensued. Jack believed the argument had reached denouement. Then he heard it—the crack of flesh against flesh. The sound was unmistakable. Afterwards, the whimpering began anew. Jack imagined the meaty back of the man's hand had caught Luz across her face. Savages, he thought. He braced himself for the sound of another strike—but none came. Instead, deep, menacing laughter echoed through the open window.

"Tu eres mio, puta," the man said.

"No," Luz said. "Por favor, no!"

The man bellowed, his voice lingering in the sparse cavern of the room. Jack heard the sofa slide across the wood floor. The sounds of a short scuffle followed. Luz cried loudly, almost yelping. She spoke rapidly—presumably pleading—although it was incomprehensible to Jack. "No," she said again. "No."

Jack needed to see what was happening. He lifted his head to peer into the window. Luz's man stood behind her, his pants dropped to his ankles. The man bent Luz face forward over the sofa and hiked her dress above her waist. He tore her underwear off.

"No," Luz said. "No."

"Sí," the man sneered, taking his erect penis in his hand. As he held her down, he thrust himself into her. He groaned. "Te gusta?" he said. "Te gusta, puta?" He pumped more rapidly, grunting as he moved in and out of her. At the end, he moaned loudly. The entire encounter took less than two minutes. He slapped Luz on her rear, but she seemed to register nothing. She stared straight ahead, her eyes vacant. The man disengaged himself, pulled up his pants, and strutted toward the kitchen. He spat on the floor before he escaped Jack's line of vision. Luz, exposed and silent, remained folded over the back of the sofa.

Jack crouched in the darkness again. Despite its disturbing nature, the scene had aroused him and he felt cheated of pleasure. He wanted to satisfy himself in a corner of the alley but worried that the bitter cold would discomfort him and prevent him from achieving release. Placing his hands in his pockets, he slunk from the alley to the sidewalk. He needed a drink to take the edge off. He proceeded down Asylum, his erection subsiding. Images from the night flitted through his mind. He felt a frustration—a fury—about the progression of events. He fumed that the Neanderthal had come home when he had been ready to make his move on Luz. To compound the insult, he then had to watch the brute take by force what he had hoped to take by seduction. Luz—and her role in this vignette—mattered little to him. In fact, he thought she had got what she deserved. That's what happens when you climb into a cage with a beast, he told himself.

Despite his inability to comprehend Luz's misery, Jack's feelings toward the brute surprised him. He found himself harboring a begrudging respect for the cretin. At least he got what he wanted, Jack thought. That, and he probably has another woman stashed away somewhere in a dingy apartment. Comparing himself to Luz's man, Jack felt tentative, weak, impotent. "Savages," he muttered to himself. "Filthy, goddamned savages. They're no better than rats." He kicked an empty beer bottle across the asphalt and watched it shatter against a nearby wall. He saw up ahead the street that marked the end of the ghetto. He sighed in relief, lit another Lucky Strike, and walked on. He didn't look back. The smoke from the cigarette trailed behind him in the moonlight.

When Jack crossed into downtown proper, the asphalt sidewalks transformed into brick pavers.

The buildings rose tall, and their windows glimmered in the white shine of the streetlights. He felt at home here—no roaches, no crumbling tenements, no savages. He walked one more block to the corner of Main. There, he faced a wall of thriving commerce. Shiny cars were parked on the streets, and passersby rushed in and out of restaurants and bars. The men wore pressed pants and wool blazers. Even in the cold weather, the women promenaded in tailored dresses and coiffed hair. Only one blemish blotted the glory of this mecca. As Jack waited at the corner across from the bar he frequented, a vagrant approached him. This was a different vagrant than the one he had seen near Luz's apartment, but a vagrant none the less. The vagrant had bloodshot eyes, red hair, and a matted beard. He smelled of booze, dirt, and stale cigarette smoke. He stumbled close to Jack. In a raspy voice, he asked Jack for a cigarette.

Jack rolled his eyes and backed away from him. "No comprendo, hombre," he said. The vagrant stood there watching him. Jack motioned for him to move on. "Scram!"

The vagrant looked at his feet, apologized to Jack for bothering him, and walked away. "God bless," he said.

"Take a bath, hobo," Jack said to himself as he watched the man walk toward the ghetto.

Once the crosswalk light changed, Jack traversed the street. Neon beer signs glowed in the bar's windows. A man and woman stood outside the door and smoked. They wore jeans and ragged sweaters. The man wore a baseball cap pulled low, the bill shading his eyes. The couple huddled close to each other in the cold. They smoked their cigarettes as quickly as possible. Jack attempted to make eye contact with them before entering the bar, but the couple stared at their feet. Their faces were plain and pockmarked. Jack wondered if the riffraff were now invading his territory. He had a good mind to let Mary the bartender know the value of keeping his refuge free from such refuse. He closed his eyes, and let his thoughts wander to Mary. He pictured her ample rear and imagined bending her over a barstool and thrusting himself into her. He began to grow hard again. He waited for his excitement to subside before opening the door to the bar.

Inside, the steady beat of classic rock pulsed. Beneath the glow of fluorescence, rosy-cheeked faces stared into their drinks. Jack's barstool was empty, as usual. He hung his coat on the rack and meandered to his seat. Mary wore a lacy, low-cut, cotton blouse and tight blue jeans. Her face was flush and clean, and her blue eyes shone brightly as she approached Jack. She wore her long blonde hair pulled back in a ponytail. She was of his kind, he thought. He understood why he desired her.

"The usual?" Mary said.

Jack nodded. He smiled at the irony. The night seemed very unusual to him. He had nearly slept with a tramp, watched a man rape her, and now sat calmly at a bar waiting for a shot and a beer. Mary sauntered back toward him, two drinks in her hands. She set them down in front of him. She leaned forward, and Jack saw the creamy whiteness of her breasts as they plunged into a scarlet bra. She caught him looking and smiled.

"That'll be twelve dollars, sweetheart," Mary said.

Jack placed a twenty-dollar bill on the bar.

As Mary took the bill, Jack grabbed her hand. The touch of skin against skin felt electric. Startled, she dropped the bill. She looked into his eyes. He thought her eyes burned with a mixture of fear and desire. She tried to draw her hand away, but he held it firmly. The skin on her arm grew gooseflesh. He had seen what he needed to see. He loosened his grip.

"I was just toying with you," Jack said before blowing her a kiss. "Keep the change."

Mary mumbled something as she walked away.

Jack believed she said, "Thank you."

While tending to other patrons, Mary repeatedly looked at Jack. He downed his shot and sipped his beer. The night had changed for the better, he thought. He placed his hands behind his head and leaned back in the barstool.

Mary fluttered nervously back-and-forth behind the bar. She looked like a frightened, caged bird.

Jack liked what he saw. "From now on, things will be different," he said to himself. "From now on, I'll take what I want."

About the Author:

Lewis J. Beilman III lives in Hamden, Connecticut, with his family, dog, and two cats. His stories have appeared in Foliate Oak Literary Magazine, ArLiJo, Reed Magazine, and other literary publications. His novella, Fourth of July, was published by Scarlet Leaf Publishing in August 2017. He is a former first-prize winner of the Fred R. Shaw Poetry Contest.

VIRTUAL PLAYGROUND: PLANET EARTH
by Sarah A. Odishoo

"It may be that our role on this planet is not to worship God but to create him."

—Arthur C. Clarke

"In a time of universal deceit, the truth is revolutionary."

—George Orwell

What if human beings are hybrid alien creatures?

That is, a Creator used matter (the earth's four elements—earth, air, water, fire) to design a "space suit"—the human body. Then the Creator injected the body with a "spirit," an alien life force from another plane of existence, to live and play and breed in this new earthly plane of Being?

A celebrated 1997 paper by Juan M. Maladacena...describes nature as a kind of hologram, in which the information about what happens inside a volume of three-dimensional space, for example, is encoded in quantum equations on its two-dimensional boundary, the way a 3-D image is encoded on the face of your bank card.

...physicists have more reason than ever to think that information cannot be lost. *

And the purpose?

For those beings to remember their source—the holographic designer—and return to it, not in their physical form (their space suits) but in spirit (their real form), the "eternal" information with which we are programmed cannot be lost. It may be that the ultimate goal would have

been to have that information transform the body so that the spirit of the body would remember where it came from and use it consciously to teach the leaden, fleshly body to learn how to navigate its spiritual powers in a material world to transform matter into psychic possibilities...

But that may be far ahead of our script.

II

Quantum entanglement, also known as "spooky action at a distance," in which particles separated by light years can still instantaneously appear to remain connected. *

Our spirit exists not only in our bodies but also in another dimension, and we can, if we become conscious, direct our activities—and here I mean thoughts and feelings and meaning—not only to others but to the Source within the body, not only to the physical body and world.

As Einstein, Boris Podolsky and Nathan Rosen pointed out in 1935, quantum theory predicts that a pair of particles can be connected in such a way that measuring the property of one—in the direction of spin, say—will immediately affect the results of measuring the other one, even if it is light-years away. *

We may be in a "boarding school" where we are in the process of awakening matter with our spirit in order to become one with that which is—that "spooky action at a distance." I suppose you could say Jesus was one of those teachers of spooky action, as were Buddha/Siddhartha, Moses, Mohatma Gandhi, Mohammed, Joan of Arc, Theresa of Avila, the ones who actually lived in corresponding universes simultaneously and suffered the double language barriers—those of this material reality and the other interior one, but all chose Spirit, against all odds.

III

The physical barriers?

We are born into a material world as beings of matter—flesh, bone, blood, air. In the womb we neither see, nor hear, nor feel the outside physical world. We understand nothing of the material world. We are spirit encased in fleshly matter. We must enter the world this way to become acclimatized to a new order and learn the ways of a system completely unlike the one from which we came in order to consciously choose to return to spirit. That freedom to choose to recognize and acknowledge the Source available to us transforms the material body into lifeforce, like electricity. Spirit taps the source of the energy we need to transform unconscious living into conscious living—seeing the Source in all that is.

Most of us completely forget our birthing and the first three years of life. Wordsworth describes that infancy in our bodies as "trailing clouds of glory," as he identifies in that beginning the essence of the unknowable in the naked appearance of a God in each newborn. Just as the child sees the world as new, so the soul looking at the world through spirit sees its miracles, its order, its wholiness.

IV

According to science, our inherited nature is created and formed by a history of ancestors, their gene pool, and the memory programmed within those genes.

...a basic tenet of modern science and of quantum theory is that information is always preserved. From the material in the smoke and flame of a burning book..., one could figure out whether it was the Bible or the Kama Sutra; the same would be true of the fizz and pop of black holes. *

Where did that Nature come from? Spooky action at a distance?

We still don't know. Three axioms:

1. All human beings alive today are related to each other; the furthest away any of us can be from one another is 42nd cousin!

2. All human beings have the same four lettered genes, yet of the seven-and-a-half billion humans on the earth, there is not one duplication of genes. Each human is a unique, singular, incomparable being. Why?

3. All human tribes and cultures have had a Source to which they turn for explanation of cause and effect and to which they feel indebted for both what they can see and feel.

Humans are programmed too. The search for meaning to this earthly life is a paramount constant in all human values and activities. And all human societies identify the translators of that alien world: parapsychics—priests, magi, ministers—who try to explain the unexplainable—smoke and flame of what is.

Scientists are the new-world magi, and like the magi who predicted a "new king is born," the scientists give us reality checks of unseen forces of creation we either don't understand or don't believe or both.

A hundred times every day I remind myself that my inner and outer life are based on the labors of other men, living and dead, and that I must exert myself in order to give in same measure as I have received and am still receiving.

—Albert Einstein (1879-1955)*

Einstein understood he was on the shoulders of a whole history of magi who tried to explain the purpose of Being—the real.

V

Consider this: The earth as God's school and playground.

VI

Entanglement: What if each of us is a virtual being: a projected image of our Self from another dimension? That self as Spirit can project its being—its imaginal Self, the actress—on the projected stage called Earth. And on that stage, she tests and refines her powers of choice, action, process, play, and replay until she perfects the roles she has chosen, accepted, and learned what she needs to know in order to return to Spirit. To do that, she needs to communicate with the Self from which she came. Entanglement. Particle whispering to particle. Known to unknown. And each pain, conflict, agony, ache, has meaning, significance, and implications that are different than joy and happiness. Pain brings conscious attention to solving the problem; joy loves its state and wants to stay in it.

So that small, still voice is the other particle that wants us to know what we don't already know.

This Stage is her testing ground to perfect her imperfect perception of spiritual wholeness. The process of living in this world is to choose to know or not to know what the other particle is whispering and to act on that knowledge instead of the earthly instructions. The progression on this earthly stage for humans is Love/Laughter/Language/Logic—in that order. If you don't receive one, the next and next are affected—Nature and its laws are affected.

In the cosmic world smoke and flame can tell us if it's the Bible or the Kama Sutra, and our lifetimes have the same residues as well.

God does not play dice.   —Albert Einstein*

VII

The Laws of Nature are interdependent for a reason—Growth. There is no act, no thought, no decision, no word that is lost, or has no consequences, or no repercussions. All affects All.

And for what reason?

The loving logic behind all the laws is to make us conscious enough to recognize that the Source is within and with-out us and the natural laws abet the Source in returning us to what feels like a "natural" state—the Source within us.

So that small, still voice that is the other particle wants us to be conscious enough to be free to choose what we already know—The Source.

VIII

No information is lost. Our lifetimes have residues billions of years in the making and remaking. The role ends, not the Being.

IX

Why Death and dying?

Every sliver of experience is part of a conspiracy,

in the best sense of the word, to reveal and reflect our relationship to the whole. The freedom to choose to know—consciousness—liberates the human from the material construct of the body to explore possibilities that are the transforming dimensions of Being and Source. Death is the end of the show. An actor's virtual life is on the stage. Her real life is in the wings, preparing to die.

Death always prioritizes the Real, and the Self begins to understand what is critical in this play of life. In the role she has chosen in which the Source has set the Stage, she can stand in the wings watching herself watching herself...

Another season, another show...

*All italicized references are from Dennis Overbye, "Einstein and the Black Hole," The New York Times, August 13, 2013.

About the Author:

Sarah A. Odishoo is a poet and writer who teaches at Columbia College Chicago and who was nominated for Best of Net Anthology for "Euclid's Bride," published by Diversevoicesquarterly.com (2014) and "Germane German" Under-the-Sun.online.com (The Pushcart Prize ,2015, and most recently, published "Virtual Reality is the Real..." (2016)

with www.michiganquarterlyreview.com.

IDENTITY CARD

Kate McCorkle

On another cloudless September morning of perfect, temperate weather, Jason and I, both twenty-four, drove the canvas-top Jeep to Fort Campbell to have our wills written. That was something the Army strongly recommended—having Jason's will drawn up—because everyone knew the guys were soon heading somewhere that would likely kill them. Sunburned, unwashed hair twisted into a sloppy bun, and wrung-out, I was going since we figured it made sense to do the wills together. After all, we were married now. Twelve days.

Getting on post, the Fort Campbell Army base in Clarksville, Tennessee, was straightforward in theory. Flash your identity card to the MP (military police) on duty at the gate, then drive through. Only post, like the whole country, was on high alert from the 9/11 terrorist attacks twenty-four hours ago. Life itself was in a horrified lockdown. And Jason and I had a problem. I didn't have a military ID.

Initially, in the other lifetime that was yesterday, I didn't understand the big deal about not having my ID yet. Couldn't my driver's license get me on post? I had a grad school ID, a credit card with my name. I knew who I was.

Wasn't that what I was always trying to prove, some way or another? With each new school, team, or move—proving myself to people who underestimated me—who called me a dumb blond. Or assumed the hair made me easy, somehow. People who thought introvert meant docile, or bookish meant passive, or blond hair and blue eyes excused smirking insinuations, made a blank

canvas for unkind projections. By now I had developed a fuck you muscle and an obstinate self-sufficiency. I might be married but I wasn't taking my husband's name. That's not me. Yet Jason and I were in this marriage, this new endeavor, together. We'd figure it out. Just like we were bumping along a back road in a Jeep that felt every rock, figuring out how to get through that gate without a mandatory ID.

Apparently a driver's license wouldn't work because it only proved I was who I claimed to be. It confirmed my Kate-ness. The driver's license didn't reveal I had any link to Jason, therefore any association with the Army—ergo, any permission to access that life.

And, as a newly minted officer's wife, life now hinged on the United States Uniformed Services Identification and Privilege Card. I couldn't register for medical, dental, or auto insurance, couldn't obtain our housing or salary information, couldn't buy groceries or go to the gym, and certainly couldn't get on post to ferry Jason to and from work without that card. I was also barred from the emergency family meetings that had erupted in the past twenty-four hours. (Ironically, I would have eagerly attended: my ignorance and fear around Jason's job was that high. By the time I finally did get my military ID, I resented being told what to do and chaffed under the groupthink.) Cristy, another officer's wife, volunteered to fill me in on anything important. The towers fell. Planes were weapons. Isn't it all important?

After waiting in a two-hour car line (in

which I nearly peed myself), it was our turn at the gate. The rifle-wielding MP ping-ponged between me and my license, reconciling the husk in the passenger seat with the smiling college girl in the photo. He eyed me warily, waved another MP over to confer, shifted his rifle on his hips—Why's a civilian with no military ID trying to get onto Fort Campbell?—but Jason assured them we had a JAG (Judge Advocate General) appointment, and a proper ID was forthcoming. Satisfied (or suckered), the MP returned our cards and waved us forward. As Jason drove through the gate, another rifle-toting guard yelled, "Balls!"

I looked at Jason. "Did he just yell balls at me?"

Jason snickered. "Yeah. Balls of the eagle."

"What?"

"Their unit is the balls of the eagle. Like we're the talons."

"Talons?"

"Our emblem. The battalion insignia. The eagle is the symbol of the Hundred and First, right? The different battalions have different symbols—"

"And someone took the balls? What the—"

"Canon balls," Jason laughed. "Canon balls. We're talons, the Rakassans are a winged sword—"

I closed my eyes and leaned against the plastic window as Jason elaborated on Army insignia. We were on post now, driving toward the JAG office, and the uncanny scene both resembled a town and not. It was my first time there, and what was normal for Jason seemed profoundly strange to me. I tried to peg the dissonance.

Identical buildings clustered together, like a dump truck spilled whatever material was handy in a designated area and they built one model until supplies ran out. Some areas, like the barracks, looked like they came from a '40s movie. Nothing was higher than two stories, save for the red brick Continuing Education Center and the massive scaffolding towers used to monitor maneuvers and parachute jumps.

The scene unsettled me, especially after living in Chicago for the past two years. I smiled recalling the energy that expanded in every direction in the city—cars and buses and the El and bikes zigzagging, intersecting, skyscrapers shooting vertical, parks and bike paths—the river—creating their own swirling vibe. The stones in the buildings seemed to sing, tell of their varied origins. Beautiful polyglot people, with their music and smells and color, were everywhere.

Alongside the Jeep units ran en masse, buzz-cut men wearing light-refracting safety belts across their chests, even at midday. Lock-step. Uniform. Precise. Everything was so organized and regulated. Like someone took nail clippers to blades of grass. The speed limit was twenty-five miles an hour. Most people wore uniforms labeled with their names. Houses were identified with family name plates by the front doors. Every building had signage visible from the road. Labeled. Categorized. Neat. A twinge of irritability kicked in.

"Why are those playgrounds so crappy?" I asked, tapping my plastic window in the direction of a splintered see-saw and rusty jungle gym.

"Enlisted housing," Jason answered, eyes on the road.

"You mean all the enlisted guys live together?"

"Same neighborhood."

"And the officers are separate?"

"Yep. Single guys are in the barracks. No one likes living there. Some guys get married, you figure it's just to get out of the barracks."

"That doesn't seem right," I said, still thinking of the segregated housing.

"Well, they're eighteen. They meet some local girl or have someone back home—"

"No. The housing," I said. "Why do the enlisted kids have a junk playground?"

"Kate," Jason sighed. "Don't start."

"I'm serious," I said, turning toward him. "Don't you think it's a problem to have housing segregated by rank? And one group's children get the shit playground?"

"That's just the way the Army is," he said, eyes on the road. "You don't—you don't get it. There's a reason for it that makes sense—"

"There's a reason for an enlisted guy's kid to get splinters from a broken see-saw?"

"There's a reason for the separate housing areas. No one wants to run into their boss or their men outside work—struggle with a lawnmower in front of their men—go outside with a beer and your boss is there. Look, we're almost at the office. Can you not do this with the lawyer?"

"I'm not doing anything. I simply asked why you treat children like shit." I waited for him to react to the you, to take the bait—Why had I even said it like that?—but he was unfazed.

"Okey-doke," Jason muttered, turning the Jeep from the road and sliding into one of the three spots beside the signage marked JAG. The office didn't look any different, any more imposing or judicial, from the other buildings in this stretch labeled LAUNDROMAT or some indecipherable acronym like JXZQKY.

I followed Jason into the office: him in drab green camo, black combat boots, and that supershort hair I hated under a cloth hat, called a cover, that was removed indoors. Until I saw the JAG lawyer in his uniform, I thought I was dressed okay. But now the surfer shorts, t-shirt with belle époque illustration, and flip-flops felt childish.

I don't know what I expected from a lawyer's office but it wasn't this. The space was basically a wood-paneled trailer colonized by a civilization of paper towers on every surface, including the floor. An office supply (like a stapler or three-hole punch) topped each stack since a large, oscillating fan in the corner created enough wind to tornado the papers. The undulating buzz from the fan and the trembling documents created a kind of call-and-response orchestra. When the lawyer jumped up to shake our hands, I was struck by how young he looked. Lawyers were my parents' age, not mine.

Nodding to the paperwork enveloping his desk, the stacks overflowing onto the floor, he apologized for his office being so messy. It wasn't normally like that, he said, clearing off a second chair so I could sit. The attacks hung in the air. He set the fan to a lower speed; picked his way back to the desk through the minefield of paper towers. Married twelve days, twenty-four years old, and we're drafting wills with a baby-faced Army lawyer. I cringed catching sight of my flip-flops, but least my toenails were done—robin's-egg blue (my something blue for the wedding). I had been happy my feet weren't calloused for once, but blue toes felt asinine now.

Jason's living will was written first—in case he came home a vegetable from wherever he was going.

The final wills weren't that complicated since we didn't own anything and we'd leave that nothing to each other anyway. I snorted when we came to the language around "future issue"—the idea of motherhood, of me capably caring for another, seemed ridiculous in light of the world ending—but Jason let out a deep sigh. Dark circles puffed under his eyes. I reached for his hand. He leaned forward and asked the lawyer if there was anything we could do about my lack of military ID. The lawyer pushed from the desk, tipped in his chair—"How'd y'all even get on post if she doesn't have an ID?"

Jason explained that he started the process of obtaining my military ID yesterday morning—his first work task after returning from the honeymoon. He needed to submit our marriage license—currently housed in the Worcester, Massachusetts, city hall—as validation that I was a dependent under him. (I grimaced; Jason and the lawyer each instinctively raised a hand to quell any protest.) Jason's request was filed and the license was scheduled to arrive in Fort Campbell, Kentucky, via air mail forty-eight hours later. Only all flights were grounded indefinitely by 9:30 after the terrorist attacks.

"We don't know how long the paperwork's going to take now," Jason concluded, twisting his cover.

"She needs to be in the system," the lawyer murmured. He and Jason exchanged a look, then averted their eyes.

I sat in my chair. Quiet. I was a dependent, a problem to be figured out by the men. I wanted to jump in, clean this mess myself, but I had no idea where to even start. There was basic stuff about the Army I didn't know—like the difference between companies, battalions, and units. I tried to reassure myself that quiet was okay. Quiet did not mean weak. I took in the framed diploma hanging on wood behind the desk, the audible rhythm of the oscillating fan.

I had made a promise to the boy sitting beside me and that changed things. A broken world is imploding. I don't know who I am.

The lawyer thought for a moment. "A power of attorney might work," he said. He strode from behind his desk to search a ream of papers on the floor (weighed down by a book), eventually standing with a document in hand.

"A power of attorney," he said, delicately making his way in combat boots through the stacks back to his chair, "isn't going to solve your problem. But it could help."

He explained that the power of attorney would allow me to legally sign Jason's name on documents when he was gone. Which was happening any day now.

Once we notarized that paperwork, I was legally Second Lieutenant Jason Voight, United States Army, at the same time I couldn't prove my own identity to the Army's satisfaction.

We'd been up since six, and I was starving when we left JAG, even though it was only ten. I fantasized about a rare hamburger and onion rings chased by a black-and-white milkshake. Writing your will as a newlywed makes a girl hungry. Jason said breakfast hours were over, and nothing on post would open for lunch for another hour since everyone was at work. As we drove to our next errand at the housing office, I saw this was true. No one was on the road. There was no need for any food service to be open. The Burger King would open at eleven, Jason said, so if I wanted to swing by after I dropped him off at work—

Forget it, I said, dreaming of the Chicago restaurants that perfumed the street with grilled onions and peppers, sautéed garlic, deep-dish pizza, Montreal-seasoned steak, even caramel corn and hot chocolate—scents that physically turned your head and transported you, fed you, even at 9:30 in the morning. Maybe, 460 miles north, my friend Lyra was chasing a spinach and feta omelet with coffee.

Lost in my gastronomic fantasy, I realized we'd arrived at the housing office only when Jason threw the car in park. The building had an actual foundation—unlike the glorified trailer that was JAG—but still managed to resemble something thrown together from leftover material.

Every soldier receives a basic allowance for housing (BAH) as part of their pay. Now that Jason had a dependent (moi), his BAH increased. It's how he could go from splitting rent with two other guys to shouldering a place on his income alone. Our rent was due but he was still pulling a bachelor's BAH because I wasn't in the system yet.

Despite being at Campbell for mere days, I knew the housing office to be both the DMV and Ellis Island of post. Along with the mind-numbing red tape and paperwork associated with the place, it was also an active social experiment: how long before tedium and the absence of logic makes a human snap?

Every minute in the waiting area, Jason grew more restless. He played with his new ring, loosened and tightened his watch, pumped his heels. He was supposed to be at work—it was already one—not chaperoning me and our paperwork. My legs suctioned to the chair. Everyone else was in uniform; I was the only dumbass in shorts. I felt like I should be popping gum or wadding spitballs, even though I'd never do either in a waiting room.

"One of these things is not like the other," I sang to Jason, leaning close so no one else could hear. "One of these things just isn't the same."

Jason looked at me blankly, shrugged.

"Can you guess which kid is doing his own thing?" I sang in a slightly different tune, waiting for recognition. Jason rolled his eyes, scooted his chair away.

"You never watched Sesame Street?" I asked.

"I guess not." He turned away, hooking and unhooking his watch.

A minute later I leaned in again and moaned, haaaaamburger. A few days ago, on our honeymoon, he would've rolled his eyes or at least smiled. He might have admitted he was hungry too. Now he waved me off, pointed at his watch. I have to get to work.

I pried my sweaty legs from the chair and, holding the power of attorney like a shield, approached the intake area that resembled a bank from the Old West (plywood, divots that could be bullet holes).

"Kate," Jason hissed as I caught the eye of the soldier/administrator behind the bar, a large-chested woman who looked old but probably wasn't.

I presented my freshly minted power of attorney, thinking I could do this and let Jason get to work. That brought an already lurching process to a screeching halt. From my periphery I saw Jason wince and fold his face into his hands.

"What's this?" the intake soldier asked. She said it like, Whazzis.

"A power of attorney."

"Why you giving me that? What number are you?"

"It's for my housing—"

"ID," she demanded, extending her hand.

"That's what this is. It's—"

"No. It's not. Where's your ID?"

"I don't have an ID yet. We were just married." I nodded toward Jason, my heart involuntarily swelling a bit. Days ago we'd say that and people—usually older women—would sigh and coo their congratulations. It annoyed me then, mostly because I found it schmaltzy. Here, though, in the Old West/DMV/Ellis Island, some cooing would have meant I was dealing with a human.

"If you're married, you have ID. No ID, no marriage." She looked past me, as if anyone else was dumb enough to get in line.

"But this is acting for that." I tapped the paper between us. "The lawyer said the power of attorney could act as my ID—"

"Wait. How'd you get power of attorney if you're not married?"

"I am married. We just don't have the license because planes are grounded."

"What do planes have to do with anything?"

"We got married in Massachusetts. The license is up there. We filed the paperwork yesterday morning, but flights were grounded two hours later."

"Why didn't you bring a copy with you?"

"I didn't know I'd need my wedding license for anything."

"You didn't know you were marrying someone in the Army?" She took a step back, like the stupidity radiating from me literally repelled her.

"Look—the point is—we don't have the license yet. It's on its way and we need to get our BAH adjusted—"

"You don't have a marriage license. So how'd you get that power of attorney?"

"From JAG."

"Here? On this post?"

"What other JAG—"

"There is no need for surliness." She lurched forward and leaned over the intake counter, the power of attorney crinkling under her abdomen. I backed up.

Jason approached the counter twirling his cover. The administrator turned to him.

"Where's her ID?" she demanded.

Jason sighed. "I'm trying to adjust my BAH—"

"You need a valid marriage license for that."

The exchange continued for a while, entertaining our fellow yearning masses in the waiting area. They were probably having a good laugh at the girl with blue toes. Eventually the intake soldier got her boss, and after quintuple-checking and many raised eyebrows (I waited for her to yell balls at me), she signed off on our BAH form. Now we could pay rent.

The process might have been messy, but I was proud I kind of got something done, greased some wheels. When I suggested this to Jason en route to his office, he shrugged. You can't make your own rules, he said, the corners of his mouth turned down. When I'm gone—this isn't a joke.

I know that.

Leaning my head against the plastic window, I watched identical buildings blur into a white wave. The germ of a thought that had sprouted in the JAG office, as I sat very still, returned. Two thoughts, together. One: My presence is a difficulty, a complication. I am intrinsically wrong for Jason or at least wrong for a military environment. Two: The bureaucracy is the problem, not me. Maybe if I fix it, things will be okay.

In this way, I will never fit became both a fear and a hope that was itself complicated by the boy. Fitting in meant I was a good wife but a little dead inside. A middle finger to the system granted me sanity but made for a shaky marriage. The careening pendulum swings between these poles would plague me most of the time Jason served in the Army. I hadn't yet learned to hold my breath and dive under the wave. I still thought my willpower could stop it.

A few days later we bought a new car—an American-made Pontiac Grand Prix. We hadn't planned on buying a second car so soon, but we needed one if I couldn't get on post, and the dealerships were offering huge discounts. I wondered if this was happening across the country or just around military bases. Guys got a bump in pay for hazardous duty, and everyone expected them to deploy soon. It was good timing for a new vehicle.

Less than a week after buying the Pontiac, the dealership called because there was some confusion with the paperwork—forms they were just now processing due to high volume. I'd have to return and resubmit the information, re-sign the documents. Jason was gone by this point—on a mystery assignment. The car salesman said to come anyway. The forms, which had to do with the title, had to be filed. You can sign your name, can't you, honey?

At the dealership I signed papers attesting that I was legally Mrs. Voight and not some rogue impersonator. (Although, legally, I'm not Mrs. Voight. I'm Ms. McCorkle.) I used the power of attorney to do this because the affidavit required Jason's signature. So, in effect, I signed Jason's name to a document vouching that I was his wife.

Until the flight ban lifted and our marriage license arrived, I was a non-person.

Kate McCorkle's stories and essays have appeared in several publications, including Barely South Review, r.kv.r.y Quarterly, Marathon Literary Review, and Penmen Review. A Pushcart nominee, she writes with the Greater Philadelphia Workshop Studio. Kate is currently working on a book-length thing about her time as a 9/11 infantry wife. A mother of four young children, she swims to keep insanity at bay.

About the Author:

Kate McCorkle's stories and essays have appeared in several publications, including Barely South Review, r.kv.r.y Quarterly, Marathon Literary Review, and Penmen Review. A Pushcart nominee, she writes with the Greater Philadelphia Workshop Studio. Kate is currently working on a book-length thing about her time as a 9/11 infantry wife. A mother of four young children, she swims to keep insanity at bay.

NEW BOY RULES

Joseph Eastburn

When my parents separated in 1962, they decided to send my older sister and me off to boarding school to get us out of the turmoil of a disintegrating marriage. For me, the decision may have saved my life; for my sister, it was a disaster.

My sister was the kind of girl who liked to wear makeup and earrings and put on dresses and nylon stockings and heels. She was an editor of her high school newspaper. She was sent off to Woodstock Country School in Vermont, where everyone wore jeans and called their headmaster "David." There are other reasons why she may not have fit in. My parents met onstage, and so we were all somewhat artistically inclined in our eccentric way—what I might call "literary," though instead of actually reading books, my parents talked about them while they drank heavily. My father was also directing and producing theater in New Jersey, and we would drive into New York City to see the world premiere of a Harold Pinter play in Greenwich Village, for instance, or a Broadway show. We were theater people—which meant high drama.

In that context, my sister being shipped off to a windswept farm full of long-haired, sad, straight-faced girls (who in my mind's eye all resembled the Manson women) was worse than my boarding school experience, even though mine looked worse. She was like a hothouse flower taken outside at full bloom and flung in the snow.

While my sister had thrived in public school, I was failing, constantly in trouble, and had already been suspended. It wasn't until my forties that I realized I got in trouble at school because I was trying to get attention—even though the only

kind I got was negative attention. I'd already been labeled a troublemaker. The school secretaries remarked that they knew I'd be the first student to try out the brand-new chairs in the principal's office. When I was catapulted off to boarding school in seventh grade, it was a new start. I was out of the upheaval of my parents' tunnel of acrimony and the crisis of their breakup. Except for a summer at sailing camp, it was the first time on my own.

There was only one catch.

I still remember the date I started attending the Peddie School in Hightstown, New Jersey: January 11. By transferring in the middle of the school year, I didn't have to go through the new-boy orientation that all the other new students had to endure.

And new-boy rules at Peddie were fairly extreme. You couldn't walk on the grass; if an upperclassman caught you, he could make you do push-ups on the spot. The school colors were blue and gold, so you had to wear a blue and gold striped school tie; a blue and gold beanie; one blue sock and one gold sock. But the worst part was the hazing. Any new boy could be physically and mentally abused at will, and it was an accepted part of being initiated into the school's community.

The culture at East Coast boys' boarding schools in the sixties was very British in tone. You had to wear a coat and tie, go to classes six days a week, attend chapel every day, eat at assigned tables in the dining hall (another venue for being ostracized), and submit to "lights out" at 9 p.m. It was strict. Once the dean saw me throw a snowball after it had been prohibited, and I had to stay on campus during a free weekend. The Junior School had emptied, so I had to move into an upperclassmen's dorm with a kid who smelled, wouldn't do his laundry, and wore my clothes.

One student who took it upon himself to put me through an impromptu (and more brutal) new-boy orientation was Albert Shaio. Eastburn was my middle name. Like everyone else, Albert started with a corruption of my last name, Blankenship. At the dining table, Albert addressed me as Blankenshit, then to save time, shortened his greeting to "Shitty." He would decide whether I was to get any food or not, or what weird inedible items would end up on my plate as it was passed down to me. Albert was of mixed ancestry: Spanish and Jewish. I mention this only because in 1962, racial stereotypes seemed much more pronounced, and kids tended to be more willing than adults to use racial slurs out loud. Peddie was also in Central Jersey, close to Pennsylvania, so there were a lot of tough kids from Trenton and Philly. Albert was the lieutenant of a group of eighth-graders who called themselves "Murder Inc.," after the 1960 movie with Peter Falk. Instead of taking a contract out on someone, they would fling a piece of lettuce down on the table in the dining hall and joke that it was a contract to beat some kid up.

Once I was invited to witness this in the privacy of a dorm room. The kid doing the beating was Murray Barrett. The kid being slapped around was Jim Snedicker, a tall, nerdy, rail-thin kid with glasses. As an audience of one, I wasn't sure what I was doing there. After it was over and Jim had left, humiliated, Murray told me it was a fake fight, and that it had been ordered by the guys on the third floor. The implication was that it could happen to me. The whole thing was a little like a boys' school variation on Lord of the Flies. Murray was our dorm go-between. He'd communicate with the tough kids on the top floor, yet he was a regular kid who had probably risen to his current status by getting beaten up himself—and who happened to be a born negotiator. At first there were only veiled threats of bullying. But because I hadn't gone through the actual new-boy orientation, it was inevitable that the kids in the dorm would have to put me through their own personalized hazing.

It all kind of erupted one night just before dinner. Even though there were two single beds in my room, I was living alone in a back, corner room on the second floor of the dorm. It was dark outside. I was getting ready to walk over to Wilson Hall, where the dining room was. There were students milling around outside my door. I heard voices and someone kicked my door. I remember I was wearing my jacket and tie under my black raincoat. When I opened my door, the hallway was full of students, all staring at me. Nobody spoke. I think I said "Hi" and walked toward the down stairwell.

Out of nowhere, a tall kid I'd never seen grabbed me, accused me of calling him a name, and slammed me against the wall. He was Ken Walsh, a tough kid with a leather jacket who wore his red hair greased back in a "Chicago duck's ass"—the greaser style of the moment—where his hair was combed around the back of his head, both sides meeting at the center in a line that grooved down to a little tail. Kids referred to it as a "D.A." Walsh had me by the lapels of my raincoat and was demanding to know if I'd called him a certain name. I kept saying "No." And he kept insisting that I had. Finally, he kind of pushed me away, threatened me, and with students lining both sides of the hallway, some kid tried to trip me and another called me "chicken" as I walked toward the stairs. That was the start of it.

That night there was a basketball game. I sat in the second row of the bleachers, and a group of five or more eighth-graders, all smiling, walked by me up into the stands. Each kid punched me in the arm, or smacked me on top of the head, until finally Walsh dragged the top of his shoe along my leg and up my side. I can still see the shoe. It was brown and extremely pointed, the kind of shoe in my hometown we had called PFCs, or Puerto Rican Fence Climbers. In the Northeast in the sixties, Puerto Ricans were the ridiculed minority—the "Mexicans" of today.

The hazing continued for several weeks, with students that I thought were friends accusing me of calling them names too. That was a common strategy. Or, kids would throw things out of the windows at me while I walked to class. At the same time, one of the eighth-graders from the third floor befriended me. Charlie Bryan, a tall dark-haired kid, used to invite me onto the lawn beside the dorm to play catch with a football. The point man for the hazing was always Albert, who kept challenging me to fight him. I just kept saying no. But the time would come when I would have to fight him—even though I didn't know that yet.

The main classroom building on campus was Memorial Hall, a gigantic three-story brick edifice near the chapel, which dominated the main campus. In the other direction, the building towered over the athletic fields. It was there—after weeks of verbal abuse, snubbing, and getting shoved around—that the time finally came.

I was standing at the rear of the third floor, outside of the 4:45 p.m. study hall that all Junior Schoolers and freshmen had to attend. I had stacked all my course books on top of a loose-leaf notebook and placed them up on the open window, leaning forward, my elbows on the sill as I gazed out across the athletic fields toward a highway in the distance, wishing I could get away. Someone, I never found out who, pushed me hard, so my own elbows knocked my books out of the third-floor window. It had recently snowed. I walked down three flights and waded across the wet, frozen ground, picking up my ruined books. For a minute, I thought it had started to rain. Then I realized students were upstairs on the third floor spitting down on me. I walked back upstairs, placed my wet books on the radiator, and stared out the window again.

Murray came over and said, "Shaio wants to fight you."

I said, "I don't want to fight."

He tried to talk me into fighting, and I just kept saying no.

Then Murray said, "But this is gonna keep happening until you do. Why don't you just fight him and get it over with?"

I had to admit, that made a lot of sense. So I finally said, "Okay, I'll fight him."

Murray smiled his approval and shook my hand. The next thing I knew, he had spread the word, because friends rushed up and said, "I hear you're going to fight Shaio." Before study hall started, Murray came back and told me the fight would take place behind the gym after study hall. He shook my hand again, as if sealing a contract. Word had spread through the entire study hall. As we were filing into study hall, I heard a kid behind me whisper, "Shaio is going to fight the new boy!" Then in a muffled tone, another voice said, "Shh. That's him."

Oddly enough, Shaio sat across the study hall in the same row of desks as I did, in the kind of wood-top desk with the metal chair attached. I remember the book we were reading in English class at that time was The Yearling, by Marjorie Rawlings. I read the book for the entire forty-five minutes of study hall, but kept reading the same paragraph over and over. I probably never retained a single syllable of print. I looked down, as if engrossed, but I was thinking only about the fight. Once in a while I would glance over at Shaio out of the corner of my eye. He looked engrossed as well, but I would guess he probably wasn't reading either.

After study hall, everything was a blur until we ended up behind the gym. There had to be thirty to forty kids there, milling around, waiting. I saw Walsh smile and place the heel of one pointed shoe up on the bricks of the gym wall and lean back with his arms crossed, as if that were the posture one should adopt watching a fight. Several kids imitated him exactly, so there was a row of kids with one shoe up and arms crossed. It was dusk on a winter evening, and the light was hitting the campus buildings at a sharp angle.

I don't remember all the words that were said, or the advice friends whispered to me, until Charlie Bryan came up to me and said, "Give me your rings."

I handed him my rings.

He looked at me and said, "All right, now hit that spic Jew in the nose."

He could have said, "Pound that Spaniard in the protuberance. Punch the Basque bastard. Aim for the nostrils of that Latino-American person." But he didn't say that.

Years later, it would occur to me that the "spic" slur meant Albert was probably of mixed Puerto Rican and Jewish ancestry—and had himself probably been bullied wherever he grew up.

"Hit that Jew in the beak as hard as you can.

That's all you have to do."

I remember saying "Okay."

"Do you understand?"

I must have said "Yes."

The sun had set and we were standing on a patch of grass, with the light fading. I remember Shaio had wisely chosen the higher ground. He was wearing a yellow shirt. I had on a striped sweater. The next thing I knew, we were facing each other with fists raised.

Shaio said, "Are you ready, Blankenship?" No "t" on the end. Looking back, I had already earned a measure of respect by just being willing to fight, even though I was clearly going to lose. We charged each other and I followed Charlie's instructions. I swung as hard as I could and hit Albert Shaio in the nose.

His nose burst and he started spouting blood down the front of this yellow shirt. I heard a roar from the kids behind the gym. We traded more blows. I remember hitting him on the side of the head. The next thing I knew, Shaio had tackled me, put me in a headlock, and was punching me in the forehead. I had my eyes closed, and each time he hit me, I remember there was a shock of light, like someone had taken my picture with an old-fashioned flash camera. A teacher showed up and stopped the fight. I remember walking away, right next to Albert, who by this time had put on his sports jacket. I heard somebody say, "The kid in the sweater just beat up the kid in the jacket."

A whole group of kids surrounded us as we crossed the main quad. When we got to the dorm, Albert disappeared. Walking up the stairs with Charlie and my classmates, I said, "Well, I guess I lost."

They all said, emphatically, "No, you didn't lose. You won."

Was it the blood?

They followed me into my room. The seventh-graders began acting out the punch with sound effects. Everyone was really excited. More and more kids crowded into my room, congratulating me. One kid grabbed my wrist, raising my arm in the air the way a referee would after a real bout. Finally Shaio walked in, wearing a new shirt. Everybody cheered and he gave us a big halfhearted

smile. He definitely looked chastened. It took guts for him to show up in enemy territory.

The next day I was walking back from the canteen and passed Ken Walsh on the road behind the dorm. He gave me a big smile and said, "Hi, Joe." Real friendly.

There was no more hazing.

I realize this is a sad commentary on the human condition—that males have to go through this violent ritual to become accepted. At a time when bullying and racial slurs have become weaponized by the Internet and prominent voices in our culture are encouraging more harassment, I'm embarrassed to feel proud about this fight. But it's what happened.

I was a troubled twelve-year-old from a broken marriage, away at school for the first time. It was maybe the first time I'd ever won at anything. And even though it took a lot of people hectoring me to stand up for myself—I finally did.

About the Author:

Joseph Eastburn was an actor and poet who began writing for the theater, which led to screenplays, books, short stories and finally essays. His first novel, Kiss Them Goodbye, was published by Morrow in 1993, and HarperCollins brought it back into print in 2016. His new book, Take, was a 3rd Place Winner in the Operation Thriller Writing Competition. And he's writing a full-length noir on Twitter, The Summer of Love and Death (http://twitter.com/darknovel). His essays and short stories have been published in fine literary journals like: Existere, storySouth, Crack the Spine, The Apalachee Review, Forge, The Penmen Review, Slow Trains, Reed Magazine, Sliver of Stone, The Tower Journal, Sand Hill Review, The Sun Magazine, and Hobo Pancakes. He lives in California, still reads the New Yorker, and drives a beautiful old wreck of a sports car, vintage 1985.

SANTA CLARA RIVERLESS

Ellen T. Birrell

We are hard to find. If you were to search our address for directions, you would only get to the end of the county maintained road about two miles away. You could spy on us with Google Earth, but only if you knew where to look. You might see an old farmhouse surrounded by citrus orchards spinning out until the gravitational pull of human order--houses, gardens, gadgets and pavement give way to the more enduring force of the Santa Clara River on our northern border, carrying the mountain away, down the valley to the sea. The river has sucked at the toe of that mountain for eons.

Green creates topography. I knew this primate truth early. When I was growing up long ago and far away, I played in my neighbor's rhododendron forest. The game was to climb a tree at one end of the yard, and not touch the ground until I had to go home for lunch. My young monkey brain discovered early on that trees offer heights to scale, shelter, safety, and probably--although I always enjoyed my peanut butter and jelly sandwich in the kitchen with Mom--food. I know; any geologist would complain too. A minion of Big Science, he would politely explain that rocks and dirt and glaciers, and rain and frost and faults create Topography, and pull out his Dibblee map to show me, yet again, the hard and soft facts of the old ground around us. His topography is brown, mineral and durable. Mine is green, breathing, and vulnerable. As a suddenly late-in-life citrus farmer, I have staked my welfare on green topography, and depend on the food part of trees pretty heavily without having climbed one in longer than I care to remember. If I had the

guts, strength, or the imagination of my earlier selves, this farm's thirty acres of citrus orchards would entertain me with lifetimes of tree-top travel.

As a thoroughly adult and grounded biped, I have had an arm's length relation to the farm. I have accounted for it through taxes and "inputs" bought and paid for, like sprinkler heads and herbicides. I have savored its aesthetic spectacle during many labyrinthine walks.

"Miracle Monocrop Under Moonlight" is highly recommended. In the stark light of day, I have

calculated its more pragmatic qualities, sometimes at my computer, sometimes in the field with the pickers, to glean and check that all is well. After all, this green has produced the green that has allowed us to live here. From my arm's length distance, any question of "how does this work" over the years has garnered a dizzying array of partial answers. In the last two years, I have learned there is no arm's length approximation for farm life.

The river has unraveled its moist embrace of our land, retreating to the hot broody hinterlands upstream. My 7 and 9-year-old friends, Metta and Josie, visited recently. They always make a trek to a sloppy mud bank off our west end with big rubber boots on, calling it "Icky Icky Island." This year they went in sneakers and reported the island "just sand." California is experiencing its worst drought in recorded history. Big Science, that assiduous analyst of tiny data, announced in the newspapers that as water disappears from the land, the geography of the state is actually changing altitude, rising measurably from the burden of the water's staggering weight. (http://www.latimes.com/local/la-me-groundwater-20140822-story.html) Luckily some previous steward of this place piped in a drinking water supply from the city of Santa Paula, but this farm has drawn irrigation water from the river since 1908.

What little river water might still flow this far downstream has been pent-up behind a dirt dam, pooled for exclusive use of a land-lease upstream from us, an industrial scale row-crop concern. They are harvesting green in all senses every three weeks—chard, kale, cilantro, watercress, celery—all fast money in the bank to them. Downstream, the river is bone dry. The 30 acre organic lemon farm and the 80 acre golf course are both irrigating with drinking water from the City of Santa Paula municipal supply, and we are too. We are all trying to keep our greens alive until it rains, until fire season passes, until the drought is over, until we run out of money, until, until, until…. The sky is, truly, falling, but not in the wet way we need.

I think of the farm's irrigation system as part of a vast plastic circulatory system insinuated just beneath the skin of the land. You might assume the analogy is only half true; the system has arteries and a pump, but no veins or lungs. I thought so too, at my desk paying bills. But as any born farmer will tell you, our green topography does the other half, fruiting, feeding, exhaling oxygen and moisture back to the ether to form clouds. The ranch's current river collection system dates from 1996. Imagine perforated plastic fingers spreading out horizontally in the gravel about 25 feet below the surface flow of the river and add a pump. When the river flows, this "infiltration gallery" collects 600 gallons of river water per minute. From a 20-thousand-gallon tank in the orchard where we planted our first tangerines, the water is distributed through 12 irrigation zones on the ranch, so normally it takes about 12 days to get all the orchards watered doing one 8-hour irrigation set a day. Irrigation and weed management is why the ranch has always had a full-time employee.

Watering the farm with our drinking water supply water now takes more than two months, with all

hands--including mine--on deck. I am up by dawn, pulling on scruffy clothes in the dark, usually the same ones I left on the floor yesterday. Dawn used to be earlier, but the nights are getting longer. With the recent mountain lion sighting on the ranch at dusk, I am content to sleep in 'til full light.

Our daily job is to shepherd tiny water (think garden hose, not fire hydrant) from one area of the orchards to another, a network of valves turned on or off, a different combination each time we change a set, two sets a day. The cardinal rule of irrigation is always having a place for the water to go; if the pump is on but the valves are closed, water pressure will rupture the pipe couplings somewhere. Our ranch foreman, Gerardo, got sick one week, and a young friend of his, Antonio, and I tried to get the irrigation done without him. It did not take us 20 minutes to blow the couplers at the pump wide open, knocking the whole damn Tinker Toy system off line for 3 days while we glued it back together.

The 12 irrigation zones have 90 sub-valves. Each one opens an underground pipe to which any number of PVC risers are connected. The risers, mounted perpendicular to the pipe, come up about a foot to 18 inches above the soil, that is unless the soil surface level has changed—sometimes we have to dig them up. There is a thumb valve about 6 inches from the top which is crowned with a T shaped coupler into which is fitted a length of irrigation hose. With the pump on, valves open, we wait for the water. We observe the day's varying pressure and decide how many valves and risers we can open. (We can tell when the golf course is running more than 3 sprinklers, because our pressure drops.) Any sets smaller than 20 trees we just walk away from, hoping there will be more pressure next time we make it around. We can't even get water to the top of the east end tangerines (zone 10). There are about 150 trees up there that will just have to hold on until rain comes.

Changing this morning's set—the tangerine trees on the firebreak above the west end—we arrived only moments after a coyote had gnawed one end of the hose out of the T-coupler to grab a drink. The water had not run long enough to wash much of Sugar Mountain away.

I got my first badge of honor about a month into this work. Gerardo gave me my own irrigator's bag; a scavenged grain sack with a shoulder strap of braided baling twine. Our bags carry plastic jars full of irrigation bits—various sprinkler heads, couplers and tiny plugs—and needle-nosed pliers, sharpened pruning shears, and compression couplers. Working under the lowest branches, I have learned to wear my baseball cap backwards, like the homies. With the brim in front, my vision is obscured and I keep hitting my head. Backwards, the cap still protects my scalp from lemon thorns.

The color of the tiny stripe on the irrigation hose probably means something—capacity, plastic grade, manufacturer or temperature range—but now as labor in the field, there is a lot I don't need to know. Just clip the hose and push the ends into the T at the top of the riser. It is a compression coupling and takes a bit of strength. The hose unfurls at the base of the trees in that row, and is sealed at the end by threading it back and forth through the two holes of a clamp shaped like a figure eight. The clamp slips off easily, and this too is useful, because the lines clot with river silt regularly.

Our capillaries are tiny hoses—3/8ths of an inch—anchored at one end in the irrigation hose with a tiny coupler from my jar, threaded through a plastic stake pushed into the dirt and capped with an emitter, also in my jar of bits, that might be simply described as a sprinkler head, except that they are marvels of miniature design, some no bigger than half an inch. They too are color coded, and manufactured in a dizzying array of volume capacities and spray patterns that I cannot and do not need to parse. These little miracles come bagged by the 50 count, and we use them in the orchards like TV cops pop donuts.

Each emitter must be checked as the water comes through the valves. Sometimes they are buried in the leaf litter or knocked over entirely. I pull up the stakes and re-set them, making sure the spray doesn't't hit the trunk—a fast way to root rot. Sometimes the tiny hoses have pulled off their coupler, or somehow the coupler has broken and must be dug out of the big hose with needle nose pliers and replaced before reconnecting the emitter tube. Gerardo tells me to cut lemon twigs sporting especially long thorns. Scary green stilettos, good ones are as much as two inches

long—no emitter harboring snail scum or river silt stands a chance against them. I stab and suck them clean. Gerardo shows me that the shorter lemon thorns are great for plugging small bites in the hoses; just cut the thorn off and stick the pointy end in the hole—the width at the base of the thorn is usually big enough to match thirsty rodent teeth. Thus, in a manner of speaking, the lemon trees repair themselves; Gera and I perform the systemic immune response with thumbs and tools and thorns.

We circulate from row to row, always in a hurry to arrive before it's too late, always in a hurry to move on. The trees stand and wait, patiently green, until suddenly, without complaint, they are not.

I can see generations of owners, myself included, who have made "check-book decisions" about expanding the orchards, tucking in a few extra trees every time we do replants, because, like donuts, nursery whips are cheaper by the dozen. This kind of arm's length thinking can get you into trouble, in my case literally—I torqued my back repeatedly on long muddy slides down the mountain. I know where those tuck-in trees are planted, and because I am old and creaky, I have a deep appreciation of the categories "nearly impossible" and "dangerous" that youth might not notice and labor has never been authorized to point out.

On the irrigation crew, I am labor--newly and once again muscle, observation and strategy--as I was as a child in the rhododendrons. I am often sore, and acutely aware that at sixty, I can no longer bid my body do as I did in my thirties. Managerial abstraction (not to say as Marx might, alienation) in this sense comes naturally with age. I cannot do everything Gerardo can—he is half my age. In joining the effort, I must draw on other strengths. With my up close and muddy point of view, I plan the lineaments of a much smaller and more productive orchard, one that generates sufficient green but also preserves firebreaks, because out here green and brown create fire topographies as well as compost.

Here, where the land leaks a muddy flux into the river and on, down to the sea, fossils reveal an older sea floor, high above our heads on Sugar Mountain, parched and flaked by our desert sun.

Skeletons of sand dollars and seafoam, little fish-ies and odd plant-life, long caught as snapshots in the slurry under the surface, translated by time and heat and pressure--and the multi-millennial meanderings of water over the surface of our globe. After two summers of the river's absence, I know none of us—neither the legged nor the leaved—does the work of living out here alone. I hope the water returns soon.

About the Author:

Ellen Birrell is an artist and lemon farmer in Ventura County, California. She co-found and edits X-TRA (www.x-traonline.org) and has taught at CalArts since 1991.

WREAK OF THE COWBOY

Ellen T. Birrell

The first time I saw Gerardo—oh, years ago—he was riding a flashy paint stallion down a country lane in the setting sun, heading into town for Sunday supper—hat, poncho, charro saddle, Sunday polished boots and a can of Bud Light. He was the foreman of the citrus ranch we moved to shortly thereafter. My mother joined us too.

He had an episode with his heart again—the second time he landed in the emergency room. He felt palpitations, dizziness, some nausea. The first event was due to dehydration and Monster Drinks, "all that caffeine and sugar," he told me, his partner Marta holding his hand. This time, three, four years later, brought a different confession; he told me that he had been using "cocaina." I suspect he meant meth, which, along with Bud Light, are the "Farmworkers of America" brands, cheap and widely available (the cocaine of my experience was precious as gold dust and evanescent as shooting stars). Gera took it, he said, to have more energy, to work all day and still break horses, rope cattle, drink, dance and romance the night away. He asked me not to tell David, my husband and fellow farm manager—he wanted to tell him, himself, when he passed his first clean blood test. By then Marta had long since taken the kids and left.

Later it was the riverless slog through the orchards all summer, Gera and I scaling hills, repairing leaks, getting drenched in our dime a dance rain, worrying the farm's trees into some productivity. I found the difference between my 60 and his 36, my eroding estrogen and his robust testosterone, my broad opportunities and his uncompromising facts.

He was preoccupied, the way an anxious person sitting right next to you can shrink a million miles away into his own uncharted distance. I kept up my bonhomie chatter, fed him coffee and breakfast, bought him groceries. His young horse friend Antonio came too sometimes; I was so grateful to have another presence with an open heart and a good giggle.

In October Gera took some vacation time, said he was going to a church retreat. Antonio and I kept the water going, inevitably getting things wrong, figuring it out and moving on. Gera returned but his voice did not, and when he could speak it was as if his voice was changing all over again: a young boy's high worry splitting the grown man's gravitas. He told me the retreat had been in a box canyon in the desert and the participants, all Catholic men, had shouted domestic violence scenarios at each other across the canyon for five days. Some time after, I came across him unexpectedly in the orchard. When he turned to face me, his countenance was split by terror and sudden tears; I took him to my mom's house.

With a glass of water and a tissue, he told us, in Spanish, how terribly frightened he was; he couldn't leave his house for long, he was convinced that someone, something was after him, he was a bad man, the ranch was full of memories of his children. Over and over

"I am a bad man." In my mother's perfect Venezuelan Spanish and my Spenglish, we attempted to reassure him that no, for us it was not so.

It got no better; Gera was too frightened to come out of his house and then only able to work a couple of hours. His brother came every night, offering vitamins and dinner, trying to get him to a doctor. His sisters came. My fellow crone Lynn pulled off miracles with County Mental Health and he was finally assigned a case worker who was very capable.

Meanwhile, Antonio filled in, with Gera when he was well enough, with me when he was not. Around Thanksgiving the rains came, densely enough to recharge the river and our irrigation pump, but Gerardo was worse. I saw him on the road going to town in the middle of one morning, that haunted look on his face.

"Cigarettes and breakfast, back in a moment."

He didn't return. That night, his brother texted me that Gera was safe and would be in touch. When Gerardo finally called me 3 days later, I told him to take this time and think about what he wanted. I would pay him for the week, with half pay the week following, but after that I needed to hire someone.

He was back in 10 days, but within weeks said simply, "I cannot do this anymore," and was gone by morning.

Edgar at the local feed store told me Gera moved to Tennessee and, more than a year later, he seems to be better, working construction and riding horses again. He came back once to the area and settled his bill, but he did not call or come to the ranch. He married Marta though, and took his children back east. It was several more months before his brother came and hauled away his beautiful paint stallion.

And the river is dry again this year.

SONS OF UNCONSCIOUS FATE

by Gabrielle Morales

Intro.

Though I was only eight, I still remember my mother's approach to the facts of death. It was like any other day in August. My best friend, Nikki, and I had on our matching pink and green bathing suits. As usual, we were in the backyard making chocolate mud pies, joking and arguing over whose was the best and most ribbon worthy. We continued on for some time, giggling and bathing in our mud baths, until my mother came to me.

She held the phone in her right hand, her left pressed hard against her lips. Dry tears and streaks of black stuck to her rosy cheeks, exposing the bare skin beneath her powdered foundation.

"Honey," she said to me. "It's…" she paused, her voice cracking, "It's Tara."

I stood up, my legs covered in mud and tears building up in my eyes, not because of the undefined news but because like most children, I adored my mother, and nothing broke my heart more than the sight of my mother's tears.

"Don't cry momma," I said, running to her, burying my face in her freckled chest.

She stuttered, "Oh… Honey… I'm… I'm so sorry. She's… She's gone." She pulled me in closer, repeating, "I'm so sorry. I'm so sorry."

As vague as it was, I knew what my mother meant by "she's gone." I had heard about this thing called death and yet, the reality of her death did not phase me. But when the day of her funeral came and a sealed, oblong brown box stood before me, I was faced with the reality of my cousin's death. At first, I did not understand why she would not come out to play. I did not understand what my mother meant by "She's in Heaven," or why I could not visit her "in Heaven," not even for my ninth birthday. And I could not quite wrap my eight-year-old mind around the fact that I was not able to see her one last time—to say goodbye—because she was "too badly hurted" for my eight-year-old eyes to see.

As I grew older—older to the point where I understood the meaning of death, or rather, the definition of murder and the circumstances of her death—I could not understand how or why someone could do such a thing and still, after the fact, toss her body like a Raggedy Ann.

For years, I have repressed my late cousin's death, thinking nothing of her killer, seeing no worth in him. The pain still devours my soul, like a paralyzing numbness in my heart. I still cringe when I hear his name and when he makes an appearance in my dreams. And the very idea that he only received thirty years for taking her life uncovers a different, a less controlled and heated, side of me, especially when I am reminded that he will be out of prison in less than twenty years.

So why exactly am I doing this? Why am I writing about him? To be honest, I don't quite know what I am looking for. Certainly, I am not waiting for a moment of enlightenment or understanding of why he did what he did but perhaps a process of the latter. With that being said, this short narrative is my attempt of understanding—of humanizing Tara's murderer.

The day Gordon Grey had revealed his secret was the same day he jumped off the Ellington Bridge. In the time before the fall, he had aligned his bare feet to its very edge. What laid behind were his clothes, tattered and soaked with the blood of his victim. He moaned in disturbance, noticing the specks of red that still remained on his glasses. He proceeded to wash them with spit. "That'll do," he muttered as he pressed the weathered frames back against the bridge of his nose. At last, stripped and lain, he had finally escaped from the echoing cries of his mind. Heartless to say, he felt no feelings towards the day's event; for he was fixed in a trance of disbelief.

He watched as the moon made its daily end, himself descending from a high. As the night went on, he grew into a panic, realizing the state of his position. "The body, the blood, all of the blood. I have to get all of this blood off," he hissed to himself, picking at the scabs on his face. A momentary rush of wind brushed up against his broken skin, filling them with an unpleasant, burning sensation. He continued to peel back and create new wounds—that is until he heard the pleasant sound of a familiar voice, a voice that reminded him of his younger brother, Jayden, when he was a child.

"Gord?" the small voice uttered from behind.

He quickly turned towards the voice, which revealed to be a small boy in Spider-Man pajamas—Jayden's favorite superhero. Indeed, it was him, Jayden, in the flesh.

"Gord?" the boy yawned as he walked barefoot towards his brother.

"Jay?" he said softly. "What—what are you doing here?"

"I've been looking for you," the boy answered in a sweet tone. "Where've you been?" he asked, looking down at the blood-stained clothes.

"I—I," he stuttered.

"Gord?" his voice softened, "What is that?" he asked, pointing at the clothes.

"I—I," he continued to stutter.

The boy's eyes grew big, "What—what did you do?" he stepped back.

"Jay—I," he stepped forward.

The boy stepped back once again. "What did you do?" his voice cracking, tears filling his eyes.

"Jay," he stepped forward, grabbing the boy's shoulder.

"What did you do?" he raised his voice, pushing him away.

"Jay," he began to cry.

"What—what did you do?" his voice quivered, "What did you do?" the boy repeated, screaming.

"Jay, please!" he cried as he covered his ears and shook his head. His heart began to pace forward, skipping in beats of twos and threes, until he could no longer catch his breath.

He pulled himself away, off and towards the sea below. As he made his descent, his time in midair appeared to accelerate as though time was a broken dial or timer of sort. And when that timer went off, in an instant, he was fully immersed and made one with the bay. He quickly barreled down the abyss, where shadows blend and lies begin, hitting its surface and coming to on his bathroom floor. A pool of water surrounded him, the tub overflowing and spilling.

It did not take him long to realize that it was all but a conscious dream, or rather the result of a near overdose. Perhaps it can be said that the dream was a hidden door in the deepest and most intimate sanctum of his soul, which opened to that primeval cosmic night that was soul long before he was conscious and will be soul far beyond what his consciousness could ever reach. It should be known here that Grey, an unemployed twenty-two-year-old, experimented with drugs.

Grey was born just East of the Anacostia River in the "Chocolate City," or what most know as D.C., where the percentage of teen pregnancies far exceeds the rate of high school graduates.

Located in the inner pocket of the city was a neighborhood called "The Springs," from which Grey belonged. The Springs was a small neighborhood, nearly populated with two-thousand people. It was common for children to roam the streets during the months of June and July. The Springs offered no other alternative to playing basketball, and when that grew tiresome, they created the havoc that The Springs' children did. In other words, drug use was a sort of sport, and Grey had started early on in life, so he was good at it.

Sure, you could say he was like most young men his age, but besides the former, he was not like the rest. You see, Grey had a bucket list, but it was no ordinary bucket list; he kept it neatly folded and tucked under a shoe in his closet. Fearing that someone would find it, he only brought it out at night. The florescent light of his desk lamp would guide him as he sat hunched over his cedar desk, re-reading and adding to the ten-page list for hours into the next day. And on the first page of that list was a startling wish. Scribbled in black ink, it read:

"#13, kill someone."

And on one Sunday in July of 2005, Grey crossed this item off his list. Though, aside from this document, he would not claim the following to be premeditated. Instead, he would simply claim to have jumped at the opportunity to complete the task. It was no more than a poor coincidence that she, his fourteen-year-old victim, had crossed his path that afternoon in July.

His body laid face up on the cold white tile. Motionless, his eyes half shut, he gathered his thoughts and attempted to recount his steps before the blackout. He continued in a trance, almost paralyzed, not knowing, or caring for the surrounding flood.

The cold surface of the wet tile pierced through his veins. His body shivered, and he brushed his hand up against his head, rubbing his temples. He groaned, raising his head, pulling himself forward

and up, supporting himself with the molded shower rail. He proceeded to turn off the faucet and stumble to the bathroom mirror.

He stood before the mounted mirror, his lip bruised and swollen from the fall and his hollow black eyes looking back at him. He bit his lip, sucked off the dry blood and turned away from himself, looking at the floor.

He placed his left hand on his forehead, "Agh... Shit," he mouthed. This had happened before, more than once.

Reaching into the cupboard above the mirror, he grabbed a towel and tossed it onto the ground. He entered his room in search of a clean pair of clothes but quickly gave up. The room was far from orderly. Stacks of magazines and piles of video game cases surrounded his bed. The base-board molding had been out of sight for more than a few years, as was the space between his mattress and the floor. It was stuffed full of dingy clothes; he did laundry less than twice every three or four months. For Grey, to clean was to go a day without shooting up. To put it simply: he was not up for such an endeavor, not today.

No one was home, so he made his way to the stash he kept hid in the shoe next to his bucket list. He lit his pipe and threw on a worn-out pair of sweats and one of his many bleach stained crewnecks. He exited the house, leaving the mess behind and hopped into his old sedan.

He drove up and down the plains for quite some time, flying high at 90MPH. When the empty light went on, he drove to the only gas station in town. The engine sputtered as he forced it to an abrupt stop, spotting the figure of a young woman in the rear-view mirror.

There she was, Tara, exiting the market with a bag of Hot Cheetos in her right hand and a bottle of Coke in the other. He watched as she walked off the lot, waiting for his tank to reach its half-way point. When she grew distant, he started his car and proceeded to follow her, casually pulling over as they made eye contact.

"Hey, need a ride?" he smiled.

About the Author:

Gabrielle Morales is the daughter of a migrant worker from Jalisco, Mexico and a farmer's daughter from rural Oregon. She is an undergraduate student attending Northwest Christian University where she studies English. As a first-generation college student and Gates Millennium Scholar, she aspires to teach adult literacy. This is her first literary publication.

WALKER

Olga Pavlinova Olenich

Sometimes when you walk along the well-trodden path following coastline, there is a moment when the suburban elements – the ugly new houses behind you, the road with its speed bumps and impatient cars, the distant metallic glint of industry – disappear from your vision. They are stripped away to reveal an old seascape, unchanged by the human story. Black rocks glistening in the brilliant sparkle of blue waters, long silver sandbanks rising up from the sea, pelicans gliding down from the sky in symmetrical formation, black swans floating between the black rocks, their long necks arched over ripples of clear water – all of these elements are caught in your one moment of vision.

And you, too, seem to be stripped back to something that is perhaps less than you are but feels as if it is more. You have lost the sense of your body and its all-consuming needs and you are separated from the perpetually recycled concerns of an ordinary life – the fears, the obsessions, the battles with your own self - they have suddenly evaporated. You are left in one of those perfect moments of contemplation that lift your existence to some other plane, if that is the way to describe the defining moment that throws up the question of existence and holds within it all the spiritual imagination of human beings in all places and at all times. Is this moment, perhaps, what life is all about, this little point of perfect understanding between the natural scene before you and the you that contemplates it? Is everything else a mirage as the Buddhists would have it or is this the mirage that makes the other bearable? The moment holds the answer within it but,

strangely, you can never remember that answer when the moment has passed. Not completely, anyway.

I try to walk this stretch as often as my crowded days will allow. I suppose I am, in some sense, pursuing that defining moment. I have acquired a thirst for it. Perhaps it is a greed that grows with every passing year and with the sense of my own mortality. Sometimes I am granted such a moment, sometimes I miss out. There are no guarantees, even if the setting is right and your mood seems receptive. On the day I first saw the walker my mind was too crowded with the detritus of days, and my eyes too affronted by a new outcrop of tightly packed houses where there had been, until recently, one rambling weatherboard place with a wire fence and an eccentric garden. I was disenchanted and bad-tempered and not prepared for a special moment or for the walker.

He materialised on the bend in the path where the revegetation program has been the most successful and the low shrubs and indigenous grasses have taken up their rightful places again, casting shifting shadows across the path so that it no longer seems as intrusive. He came out of those shadows, a tall man with a shock of silver hair. I was annoyed. I was used to having this stretch to myself, especially during the week at a time when children were at school and adults were at work or having their coffee in some cafe near the public beach.

We walked towards each other on the narrow path, knowing there was only room for one. One of us would have to step aside into the grasses between the shrubs so that the other might pass. I looked around searching for a spot where

I might step off the path without scratching my legs or crashing into a bush and appearing to be a complete fool. He did not look as if he would veer from the path. He looked as if he belonged on it, his long strides taking easy control of its distances, his silver hair another kind of seaside plant rippling in the wind.

He approached. I became defensive. Would stepping off the path now show a submission that I did not wish to show? Why did I have to be the one to step off the path anyway? After all, it was my path as much as it was his. Just because he was taller, just because of his hair, just because he was. And just then, he stepped off the path to let me pass. He stood in the grasses with a slight smile playing around his mouth and I hurried on, wondering if I should have said thanks but reassuring myself that it was, after all, my path as much as his.

After that, I came across the walker regularly. I would see him walking along at his particular pace that had its quiet determined rhythm and never seemed to change in response to some external urgency or a shift in the weather. At different points on the path we would pass each other. Sometimes, in the narrow stretches, we would repeat the same small ritual. I would approach and he would step sideways, standing silently against the silvery undergrowth and the glistening sea. It didn't seem right to thank him. It was just something he did.

I had waded out from a small inlet where the beach came and went with the tide but where the black rocks remained above water so that the seabirds gathered on them to dry off their wings. I sat very still on one of the rocks and watched the sea. The birds were generally undisturbed by my presence. The seagulls gathered on a long sandbank, their silver white breasts caught in the afternoon light and the great pelicans came in, gliding in formation, skimming the water and settling on it in a perfectly formed arrowhead. The wading birds,

I can never remember their names - egrets perhaps - balanced on their impossibly thin orange legs near the edge of the water and were as untouched by my intrusion in their wavering

reflections as they were in their reality. Only the swans kept their elegant distance. They were just on the periphery of my vision partially merging into the dark reflections of the black rocks on the other side of the beach and then separating out in the brackish water near the old boat enclosure. Floating spots in the corner of my eye. I concentrated on the mesmerising pelicans. Larger than the other birds, stranger, belonging to some ancient time in which our species did not figure. And yet there was a familiarity about them and their presence was a quietening one. I sank into one of those moments.

"Pelicans have an extraordinary sense of symmetry," he said. And I knew it was the walker. I turned to see that he was just behind me, his trousers rolled up and his feet in the water. A giant egret with tanned legs, not really orange but in the same spectrum of colour. He waded a few steps and sat down on a rock near enough to mine so that I could see him properly for the first time but far enough for the water and the breeze to separate us on our own rocks and in our own moments.

I looked at his reflection in the water. It was long and indistinct and it stretched between us like a bridge.

"I think it is their positioning in relation to each other that makes them so beautiful." He had a nice voice. It hung in the air without disturbing it. I did not feel an obligation to reply. What he said was what I had been thinking, or so it seemed. I continued to watch the pelicans but I felt that I was watching them a little differently, now that there was another set of eyes on them. They had been on the water for a full minute, bobbing slightly on the wide ripples but keeping their formation.

"It's like a trust," I said, "they don't even have to look at each other." And I smiled to myself more than at him because I realised we were, both of us, also saying something else. It was a pleasant thought, easy to encompass because of our surroundings. Anywhere else and I might have kept it to myself. We sat there for a while, looking at the pelicans. The afternoon took hold of the sea. The blues took on purple. At the very edge of the water there was a show of silver. He left as quietly as he had come. I hardly noticed him go but the seagulls were alerted by his movement and took off from their sandbank, a great cloud of them spreading out above my head.

After that, we met regularly on our walks, but only for a few quiet moments. He would appear, we would exchange a few thoughts or perhaps the same thought and then he would walk away. I never thought of following him. It didn't seem necessary.

One day I was standing on the observation platform that has been built above the salt marshes. This is the one point in my walks where I expect to see people. I catch them reading the information about plants that cleverly convert salt water into fresh, birds that visit at different times of the year from as far away as Siberia, fish and other creatures that complete their secret cycles of life under water, never comprehending what it is to walk on land. The local council has done a good job. The wooden walkway and the weathered platform are unobtrusive in the landscape. On this particular day, in the quiet of a late March afternoon, there was nobody around. For some reason, I felt a surge of disappointment. Perhaps I needed somebody else to be witness to the season's turning. The breeze was cool, the sea was choppy and the clouds hung low over the grey-blue horizon. Summer was over. I shivered. And then I heard his footsteps. I did not turn around but for the first time, I was not entirely easy with his coming. I deliberately leaned over the wooden rail and looked into the pools of water below. I had to find a focus to still my mind. The pools reflected the grey clouds, their surfaces were rippled with all the shades of the sky and something else besides – their own green-blue translucency. Suddenly the sun appeared between the clouds and everything below the platform turned into diamonds. Every ripple shone and threw out a cutting light that hurt my eyes. I took in my breath. The walker was beside me, looking down too.

"It's beautiful," he said.

"Yes." Together and, I think, also apart, we continued to watch the sun dancing on the water. I wanted to say something important or nothing at all but nonetheless words came out of my mouth, very slowly, it seemed to me. "We live in these moments," I said. There were swans in the distance and the seagulls were somewhere, their cries scattered on the cold breeze that was beginning to work itself up to being a wind. I hadn't seen a pelican all day and the egrets had taken off for a different world at least a week ago. He was silent for a while and then he said, very quietly,

"Perhaps we also die."

I heard him walk away and I did not turn around. I wonder if I missed an important moment. I never saw him again. I continue to walk the path whenever I can. I suppose I am still looking for those extraordinary moments. Sometimes

I find them. As has always been the case, they come when I least expect them to come -the soft splash as a pair of pelicans descend onto a stretch of water, the delicate feathers of a wading bird caught in a shaft of light, the horizon suddenly turning an impossible shade of turquoise. I come back again and again but I don't know if I am looking for the walker any more.

About the Author:

Olga Pavlinova Olenich is an Australian writer whose work appears in local and international publications. Her prose and poems have been broadcast on national radio and have featured in national newspapers. Her memoirs have been included in the collection Best Australian Humorous Writing (Melbourne University Press, 2008) and The Best Travel Writing Volume 11. (Travelers' Tales Series. Solis House Palo Alto, 2016) Her poetry is included in several anthologies including Australian Poetry Anthology 2006,2016 and Best Australian Poems (Black inc. 2015)

IN THE COMPANY OF MEN, MUSCLE, AND MACHISMO

David Boyle

For more than fifteen years I have not given one iota of attention to sports; that is, professional sports. Sorry, gentlemen, treat me like a leper if you must, it wouldn't be the first time. There's no turning back for me at this point: I've come quite a distance on the important journey known as self -discovery, a journey of life-altering twists and turns and revelations. Men might think that for anyone of their kind to maintain such remoteness from the world of sports is not only unusual but unnatural—much like the women who ostracize others of their gender for not sharing their penchant for gossip, clothes, makeup, cooking, dancing, massages, facials, manicures/pedicures, etc. Regardless of gender, people are from time to time faced with identity crises, having to either join the clique or resist belonging. As for my separation from sports in general (not from exercise or from staying physically fit, mind you), one day it just happened. Nothing and no one indicated imminent change. I have no recollection of how, when, or where my priorities changed. And I have no regrets, either, moving on was a veritable cinch. The "why," on the other hand, is much easier to illustrate, and I'm inclined to cite a reason or two—chief among them, believe it or not, the fans themselves, who don't shy away from complaining when their favorite team loses or from assigning blame rather arbitrarily; who offer critique whenever a player commits a blunder, and who pontificate at length before, during, and after a game, laying out all forms of commentary, from detailed analysis to alternative strategies, sounding in tone and delivery like a general outlining a war plan and addressing his battalion. Men, many of whom couldn't make the cut in any

sport even in their wildest fantasies, believe themselves to be experts irrespective of the game they enjoy watching, irrespective of who's within striking distance of their critical whip. As some of us know, even those who have spent enough time around men (as I have), a good many, I've reason to believe, are envious of athletes, jealous of, among other aspects, their money, fame, and social status. Have you ever heard a man say, when a baseball player strikes out with the game on the line, or when a football player throws an interception or drops the ball, or when a hockey goalie lets one slip by into the net, or when a basketball player misses what's considered a sure shot: "How can you choke like that? You get millions a year!" I'd be the first to admit, by the way, that professional athletes are not only pampered and overpaid but over-privileged. But that's another entirely different discussion. Often drawn to power and prestige of one sort or another, men can find it, and worship it, in high-level professional athletes, in their posturing and in their swagger. Or even feel empowered by participating in and contributing to their kids' sports-related activities, serving as coaches and mentors, as well as in other capacities, reawakening through their children their own long-dormant dreams of glory and acclaim and attention from the community.

In my experience, being around men embroiled in a sports-related conversation calls to mind the consequences of being an outsider: It's not uncommon for me to be perceived as an inferior, as less of a man, though I can shrug off the harshest judgment and, unfazed by the source and the style, still feel whole and adequate as an individual. After all, I'd much rather read good writing, attempt to write something of substance myself, or watch a thought-provoking movie. These activities, for me at least, bear fruit, both emotional and psychological, paying long-term intellectual dividends. Besides, athletes earn staggering amounts of money, and good for them, I begrudge them nothing: A month of any top athlete's salary is more than I'll ever see in my lifetime, all for having fun and for avoiding the banality of a real year-round job. With that in mind, think of the athletes who cannot even complete a full sentence, who barely speak a word of comprehensible English. Think of the athletes who fail on every level to conduct themselves as decent citizens in public, who can't get through a game without fighting or instigating a conflict, yet are rewarded with commercials and endorsement deals, movie/television roles and luxuries normal people can only visualize in their most outlandish dreams. Some of these athletes, of course, are good-hearted, generous, intelligent, and, when interviewed on TV or when appearing in public, come across as humble, upstanding people who from time to time even downplay their own talents. Not all players fit the dysfunctional mold. There are athletes from all walks who are grateful for the life they've been given and demonstrate their appreciation at every opportunity. No matter. I myself have simply outgrown the sports mindset and the superficial bonding and team pride that tend to accompany life as a devotee. I do not wish to wear a team jersey. Nor do I wish to paint my body for a game or get a tattoo. I do not wish to conjecture as to why a team lost, when the answer a majority of the time—if not all of the time—is that the losing team was outplayed. Period. What do obsessive fans do as a result? They sulk the next day as if their world has fallen apart; sporadically come to heated exchanges or fisticuffs with their "adversaries." Sure, to be honest, I went through that fanatical phase as a very young man, hoping to feel I was part of something that had a purpose, a benefit or two, only to come out without having gained much of consequence. In fact, I have nothing to show for my years of being sports-minded. And, needless to say, I can't get that time back, but I sure can make up for it, which is what I've been doing for more than two decades.

With respect to the physical elements of sports, playing and competing on an athletic level is the only time when men express emotion and get away with discreet groping. It's true, and I'm not trying to disparage sports or its followers or offend anyone. I'm merely trying to emphasize a subtle point about men, about their ambiguous behavior. Players often cry, and hug one another, whether in victory or in defeat, and pile on one another in celebration. Players and coaches pat their colleagues on the back and on the buttocks, on the arms and legs; tap their teammate's fists, forearms, and chests with their own; shower together, snap each other with towels and make primitive sounds. Peculiar behavior for any male-dominated sport, don't you think? Do women engage in such antics on the field or in locker rooms? I'm not sure, though I suppose some do and some don't. In any case, with age I've become more attuned to the male psyche, the way they, like others of their ilk, hunger to fit in with a group while at the same time grapple with the inner conflict of wanting to stand alone without being mocked or judged. Not an easy situation to be in, but one must navigate the potholed road of indecision on his or her own.

Sports, as I've attempted to explain here, fall dismally short of nourishing my soul, fortifying my mind, or engendering within me any meaningful thoughts or ideas or inspirations. Since I'm not the competitive type (I never have been, a weakness of mine, perhaps.), maybe that's why I no longer find anything enthralling about sporting events and those who avidly play them and watch them and attend them. When I happen to glance at a TV screen in a restaurant or pub, or hear others discussing the latest contest, my mind goes blank. That part of my brain has become a self-sealing fissure which no longer allows the passage of stale, unnecessary information. Besides, when sports on TV occasionally enter my eye-line, I never know what I'm supposed to feel, if anything. What I do know, if I may be honest and direct, is that when I'm reading, writing, or entertaining myself according to my own needs, tastes, and desires, I become imbued with sensations and emotions and energies which stimulate my mind, body, and imagination—as if I were an easily crazed fan watching a sporting event and experiencing the rush they so desperately crave—

persuading me not only to explore more deeply who and what I am but what I aspire to be, even if I should never reach all goals. And although I seldom yearn for the company of other "typical" men and what nowadays constitutes "male bonding," I wouldn't change my outlook, my trajectory, a smidgen. Why would I? I like literature. I like art, music, film, etc. I like educating myself, sharpening my assets, my own definition of myself, on my own terms. And I admire creative people because they are forced to apply their intellect and imagination to make something fresh and unique out of nothing. There's no playbook. No coach overseeing your daily progress. Nobody orchestrating or cheering your next move. And rarely, to my knowledge, is there a big payday. Insofar as I am aware, no drug or supplement will speed up or make possible a work of artistic merit, unless we take into account those feckless artists who've become ensnared in the habit of using alcohol, marijuana, or cocaine (or various drugs) to alter their state of mind—to get their creative juices flowing, as the phrase goes. Athletes, on the contrary, can be aided by any number of performance-enhancing drugs and supplements, team approval and audience and community support. Hefty paychecks. This data notwithstanding, I derive steady and irreducible pleasure and fulfillment from studying, researching, and immersing myself in my pursuits, using my findings to improve my life and to attain emotional and physical balance as well as inner strength. Sports do not fill me with awe and wonder and curiosity, and cannot provide for me what I long for the most: sustained growth. For years and years, books, movies, music—art in all its forms, essentially—have been keeping me company. And, in consequence, I'm wiser and more impressionable, learning and evolving with each new day—an existence which I'm faithful to and one that hasn't come close to letting me down. As each promising opportunity comes my way, I hope to never drop the ball and blow the all-important game—the game of life—since I'm having a tremendous amount of fun playing.

About the Author:

A versatile writer, **David Boyle** has written two short story collections, published by independent presses. Five of his stories have been adapted to film. In 2014 four stories from his second book, Abandoned in the Dark, were made into a full-length anthology film of the same name. Though he earned his readership by writing reality-based dark fiction, Boyle has gained a reputation for literary stories, essays, articles, aphorisms, reviews, interviews, analyses, travel writing, and poems, a good number of which have appeared in both print and online magazines as well as in anthologies.

Discover David Boyle:
www.facebook.com/authordavidboyle.

ASSOCIATIVE LEAPING

Lydia A. Cyrus

1.

My mom told me that a red chicken was dying. How? I asked but no one knew how. My brother, the reaper, slid into a pair of black, heavy rubber boots and went to retrieve a dying hen. With gloved hands, he stuffed her into a white garbage bag. He tied the yellow plastic string into a tight knot and left the bag on the ground. He said she smelled bad. At the bottom of the bag the hen lay—still breathing. We watched the bag expand and stifle over and over. I remember red chicks, small enough to fit in my piano hands, small balls of centimeter long feathers. But little red chicks grow into hens and sometimes you put their lives in your hands. Only you don't stroke it and marvel over the size of it. So my brother buried a still breathing chicken. I know she was still expanding but what could you do? She smelled so bad. In the same spots we have buried dogs, cats, and even people, we have buried a small red hen.

2.

When you stifle a fire you put it out. You pour water over it, you can even give back to the earth and piss on it but, ultimately, you put it out. When I was a kid, we had bonfires in the mouth of the holler. Together we sat in stiff, blue plastic chairs and wore glow sticks around our necks and on our wrists. Sticks of neon pink and green, sticks of vigilance to ensure no child would wander or disappear. Once, my aunt told a scary story and it frightened my cousin John so badly that he fell backwards in his chair. His head of sandy blonde hair landed right at the start of the fire, right at the thin red line.

3.

My brother has ADD. With his diagnosis came his extreme "fondness" of open flames. Matches, lighters, candles, and fireworks all became the Holy Grail he sought to find and stake his claim upon. He sought to watch the orange brilliance spring up like a stalk of summer corn. The doctor said that if he doesn't take his morning and evening medication he would be drawn to the chaos of fire. My ears have learned to pick out of a crowd the sound of the soft tisk a cigarette lighter. On one occasion, he caught a piece of fly tape on fire and it left a dish size circle of soot on the kitchen ceiling. My mother tried to whip it away but a halo of grey, of remembrance, remains. One rainy summer day I caught him striking matches and tossing them into a plastic Folgers's can. Inside the can was a bed of cedar chips and firecrackers. He admitted to me that he had no plan for the actual sparking of the fireworks; he just wanted to see the flame.

4.

The power goes out often where we live. Trees, rain, snow, and car accidents all have the ability to leave us in darkened houses. One spring when I was a college freshman, it snowed and we lost power for over three days. We boiled water and took "GI Joe" baths and ate food cooked on gas stovetops. We slept with thick blankets and socks and woke in black bedrooms. I like it when the power goes out in cold weather. When it goes out in June, we suffocate from the entrenchment of humidity and I sit with my head cocked out a window and into the visible constellation above.

When it goes out due to snow I can add blankets, I can add socks, and Carhart coats. The spring of freshman year I lay bundled next to a red Coleman lantern and I read The Return of the King. The darkness in my bedroom battled the lantern light as wars in far off places waged, as a wizards sought out light as he crossed mountains.

5.

We live at the bottom of the mountain. The road, Mountain Union, leads to a valley of modest homes and trees. A one-lane road runs through the neighborhood and there are only three streetlights. I'm related to everyone on the right side of the creek. Or the left side depending on perspective. At the start of the concrete bridge leading to my driveway there is a walnut tree. When the air seems damp and warm the leaves on the tree turn inside out: rain is on the horizon. At the top of the hill, what the older neighbors call the start of Mountain Union, to the right there is a family cemetery. It's on the left side depending on which side of the road you are driving on. One of the men buried there is the father of a woman who lives two houses down from me. We are not related. The man, Jim, was hit by a car one night while he was walking. It was Super Bowl Sunday and it was snowing outside. He was pinned under the car while one of his daughters watched. The driver took his license plate off of his car and ran into the woods. That's where the police found him. This is why my mother doesn't want me to walk on the road at night, the road that leads up to the cemetery.

About the Author:

Lydia A. Cyrus is a creative nonfiction writer and poet living in Southern Appalachia where she focuses on volunteering and education. She is a proud Mountain Woman who hails from the Western most county of West Virginia.

LOLITA'S GLASSES

Carrie Bailey

I've read the novel, Lolita at least three full times. The first of which, and I'm no longer afraid to admit this, 30 years after the fact, I could identify with Lolita, not necessarily the girl, but the narrative. I read Lolita, the first time, as a love story. I went so far as to sign teen age love letters to my own significant other as, "Lo." Typed and written in pen all over sassy fashion magazine spreads with seductive poses in unusual places. The glossy pages of Vogue, Elle, and Harper's Bazaar became personal high fashion stationary. My favorites were ridiculously ornate and imperial dresses worn in wild fields and treated with the disdain of a ranch hand. The more impractical and sultry the better. I even committed petty theft by stealing a House of Lo menu from a restaurant, just for the slight link to this namesake. This childish, heart-shaped view emanated from the hundreds of pages of objectification, through the eyes of Humbert Humbert and his class of "Dads, including the sophistication, cosmopolitanism, and any of those cute, vogue, French phrases that I could understand. I wanted to be the object of such a narrative. Un triangle amoureux. I don't think this anymore. I hated Lolita for getting old: 17! I did not realize what I thought was a love story was also a control story and it had worked on me—for a while at least.

My graduate school writing sample was on, "How Lolita, the girl, becomes Lolita the text." I rambled on those textual freeways of Nabokov's Great American Novel with a sharp pencil as my brake. Like for so many other readers, the aesthetics bedazzled. I tried to tap into Nabovok's magic by reading about his butterflies, Pale Fire, and digging deep into Russian history. I learned

that Slavic once stood for slave. Nothing was as regal as it seemed, except for the Faberge eggs; however, I stood by the mighty artistry, identifying with the power of the words in the book, power by pen (or typewriter). When I used Lolita as reading material, while teaching an Introduction to Fiction course, some students, especially those whose lives overlapped with some of the unfortunate experiences shared with Lolita the character, made argument about Nabokov being an evil man. I would push those concerns off and ask them to focus on the superior art: to just ask more of Nabokov's magic.

If you Google the two words, "Lolita Sunglasses," you will find most results yield red heart-shaped glasses. (Although a glassware company has cleverly called its range of "dressed up" wine glasses, Lolita, to maximize "Lolita glasses" web searches. You will get those, too.) The heart-shaped sunglasses have become iconic, even though they never appear in the novel or Stanley Kubrick film, just the photo promoting the 1963 film. In the image, the young Lolita actress, Sue Lyon, peers over the heart-shaped glass, a red lollipop pressed to her red lips. The heart-shaped glasses form a cultural illusion of sorts, which brings me to a revealing comment in the Afterward of the novel, in which. Nabokov recalls the inspiration for Lolita: how an animal in a zoo's first artistic expression is only the bars of its own cage. A few literary historians have dug up some images from magazines of Nabokov's and Kubrick's time period that show photos of people gawking at animals in a cage—from the animal's point of view. The bars of the cage fade behind girls, boys, men, and women, Americans staring through the cage and at the novelty.

If we were to imagine Lolita's cage in Humbert Humbert's torrid narrative about his passion for girls of a certain (under)age, it would consist of manipulations instead of iron. In one of the final scenes of the novel and film, which shows an older Lolita, no longer vibrant, she trades in her aesthetics for practicality. she wears a very practical set of glasses as she looks back at him: no longer with the rose, heart-shaped or cat's eye glasses. These are very basic, far less fashionable glasses. They resemble the GI glasses, lovingly referred to as Birth Control Glasses, which are named for the lack of sex appeal given to those who wear them. This choice in eyewear could mark a step up in maturity in Lolita's style, but it also shows consistency in being framed. Looking at this series of fashionable eyewear, heart-shaped, cat's eye, and unstylish, it's not too much of a jump to see the ever-changing shift of an encultured lens. In order to be wanted and visible, you wear the right fashion. To be seen, you shade something of yourself.

In a lamenting sonnet, after Lolita escapes him, Humbert poetically envisions his version of a Wanted Poster: Wanted Dolores Haze, giving her "Profession: "none" or 'starlet'" (271). This is an ironic pair of job descriptions, in that it implies that you are the star of a scene in Dad's movie or you are nothing. Yet, the belief that there is a film and performing in it might be more of a problem. So, in the fiction of Humbert's love lens, in the literature, it's a zero-sum game; Lolita is nothing or the subject and starlet of the word. Doomed to the life cycle of a star. but attached to the long tail of someone else's supernova.

Another adaptation made In the Kubrick film, Lolita, was to leave out the news about Lolita dying in childbirth with daughter, which is sneakily previewed in the Foreword of the book (if you know her alias, Mrs. Richard F. Schiller). In Nabokov's Lolita, Mrs. Richard F. Schiller is already dead before the adventure begins. So, Nabokov kills off the girl and her female heir, leaving the book as an artifact in her place. Kubrick leaves their demise out. While the novel closes the story of Lolita as a mother before it begins, Kubrick leaves that possible narrative open in his film. This is the electricity of hope in literature that I

felt on Nabokov's word highways and in Kubrick's visual flyovers of those words—that anything can happen. The hope in creativity bringing light in even in the darkest circumstances, even on Hunter Road, upholds that in aesthetics, there is a freedom that one rarely finds in other places, which precludes asking anyone's permission.

Afterward

Recently there was a new monkey photo controversy. A macaque named Naruto took a selfie of himself in 2011 with the photographer David Slater's camera. In Naruto's image, the primate grins and stared directly into the lens, in a vivid self portrait. Slater holds a British copyright for the photo; however, in America, things run a bit differently. Despite legal appeals from PETA, the picture taken by a monkey cannot be copyrighted. Going back to Nabokov's inspiration for Lolita as an animal drawing its own cage, in the days of digital photography, Naruto sees himself without a cage, unframed like Stanley Kubrick's adaptation of Lolita and her daughter's future. Naruto's photo remains a lot like mother and daughter—in the public domain—where no one can ever own it.

About the Author:

Carrie Bailey is a college instructor from the Portland Metropolitan Area. Her latest creative projects include a book on parenting adult children and a novel that includes accompanying fragrances. Grounded: she is a Taurus and was born in the year of the boar. Lolita has been on her bookshelf since 1989.

THE GOLD CHAIR

Rebecca Johnson

It was The Gold Chair that turned everything upside down. It was not an ornate kind of chair. It was not made for Medieval Kings with real gold, fancy scrolling, and a dignified red or royal purple velvet cushion. In fact, it didn't have a single fleck of gold at all. It was stout, plush, and upholstered.

The Gold Chair was from the 70's, I assume, when gold was the in-color. Our house was never the type to be filled with trendy or flashy furniture. The kind of furniture found on the marbled tile of expensive showroom floors. More likely it was a hand-me-down from my grandmother, who always disposed of her out-of-style furniture to our garage or our least furnished room. Our living room, becoming merely a cemetery plot of old and invaluable things.

On more than one occasion she said our house didn't warrant nice things. After a while, I think my mother believed her or I doubt the out-of-date Gold Chair would have stuck around for so long. From my earliest memories, The Gold Chair, that gold chair, dumped from my grandmother's house to ours, sat in my parent's bedroom against the wall near the telephone. "It's always nice to have a comfortable chair in the bedroom," my mother still tells me.

Since giving up a wealthy childhood for a just-getting-by adulthood, she no longer had pretty or new things. To her, only an insignificant and obvious exchange for the truest kind of love from a man, who grew up with three brothers, on the side of town without slate roves. True love must do that to a person – place importance on things like comfort over beauty or style. The Gold Chair would sit in my parent's bedroom, in the same spot, for decades.

My grandmother replaced The Gold Chair with a new, store bought, peachy or pinkish one to match the newest 80's décor pallet. She was unconcerned with a furniture's ability to offer comfort – that is if it were just the right style. After all, she was the type of lady who wore shoes that pinched your toes if they had colored sequins. She even had purple leather pants. That became her identifier if anyone asked me about my grandmother. Not that she made the most glorious peanut butter cookies. Because she didn't. Or how as a small child I loved to sit on her lap. Because I didn't. Or that she colored with me so few times, at age thirty-six, most of the crayons resting in the same box are still sharp. But that she had purple leather pants. That was all they needed to know.

We never had store bought furniture. But it was okay with me. I didn't mind much. At least not until high school when I became aware my classmates had store bought furniture. Or antique furniture. And carpet that wasn't twenty-years-old. Their dad's had jobs like doctors. While mine sold insurance for his father-in-law's business out of respect. Though he secretly wanted to have a greenhouse. That was the kind of man he was.

I loved my father. Before I hated him. Before I started to miss him. And so I, too, learned having store bought and stylish furniture, or the newest carpet, wasn't more important than the comfort of a father's love.

My first intimate acquaintance with The Gold Chair happened when I was quite young. Three or four. The 80's weren't known for time-outs but if I did something especially naughty – which I often did, my mother would say, "Go to The Gold Chair." I would be sentenced there for an unknown amount of time. The directions were to, "Sit here and think about what you did." Except I wouldn't think about it. I would make sure I thought about anything except what I did.

It was also next to my mother's sewing things. A delicious, red pincushion shaped like a tomato. And a jar of buttons I wasn't allowed to play with – but always longed to. When punished and sent to The Gold Chair I would open the jar and handle the smooth buttons. And then prick the pincushion with my favorite pins – the long kind with the pearly tops. After a while my mother caught me and removed her sewing things. The Gold Chair was not meant to be a place of forbidden pleasure.

Once those sewing things were taken away I started peeing in the chair. After a few peeing incidents I never had to go back to The Gold Chair. Instead my mother would say, "Go get the yardstick," and I would be spanked. It never hurt. But I kept that to myself.

The morning my father died my mother told me from The Gold Chair.

That God damn gold chair. In that moment, only a little girl, I hated nothing more than The Gold Chair. As if it were its fault for taking my father from me. I wanted to pee on it. Punch it. Tear it's upholstery until it was nothing more than decades of dirtied golden thread. It was Mother's Day. But we didn't celebrate. My mother sat in The Gold Chair.

All day. Stoic. Motionless. Stunned.

After my father died my mother was never the same. I imagine losing the love of your life at forty-two would do that to anyone. One afternoon, as she sat in The Gold Chair putting on her shoes, she asked me to tie them for her. "Why?" I asked.

"Sometimes it's just nice to be taken care of," she said, asking me not to tell anyone. I tied them. My childhood was over.

About the Author:

Rebecca Johnson is an Annapolis-based writer whose creative nonfiction, personal essays, and flash drama has appeared in 'Fresh, Young, and Relevant,' 'Number Eleven,' and 'Headquarter Press.' Her work has also been anthologized in The Geography of Loss. Her first collection, An Abnormal Love of Light, is forthcoming.

WHAT IT TAKES

Carla Sofia Ferreira

I cannot imagine
a greater strength
than what it takes
for an immigrant
to leave their homeland.

Remember your hardest goodbye
the one that returns to you
when you least expect
the one that keeps you awake
sometimes.
Imagine if you can
that goodbye stretched
over mountains and rivers
and houses you have known
and even the lilt and turn
of language. Imagine that
goodbye times an entire country.
Imagine it happening
without you asking.

In Portuguese, we never say goodbye
once. We say it over and over like
the end of an important prayer.
We say it in English and in Portuguese.
We repeat our goodbyes
because we never want a goodbye
to be final. We love and fear the oceans
that divide us. Perhaps fear, too,
is a type of love.

I can talk to you of saudade
and of the longing in be-
longing but there is no language
for it—
for the leaving.
It is beyond translation.

About the Author:

Carla Sofia Ferreira, originally from the Ironbound community in Newark, New Jersey, she studied at Harvard where she wrote a creative thesis: a compilation of 52 original poems, In Transit, focusing on urban ecology and transience in (im) migration. Currently, Carla teaches intermediate English language acquisition to first-generation immigrants in high school. Her parents emigrated from Portugal to the United States. When she's not teaching, Carla is likely trying to keep small succulents alive, reading poetry, or watching telenovelas.

MOON SILENCE

Pierre Sotér

Alvorada

Anuncia-se a alvorada.
Um galo canta
e toda a terra, repousada,
a pouco e pouco se levanta.
Os primeiros raios de luz
prescutam a leve névoa,
que se dissolve e nos conduz
aos cumes da grande serra,
à nobre fonte que introduz
a vida e a sua regra.
Anuncia-se a caminhada
que o Sol aquece,
e as feras e a passarada
seguem a forma encantada
em que a vida acontece.
Apenas os homens se esquecem
que os Deuses não são tolos,
que com ou sem jóias e bolos
da mesma forma nascem e crescem
gafanhotos e bisontes,
que do outro lado dos montes
onde todos envelhecem,
vive mais quem ouve o galo,
e sente o vento, e sabe amá-lo.

Moon silence

Silence and a full moon are perfect mates,
the moon twinkles and silences infest
lightless skies with old starry silent states,
hanging in the spheres of Almagest.
Lions rule at land and the vaulted seas,
and an eagle flies over Aquarius,
while the seven sisters, the Pleiades,
sail against Scorpio and Sagittarius.
And souls dance to the heavens' symphonies,
and minds travel through the epicycles,
and man's will creates divine dynasties
while man's power dreams with cosmic titles.

But I just enjoy looking at the moon,
when it's silent and clad in silver, soon.

Rien que l'éternité

Entre nous et le ciel, l'enfer ou le néant,
pendant qu'on s'interroge sur ce qui nous suffit,
il n'y a qu'une si fragile vie, Pascal nous a dit,
un temps qui cours vite, et tant de fois méchant.

Souvent, on ne prends pas la peine d'y penser,
et sans se mettre en vers, et sans se faire une clé,
on court tous les chemins sans un demin trouver,
on vit autour d'un cercle ou dans un carré.

On se fait la tête, on peste et on pars,
sans une raison d'être, non plus nos espoirs,
on se plaît à rester part de l'humanité.

Même si cependant on donne sa langue au chat,
rien n'est si important à l'homme que son état,
rien ne lui est si redoutable que l'eternité.

Things I forget

When in my thoughts simple feelings I forget,
and meaner things forcefully I overdo,
unawareness becomes a state of fret,
which unchecked will last long, unaware too.
When in my thoughts all my dreams I neglect,
and magic things haughtily I disregard,
weariness sets in before the Sun is set,
sleep will be less deep, and the night more hard.
When in my thoughts logic is incorrect
and intuition fails or is overruled,
I will have to believe my luck and bet,
and hope my soul won't tell me I'm a fool.

When in our minds thoughts and sense are lost,
sometime, somewhere, somehow we'll pay the cost.

About the Author:

Pierre Sotér is the pen name of a well-established Portuguese author. After thirty years of successful professional life and intensive soul-searching, he now dedicates his time to poetry and philosophy. "Dawn," the first book in his Book Series "Poems and Thoughts of Pierre Sotér." has been published in July 2017 by Adelaide Books. Pierre writes in Portuguese, English, and French.

ANA AHMATOVA POETRY
translated by Donald Mager

untitled

To Vera Ivanova-Shvarsalon

Mist lightly filled the park,
And a gaslight flared at the gate.
I only remember a certain look,
Eyes oblivious and sedate.

To others your sadness was not clear,
But right away attracted me,
And you discerned that some despair
Was choking and poisoning me.

I love this day's pure indolence,
And will come to you if you call,
My waywardness and indolence,
You've not rebuked, nor will.

April 1911

Вера Ивановой-Шварсалон

Туманом легким парк наполнился,
И вспыхнул на воротах газ.
Мне только взгляд один запомнился
Незнающих, спокойных глаз.

Твоя печаль, для всех неявная,
Мне сразу сделалась близка,
И поняла ты, что отравная
И душная во мне тоска.

Я этот день люблю и праздную,
Приду, как только позовешь.
Меня, и грешную и праздную,
Лушь ты одна не упрекнешь.

Апрель 1911

Vera Ivanova-Shvarsalon (1890-1920) was an acquaintance of Akhmatova's and 21 years old at the time of this poem. Her mother, the novelist Lidiia Zinov'eva-Annibal, married to the poet Viacheslav Ivanov was recently deceased. Vera's father was from Lidiia's first marriage. In 1913 Vera became her stepfather's third wife. In later years Akhmatova referred to the family as incestuous.

untitled

We are all tramps and floozies here,
Together how unhappy we are!
On the wall, flowers and birds
Continue to pine for clouds.

The pipe you puff is black,
Above you, an odd drift of smoke.
I slipped on a tight skirt,
It shows me off just right.

The windows are sealed. That sound?
Frost? Storm coming on?
Like unblinking cat eyes,
Peering out are your eyes.

O my anxious heart,
Is it death or time I wait?
But she who dances now will
Not fail to be in hell.

1 January 1913

Все мы бражники здесы, блудницы,
Как невесело вместе нам!
На стенах цветы и птицы
Томятся по облакам.

Ты куришь черную трубку,
Так странен дымок над ней.
Я надела узкую юбку,
Чтоб казаться еще стройней.

Навсегда забиты окошки:
Что там, изморозь иль гроза?
На глаза осторожной кошки
Похожи твои глаза.

О, как сердце мое тоскует!
Не смертельного ль часа жду?
А та, что сейчас танцует,
Непременно будет в аду.

1 января 1913

In one of the poet's most often cited early poems, the poet describes the very Petersburg cabaret, The Stray Dog,
which was a popular gathering place for writers, musicians and social celebrities during the 1910s. She often read
her poems there.

Dream

I knew you were dreaming me
For I could not fall asleep.
From the dim blue lamp
My way revealed itself.

You saw the tsarina's garden,
The ornamented white palace
And black wrought iron fences
Around deserted stone porches.

Not knowing the way, you went on
Assuming: "O, quick, quick,
If only I can find her,
For our meeting, no yet awake."

And the guard at the red gate
Hailed to you: "Where to!"
The ice cracked and broke,
Black water underfoot.

"This is the lake," you assumed.
"In the lake is a small island . . ."
And suddenly out of the dark
A small blue light showed itself.

In the harsh light of a meager day,
Waking up, you groaned
And identified me out loud
For the first time, by name.

1915

СОН

Я знала, я снюсь тебе,
Оттого не могла заснуть.
Мутный фонарь голубел
И мне указывал путь.

Ты видел царицын сад,
Затейливый белый дворец
И черный узор оград
У каменных гулких крылец.

Ты шел, не зная пути,
И думал: «Скорей, скорей,
О, только б ее найти,
Не проснуться до встречи с ней».

А сторож у красных ворот
Окликнул тебя: «Куда!»
Хрустел и ломался лед,
Под ногой чкрнела вода.

«Это озеро, — думал ты, —
На озере есть островок . . .»
И вдруг из темноты
Поглядел голубой огонек.

В жестьком свете скудного дня
Проснувшись, ты застонал
И в первый раз меня
По имени громко назвал.

1915

Ахматова, Анна Андреевна. Сование Сочнеий В Шести Томах. [Akhmatova, Anna Andreevna. Complete Works in Six Volumes.] Ed. T. A. Gorkova. Moscow: Ellis-Lak [Эллис Лак], 1998-2005: 1, 120-121)

To the Poema

. . . And turn words back to music.
O. M<andelstam>

You grow, you flourish, you—take voice.
To new torments, I
Resurrected you—gave you to the enemy . . .
Eight thousand miles is no obstruction,
As if song resounded in the garden,
I can sense every sigh.
And I know—he can do the same,
Nor can I be indignant and chide him,
This bond is stronger than either of our wills,—
Neither of us is guilty of any charge,
We, the bloodless sacrifices—
I forgot, and he—forgot.

20 September 1960
Komarovo

САМОЙ ПОЭМА

. . . и слово в музыку вернись.
О. М <андельштам>

Ты растешь, ты цветешь, ты—в звуке.
Я тебя на новые муки
Воскресила—дала врагу . . .
Восемь тысяч миль не преграда,
Песня словно звучит из сада,
Каждый вздох проверить могу.
И я знаю—с ним ровно то же,
Мне его попрекать негоже,
Эта связь выше наших сил,—
Оба мы ни в чем не виновны,
Были наши жертвы бескровны—
Я забыла, и он—забыл.

20 сентября 1960
Комарово

The line comes from Mandelstam's "Silentium"(1910).

The poem is addressed to the poet's masterpiece, the poema Poem Without A Hero—which underwent many revisions and additions over 20 years and was not published during her life. The "he" would seem to be Mandelstam who had been dead some twenty years at this point.

Ахматова, Анна Андреевна. Сование Сочнеий В Шести Томах. [Akhmatova, Anna Andreevna. Complete Works in Six Volumes.] Ed. T. A. Gorkova. Moscow: Ellis-Lak [Эллис Лак], 1998-2005: 42, 80.

Anna Akhmatova (1889-1961)

Akhmatova's early Acmeist poems were sensationally popular during the teens and 20s of the twentieth century. After the Bolshevik revolution her personal life and public career went from crisis to crisis. She was effectively barred from publishing. She continued to write "for the bottom of her chest" as she said. Her third husband and adult son were imprisoned and sent to Siberia during the Stalinist purges of the 1930s. Her great poem "Requiem" reflects this experience. It circulated among friends and later in samizdat, but was not published in the Soviet Union until the "thaw" in the 1950s. This was followed by a second long political poem "The Way of All the World." In 1942 she began her long masterpiece Poem Without a Hero, which occupied her for much of the rest of her life. After Stalin's death, she was gradually rehabilitated and her work was again widely published in the Soviet Union. In 1998 Ellis Lak Publishers began a comprehensive collected edition of her works including, drafts, sketches and variant. The eighth and final volume came out in 2005. It supersedes all previous editions both in the West and in Russia.

Don Mager's chapbooks and volumes of poetry are: *To Track The Wounded One, Glosses, That Which Is Owed to Death, Borderings, Good Turns, The Elegance of the Ungraspable, Birth Daybook, Drive Time and Russian Riffs.* He is retired and was the Mott University Professor of English at Johnson C. Smith University where he also served as Dean of the College of Arts and Letters (2005-2011). As well as a number of scholarly articles, he has published over 200 poems and translations from German, Czech and Russian. He lives in Charlotte, NC with his partner of 36 years, Bill.

Us Four Plus Four is an anthology of translations from eight major Soviet-era Russian poets. It is unique because it tracks almost a half century of their careers by simply placing the poems each wrote to the others in chronological order. The 85 poems represent one of the most fascinating conversations in poems produced by any group of poets in any language or time period. From poems and infatuation and admiration to anger and grief and finally to deep tribute, this anthology invites readers into the unfolding lives of such inimitable creative forces as Anna Akhmatova, Boris Pasternak, Marina Tsvetaeva and Osip Mandelstam.

HOMEGROWN ATROCITIES
Richard Pacheco

HOMEGROWN ATROCITIES

I watch my children grow
more like me each day.
I see their sneers
their obvious revenge
repeating my habits
and mannerisms
in an attempt to drive me mad.
They build pyramids of dishes
by the sink in the hope of a flood.
An avalanche of laundry
tumbles into the hallway
almost alive-- and they smile.
In their teenage years
they have built the Great Wall of China
between us as I struggle ·
to maintain some trace of civilization
they prefer to be barbarians
just for the fun of it.

So I smirk to hide my fear I
knowing they know me too well
and my little charade
is too pat and predictable
to work.
And we retrace our steps
with each fresh day
and mock each other
behind our backs.
It is a careless strategy
so sad and sterile
Unmade restitutions
accumulate too fast
and we remain
destiny's deliberate malcontents.

Looking for Absolution

They calculate prayers A

meticulous as mathematicians

devotee of empiricism.

Prayer

Their beads are fine baby teeth

plucked from Dachau corpses

strung together....phantom faith

They march by candlelight.

a procession

across the windy places

the sandy expanses of

the despairing hearts

Quick & silent as nomads

(mounting the crested dunes

they move

whispering

the names of the dead

into the sirocco

About the Author:

Richard Pacheco is an award-winning playwright, poet, artist, journalist, filmmaker and educator. A finalist in the grant competition in playwrighting at Massachusetts Artists Foundation (1976) he won the 1986 American Regional Theatre Award best new play. His plays have been seen throughout Massachusetts. He won the best actor Award from New England Russian in Boston, He acts on stage, in film and television. He is a member of SAG-AFTRA.. He holds a BFA in painting and an MFA in printmaking from U. Mass. Dartmouth His poetry book, "Geography" was nominated for a 2015 Pulitzer Prize in poetry.

Footsteps

The women walk by in the rain

their heels clattering

like frightened crickets...

PIECES OF A LIFE HISTORY
Larry Smith

PIECES OF A LIFE HISTORY

Finally, he saw the commonplace, that gods
ever punish wicked adolescence
by making its dreams come true.
But sleep now, the years are numb.

A bed in Bedlam, pretty pilgrims
succored at the teat of a squall,
highwaymen in the snow, rhomboid winds...
but sleep now, the celebrants are dead.

Exile and age formulate deserts and riddles
and riddles that rise in deserts just for him--
the answer, man, just for him.
But sleep now, wisdom is dust.

And it was the desert lady flew him home
but Thebes was just a Thebes like any other Thebes.
Finally his mother bore him down and she crushed him.
So sleep now, the women are defeated.

CHRIST

You'll never be more of anything
than what you are of love right now

What a lucky man this Jesus
to know life a meaning
and death but sweaty spasm
in mid afternoon

Bless Him
and the ass he rode in on

Pure music
No melody
Jesus is just like Schoenberg
In that respect

Dead so long and still fat

SEMBLANCE OF ORDER AT HARTFORD ACCIDENT AND INDEMNITY

Janet Yellin's Talmud is a couplet to counter Pound:
With Usura hath no man a house of good stone
But without Usura hath no man no house no how.

By such irony the world reasserts order.
The coins jingle because God gave us the pockets,
Yet what a small music to lay claim to consonance!

Render unto this one and render unto that one--
Christ's indifference thuds down through the centuries,
And on the architectonics of economics, no comment at all.

Though how insistently mortals resist the divorce,
Insist their symmetries partake of bigger bread.
Prime rates, discount rates fugue-like frame the balance sheets.

Hartford's light's a semaphore through louvers at dusk.
Ink still wet on policies begs the questions,
Do equities harmonize? Do the spheres hum here?

Pythagoras assumed ever-lasting sound
While our prolix clauses dim fast in moonlight.
The deer go one way and the dachshunds another.

Yet some nostalgia for order outlives this undoing.
Moonsoil holds the Indian summer song;
We burrow in that warmth and play with geometry.

Heaven's plane arrests our eye, so does hell's--
Can fiscal conceits adventure either shrine,
Or form a third, a hierarchy limbo's very own?

Actuarial tables by any other name...
Shall I with sunup dare adopt new tact,
Engird all worlds, string the lyre from cloud to client?

Not when morning shows me fear in a globule of dew.
Proportion's but a chimera amid the indices:
Flee, you music, sleep deep in the fur of a warm bed.

The body gets up and goes to work like Christ preached tax law.
It does what it has to do, and doesn't dream.
Office order's moot. Areopagite, pass by!

A noontime sun bleaches the gray-brown bow ties.
Deductibles beat unsung time, unhallowed song,
And I walk the two ways of worlds that never touch.

Larry Smith's poetry has appeared in Descant (Canada) and Elimae, among others. His novella, Patrick Fitzmike and Mike Fitzpatrick, was published in 2016 by Outpost 19. His stories have appeared in McSweeney's Quarterly Concern, Low Rent (nominated for a Pushcart Prize), Exquisite Corpse, The Collagist, Curbside Splendor, Sequestrum, PANK, among numerous others. His articles and essays have appeared in Modern Fiction Studies, Social Text, The Boston Phoenix, and others. Visit larrysmithfiction.com.

I ATE MY POEM
Seamus O Sparks

I ate my poem last night
We got into a vicious fight
It tasted wasted sunken drunken
Then I lumbered then I slumbered
Long I slept and loud I wept
At once I was awakened and once again mistaken
To try and sit and try and write
About the poem I ate last night
Because my thoughts could not agree
Did I eat the poem
Or did the poem eat me

Thoughts while eating Pad Thai after therapy

There is the word, there is man
Of the world, and the light
To puke his way past
To reason his way out
Liver of life
Dier of deaths
He can't remember when the sun wasn't a hard-boiled egg yolk
Stuck to the sky
The man, created he shopping malls and soda pop in his own image
That he be sick with life
Long before he dies
By which time the game will already be fixed
And the peace already broken
Between the pig animals and the cannibal babies
All men are created equal until they eat shit
And then it's another story
But for today, blessed are the meek, and the actuaries, and the direct TV subscribers
And the man
For thine is the sex: to measure his dick
The drugs: to measure his doom
The rock-n-roll: to measure his sins
And he looked around and saw that it was good...
Or, at least, as good as it was ever gonna' get

Everybody needs a hobby

It's remarkable how you can lay in bed
And dangle on thoughts
As the brain uncoils
The great words come
Thru the breach
Of deprograming in the idle hours
It's the wonderful time
Articulations of a mind that isn't trying to say
Anything

So you hop up, grabbing pen and paper
Attempting to cast your gut in language
And there is nothing
Dire scribbles on an aggravated night
The piece won't break out (the fucker)
Just rusty gears cranking and a pile of wadded papers
More crumpled pages
To tell the story of your life

No matter what you do: smoke, pull the cat's tail, rub your nipples
It's all a fat bust
Thought constipation
Another brutal round of pulling words to death
And swatting at gnats
And mindless television
Then your ear begins to itch
The commercial telling you to spend 30% less for 20% more
Makes the itch deep and unbearable
So you jab pen in earhole
And go to work
Scratching like hell

At the emergency room
You stick out
Amidst the witching hour weirdos:
Night victims
Drug freak outs, drunks, wolfmen

Everyone staring

At the pen sticking out of your head

Your insurance sucks, the receptionist is all paperwork and no soul

The doctor gives you shit for smoking

And asks how you came to have a pen

Stuck in your head

You tell him, "writer's block"

He goes into a half-hearted spiel about his son

Who is a writer

And graduated Summa Cum Laude

Travels the world, wins prizes, publishes, flourishes

With a fast car and a leggy blonde nibbling his

Fancy leather belt

You tell the doc that you're not really a "writer" writer

Just some guy with a pen stuck in his head

He tells you, "Everybody needs a hobby"

As he removes the pen

You look at the pen, you see the blood

You think of the thousands of crumpled pages

And the crumpled lovers, friendships, evenings, brain folds, blankets, nerve endings, conversations, choices, opportunities, plans, hopes, strategies and dreams it took to bring you to this moment

Then he wishes you luck with the writer's block

About the Author:

Seamus O Sparks is an unpublished writer from San Marcos, TX. He works a menial job and doesn't interview well. Besides writing Seamus likes to sit and worry and generally waste time.

FORGOTTEN

Sergio Ortiz

The Things We Draw on Maps

There are men who write
where men don't speak

peaceful revolts
which overthrow bloodthirsty kings

business men who give undeserved gifts
music in the middle of a battlefield

strawberries in the woods
people who meet & understand each other

amazing triumphs of love with no strings attached
There are small precarious paradises

along the path we walk
on the shore of a wild monstrous sea

where it smells like grilled fish
& festive laughter

where we play without rules and balance
in unison on large red hammocks

where we embrace & lose track of time.
Where we forget with cheerful vehemence

Forgotten

He arrived from Lebanon
ready to repair and sell carpets.
Gold and ruby fibers
put the mystery of time to rest.

He doesn't know
the twentieth century
will part like a blizzard,
same as every other century.

When night barges in
without hands
ticking won't be necessary
—mountains
and magical mango trees
will shed the last light
of a lost recollection.

Blood says nothing
of his Maronite prayers
or of his grief in an old
Kobayat alley
where he scattered
his childhood.

A longing for an Arabic
call to prayer is rare.

Mr. Man's Man

One day I'll know you're not eternal
and that you don't exhale lavender,

that your sweat isn't honey. I'll learn
your hands don't shape my world,

your laughter doesn't own my hours.
I'll undergo the loneliness of stars,

the impotence of the sea before the moon.
That'll be the day my sunsets end.

Voodoo

He offered me
a handmade box

with floral motifs
and voodoo pins

inside, four tiny children
nailed to my body.

He said: I'm yours
even if required to prick

the bolt between my legs
and that viscera, the heart.

Pessimistic butterflies flew.
I heard their flapping

in the shadows. The snap
of a nonexistent tongue.

Ephemeral Hatchling

A bird lands on my garden.
I know it's thanks to the discontinuous
pixel movements of its brief
leaps on the grass.
Its slight figure rummages for supplies
with its childlike beak
between the tiny leaves
on the ground.

The grass, I tell myself, the grass
is where the food is hidden.

I'm about to decipher this mystery,
it's like the poetic breath that precedes it.
Always something violent, the breeze
blowing stronger,
or the very sensitivity
of the hatchling sensing
my garden is non-garden
a wasteland
a fiction
a reduced green apparition
in the courtyard of the house.

When just like that, the bird flaps,
flits— drawing pixels like it arrived,
and disappears.

Then the house faces

the reality of its troublesome stay.
The common everyday trappings
feel enlightened
as if its ephemeral presence
provided them with fleeting certainties
and endless senses.

About the Author:

Sergio A. Ortiz is a two-time Pushcart nominee, a four-time Best of the Web nominee, and 2016 Best of the Net nominee. His poems have appeared or are forthcoming in Valparaiso Poetry Review, Loch Raven Review, Drunk Monkeys, Algebra Of Owls, Free State Review, and The Paragon Journal. He is currently working on his first full-length collection of poems, Elephant Graveyard.

LUNA
Clint Davis

Speak for me
I am Luna, I was only Three,
this was what they done to me,
train ride with family,
no room to sit, only stand,
my legs so tired,
mom can you hold my hand?
No windows, I can't see out, all
the people all scream and shout, but,
only silence from me,
could someone please, speak for me?
through the cracks,
I try to see, everything that passes by me, I see tall trees,
grass blows in the wind, as we pass by,
so much thirst, my lips so dry,
legs so weak, can barely stand,
mom could you hold my hand?
this is what they done to me,
I am Luna, was only Three,
tell everybody that you see,
tell them all, speak for me.
the wheels of the train,
sound so loud, when we stop, the
men in boots, begin to shout,
those with stripe suits, look down at the ground,
a terrible dog begins to growl,
they take my dad and brother away,
Mom and I, are led astray,
my legs are so weak, can barely stand,
mom could you hold my hand?
they take us to a room, with dark walls, with white scratches,
heavy doors, with loud latches, I can hear,
foot steps over head,
mom, can we go?, to another place instead?

they take my doll, and my clothes too,
mom, what have they done with my shoes?
so alone, with so many, so hungry, we look
so skinny.
we cry out! can God hear us?
we all know, death is near to us!
Its quiet now, no one is listening,
I am no longer here, is
Luna gone I fear!
but, I am only three, look what they have done to me!
oh, they pick me up, they take my hair,
its so pretty, don't they care?
put me in a little room,
with heavy doors, with loud latches,
they burn me, without any matches,
my name is Luna, I was only three,
why did they do this, this terrible thing,
I was so precious, can't you see,
so tell everyone, tell them all,
tell all you see, please, speak,
speak for me,
so now they take poor Luna out,
spread her ashes upon the ground,
gentle breeze blows her all around,
Luna no longer makes a sound,
so quiet now... she wants to speak,
she can't now... her words don't come out!
God takes her by the hand, he holds her near,
she says the words only he can hear.
I'm Luna, I'm only Three,
on a train, mother sits with me,
I clutch my doll,
I feel so free, I look to the window,
I can finally see, trees pass by us,
grass blows by the wind, so happy,
I no longer stand, My lips no longer dry,
my dad and brother they look and smile,
though I try to speak, and I am finally free,
no words come from me, so won't you speak.
speak for me...

ELM STREET NEIGHBOR

Dianne Moritz

From curtainless
Kitchen windows,
Light pools on
A mid-night lawn.

The old woman sits
In shabby housecoat,
Hunched over
Her formica table,

Limp hair hiding
Her shaggy profile,
Shuffling worn cards
For games of solitaire.

Walking my dog
Down shadowed streets,
I watch this pantomine:
Slap of cards,

Thin wrist reaching
For a glass rattling
With amber ice.
Sadness drenches me
Like warm rain.

BEACH HOUSE

That house is lonely now.
First my dog, next your old cat.
No one expected a cancer,
so quick and greedy.

How I miss your laugh,
Blaze of blue eyes as you
Spoke of love and work,
Offering sage advice.
I miss these sounds: ice
Tossed in a glass, jazz
Humming, the unlikeliness
Of us together there.

How the mind tricks!
Moments and memories
So clear, while that house
Stands bereft and cold.
Empty as air.

Dianne Moritz published poems in Poets On, Live Poets Society, Poetry Motel, Earth's Daughters, Long Island Quarterly and others. Essays have appeared in the NY Times, LA Times, Romantic Homes and many others. She co-authored 2 picture books with Kane Miller and is a frequent contributor to Highlights three magazines for kids.

SAMAEL'S LYCHGATE
Joseph Harms

SAMAEL'S LYCHGATE

Debrided Let returned to New York once unrecognizable,
austere as hell, his lychgate rented for the week to pay
for it, rogating friend to friend who'd ask about his missing
wife then nightjarring from zenana to zenana pied
and piing, somaed, nights unslept or slept spiculed into
a new facsimile, the life they'd shared less than a watercolored

dream. Love reduced is a detective story. Cocted solved
solutey. Light so light it's black. Back home he burned what leaves
he could and read the volitantes' asterism, woke
bedmade unselved as rote and clung to that. To live in Would.
Negating bout the garden eschewed by rabbits even
Let would unclimb the trellissy holdfasts but not deracinate

rather feed them into moleholes. Commuted. Expelled. Pall-
Malled round the 22nd of each month, parhelion
nevernevered, missed missing...We would at times we would and then
we wouldn't...The space the horror the forgetfulness the utter
lack of substance. Anchoritic ouroborossatisfaction.
The lychgate rent to own even...God beyond God...apolytrosis...

ROMA/MEIROTHEA: THE HEAVY HAND

Estranged the lawns aspersed, gazeboed parks, the depotpunks
and gravelledalley fireworks, the harlequined rill holyspiriting,
the dusty elms and aspens, shinhigh soy phalanged to earthend,
nostalgic cumuli etcet as liebestod etcets
as Let extrops from hebdomad to hebdomad etcetting
what's there. Black suits are all that's left scarecrowed by nails about

Let's room. He berths the Dairy Queen. A queue cannot be joined.
A tree cannot be climbed beneath this sun's etcetting sublim'ing.
The dirtroads bleached like snowy lanes beneath the sieving pollen.
Earthhum. Meirothea around each corner. Evoe. Evoe.
It's from the interstice the vista's gained. The keyhole is
the architect. Vejer Pinilla Roma madeleine

no more than Dexter's terminus ad quem. A hawkdropped daysold
fawn bounced from parasol to picnictable where it licked
a Blizzard bleeding from the ribs onto the carved names dates
profanities as people backed away, the limestonedust
by interstitial enfilade mushrooming till it stood
as if atop a rocket. Let with fawn in coat unstoppered left

unseen almost.

THE BOATS

From charybdis awoke to charybdis toward charybdis
within the scaph where February's augustlight scyphates
the sadly longing days iridized by snow honeylocast,
fissuring doorways felledthrough by the sun, the berm away
always in view beneath the moony berm (some distant headstone
for Dis, Let'd think when thinking allowed)…Necrophored from shore

to shore, scybaaling heart resuring the nonsensing days
where worst yet everything linesup—purpura purpura…
purpura purpura: Gloam! How spifli it comes! molling
about the scary shirring outremer spouting and spouting Now.
A blackhole's whitefountain. Orgasmic Recognition. It
glitches smally all about—the antipode of oneself.

You as well sleep beneath this drumlin scyphate un undrummed.
I see just where you dream, their map. Ab(r)axial. The sun
is shining plumbeous as wont as rote resuring everything
that's done (as nothing's done It's true). I see us there Genevaed
laked, pebbles black with white streaks, speckles—how we held ourselves
itall longshuttered, heavy boredom trephinating

the porcelain welkin.

FINELESS

> *Every nerve in my body is so vacant and numb*
> *I can't even remember what it was I came here to get away from*
> Dylan

To bring unchanged a deadroom continent to continent
and town to town: it's all affined, Ophion. Phlegethon's
prismatic mobiles about procumbent boughs whose limp
wintered limpets moth unstelled or stell unmothed yet never
are leaves kiting in the Boreas beneath regardant
cumuli zounds, the ferrous pines belittled by the zoundsy

sun that needsbe affining everything. Corsive, ma'am, Let.
Let Corsive. Son of Asmadai—Nullipper offtheclock.
A kiter, yes. I haven't been myself these days or someone
else for that matter (cognomen: Nomatter). 86'd
unvaled boohooing livedlongdays. I've come for your youngest
daughter. Yes, her. Please shave her eyebrows, ma'am. Acquaint her with

blackmetal. I'll return in two lustrums. / The airports that
we lived through! Life! That last as escalated I watched you
shrink queued, the Xing planes, the glass milieu.   The certainty.

About the Author:

A finalist for the 2015 National Poetry Series Award for his sonnet sequence Bel (Expat Press), **Joseph Harms is** the author of the novels Baal and Cant (Expat Press, 2nd Editions forthcoming). His work has appeared in numerous literary journals, including Boulevard, The Alaskan Quarterly Review, The International Poetry Review, The Opiate and Bayou Magazine. Currently, he is an MFA candidate in the University of Michigan's Helen Zell Writers' Program.

CALL ME ISHMAEL

Gayle Compton

Reflections on *Beowulf*

We swore she was of the race of Cain.

Wyrd is, and will always be, God's equal in the universe,
Professor George proclaimed.
But for now, I am the master of your fate.
Fail this class and you draft dodgers, pacifists
and dumb asses will pack your duffels for Vietnam!

Poor Whitey Joe, who misspelled Hrathgar, grand mogul
of the Mead-hall and mid-term ten-pointer,
was blown neatly in half west of Saigon.

Wendell Lee, who mistook "tatters of food" for "taters,"
the Irish kind he ate with beans in West Virginia,
lost both legs in Da Nang and went mad with Agent Orange.

I, who stayed up all night until my brain was a Scandinavian
stew of moors and moats, dragons, bards and kings—
Old English verbs dripping off my chin like Unferth's hot ale—
got Dr. George's only "A."

Now, for the life of me, I can't recall just who the hell Wyrd was,
or how Beowulf fared in the fenlands.
But I remember Wendell Lee, scrubbing toilets in the men's dorm,
thinking about his girl in Boone County;
and Whitey Joe, who wept when Bobby Kennedy died,
locked in his room with Bob Dylan.

And how we put a name to the nameless beast
the bard called "Grendel's Mother."

Call Me Ishmael

Once I believed in Endymion.

Once Keats, the bard of Joy,
sang to me in "mused rhyme."

I read Moby Dick in a front porch swing,
heard the sea's rolling symphony
beneath the swinging bridge.

Once my mother drew water
and the rusty voice of the well chain
was the Pequoid's
farewell to Nantucket.

Hanging off a C & O coal gon
I blew in at the Cape,
bearded, unbathed and swarthy.

With my clothes in a cardboard box
I rode a Greyhound bus
to the mills of East Chicago, Indiana.

I saw hell fire trundled
on an ingot buggy
and breathed the sulfurous
breath of Satan.

Clinging to a wheel of a '54 Mercury
like Queequeg's floating coffin,
I found the road to Peabrook.

Abraham, my dear old redbone,
rose stiff-legged from the porch,
whining and stretching,
his eyes full of memory and forgiveness.

Paul Newsome's Grass is High

Paul Newsome's grass
is getting high.
See how the honeybees
work the clover,
how the blue wings
nurse the dandelion!
Paul Newsome is dead.
His widow has locked the doors
and closed the blinds.
All day she sits in darkness
waiting for the night.
The grass grows
and honeysuckle climbs the gate.

The man who killed Paul Newsome
has gone away.
His chickens roost
in the unfinished shed.
The lizard waits for flies
on the new pine boards.
Strange, how his wife wears
the old coat he left.
Wrapped against the eye
of the mid-day sun
she walks alone--
easy as the bees in the wild grass.

Nine Cedars

Damn a woman thinks she's too good—too good to wash clothes on a board.
Damn that woman to everlasting hell!

You could hear him cussing, coming up the holler, Grandpa Gus,
cussing everybody on Lykens Creek, everybody from Spewing Camp to
Possum Trot, damning them all to hell.

Swinging his cane and cussing, damning the Lord, damning Grandmother,
a righteous woman with her hair in a bun,
dreading Grandpa, crawling through the drawbars, blood in his eye.

Grandpa Gus, who planted 10 cedars, one for each child, staid drunk two weeks
when they buried Sally Jane.
Strange, how the third tree died in the flush of spring.

Tanked up and coming home, nine cedars marking the path, nine cedars
taller than the house,
two rooms propped on hickory poles, horse shoe over the door,
Jesus on the wall.

Cussing "old Mert," a good woman with supper on the stove,
mocking the liver spotted hands that made the quilts that bought the cheap Maytag
with dollars saved and counted in a Prince Albert can.

Grandpa, the whore hopper, spending his old-age pension on the red-lipped floozies
at the Lloyd Hotel,
rode me on the corn sled pulled by old Dobbin, driving ahead of the thieving crows, showed me where
to drop the golden seed into the fresh turned earth.

Grandpa Gus, out all night at the Greenfly hoedown, up all night shaking a leg,
fought an oil lamp by a corn shuck bed,
lit the house on sawmill road, burned off both ears and singed his head,
saving a pint of Early Times.

Loaded to the gills with West Virginia rotgut, Old Man Gus kicking the door,
slinging the bean kettle slap in the creek,
rolling a brand new Maytag over the hill.

Grandpa Gus, high as a kite, damning that high faulting woman
hiding in the barn with two grown girls,
taught me how to milk old Pet, sitting on a bucket, squeezing the full teats,
laughing out loud, squirting my tongue with the sweet rich cream.

With his big hand led me to the spring under the papaws
where the fresh milk and white churned butter chilled in the
moss green rocks.

I was 16 when the house burned on Lykens Creek,
when two ladder back chairs held a cheap grey casket
in the green shade of nine cedars.
I saw the liver spotted hands lay a new white Bible
gently, gently over charred bones.

Three days later, in the smoldering ruins, Morgan and Ed,
two sons left to fight over the land,
two brothers who would never speak again,
found his bottle.

Alone, reaching deep into the cursed ashes,
searching for something without a name,
something beyond the specter of blue smoke,
it was I who found his heart.

About the Author:

Gayle Compton is a hillbilly living in Pike County, Kentucky, center of coal mining and internecine feuding. His prize-winning poems, stories and essays have been published in numerous journals and anthologies, including Appalachian Heritage, Main Street Rag, Now and Then, New Southerner and The Kentucky Anthology. His novella Countdown to Glory is forthcoming from Prolific Press. Should his androgynous first name suggest otherwise, he is a male.

THOUGHT ON A MONDAY MORNING
Mark Martyre

She continues to grow
more beautiful
as each day passes.
As I continue to rot.

The fates launched us to opposite ends
of the arc, but my heart always finds hers
like a magnet,
and I'm always being drawn to its pull.

I can never escape my love for her,
I will always hold her in my heart
and in my mind
while I know that our skin will never touch.

She continues to grow
more beautiful
every time I see her.
While I keep wilting away.

I have nothing but good things to say about her.
Nothing but loving things to tell her.
But, it's often better
if I say nothing at all.

Silhouettes

We walked together;
it was the longest day of the year.

We walked together the river's edge,
among families of geese,
under the quiet rustling trees,
bathed in the orange glow
that bounced off the water,
that spread across the grass,
that danced with the bugs fluttering in the bushes,
that shone on your face, through your eyes,
and within the gentle words
you spoke.

And then the sun began to set, on that warm day,
and we turned, with the sun at our back,
to head back home:
me to mine and
you to yours.

Long shadows, we cast,
that pushed into the future,
that raced across the waters, and fields,
and gravel paths.
Our silhouettes stretched out
ahead of us
as we walked.
as they continue to stretch to this day,
as they reach me here
now.

And, I know, they'll reach into the next life
when we both come back as stray dogs,
and I spend that lifetime picking up your scent,
always trying to find the air around your heart.

And then again when we're birds,
and our shadows fly high above the earth.
But each with our own migrating pattern
that never aligns.

And the shadows will reach into the life after that:
me as a peasant, you as a queen,
me sitting outside the palace walls
hoping for glimpse of your silhouette in the window.

And on and on the long shadows stretch,
finding us reborn again and again in South America,
then in India, then as turtles, then as elephants,
then as Parisians - where our smiling eyes meet
as we both browse the book vendors on the quai,
along The Seine.

And on and on the long shadows stretch,
just as they had stretched up to today
through conquests of Alexander the Great,
through the Renaissance,
through me seeing you across a 1920's speakeasy,
dancing with other flapper girls.

And then, finally,
after many eras have come and gone.
After our hairstyles, and clothing
have moved forward,
and then come back around.
After we've explored the far reaches of space
and I've loved you from the surfaces of Mars,
and from the moons of Jupiter.

After my heart has spent thousands of years searching for yours,

we'll return, once more,
to walk on the longest day of the year,
along the edges of the river,
with the sun setting before our eyes.

But, this time, hand in hand,
as partners, as lovers,
finally sharing the
same shadow.

photo ©Matthew ......di

About the Author:

Mark Martyre is a Canadian writer and musician. He has written and produced five studio albums since 2012, which have garnered critical acclaim, both nationally and internationally. Mark's poems have recently been published in Peacock Journal, The Littlest Voice, Poetry Breakfast, and The Spadina Literary Review. For more information visit http://www.markmartyre.com

THE WAY IT IS

Eduardo Escalante

Some signs

Under

the wave an invisible sound breaks it. The ancient wood

does not survive to the sound of the steps sprung with an admonitory

message. Leaves fall from the trees with time hanging on their necks.

A flock of tanned birds with a fervid injunction to look alerts to

falling seed. The dismembered trunk betrays the inhabitants,

their toes immersed in the arteries of the roots,

leaving stunned footsteps in the tangled forest.

Nothing paralyzed, flow or break. The window

opens, a world of shadow and lights reflecting

the way my mind unrolls under this spectacle.

I picture them: speckled palely at my page,

their flare of colors trailing in me. I raise

my eyes. The next naked unlearned

shape I must sign for the laughter

Dreams return to the world from

within and the past is circular,

like consequence. Until I can

reach the finish and the death

wakes me at midnight.

The way it is

An invisible sound,
Beneath the wave,

He breaks it. old timber
does not survive to

the sound of footsteps.
The leaves fall from the trees

the day hangs
from their necks.

Flock of birds
Round in the afternoons,

Alerts to falling seed.
The dismembered trunk

betray inhabitants. Toes
submerge in the arteries of

The sunken roots in the earth.
They leave stunning prints.

Nothing paralyzed
Flow or crunch

attending to these life events
I will grasp them with my hand

– its urgent here

About the Author:

Eduardo Escalante is a writer and researcher living in Valparaíso, Chile; he publishes regularly in Hispanic Reviews (Signum Nous, Ariadna, Nagari, Espacio Luke, Lakuma Pusaki, among others); and reviews in English (StlylusLit, Writer Resits, Spillwords, Slamchop and in Gramma Poetry).

IN A PEAR TREE

Lydia A. Cyrus

She grew pears instead of apples, my aunt did. Four medium height pear trees beside a creek bed. Except, no one ate pears in our family, so they would fall off the branches rotten with readiness. They were green and brown, soft and sweet smelling. As children we would walk, holding someone's hand. The youngest of us would be in a plastic red wagon, rolling through knee high grass. We admired the leaves of sycamore trees and the tuffs of milkweed plants as they all blew away. But you can't make a pie out of pears. So the fruit of nature's labor would roll into the grass and decompose but before that they would find their way into the wagon, into our hands. Leaving our hands sticky with something we had no intention of taking home.

SMALL TOWN IN OHIO
John Grey

JUST WHEN I THINK I CAN RELAX

I'm slowed to evening's speed,
breakneck frozen, filled with, comfort,
arid then a door-knock; the last word
in disturbance.
Silence and newspaper
interrupted by a neighbor's need
to talk by rote,
his body on the step
preventing the moon
from harvesting inside.
Same measures by which
the human frailty is exposed...
sports talk, politics, even a word
or two about the wife who left
him for the butcher.
From time to time,
the giant blade comes down,
severs the squealing pig.
He's caught me at a moment
when I'm nothing but myself,
no wish, to share that slow growing epiphany.
For an hour or more of small talk,
I ache to return to who I am.
My life,
the one thing I thought
was safe to try at home.

SMALL TOWN IN OHIO

There was a father once
who raged from Maine to California,
who must have figured only metal survives,
so he would always be metal,
backed up with fists
thick and hard as the stone blocks of sculptors,
and a thirst like a desert lion's.

He is not here
in this simple cottage.
This is the sober father,
the one awkward, timid even,
who cries while reading in a parlor chair
when a book plot requires a dog's demise.

These are eyes continuously washed clean
so that the inside light shows
to whoever might go looking.
He had one of those other fathers for his own.
It's a secret he occasionally spills
like a drop or two of coffee
that he immediately mops up.

The book is of lives gone dreadfully wrong.
Not just the dog but the people in it end badly.
He regrets ever starting it
but then again, life can't always be about
the smooth, even boring passages,
or the occasional dark time
with its miraculously happy ending.

He often says that the last chapter
is like the boy who tries to be good
but is overwhelmed by what it takes to please some people.
Of course, it could be that
the writer just didn't love his protagonist enough
to want to save him.
Either way it's just fiction.
Or a small town in Ohio.

TEACHER MAN

I remember you showing me your words
in an East Side coffee shop,
the awkward giddy ones
that bridged girlishness and young womanhood.

I was overcome by the roles
the situation forced me into -
audience, teacher, protector
and the one I feared the most -
prospective lover.

Beauty, being skin deep,
should remain that way
until a man can catch his breath.
But I had little time to deal with the surfaces.
Your poems immersed me
before I was even ready.

All I could do was pontificate
and I hate that in me.
I felt like an older brother.
And, heaven forbid, a father.

I was nervous offering you advice
because, whatever I gave you
would have to include me.
Any comment from biased lips
was just me making up your mind for you.
You wanted, at worst help,
at best, confirmation.
I was neither one of those.

In the end, I really did have nothing to say.
I left you with what you knew already.
Your own way through the world is how we left it.
And a clink of cups, maybe the nervous stir of a spoon

About the Author:

John Grey is an Australian poet, US resident. Recently published in Front Range Review, Studio One and Columbia Review with work upcoming in Naugatuck River Review, Abyss and Apex and Midwest Quarterly.

TRISTESSA

T. William Wallin

A heavy downpour of lucid thoughts
And sensitive droplets of fuel for dreams
Ravaging the pale grey night
The banging atop the aluminum tin roof created
And manipulated shivers down the spine of the Kerouac novel
Whose words struck my heart and rang true
The innocent savage slavery of hands that grapple
And strangle a hold the junkie
No matter what country, America
Mexico
India
The manners and characters of a sick dog stuck
In Samsara
Unable to flee the obsession
But that is also what we beings, stuck in dillusion
All share in common
The collective conscious of suffering
No one unable to break free the chains
As the addict to the fix
Except when one can become awaken
Dive deeper into understanding
And inherent wisdom of no birth, no death, no coming, no going
To see the joy through sorrow and of sorrow
To see and feel love through hatred
To escape Mara the tempter
While these thoughts appear there is a break in the early morning storm
Of downpour to allow a brisk walk
For a wake-me up of fresh café as my southern brother would call it
And I contemplate the junkie, samsara, foreign ravage torn lands and myself
The mirror always reflects back

An American River Ramble

A rolling over of the mattress towards the window
Paints a picture of the days direction
A comforting overcast is making its way over the American River
Barreling down from the north
Tahoe has heaved a cold front down to the valley
as if commanded by Twain himself
Along the bike trail puddles start to emerge and fill up
Making new homes for creatures of the banks
The trail leads behind a college campus with students ducking for cover
Trying to stay dry from the downpour beginning to fall
Umbrellas are raised
I don't see anyone dancing
The trail leads to the East
Through midtown café's and tree tunnels
Again I see no one dancing
I follow the muddy path passed tent cities
People ive known and witnessed firsthand
Walked in the same lopsided shoes of debauchery
forced upon by society
Discovery park is full of life and death
I can't stand the sight and my feet start moving themselves
There is a carnival fueled by both love and grief going on
I drift with the wind
Trying to be carried by the showering storm
Rain begins to fall heavier and heavier
Still I see no one moving their feet in rhythm to the liquid orchestra
Just ducking for cover as if acid is being sprayed from canisters
to unnoticed protesters on sidewalks
I graze behind garden state highway and cheap motel stays
Memories flood the gates of my mind
Until I get to the bridge
A familiar train rolls over, effortlessly, bringing destination exploration
The other golden metal link over the river is raised
like hands holding the sky in place, a bodhisattva of an older time
Grasping for the clouds but aiming for the moon
I can relate
I start to dance in the storm because that is what Whitman would do
and no one else is

My Grandfathers
Last Breath

We spread your ashes out at sea,
at the dock, where you once fished
and brought grandma because it reminded her of Japan

the winds were fierce and blowing sand
from the dunes in every direction
your daughter and grandsons

we're standing in silence,
trying to ease the pain
of your distraught wife

waiting for the rickety boat
owned by a friend
of yours in the war

the peninsula was empty
only scattered boats rocking at the pier
with no captains, waves breaking at the masts

we flew through choppy water
tasting salt and sea kelp
the engine was cut where the mainland became a mirage

grandma cried and sang
a song in Japanese I hadn't heard
since I was a little boy

when she finished, her delicate
fingers wrapped around your urn
with trembling hands

a family of whales surfaced
blowing the sea into the sky, the wind
died and the air was silent

your ashes were scattered
like falling stars, absorbed
by the ocean

your last breath
assuring us
it was time

My Okaachan (mother in Japanese)

My Okaachan is beautiful but crazy
raised by a mother still haunted by
Hiroshima, telling stories of death and starvation
Disowned for falling in love with the enemy
a young American soldier
who too was only 13 when WWII broke out
My Japanese ancestors were so prideful
I understand where my mother gets it
A school girl innocent as the cherry blossoms scattered
across Okinawa dirt roads
Big Buddhist statues guarding the village
like a glowing western angel
As her Sensei teaches her class math and history,
history is taken place North, student protestors
against the Vietnam war and American bases
on Japanese soil overtake Tokyo University
My mother is studying the Edo period
before Tokyo even existed
The first Asian to win the noble peace prize
is in 1974, the same year
my Okaachan was uprooted into the counter culture
revolution of America
6 years after Martin Luther King JR was assassinated
and the southern states retrograded into
segregation once again
Japanese are not welcomed in Georgia
and they let my Okaachan know
Dirty Jap is a common name spit
from prejudice mouths
on the overpopulated white bus
even the bus driver makes comments
about slanted eyes and white supremacy
There are no cherry blossoms to soothe
her degradation
she stays shy and quiet, trying to stay unnoticed
and a sight unseen, the shadows are her friend
empty fields a safe haven and loneliness a comfort blanket

My okaachan is only a teenager wondering
why the buddha said she should live in harmony with each other
and nature, but she does not experience harmony
Then a miracle happens, she moves to California
where there are communities of Japanese immigrants and citizens,
intermingling with every other race on this planet in one place
Excited and culture shocked, again, she matures
and learns normalcy, but harbors hate
and resentment from racial discrimination
that scars her psyche
My okaachan is beautiful but crazy
Using the wooden rice spoon as
a disciplinary tool to her wild trouble-making boys
She sometimes becomes sad, for no reason
I can think of, I try to make her feel better
as a tear rolls down her cheek
but the past surfaces when we least expect it,
shoveling down life experiences under masks
and pharmaceuticals, co-dependency
and materialistic waste
There are not enough Buddhist statues to guard us
reminding us of the beauty in all experience

She's Asleep

she is curled up like a Maine coon, rolled in a ball
clutching the pillow
I lay behind her on my side listening to her breathing
and deciphered jibberish that exits with each exhale
words escaping her dream state unconscious into the reality
I am still awake in
I wrap my arm around her, clutching her smooth soft stomach
so as not to float away in space
she grounds me in an ungrounded world, a boundless
world with no attachments
I am awake and she is in another realm as most nights
I get pleasure from being able to old her
in such vulnerability, such nakedness, she is safe
and she knows this
all I want to do is protect her and shield her from the evil
that walks among us in both the physical
and spiritual realms

About the Author:

T.William Wallin is a Japanese/American studying journalism in Northern California. He has been study-ing Buddhism since the age of 12 and finds it to be his key source of inspiration. He writes of experienc-es as they happen through his own eyes and from what he perceives in the constant world around him in full motion. When he isn't writing he can be found in the woods or along the river banks counting his breaths. He puts to words what he feels through emotion and sense perception, interacting with as many strangers as possible to bring both smiles and hear stories of how others human beings are living life.

HONEYMOON

Meg Eden Kuyatt

We drive through an industrial park
to get to the luau, where old men link arms
with girls in dime store mumus,

while their wives pose for pictures
next to tan men in thongs. Behind them, a sign says:
We are not responsible for any claim by reasons of fire.

The same middle-aged man keeps lining up
at the bar, as if there's a magic number
of Blue Hawaiis that makes you forget something important.

The gift shop clerk sings that song
that was popular on the radio
ten years ago. Was it really that long ago?

Looking just above the tiki fence, we can see
the horizon of white tour bus roofs. So many people
who have saved their whole lives to be here

and we are in our twenties, talking over
the buffet pork sandwiches and jello
about where we might go next.

Preparing my Hair for the Wedding

In the kitchen, my fifth grade teacher
does my hair. She says, I'd kill
for hair as thick as yours, and from the way
she combs out my tangles, I can believe it.

In the living room, her husband sits
on the floor with a 12" tube TV,
watching what must be a soccer game
fizzling in and out of reception.

The room gives off the feeling
of a college apartment just emptied out
for summer. I remember now—growing up,
how we gave my old clothes to her daughter.

She's plugged in the curlers, they look
exactly like my mother's purple pink
Conair Hot Sticks, warming the kitchen
with the smell of burning plastic.

Once they're done, she wraps my hair
around each curler, telling me stories
of the girls from my class who have gotten
married, how she did their hair.

She tells me that before she taught at my school,
one students called her a white bitch.
Her husband still won't go to church with her.
Her daughter's just moved out to go to college.
⬚Fifth grade was the year I lived inside Pokémon
tapes. When did I ever think about my teacher,
coming home to her school salary:
to the loneliness even in marriage?

She takes the curls in bunches,
like freshly cut flowers. She pins them
into place, and I feel the pang of bobby pins
against my scalp. This is the trial run.

She leads me to the bathroom, carpeted
and incredibly blue, giving me a mirror.
I move it, trying to catch even a glimpse
of my back—It's then I see myself.

241

Gift

From the basement pantry shelf,
my mother pulls out a dead mink
in a ziplock bag, its white fur
falling out in generous clumps.

A gift from when she was a girl,
my mother tells me how her aunt
wrapped it around her neck & she felt
the dead of its body against her skin & cried.

She must've meant well, my mother says—
Probably meant to make me feel
extravagant. But we never really know
what kids are thinking, do we?

She weighs it in her hands, says,
It's funny, how we keep these things—
the falling apart mink would probably
enjoy the relief of being discarded.

She asks me if I want it—she's asked me
about so many things & I'm tired of lying
& saying yes. My mother died when I was
your age, she says but doesn't say.

I know this won't be the last thing
I inherit but do not want:
the bedroom downstairs, filled
with boxes I will never take.

Production Costs

In seventh grade during science class
we were talking about planets
when James Cochran asked me:

*Do you know we all inadvertently consume
about seven pounds of insects in our lifetime?*
(He became an accountant.)

If I consume so many insects, what other things
must I take in unknowingly as well:
years, compliments, calories, people's good intentions—

How much of our lives are lost to sleep! Think of all
the poems that could be written! My mother's pantry:
full of expired cans, waiting to be consumed.

About the Author:

Meg Eden's work has been published in various magazines, including Rattle, Drunken Boat, Poet Lore, RHINO and Gargoyle. She teaches creative writing at the University of Maryland. She has five poetry chapbooks, and her novel "Post-High School Reality Quest" is published with California Coldblood, an imprint of Rare Bird Books. Find her online at www.megedenbooks.com or on Twitter at @ConfusedNarwhal.

PARODY

Joseph Buehler

Notes From A Padded Cell

The rabid rabbit runs
around the ragged rocks.

The pitiful old bum
forgets to change his socks.

A wary eyed wolf
feeds on defenseless flocks.

The inexperienced sailor
keeps crashing into docks.

A young drunken clock setter
forgets to set his clocks.

We don't care so much for the ticks,
but we really love the tocks.

Revolve, Revolve

"I came for the waters."
"But this is the desert."
"Then I must have been misinformed."
. . .A handsome man and a beautiful woman
are in close profile (deep red sky in the background):
"You are sending a soldier off to fight for a lost
cause, so kiss me---kiss me just once." . . . A young
muscular husband, holding his head in his hands,
bellows for his wife; will she return to him?
Probably yes. . . . A rich old man lets a snow globe
slip from his fingers as he dies; he utters a single
word; the globe bounces erratically down a carpeted
staircase and then smashes into a thousand tiny pieces.
. . .An ugly mean looking man with a broad strap in his
hand glares at you and snarls, "You, you're next!"
. . .Finally try to envision a night time scene: a young
fellow in a tight-fitting suit runs joyously around a
lighted gushing splashing New York City fountain
back toward an older fat man who is wearing a cheap
suit with a cardboard belt; they embrace and the picture
instantly freezes and the credits begin to appear.

Parody

Parody and satire are easy; truth is difficult.
Obscenity is the first refuge of the morally illiterate.
Like baseball, there is no crying in poetry.
Too many poems have already been written about the moon.
"Mother Nature" is, of course, a myth.
Dreams display our illogically sweeter self.
Dogs, as a rule, don't like oatmeal or coffee or lettuce.

Danbury, Connecticut

There are too many people in Danbury, Connecticut.
You might expect to see a lot of people in New York
City or, say, Chicago, but why in Danbury, Connecticut?

The restaurants and the motels and everything else is
jammed full of them. People are everywhere; they get
in your way---whole unruly families of them---and the
roads are full of them and once you get on a highway
near Danbury, Connecticut, and you find out that you
are on the wrong highway, you can never turn around
and go back. You are doomed to stay on that highway
forever or until you get a chance to look at your map
(or, if you are fortunate enough to have some one else
with you, have them look at a map) and figure out a way
back through a maze of conflicting and extremely busy
and dangerous highways full of impatient drivers who
seem to know where they are going and who look down
on you with hatred and contempt and who do not hesitate
to blow their raucous angry horns at you.

Ruminations

You go to the door.
You sit in the chair and stare.
You remember your mother.
Then you remember your father.
Your wife comes into the room.
You remember one of your sisters, the fat one.
No one sees you in the lobby of the hotel. You see no one except
the person at the desk. He knows you're there, but he doesn't look at you.
You ask someone for your umbrella. They say they don't know what you're
talking about and they don't have it.
Your fat sister yells at you; you remain silent. She brings up an argument that
you had with her years ago.
Nothing deters you from loving yourself.
Sometimes you hate yourself.
A dog comes around the corner and barks at you. You see the dog and try to
ignore it.
You like flowers, but not too much.
You try your best not to get angry with people.
You like to look at the ocean.

About the Author:

Joseph Buehler has published over 60 poems by the summer of 2017 in ArLiJo, Nine Mile Magazine, Sentinel Literary Quarterly in the U.K., Serving House Journal, Futures Trading, Green Hills Literary Lantern, Indiana Voice Journal and elsewhere. He is retired and lives in Georgia with his wife Trish.

CONFESSION

John Garmon

Forgive me my many sins
I didn't tend the setting hens
I didn't water and feed them well
They got up and walked away
Hungry and thirsty
Leaving their eggs unhatched

Of all the sins I have to tell
This one haunts me still
The lives I could have saved
You may think it was trivial
I don't know how to explain
My negligence so murderous
The lasting of the pain

SUNBREAK AND MOONDOWN

Sunbreak and moondown
Morning of looking east
I saw mallards flying south
I thought how peaceful
Like getting out of prison
Only a few dollars to my name
Going out under a new sky
Everywhere mockingbirds
Bees around new roses
Sparrows taunting each other
Landing on fragile branches
Sorrows at bay for a while
Of a god abiding in sunbreak
Giving race for all

HERE IN VEGAS

Here in Vegas a homeless black man came up with what he said
Was evidence that Langston Hughes was a great ancestor of
The billionaire Howard Hughes who once was a famous man in Vegas
And famous throughout the world for many memorable things
What unbelievable news the local literati guffawed

The homeless man claimed the Hughes family
Hushed up the details of Howard and Langston's kin
The homeless black man said his black grandfather in Texas was acquainted
With the father of Howard Hughes and actually knew the family
And in those days there was a slight chance of miscegenation happening
The details were sketchy and the local Vegas newspaper
Treated the story as the mad imaginations of an irresponsible indigent
However, the homeless man did not give up and one day came forward
To a crowd of curious onlookers who just wanted to laugh and ridicule
Undaunted the homeless black man gave a short speech
The reason Howard Hughes hated black people so much was not known
But I have it on good authority that Howard was highly indignant
About the hidden things that went on in the Hughes family which resulted
In that little drop of blood that joined the rich man and the poet
Everyone laughed about it and the whole thing was soon forgotten
But to this day depraved gossip mongers like me continue to wonder.

BUCKSHOT

Sleet drives down the dark street
        A homeless man puts a shawl
            Across his wife's shoulders
                And she sleeps
                    Or tries to sleep
            Propped
              Against a stucco wall
                    Behind an empty store

    It's getting cold
        This time of year
            Hunger this evening
                Pelts her dreams
                    Like buckshot.

    And the night
        Crawls along
          The alley
            Like a cold snake.

And the moon appears to rise
      From the mountains
        Like a slow mirage

About the Author:

John Garmon's poems have been published in Ploughshares, Prairie Schooner, Commonweal, Midwest Quarterly Review, Southern Poetry Review, Southern Humanities Review, and many other places. He is a writing assistant at the College of Southern Nevada, Las Vegas.

AN END OF THINGS
Daniel Kenitz

I broke a log to find its truth;
the light was bent.
Observer's Folly spent the rest.
The sap was crisp and clean—
the dew's deposit to the dawn—
but like ceasing, pounding rain
everything ends up dry.
The log was rotted up inside,
a home uncivilized.
But had I kept the log upright,
it would have sheltered them instead.
Goodbye, my friends—
I found the truth—
The home is gone and dead as youth.

Three Haikus

introductions sting
with each new sigh of greeting
but how mom forgets

-

her 255 lips
smile through a little window
on his distant screen

-

she drove west to home
into memory's gullet
then east forever

About the Author:

Daniel Kenitz is a writer and poet whose previous fiction has appeared in "Strangelet," "L'Allure Des Mots," and the University of Kentucky's "Limestone Journal." Kenitz is a graduate of the Writing Program at Cardinal Stritch University and writes out of southeast Wisconsin.

"With reason, we go beyond what we can sense.

With emotions, we go beyond what we can reason."

A CHAT WITH PIERRE SOTÉR
the Author of the
Poems & Thoughts Book Series

ALM: We know that, as an author, you prefer to use your pen name Pierre Sotér and keep your true identity a secret for now. Tell us a bit about Pierre Sotér, a poet, your artistic philosophy, and how many poems you have written.

PS: Heraclitus reminds us that "No man ever steps in the same river twice, for it's not the same river and he's not the same man." At one point in my life I decided to adventure in the forests around the river and when I came back the river looked rather different, and I tried another boat. The boat of poetry. It's a passionate boat that likes to speed through dire straits. But so do I. In my teen-age years I wrote a few poems that I may never find again. But while I'm letting this new boat steer my voyage, I'm writing about what I've seen

and about what I see with my eyes and my soul wide open. One way or another, I wrote so far almost 700 poems. But I don't have the slightest idea when this river will reach the sea and I don't know if I will be able to write in the rough sway of high waves.

ALM: Do you remember what was your first ever poem about and when did you write it?

PS: The very first poem I wrote inside this new boat, is a small poem called "Without a Clue", which is included in my first book, Dawn. It is an attempt to compress in 12 short lines the history of philosophy. A crazy idea. And I can see that I bluntly disrespected the advice of Einstein: "Everything should be made as simple as possible, but not simpler." But poetry can do some magic. I only tried.

ALM: Why do you write poetry? Why is the poetry a literary form of your choice and have you ever think of writing a prose?

PS: When my mood is taken over by poetry, everything is poetry. I'm starting to look at the old complex equations I used to solve, as a poetic sequence of numbers. There is indeed poetry in numbers and in the way they describe nature. For Pythagoras numbers were the very essence of existence. And the universal irrational constant 2.71828182845904523536028747... is simply everywhere. So, in a way, I've been writing poetry all my life. And if I follow this line of thought I will arrive to the conclusion that prose is just another form of poetry. Still, I don't know if I will ever write prose. Only if I will have an idea that I believe is good enough to write about, and interesting enough for others to read.

ALM: What is the title of your latest poem and what inspired it?

PS: It's a poem I just wrote about the devil. He is taking the life of my best friend.

ALM: How long it took you to write your latest poem and how fast do you write?

PS: This one has been written out of rage. Therefore it took just a few minutes. But for me, to write a poem can take anything from a few minutes to many long days. In the process, some are sent to the garbage can and others are given a second chance. But those are normally the poems I write myself. The ones that write themselves I don't dare to change. And they are the ones I like best.

ALM: Do you have any unusual writing habits?

PS: I don't know if my writing habits are so different from other writers. I guess not. Basically, when I feel like writing, I write anywhere. But, I like to read at night, as I believe many people do, and since I always wake up in the middle of it, I had to find a pleasant way to avoid staring at the ceiling. Thus, I write poetry in dim light. That's my favorite way and time to write. And gives me plenty of free time during day, if I'm not sleeping.

ALM: You are a Portuguese native, but you write in English, Portuguese, and French. How you decide in which language you will write and do you have any preferences about the language used when it comes to poetic expressions?

PS: This is really a difficult question. First, the easier part. French is the first foreign language I learned. It has been with me since my childhood. And I like a lot to read French poetry. Victor Hugo, Baudelaire, for example. And in fact, the first sonnets I tried to write were in French. But it's also the language I have more difficulties to write in, as I no longer use it daily. Portuguese is my mother language, and in our mother language words are always more plastic and camaleonic. This is the only "advantage" I feel when I write in Portuguese. But until now I've been writing mostly in English, may be because English is the language that surrounds me most of the time. And I find much more to read in English than in any other language. I also read Spanish and make some incursions into Danish.

ALM: Is it poetry or writing the only form of artistic expression that you utilize, or there is more to Pierre Sotér than just a poetry?

PS: Our minds have not been made for any specific type of knowledge or practice, otherwise we would be robots. I have and always had different interests in my life. Sometimes they complement each other, sometimes they are an escape from each other. Now I'm mostly playing and fighting with words. If the devil doesn't defeat me, I like to think that one day I will be a shepherd. And the thing I mostly regret is that I don't have enough skills to play music. So I listen more to music than I ever made calculations or wrote. And I cannot make paintings nor sculptures, which is also a shame. So I look at them. Photography is also a form of art for me. There I take some revenge.

ALM: What authors or poets have influenced you?

PS: In my childhood and teenage years, Edgar Rice Burroughs and Jules Verne took me on many adventures. Then I jumped almost directly into science fiction, where I found fantastic worlds and stories by authors like H. G. Wells, Ray Bradbury, Isaac Asimov and Frank Herbert. The classics came later, slowly substituting for my readings of the theories of Galileo, Pascal, Euler, Newton, Adam Smith, Einstein and the like. And the classical world is so vast and fantastic that any attempt to choose is a trap. But I won't avoid it. Sophocles, Dante, Camões, Cervantes, Shakespeare and Kierkegaard. Those are my favorites. So far.

ALM: As an author and poet what are you working on now?

PS: My first book of poetry and thoughts, DAWN, has just been released by Adelaide Books. This book has an approach and format that I will use for my next works. Drawing mostly from the poems I've been writing lately, I'm working on my next two poetry books that will be released till the end of next year.

ALM: In your opinion, what is the best way when it comes to promoting poetry? Did you ever think about the profile of your readers? What do you think – who reads Pierre Sotér?

PS: I will try to answer this question starting at the end. My life experience and original brain wiring led to a moderately skeptical way of being, that treats data and logic with the same deference, and leaves an important space for intuition, emotions and faith. But above all, data, logic, intuition, emotions and faith have to be true and fair. So, people that identify with these principles and can discuss anything without any preconceived idea, and can change their views and opinions if evidence is provided by data, logic, intuition, emotions and faith, they may find some interest in reading my poetry. I would add to this that poetry, for me, belongs to the domain where words are free to mean what they want, in the logic that nature uses to minimize energy. Do more, spending less. Say more, writing less. Now to the difficult part of the question. I don't know what should be the best way of promoting poetry as a whole. Maybe it's good for our mental health. I hope. The only general rule I can think of is that what any poet writes should be written in a way that after reading a poem for the first time, the reader needs to read it again. A bit like music. Beauty and rhythm that take over our nervous system. And hopefully delivers a message. There are many poems that I read hundreds of times, and some became a part of my feelings. Poetry has to reach deep into our minds and souls. I simply don't consider as poetry any words that try to tell me what the author has been doing since he woke up. Poetry should not be used to fill pages with useless details. When readers start believing that any poetry book in a bookshop will stimulate their emotions, I believe poetry will start having a more important role in our lives. As Charles Darwin puts it: "If I had my life to live over again, I would have made a rule to read some poetry and listen to some music at least once every week."

ALM: Do you have any advice for new poets/authors?

PS: Write with your soul and don't bother your readers with details that are only important for you.

ALM: What is the best advice you have ever heard?

PS: Avoid adjectives. Easier said than done. Very difficult to follow when one is writing poetry.

ALM: What are you reading now?

PS: I usually do parallel reading. On my side table I have now three books: The Man Without Qualities from Robert Musil, Blood and Thunder from

"When my mood is taken over by poetry, everything is poetry. I'm starting to look at the old complex equations I used to solve, as a poetic sequence of numbers. There is indeed poetry in numbers and in the way they describe nature. For Pythagoras numbers were the very essence of existence."

Hampton Sides and The Lady of the Lake from Walter Scott. A combination of a remarkable novel with well written and researched history and brilliant poetry, which add to the sense that the night has never been meant for sleeping.

ALM: Who are your favorite authors and poets, and what are your favorite books ever?

PS: Part of the answer has been given above. But requires clarification because the same way rivers change, we change. For me, right now, there is a particular book that takes alone the highest position of my podium: Niels Lyhne, written in 1880 by Jens Peter Jacobsen. A monumental (should spare on adjectives) book that I have read twice and will certainly read again. Now, whatever the reasons of my bias, and after a bit of searching in the corners of my memory, I would include in my favorites, without any concern of order: The tragedies of Sophocles, "Don Quixote de la Mancha" by Cervantes, "Os Lusíadas" by Camões, "Candide" by Voltaire, "Divine Comedy" by Dante, "Thus Spoke Zarathustra" by Nietzsche, "Either-Or" by Kierkegaard, "The Importance of Being Earnest" by Wilde, "I Robot" by Isaac Asimov, "Out of Africa" by Karen Blixen, "Uncle Tom's Cabin" by Stowe and "Jerusalem" by Montefiore, to stick to a dozen. In the world of poetry I have more difficulty in selecting. Still, for me, Luís de Camões, Fernando Pessoa, William Shakespeare and Thomas Hardy stand at the top of the best. To this list I would add a few more: Alexander Pope, Victor Hugo, Lord Byron, William Butler Yeats, Dylan Thomas, Robert Frost, John Masefield and Florbela Espanca. And all sincere poets with a poetic soul.

ALM: What do you deem the most relevant about your writing?

PS: That I won't dare to answer. I'm even afraid that I may spoil whatever ability I may have to write if I start thinking about it. But I am expecting to hear many different opinions and critics. And I hope that the way I write will contribute, even if modestly, to the perception of poetry as an art that can help and increase the quality of our inner and spiritual life.

ALM: Thank you Pierre. Good luck with your writing and your photography.

The tracks of life are long and winding,

brief the encounters of love and sin,

and bitter-dry the taste of finding

that someone will lose and none will win.

SORROWS AND JOYS
By Colin Ian Jeffery

Paperback: 152 pages

Publisher: CreateSpace Independent Publishing Platform (August 16, 2017)

Language: English

ISBN-10: 1974598381

ISBN-13: 978-1974598380

Product Dimensions: 6 x 0.4 x 9 inches

Collection of 212 poems

Colin Ian Jeffery is a leading Christian poet and all poems in this collection have been published in newspapers, magazines and anthologies. The collection gives an insight into the driving forces behind his poetry, with the main influence, seen in such poems as 'Christians' and 'King of Kings,' being his spirituality. 'Pope Francis,' is a poem that acknowledges his Roman Catholic background, and gives insight into the poet's spiritual formation in the Roman Catholic Church.

The poem 'True Love' shows his passion and belief that love must be free and never held captive.

Love must be set free

For this I know

The caged bird sings for flight

Dying captive

Looking through the bars.

Some of the sonnets are addressed to the great love of his life, the mysterious lover who moved the poet to compose some of the most poignant love poems ever written, a love for the poet that was a rock within a stormy sea giving support against raging purple storms.

The collection covers many different topics dealt with powerfully and artistically with a variety of topics such as peace, war, history, love, sorrow, death, and childhood memories in such poems as 'Wally Gog' and 'When I was young.' The poet is a modernist with the development of imagism stressing clarity, precision and economy of language. He has a strong reaction against war and the oppression of innocence, but unlike others poets in the modernism movement like Dylan Thomas and Ezra Pound he has a profound faith in God.

(Reverend Dr. Paul James Dunn)

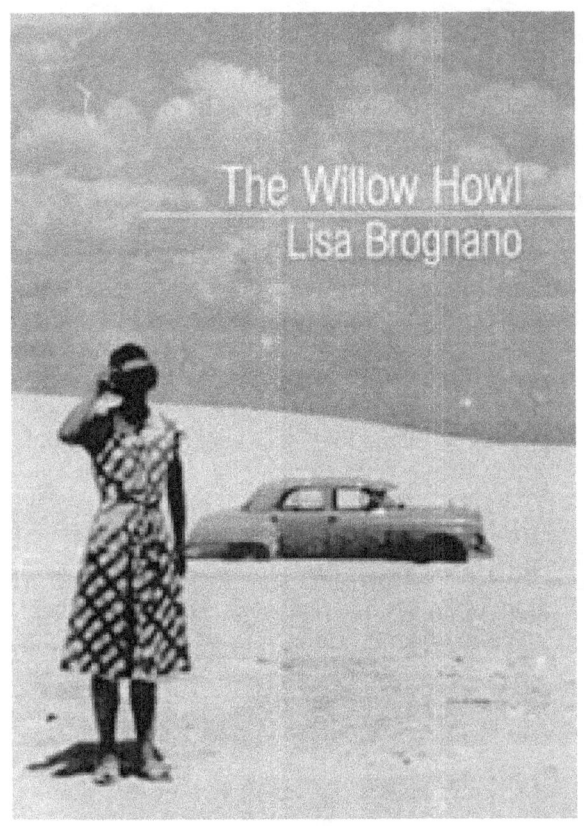

Lisa Brognano brings the reader into her poems much like a viewer becomes interested in a movie, as if one were watching the event unfold in real-time. She takes the ordinary and creates a mood, challenging the reader to feel the emotions of a poem's character. As the reader absorbs each poem, it is as if her subjects become sentient beings. As the reader digests the lyrics and is drawn into conversation with the subject of one poem, there is subtle anticipation for what she will write about next. I highly recommend The Willow Howl. (Deanne Johnson, Librarian)

AUTHOR BIO

Lisa Brognano is the author of the novels, A Man for Prue (Resplendence, 2017), and In the Interest of Faye (Golden Antelope Press, forthcoming), as well as a book of poetry, The Willow Howl (Nixes Mate Books, 2017). Her poems and short fiction have appeared in national and international literary journals, including Adelaide Magazine, Neologism Poetry Journal, The Wagon Magazine, Nixes Mate Review, and elsewhere. She holds two master's degrees, one in English and one in Fine Art. Currently, she lives in New York with her husband.

THE WILLOW HOWL

A book of Poetry By Lisa Brognano

Paperback: 64 pages

Publisher: Nixes Mate Books (August 25, 2017)

Language: English

ISBN-10: 0999188232

ISBN-13: 978-0999188231

Product Dimensions: 5.1 x 0.2 x 7.8 inches

DAWN
Poems and Thoughts
By Pierre Sotér

Paperback: 174 pages

Publisher: Adelaide Books (July 29, 2017)

Language: English

ISBN-10: 0999214802

ISBN-13: 978-0999214800

Product Dimensions: 6 x 0.4 x 9 inches

*"And after my wanderings, I hope I will arrive
where love is not alone, and hate is not alive."*

*"I shall try to follow reason & faith,
and trust that where they join it is my place."*

From the foreword:

"Writing a poem is like sailing deep oceans at the mercy of shifting winds and streams that carry uncountable words, some emanating from the still, unseen deep, others from the ever changing emotions that flutter and sometimes rage at the surface. It may also happen that a poem wants to write itself, for poems can have feelings and secrets of their own that we never imagined, and are only revealed when one begins to write. The extraordinary discovery that it implies, is what makes the adventure of writing poetry the more exciting and worthwhile. Unique.

Within my limitations, I wrote this book with deep respect and admiration for the art of many great classical and modern poets, and sympathy for all those that have courage to expose their feelings. The book reveals some feelings of mine and a few opinions. It is a book about emotions, love, joy and sorrow, beliefs, and thoughts on life. About the world we live in, the Universe from where we came, and to where we will return one day. It is a book about lions too, birds, rain, the sun and the sea. It is about living creatures and stones. And Gods, time, existence and the naive hope of an eternal restart. It starts at Dawn."

*"Tomorrow, I'll travel,
I'll dream of adventures and gavel
the tempers, all seven,
to check if there's fire in heaven."*

Pierre Sotér is the pen name of a well-established Portuguese author. After thirty years of successful professional life and intensive soul-searching, he now dedicates his time to poetry and philosophy. The DAWN is the first book in the Book Series "Poems and Thoughts of Pierre Sotér." Pierre writes in Portuguese, English, and French.

A BOX OF DREAMS

A Collection of Short Stories
By Denis Bell
Illustrations by
Louise Freshman Brown

156 pages

Adelaide Books

ISBN-13: 978-0999214817

ISBN-10: 0999214810

6" x 9" (15.24 x 22.86 cm)

Denis Bell's stories are short only in length; in insight, vision, humor and style they have a far-seeing distance and depth that will keep you wedded to the page, either laughing, marveling, or scratching your head."
- David L. Robbins, author of War of the Rats

"A thought-provoking collection of flashes and longer stories: poignant, strange, humorous and humane. A Box of Dreams should be opened by all."
- Peter Blair and Ashley Chantler, Editors of Flash: The International Short-Short Story Magazine

"The author's wit and the sense of humor is obvious and there are quite a few scenes that will bring smile to the reader's face and make a pleasant read. Life dilemmas that the characters in his stories are facing are real and believable. While I am really impressed with A Box of Dreams, I am even more fascinated with the potential that Mr. Bell's fictional world has for the creation of future adventures, maybe even a whole series of books. With the writing skills that Denis Bell displayed in this collection of short stories, it is quite possible to become a great success."
- Stevan V. Nikolic, Editor of the Adelaide Literary Magazine

"Denis Bell has a subtle hand and a crafter's light touch; he's able to tickle the bizarre from the familiarities of reality so smoothly that you are forced to look twice."
Nancy Stohlman, author of The Vixen Scream and Other Bible Stories

"You'll find a number of gems in Denis Bell's first collection of stories, "A Box of Dreams." The selections, though comfortably brief, are disturbingly bright, and their buffed shine holds up after repeated readings."
Bob Thurber, author of Nothing But Trouble and Paperboy: A Dysfunctional Novel

"Dokey is a writer who can take common people and ordinary places and make them resonate with meanings that suggest themselves to the reader long after the book is closed."
San Francisco Chronicle

"He is able to tackle enormous themes (birth, love, marriage, old age) and successfully incorporate them into relatively brief, carefully tailored stories. The author should be commended also for his ability to move effortlessly among a range of narrative voices."

Publishers Weekly

"Readers will be taken aback, too, by Dokey's candor and eloquence" Chicago Tribune

"The complexity of Dokey's fiction creeps up, unveiling striking layers of humanity to quietly reward the patient observer"

The Sacramento Bee

"He speaks to us in a solitary, moving language that only writers as skilled as Dokey can record. We are transported to the highest levels of human experience."

Milwaukee Journal

THE LONELINESS CAFE

A Collection of Short Stories
By Richard Dokey

Paperback: 206 pages

Publisher: Adelaide Books (August 18, 2017)

Language: English

ISBN-10: 0999214829

ISBN-13: 978-0999214824

Product Dimensions: 6 x 0.5 x 9 inches

Richard Dokey's stories have won awards and prizes, have been cited in Best American Short Stories, Best of the West, have been nominated for the Pushcart Prize and have been reprinted in numerous regional and national literary reviews and anthologies. Pale Morning Dun, his collection of short stories, published by University of Missouri Press, was nominated for the American Book Award. His writings have appeared most recently in Adelaide Literary Magazine, Alaska Quarterly Review, Grain(Canada), Natural Bridge, Southern Humanities Review, Lumina and The Chattahooc-hee Review.

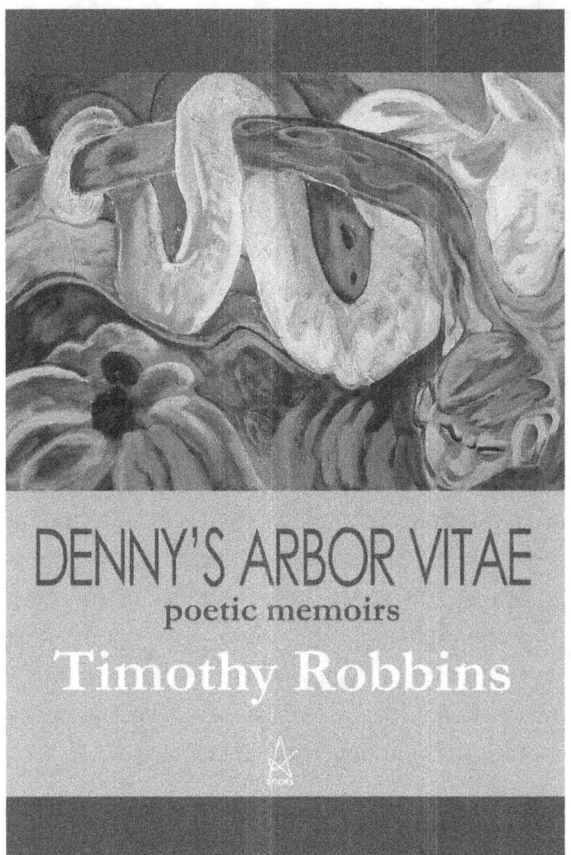

*"...Read books with words dark as
rained-on grass, tree trunks, blacktop, clothes
sucking up to skin. Each word slides like mascara.
The water on my cheek, pressing down my hair,
hanging
like spiders from my eyelashes — these are all
part
of the book, the part that makes it worth reading.
Let these be the last lines you write — not a suicide
note, but as final as one. Beware the greed good
poetry
breeds, greed for more and more verse. Soon you
won't get through the day without a shot."*

Timothy Robbins teaches ESL and does freelance translation in Wisconsin. He has a BA in French and an MA in Applied Linguistics from Indiana University. He has been a regular contributor to "Hanging Loose" since 1978. His poems have also appeared in Adelaide Literary Magazine, Three New Poets, The James White Review, Slant, Main Street Rag, Two Thirds North, The Pinyon Review, Wisconsin Review, and others.

DENNY'S ARBOR VITAE

Poetic Memoirs
By Timothy Robbins

Paperback: 200 pages

Publisher: Adelaide Books (August 18, 2017)

Language: English

ISBN-10: 0999214837

ISBN-13: 978-0999214831

Product Dimensions: 6 x 0.5 x 9 inches

ART & PHOTOGRAPHY

DAWN

Photograhy By

Viktor Tegner

Of the 23 photos that have been selected to accompany the poems of DAWN, eight have been taken at the Portuguese western coast and eight in the city of Copenhagen. That strongly reflects how inspiring it is to look at the sea and the big waves that break on the Portuguese shores, and how much I like to see my native city through my lenses. In Lisbon I took a picture through a window over the romantic Tagus estuary and after a coffee and the traditional "pastel de nata" at Brasileira do Chiado, I could not leave without a photo of the poetic genius sitting on my side, Fernando Pessoa. And there is a photo of a majestic Lion, a flying Swan, a pretty Tulip and a melancholic Dove in Venice. And a special photo by the author in the centre of Edinburgh.

Viktor Tegner is a student of Computing and Information Technologies, a clarinet player and a lover of photography. He is in charge and the main photographer of the photo sets included in the Book Series of Poetry & Thoughts by Pierre Sotér, and is working on a series of city books. Viktor Tegner speaks fluently Danish, Portuguese and English.

All photo illustrations in this issue of the Adelaide Literary Magazine are from the photo collection DAWN by Viktor Tegner.

Photos by Viktor Tegner in full resolution and in color could be seen in our online gallery at:

http://photography.adelaidemagazine.org

ACEITAMOS SUBMISSÓES
Convite a todos os autores independentes: Vamos tornar esta revista um sucesso!

Looking for contributors and guest editors.

We are accepting fiction, nonfiction, poetry, book reviews, interviews, event announcements, artwork and photography.

Check our submission guidelines at:

http://adelaidemagazine.org/submit.html

In our magazine you can promote your book for free, list your book on the new titles page, submit an interview or book review, and place an ad for free on our classifieds page, offering your writing, editing, design, translation, or other publishing services. You can be a guest editor for the issue!

Check out our website and don't be shy to send us your work. This is a literary magazine by indie authors for indie authors!

A Adelaide Magazine é uma publicação internacional independente publicada trimestralmente em inglês e português, de momento, à procura de submissões.

Pretendemos publicar ficção, não-ficção e poesia excepcionais assim como promover os escritores que publicamos, ajudando os autores novos e emergentes a atingir uma audiência literária mais vasta. Na Adelaide Magazine, os autores podem promover o seu livro de modo grátis, listando o seu livro na página dedicada a Novos Títulos, submeter uma entrevista e uma crítica literária, e ainda oferecer os seus serviços de escrita, edição, design e tradução assim como outros serviços na área da edição, gratuitamente, na secção de Anúncios Classificados.

Esta é uma revista literária de autores independentes para autores independentes! Seja parte do nosso sucesso! Seja um dos editores convidados desta edição!

http://adelaidemagazine.org

www.ingramcontent.com/pod-product-compliance
Lightning Source LLC
Chambersburg PA
CBHW080719020726
47502CB00009B/2475